ACTION FRONT! AND THE GRAY SEA RAIDERS

Two Full-Length Historical Novels of the American Civil War

GORDON D. SHIRREFFS

WOLFPACK PUBLISHING
— EST 2013 —

Action Front! and The Gray Sea Raiders
Paperback Edition
Copyright © 2022 (As Revised) Gordon D. Shirreffs

Wolfpack Publishing
5130 S. Fort Apache Rd. 215-380
Las Vegas, NV 89148

wolfpackpublishing.com

This book is a work of fiction. Any references to historical events, real people or real places are used fictitiously. Other names, characters, places and events are products of the author's imagination, and any resemblance to actual events, places or persons, living or dead, is entirely coincidental.

All rights reserved. No part of this book may be reproduced by any means without the prior written consent of the publisher, other than brief quotes for reviews.

Paperback ISBN 978-1-63977-879-9
eBook ISBN 978-1-63977-880-5

ACTION FRONT! AND THE GRAY SEA RAIDERS

ACTION FRONT!

To my comrades of Combat Train and Battery B, 202d Coast Artillery (AA) and Battery G, 210th Coast Artillery (AA)

CHAPTER ONE

The small herd of trotting coach and light draft horses had reached the far end of the wide green meadow, close to the bank of the stream, and had slowed their pace, ready to spend the rest of the hot summer afternoon in the shade of the trees. Ben Buell came down the shady lane and climbed the gate to perch on the top, shading his eyes to look for the biggest horse of them all. Then he saw him, a light bay with dark points, standing off from the others, head raised high, drawing in the fresh wind almost as though he were drinking it.

Ben stood up on a gate rail and cupped his hands about his mouth. "Dandy! Dandy!" he called. The big bay quickly turned his head and thrust his ears forward. "Bring them up here, Dandy!" called Ben.

The bay reared and pawed the air rapidly, then moved around behind the other horses. In a moment the horses were on the move, pounding forth from the dappled shade of the trees into the bright Pennsylvania sunlight, a picture of grace and strength. The best of them all was Dandy, who, now that he had moved the herd out, was racing alongside them to take his place in front. Dandy was no driver; he was a leader.

Ben whistled sharply. The bay swung away from the herd and came up close to the gate, allowing Ben to drop onto his back and grip his thick, flowing mane. Horse and boy were off, racing pell-mell down the meadow toward the western fence line, with the rest of the horses slamming along behind them in obvious enjoyment of the daily game they played with the huge bay and the dark-haired boy who rode him as though the two of them were but one, a modern-day centaur.

Ben swung the bay as they reached the stone fence that bordered the dusty road which led past the Buell farm to join the Taneytown Road on its way north to Gettysburg. A horse and buggy stood on the road and a man in civilian clothing was standing up in the buggy, watching the Buell horses as they milled about Ben and Dandy.

"You Walt Buell?" the man called out.

"No," answered Ben as he kneed the bay close to the fence. "That's my brother. He's up to the house, I think."

"Them all your horses?"

Ben nodded. He knew who the man was now—a Government contractor looking for horses to purchase for the Government. It was the beginning of the third year of the War Between the States, and the Union armies were using thousands of horses. The appetite of cavalry regiments, artillery batteries, and wagon trains for horses, horses, and yet more horses seemed insatiable, and the war itself was not decided as yet, by any means. Walt had sold a round dozen of the Buell herd a few months back, good horses for coaches and light draft work but destined in all probability for light artillery and horse artillery batteries. Destined, too, for mutilation and death on some smoking battlefield if they did not die of fatigue and neglect as many other horses had done before them. The cold thought was Ben's as he looked toward the farmhouse and saw Walt walking down toward the road with his slightly awkward gait. Walt Buell had not yet gotten used to the loss of his left arm, which he had left behind at Marye's Heights during the bloody repulse of the Army of the Potomac at Fredericksburg last December.

"That him?" asked the man.

Ben nodded. He watched the contractor drive toward the gate and engage Walt in conversation. Sure enough, Walt turned and held his right hand to his mouth. "Ben! You get those horses over here, boy!" he called out.

Ben rode around behind the herd and drove them toward the gate. He looked down at the sleek backs of the well-fed horses. The horses stopped alongside the fence, and Ben kneed Dandy away from them. He slid from the big bay's back and opened the gate so that Walt and the contractor could get through into the meadow.

"You won't find better light draft horses in all of Adams County, Mister Swan," said Walt.

"I've seen better," said the contractor casually.

Walt flushed a little. "Not like these," he said a little sharply. Walt had always had a bit of a temper, and the loss of his arm had honed that temper to an edge that sometimes was almost dangerous. "These horses are mostly Thoroughbred and Clydesdale bred," continued Walt. "Hardly a one o£ them much less than fifteen hands tall."

Mister Swan nodded. He half closed his eyes. "I'll give you a hundred dollars apiece for them."

"And you get one hundred and sixty from the Government for them!"

Mister Swan casually inspected his nails. "That's my price," he said.

"I'll take them to Harrisburg myself and sell them before I'll sell them to you at that price! "

Mister Swan smiled. "You have a contract with the Government?"

"No."

"Then you'd better let me take these horses."

Ben wet his lips, watching Walt out of the corner of his eye. Times had been a little hard on the Buell farm because of the war. Ben's father, Captain Maynard Buell, a retired Regular Army artillery officer, a veteran of the Mexican War, had marched away as soon as the war had started, to die later of wounds received at Gaines' Mill during the Seven Days. But he had lived for months after his death wound and most of the Buell money had gone into medicines and doctor's services. Then Walt had been away too, to get his crippling wound at Fredericksburg. There had been only Ben and his mother to keep the place going, and a frail woman and a fifteen-year-old boy had hardly been capable of keeping up the place, with most of the able-bodied farmhands in the Army. There were other bills due — and soon — and Walt had neither the time nor strength to take the horses up to the big Cavalry Bureau Depot at Harrisburg.

"One hundred and ten apiece," said Mister Swan.

"One hundred and twenty!" echoed Walt.

Mister Swan yawned. "One fifteen, no more."

In the silence that followed Ben heard the soft sighing of the wind through the trees and the faint buzzing of the bees.

"All right," said Walt at last.

Mister Swan stuck out a hand. "I'll make out the bill of sale," he said quickly. "My drivers will be by tomorrow to pick up the horses." He eyed the herd. "Nineteen of them. Right?"

"Eighteen," said Ben quietly. "This bay is not for sale."

"I figured on *all* of them, Mister Buell."

"The big bay is Ben's pet, Mister Swan."

"Fine horse."

"Fifteen hands, thirteen hundred pounds, and only four years old," said Ben with a smile.

"Some *pet*," said Mister Swan. He walked toward Ben.

"Let me take a better look at him. Might be able to make a better deal on him."

"He's not for sale," said Ben.

"Maybe you'd better wait until I make an offer, sonny," said Mister Swan.

Dandy raised his head, and his nostrils flared a little.

"He's touchy," said Ben. He slid from Dandy's back. "He doesn't like to be handled by anyone but me."

"Let him look at the horse, Ben," said Walt sharply.

Ben looked at his brother. They had always gotten on well before Walt had gone away to the war, but since his return there was no pleasing him, and the proud Buell blood was just as thick in Ben as it was in Walt.

"You heard me, Ben," said Walt.

Dandy moved about a little and eyed the contractor. Ben could almost feel the danger in the situation. Then, as he had expected, a hoof shot out, missing Mister Swan by inches. Ben knew that the bay had missed deliberately. Dandy was not mean or vicious. That had been only a warning.

Mister Swan stepped back. "Hold him!" he said angrily.

Walt came forward. "I'll keep him calm, Mister Swan," he said.

Again the nostrils flared, but this time the ears flicked. Dandy eyed Walt out of the corner of his eye.

"Let him alone, Walt," said Ben.

"Keep quiet, young'un'," snapped Walt. " I can handle any horse on this farm or any other farm and could do it before you were out of swaddling clothes."

"Not Dandy! Let him alone, Walt," pleaded Ben.

Dandy moved quickly. The hoof shot out again, and Ben knew the big bay did not mean to strike Walt, but Walt had not quite become accustomed to moving about without an arm. As he jumped back he staggered a little and the hoof grazed the stump of Walt's arm. He seemed to choke in agony as he reeled back to the fence, clutching at the stub. His face was white and drawn and great beads of sweat formed on his forehead.

Ben got between Dandy and the two men. "Let him alone," he said.

Mister Swan's eyes narrowed. "I'll give you a hundred dollars for him, Buell," he said. "Dangerous beast. But the Army boys will make him shape up. I'll take him along, eh? One hundred dollars! Cash on the line!"

Walt looked up with tortured eyes. "A deal," he gasped. "But get him out of here right now!"

"No, Walt!" cried Ben.

Walt straightened himself up. "Get to the house," he said. "Get to work on your chores! You've played enough these past few months with the horses and with that third rate militia company in town. Hear me, Ben Buell! I'm running this farm and don't you ever forget it!"

Ben closed his fists and for one awful moment the wild thought of battering away at Walt with those hard fists raced through his mind, then taking Dandy with him as he fled anywhere, as long as it was away from his home.

"Ben!" said Walt. He drew himself up.

There was pride in the Buells, but there was discipline too. Captain Buell had seen to it that his two sons had learned the meaning of discipline. Ben dared not look at Dandy.

"You'd better have him tether the bay to the back of my buggy, Buell," said Mister Swan.

"I can do it," said Walt.

"That bay won't let you near him no more than he would me. Have the boy do it, Buell, while we go to the house and make out the bill of sale."

Ben, sick at heart, led his horse out onto the dusty road and tethered him to the rear of the buggy. For a moment he pressed his face against that of the bay, then he turned quickly and walked toward the farmhouse, not looking back when Dandy neighed again and again.

Ben heard the hum of voices in the house as he entered by the back door, passed through the kitchen, and went upstairs to his room. It was too early for him to start for militia drill in Hinckley's Corners, but he knew he couldn't stay around the farm that day. He undressed and put on his ill-fitting uniform, placed his forage cap on his head, and took his rifle and equipment from the closet. He had just buckled on his belt when he looked up to see his mother standing in the doorway. "You're leaving early, Ben," she said quietly.

"Yes, Mother."

She studied him. "Is it true that Walt sold Dandy?" she asked.

He nodded. "He had no right to," he said bitterly.

"Walt is not well, Ben."

"I know! The loss of his arm has changed him! Well, I've been hearing that for months, and I'm getting sick of it!"

She came into the room and placed her thin hands on his shoulders. "Go to drill then, Ben," she said. "I'll talk to Walt. You and Walt are all I have left now."

He looked away from her.

"You said you would not enlist until you were eighteen," she said.

It was as though she had read his mind. "That's almost two years from now," he said. "The war could be over by then."

"I know," she said quietly.

"There are a lot of other Hinckley's Corners' boys in the Army," he said. "Joe Cash is a drummer with the Sixth Corps. Frank Ferris is a trooper in Rush's Pennsylvania Lancers, and he's only a few months older than me!

The sound of the front door opening and closing came to them. Then the sound of feet on the gravel walk. A moment later the gate squeaked open, then closed again. There was a pause, followed by the sound of reins being slapped on the back of a horse, then the sound of hoofs striking the hard, dusty road. Mister Swan was on his way.

Mrs. Buell stood there looking at her second son, the youngest of her three men. "It's part of the long and painful process of growing up, Ben," she said softly.

"Yes, Mother."

She stood to one side. "Go on then," she said.

He kissed her cheek and walked from the room, and her eyes had a sadness in them as she watched his strong back and shoulders, clad in army blue, and saw the dull sheen of the heavy rifle barrel against the papered wall.

Ben passed the big barn and heard Walt talking to old Henry Harker, who had worked on the Buell farm since before Ben and Walt had been born. "Sure, Henry," Walt was saying, "I'm sorry I lost my temper and sold Dandy, but I won't have a horse on this farm I can't handle."

"You could have handled him, Walt," said Henry. "Of all the horses we've ever had here, he was the best by far. You should never have sold him."

"You telling me how to run this place? "

There was a long pause. "No, Walt," said Henry quietly. "I think you're doing a fine job. One thing I do know though: you'll have a long, hard time ahead of you making this thing up to Ben. That's all I have to say."

Ben passed the outbuildings, climbed a low stone fence, and cut across the wide pasture to the creek. Here he walked across the big log that had served as a footbridge as far back as he could remember and passed on into the soft light of the woods. He drifted quietly along, rifle at the ready, trying to forget his loss of Dandy, while he practiced the art of scouting and reconnoitering as taught to his militia company by Sergeant Seth Pomeroy. "The scouts are the eyes and ears of the infantry," Seth would say, with his earnest eyes peering into each face lined up before him. "The lives of their comrades may depend on their alertness and thoroughness."

Ben moved on, hardly heard except for the soft rustling of his feet and the soft slapping of his bayonet scabbard against his left hip and the empty canteen against his right hip, the very picture of an alert scout.

It was all right until he reached the Hinckley's Corners Road where it joined the Taneytown Road. There the little grass-grown cemetery seemed to nestle in a wide hollow, rimmed by gently swaying trees. Here some generations of Buells and Pattersons had been buried, his mother having been a Patterson. One of the newer graves was that of Ben's father. He did not look at it as he passed the cemetery to strike out on the road toward Hinckley's Corners, for he had never gotten over the wasting death of his father.

The sun was low in the west as he neared the town. Smoke drifted up from chimneys as housewives prepared the evening meal. Far off down the valley came the mournful whistling of a locomotive. The sound was enough to plunge Ben's spirits into the very depths of despair. Dandy probably was on his way north by now. They'd try to tame him, and they'd break his spirit to do it. A sudden urge came over Ben to keep plodding on to Harrisburg, where he could lie about his age and enlist. But his mother's careworn face seemed to appear before him. *"You said you would not enlist until you were eighteen,"* she had said. And again: *"It's part of the long and painful process of growing up, Ben —"*

He looked down at his uniform as he walked along, and some of the emotion he had experienced as he had practiced scouting through the woods faded away. A uniform didn't make a soldier, and the militia was little more than a scarecrow collection of men and boys, too young or too old for the Regulars or Volunteers, and men physically unfit for active field duty. "The Pennsylvania Volunteer Militia," said Ben bitterly. Everything was ashes in his mouth now. The loss of Dandy, his quarrel with his brother, the promise he had made to his mother not to enlist until he was eighteen. For the first time in his sixteen years of life the future was of little or no interest to Ben Buell, private in the rearmost rank, Pennsylvania Volunteer Militia.

CHAPTER TWO

A whispering breeze rustled through the trees of the village square as the men and boys of B Company, Pennsylvania Volunteer Militia, drifted down the streets to gather for the evening drill. Sergeant Seth Pomeroy usually acted as orderly sergeant and indeed was in charge of the company most of the time. Captain Eb Waycross, who had served briefly during the Mexican War and who had never heard a shot fired, was a veterinarian and as such was quite often out on calls when he should have been drilling his command. First Lieutenant Oscar Mills, the local druggist, kept his shop open late as long as he anticipated a customer, and even when he appeared for drill he could not last long, for his enormous weight slowed him down and after a few minutes of exertion his breath was so wheezy none of the men could understand his commands anyway.

Ben Buell leaned against a thick-boled tree at the edge of the drilling area, with hardly a second glance at the girls who usually lined the drill field to watch the brave boys of Hinckley's Corners perform the times and numbers of drilling. Seth Pomeroy was earnestly scanning the roster roll in the fading light. Seth was the local schoolmaster and a good one despite the fact that he had just turned twenty years of age. But Seth had always had visions of martial glory and when his working day at school was over he would retire to his little bachelor's cottage near the school and devour such light reading material as *Rifle and Infantry Tactics; Evolution of Field Batteries of Artillery* in the original French text; *The United States Infantry Tactics for the Instruction of Infantry of the Line and Light Infantry, Together with Bayonet Exercises; Regulations and Instructions for the Field Service of the U.S. Cavalry in Time of War; The Manual for Light Infantry; Hardee's Rifle and Infantry Tactics;* and many, many others.

Ben liked Seth. They were actually second cousins on the Patterson side of the Buell family. He eyed Seth's serious face, and suddenly realized that Seth was a good-looking man with his clear gray eyes and light blond hair set off by the dark blue of his blouse and forage cap. The lamplight shone on the brass infantry insignia bugle on his cap as he turned to look about. He saw Ben and started across toward him. It was then that the illusion of a perfect-looking soldier faded away, for Seth Pomeroy had been born with one leg a little shorter than the other and he had a sort of rolling limp that he fought to control as he walked, even though dewy sweat sometimes appeared on his high forehead because of the effort he put out to do so.

"Private Buell?" said Seth.

Ben straightened up. He hardly felt like playing soldiers that night. "Yes, Sergeant Pomeroy," he said.

"Carry the company guidon tonight, Buell."

Ben's heart sank a little as he walked to the cased guidon and took it out of the waterproof cover. It was a beautiful piece of work proudly stitched by Mrs. Abernethy, the village seamstress. The legend on it was B Company, over the letters P.V.M., but it was the elaborately stitched company nickname that made Ben Buell shudder a little. He had thought it was quite fitting when he had joined up the year before, but when the bronzed veterans of the Army of the Potomac came home on leave they would grin and snicker at that very nickname. "The Hinckley's Corners Tiger Rifles," he said as he folded the cover and placed it in the crotch of a tree. The wind rustled the silk of the guidon as though in answer.

The company was almost fully assembled. Boys, some of them hardly fifteen, and old men, some of whom had been along in years when the Mexican War had been fought seventeen years before. Some of the members limped, one had three fingers missing from his left hand, two of them had but one eye, and aging Harry Rinders had no teeth, which hardly qualified him to tear open a paper cartridge for loading, but Harry was a fair drummer and despite his age had been made company drummer. He took the job quite seriously, and the Hinckley's Corners Tiger Rifles had no complaints about his beatings.

Sergeant Pomeroy listened gravely to a small boy who gave him the urgent message that Captain Eb Waycross was out on a call, and Lieutenant Oscar Mills was making up a prescription for ailing Mrs. Home. Pomeroy glanced at Harry Rinders. "Sound the 'Assembly,' Rinders," he said crisply.

As the lamplighter went around the square and lighted the streetlamps the steady beatings of Rinders' deep-bellied infantry drum echoed from the fronts of the buildings facing the square and the men and boys of B Company fell in with a rustling of leather and rattling of steel. When the drumming died away Sergeant Pomeroy called the roll, then took the company through a steady fifty-minute period of the manual of arms. In the dim light of the lamps, B Company looked pretty good. The thought was Guidon-bearer Ben Buell's. No one else could take the credit except Seth Pomeroy, but Ben knew well enough what was in the militant schoolteacher's heart of hearts. Seth had tried for months to get into the service. Artillery had been Seth's first love, but they had turned him down, as most of the artillery batteries were more or less composed of picked men, and in many cases commanded by strait-laced Regulars who wanted no cripples in *their* batteries. Cavalry units were always popular and the mounted regiments had their choice of fit men without taking in a man like Seth. In the infantry he would have been useless because of his limp. So Seth had returned to Hinckley's Corners and to his books and dreams, but he had never satisfied himself that his destiny was to be Sergeant Pomeroy of the Hinckley's Corners Tiger Rifles. Fate surely could not be so unkind.

It was Sergeant Pomeroy's custom to pass his company in review after drill on the nights when he was in command. Captain Eb Waycross thought it was stuff and nonsense, while Lieutenant Oscar Mills would usually be too tired to march about the square. But it was Sergeant Pomeroy's deep pleasure to do so and indeed it was a pleasure for Ben Buell too, because of the fife and drum music that set the pace. Harry Rinders was a good drummer, but Fifer Zack Pascoe had the skill and talent to coax the very breath of life into the cocoa wood fife when he played "The Belle of the Mohawk Vale" or perhaps the wild quickstep "The Wrecker's Daughter." It was then that Ben Buell was no longer a high private in the rear rank of the Hinckley's Corners Tiger Rifles but rather a rifleman in perhaps the Pennsylvania Bucktails or the famed Iron Brigade.

This night the drum rattled and the fife took up the sharp clear notes of "The White Cockade." The company stepped out smartly, led by Sergeant Seth Pomeroy, face set and stern, followed by Ben Buell proudly carrying the silken guidon, while the remainder of the company, for a miracle, were all in step and keeping perfect time. The illusion was wonderful until the company reached the eastern end of the little square not far from the white-painted bandstand where the girls and the idlers had congregated. Lamplight shone on brass buttons and on a rakishly tilted forage cap set upon dark-brown curls. The white trefoil badge of the Second Division of the Second Corps of the Army of the Potomac seemed etched on the dark-blue material of the cap top. Ben recognized Corporal Milas Gilson, hardly more than twenty years old, but already a veteran of the Seven Days, Antietam, Fredericksburg, and Chancellorsville, home in Hinckley's Corners recovering from a wound received at Chancellorsville.

Sergeant Pomeroy was almost even with Milas Gilson, striding along with no trace of his lifelong limp,

when Milas spoke out in a humorously dry voice. "The Hinckley's Corners Tiger Rifles." It was all he said. There was no need to say more. Almost instantly Seth's limp became apparent. Harry Rinders' timing became faulty, Fifer Zack Pascoe's fife flatted off, and the company began to lose step, to end up in a shambles as Sergeant Pomeroy forgot to turn the little column and they plodded manfully into a thicket. Ben Buell flushed. The gaudy guidon became a hateful thing to him. When the company was dismissed, Ben took the guidon to where he had left the case and covered it up as quickly as he could. He got his rifle and plodded listlessly across the dark park to where the shadowy figure of Sergeant Pomeroy stood. Seth was looking across the open area at Milas Gilson, who was laughing and joking with the girls. The girl closest to him, hanging onto his arm, was Sally Carr, and up until the time Milas Gilson had come home to Hinckley's Corners, it had always been Sergeant Seth Pomeroy who had walked her home, studiously elucidating on military science and tactics.

"Sergeant?" said Ben.

"Yes?"

"The guidon, Sergeant."

Pomeroy nodded.

"It isn't your fault that you're a cripple, Sergeant

Pomeroy." Then Ben flushed. He hadn't meant to say it quite that way.

Seth smiled. "It's all right, Ben. I'll walk you to your horse. I liked the way you handled the guidon tonight. How would you like to carry it on all of the drills? It's quite an honor to carry the colors, you know."

Ben shook his head. "I'd rather not, Sergeant."

Seth took the cased guidon. "I understand," he said quietly. The Hinckley's Corners Tiger Rifles." Pomeroy smiled again. "We do the best we can. Where's Dandy?"

"I didn't ride him tonight, Seth."

"Why not?"

Ben tried to talk, but his throat dried up on him.

"Is something wrong, Ben?"

"Walt sold Dandy today, Seth. Sold him to a Government contractor." The words came in a sudden rush.

"No!"

Ben nodded. "I just can't go back home tonight, Seth."

"You can stay with me. Phil Abbott goes past your place on the way home. He can tell them you're staying the night with me."

Ben and Seth entered Seth's tiny living room and peeled off their heavy blouses. Seth got a pitcher of lemonade and a platter of slightly stale cookies. He glanced at the big map that he had pinned to the wall of the room. It covered almost the entire wall. Pins of different colors and little flags dotted the map, indicating the positions of various bodies of troops of both contending armies in Virginia. No one, with possibly the exception of General Halleck, General in Chief in Washington, could have followed the maneuvers and campaigning in Virginia more closely than Seth Pomeroy of the Pennsylvania Volunteer Militia.

"Tell me about the war, Seth," said Ben.

"You really want to know?"

"Yes." Ben wanted Seth to get his mind off Milas

Gilson and the Hinckley's Corners Tiger Rifles, and he wanted to get his own mind off Dandy.

Seth stood up, adjusted the lamp so that the light fell upon the map, pursed his lips, then began to talk, indicating the movements of the armies with his pointer. "It's obvious that the Confederacy is already feeling the manpower shortage I expected they would, Ben. Fighting Joe Hooker's strategy in leaving a third of his army to hold Lee at Fredericksburg, then marching up the Rappahannock to move in on Lee's unprotected left flank and rear was excellent. His tactics were terrible. He lost his nerve at the critical moment, and Lee smashed him by daring tactics. Hooker retreated after losing seventeen thousand men. A brilliant victory for Lee and the Army of Northern Virginia."

"And now what, Seth?" asked Ben with deep interest. He heard little of the war on the farm, and Walt would never speak of it.

Seth rubbed his nose with the pointer. "I personally believe that it's to the best interests of the South for Lee to move north. An invasion, as it were, of the North."

"I find that hard to believe, Seth."

"It *is* hard to believe, but an offensive thrust northward by the Army of Northern Virginia, flushed with victories and led by the genius of Robert E. Lee, might well decide the war for the Confederacy."

"How could this happen?"

"You know that General Grant and his Army of the Tennessee have a firm grip on Vicksburg. A victory by Lee might well cause Grant to be withdrawn for use in other areas, rather than in laying siege to Vicksburg. The North is tired of war, and a Southern victory could raise a clamoring for peace in the Union. Then, too, the northern part of Virginia is practically a ravaged wilderness, hardly able to support Lee's forces. Lee and his army are known to be in the Valley of the Shenandoah.

This is almost a direct and sheltered approach to the North!

"Go on, Seth," said Ben with deep interest.

Seth eyed the map. "Our Army of the Potomac is therefore east of Lee and his Army of Northern Virginia. If Lee moves north, then Hooker also must move north, to fend Lee away from Washington and bring him to battle. Perhaps in Maryland —"

Ben nodded. "But certainly not as far north as our state, Seth."

The schoolmaster turned slowly. "Why not, Ben?" he asked.

"Why, he wouldn't have a chance, Seth! Hooker would stop him. The people would rally. Even the militia might have to be called out. I—" Ben's voice died away as he saw the intense look on Seth's face.

"Yes," said Seth in a low voice. "They just *might* call out the Hinckley's Corners Tiger Rifles, Ben. We'd show 'em, Ben. We'd show them!"

Seth paced back and forth. "They might need *us,* Ben."

The quick elation that had poured through Ben began to fade. They'd hardly have to call on the militia, with the tough veterans of the First, Second, Third, Fifth, Sixth, Eleventh, and Twelfth Corps standing in the way of Lee and his rebels. "Sure," he said bitterly, "they'd call us out to guard crossroads or bridges or something like that, Seth."

Seth stopped his pacing. "We'd see action, Ben! It would be our only chance!"

Ben helped himself to a cookie, but he took it away from his mouth untasted. If Lee was marching north there would be hard fighting. Men would be killed and wounded. Horses would be killed and wounded. Horses . . . Dandy . . .

Ben suddenly felt very tired It had been a long day.

Seth eyed him. "Best get to bed, Ben. I'm sorry about Dandy. Is there any chance of getting him back?"

"I don't think so."

"That isn't like Walt at all."

Ben looked up and his mother's words came quickly to his lips. "The loss of his arm changed him, Seth! It's hard for a young man like Walt to be a cripple the rest of his life."

Seth flushed a little. "I know, Ben. I ought to know."

Later, as they lay in the wide bed in the second floor bedroom of the little house, watching the June moonlight playing through the leaves of the trees outside of the window, Seth Pomeroy hunched his pillow up behind his head and locked his hands behind his neck. "If we get a chance, Ben. If we get one crack at those Johnny Rebs, you can bet that Seth Pomeroy will make a record! A record that will force them to take me into the Volunteers or the Regulars!"

"I hope so, Seth," said Ben sleepily.

"Let them laugh at us then!"

Ben glanced sideways at Seth, and he knew well enough what his cousin was thinking. Maybe Seth Pomeroy wanted glory, a chance to defeat the enemies of his country, but Ben was also pretty sure that Seth Pomeroy wanted to impress Milas Gilson, and even more so, Sally Carr of the laughing blue eyes and corn-silk hair.

The last thing Ben remembered before he fell into a dreamless sleep was Dandy's pitiful neighing after Ben had tethered him to the rear of Mister Swan's buggy and had walked away from him, never looking back, for to do so would have completely broken Ben's heart.

The tattoo of hoofbeats on the hard pike road that ran past Seth Pomeroy's house awakened Ben Buell. He sat up. *Maybe it was Dandy!* There seemed to be a frantic urgency in those hard-hitting hoofs. They struck the wooden decking of the bridge that crossed the stream several hundred yards beyond Seth's house, raising low thunder in the quiet summer night. Ben swung his legs over the side of the bed and ran to the open window to look down upon the moonlit pike. The horseman was pelting up the rise, and Ben could see the sweat-lathered hide of the horse, glistening in the moonlight.

The horseman looked up and saw Ben framed in the window. "You, boy!" he called. "Where can I find the commander of the local militia company?" He reined in his tired mount.

"Sergeant Pomeroy lives here," answered Ben. "What is up, sir?"

The man shoved back his hat. "Invasion," he said in a dust-hoarse voice. " Lee and the Army of Northern Virginia have crossed the state line into Pennsylvania and are marching on Chambersburg. Rebel cavalry in force have already occupied Chambersburg."

A stern voice broke in over Ben's shoulder. "General Hooker and the Army of the Potomac will stop them, sir!" It was Seth Pomeroy.

"General Hooker has been relieved of command," said the horseman. "The Army of the Potomac is now commanded by Major General George Gordon Meade of the Fifth Corps. The Army of the Potomac is on the move north also, guarding the Potomac crossings above Washington, or so it is said. The boy said you were a sergeant in the local militia. Is that so?"

"Yes," said Seth as he struggled into his trousers.

"Then you'd best get to your commanding officer! Governor Curtin is calling out the militia for the defense of the state. The term of service will be as long as the state is endangered. Will you carry that news to your commanding officer? I must get on to Gettysburg to alert the militia there."

"Godspeed then," said Seth as he pulled on his shoes.

Ben wasted no time in getting dressed. Now and then he looked at the pale, determined face of his cousin. The schoolmaster's face seemed almost to shine from within.

Ben remembered his impassioned words of the evening before. *They just* might *call out the Hinckley's Corners Tiger Rifles, Ben. We'd show 'em, Ben. We'd show them!*

"What kind of a soldier is Meade, Seth?" asked Ben as he buttoned his blouse.

Seth looked up. "He's a good corps commander. Personally, I think General Reynolds of the First Corps would have been a better choice. But Meade's a fighter! He's no picture book soldier though. There are two reasons I think he'll do well against Lee, Ben."

"Yes?"

Seth placed his forage cap on his head and raked it slightly. "He has a fine army under his command, toughened by two years of war. There's nothing wrong with them, but rather in the way they've been led. They'll fight and fight well."

"And the other reason, Seth"?

Seth looked steadily at Ben. "General Meade is a Pennsylvanian. He will not be defeated on the soil of his own state!"

The words were a little highfalutin' for Ben, but the thought behind them was good. He followed Seth downstairs. They got their rifles and the cased guidon and hurried toward the middle of Hinckley's Corners along the moonlit road. This was the moment for which they both had waited. The road to war! Nothing could stop them now. Not Ben's youth and his promise to his mother, nor Seth Pomeroy's shortened leg. The Union would need boys and cripples, and they were ready.

CHAPTER THREE

The Hinckley's Corners Tiger Rifles, Company B of the Pennsylvania Volunteer Militia, formed in the village square in the watery light of the false dawn, ready to march out on the road to glory. There had been noise and confusion in Hinckley's Corners in the hours before dawn as the militiamen dressed in their uniforms, buckled on their belts heavy with bayonet and scabbard, canteen, cartridge pouch and cap pouch, slung their haversacks over their right shoulders and let them rest on the left hip, took their rifled muskets, and then double timed to the assembly area in the square where they were issued knapsacks with rolled blankets strapped on the top. Official orders had come through channels to Captain Eb Waycross, but Captain Waycross had not yet returned from his call somewhere east of Hinckley's Corners. Lieutenant Oscar Mills took command of the company, and since he was far too heavy to ride, had hitched his mare to a buggy and would command Company B from there. "In all likelihood, Sergeant Pomeroy," he had said, "there will be little fighting for us to do, if any at all. But thanks to you, Pomeroy, we're ready for duty. It is you who should command this company. I should have resigned in favor of you, but it's too late now, and I cannot very well resign in the face of the enemy."

"I understand, sir," said Seth.

"We are to rendezvous with other militia units to the north, at Freeman's Crossroads, no later than noon this day."

So the Tiger Rifles moved out, on the dusty road toward Freeman's Crossroads, with Harry Rinders beating his drum and Zack Pascoe tootling the brave six-eight, "The Tattered Jack." Ben Buell marched behind Sergeant Pomeroy, bearing the company guidon, with his rifle carried in the lone supply wagon that brought up the rear of the trudging company.

It didn't take them long to reach the Buell farm and as they neared the gate Ben could see his mother and his brother Walt and white-haired Henry Harker, standing at the edge of the road. Seth spoke out of the side of his mouth to Ben. "You can skip out of ranks long enough to say good-bye, Ben."

Ben nodded, and as they reached the gateway he stepped out of formation. His mother said nothing. She held his arm, and her eyes were misty. Walt cleared his throat. "I'm sorry about the bay, Ben. I sent Henry after Mister Swan, but the man could not be found."

"It's all right, Walt," said Ben quietly.

Walt eyed the guidon. "Pretty gaudy, Ben. Well, it isn't likely they'll send you in to face the Johnnies, green as you are. If you do face them, don't try to win the war alone. I know you won't run."

"Why do they send boys and older men to fight?" asked Mrs. Buell.

"Just a precaution, Mother," said Walt.

"I have to catch up now, Mother," said Ben. He kissed her. Henry Harker gripped Ben's hand. Walt placed his arm about Ben's shoulders and squeezed him hard, then he reached inside his coat and withdrew a Colt revolving pistol. He handed it to Ben. "Captured this from a rebel officer at Manassas," he said. "Take it along, Ben, and I hope you never have to use it."

Ben slid the heavy pistol beneath his blouse and hurried after his trudging company. The first true light of the day was beginning to show over the low hills to the east.

The sun was hardly up before the heat of the day began to be felt, and the equipment carried by the green militia seemed to get heavier by the minute. The heat began to reflect from the hard road as they crossed through the open areas and only in the places where the pike ran through groves and woods did the heat seem to abate. It was quite different from marching back and forth on the cool grass in the square at Hinckley's Corners in the half-light of a summer evening.

By the time the company had marched to within three miles of Freeman's Crossroads the straggling was getting pretty bad. A quarter of the company limped along far behind the single rattling supply wagon, and in the wagon rode some of the weariest men. It carried some of the rifles of the men who still marched as well and Lieutenant Mills' buggy was also loaded with rifles and knapsacks.

Seth Pomeroy was having a bad time of it, and his limp became more pronounced with each mile, but he would not quit. Ben Buell felt the sticky sweat coursing down his body beneath the thick woolen fatigue blouse he wore and there was the suspicion in his mind that blisters were forming on his feet. If he had been able to march barefooted, he was sure he wouldn't have suffered blisters, but then that would not have been quite military, at least in the Union Army. Many of the rebels, or so he had been told, marched miles upon miles in their bare feet, through choice or necessity, and it never seemed to affect *their* fighting ability.

"Sergeant Pomeroy, do we have to carry all this stuff?"

asked Sam Dennis wearily. " Seems to me we'll be all worn out before we get a chance to fight."

"They won't use *us* for fighting," said Jim Vickers. " If they do, you can bet we're losing the war."

"That's enough of that talk!" snapped Seth Pomeroy.

"That's Freeman's Crossroads ahead there," said Harry Rinders. He hitched his drum up higher on his shoulders. " Nice and cool in them woods and there's a good spring there."

"Ain't no sign of anyone else there," said Zack Pascoe quietly.

"We're probably the first ones here," said Ben.

Seth Pomeroy nodded. "Lieutenant Mills told me he heard that the Pennsylvania militia were to mobilize at Harrisburg. Maybe they'll send us up there."

"That's the wrong way to go," said Corporal Dan Caxton. "The Johnnies are south of us."

Seth wiped the sweat from his dusty face. " Maybe," he said quietly.

"What do you mean by that?" asked Caxton.

Seth waved a hand toward the west. "The way the Army of Northern Virginia can march, they might be farther north than we think they are. Maybe farther north than *we* are."

The men looked quickly at one another, then apprehensively toward the west and the distant hills. It was disquieting to think of those ragged and fierce "foot cavalry" of the Army of Northern Virginia marching swiftly to the north.

"Wonder where is the Army of the Potomac?" said Harry Rinders. He had spoken the thought that was in all their minds.

Jim Vickers spat casually and shifted his heavy musket from his right shoulder to his left. "Why worry?" he said loftily. "The ol' Hinckley's Corners Tiger Rifles can fend off the Johnnies while the Army of the Pot-o-mac gets around to thinking *they'd* better get on the move."

Seth Pomeroy flushed beneath the dust on his face. He looked back at Zack Pascoe. "Zack," he said, "have you got a tune to take us into the Crossroads?"

Zack shrugged. "Probably fill my fife with dust, but I'll try my best."

Harry Rinders took his drum from his shoulders and removed his sticks from the brass drumstick carriage hooked onto the front of his drum sling. "What will it be, Zack?" he asked.

The quiet fifer looked thoughtful. "How about 'Sergeant O'Leary,' six-eight?"

"Fair enough," said Harry.

The drum sounded dull and flat in the heat-laden air, but the fife seemed to have a shrill life of its own as Zack picked out the marching tune. The ranks of Company B straightened up. The hot wind fluttered the gay but dusty guidon. Lieutenant Mills' old mare seemed to come to life. The tired militiamen tramped steadily through the sunlight until at last they entered the comparatively cool grove that held Freeman's Crossroads in its green depths. There was no sight of blue uniforms in the shifting light that came down through the thick foliage of the trees.

The straggling company halted at Lieutenant Mills' command. The fat officer's face was dewed with sweat, and his breath was harsh and irregular. "Help me down, Pomeroy," he said. "I've got to get some cold water."

There was a thudding of equipment on the ground as the tired and dusty militiamen broke ranks, stacked their heavy rifles, and headed for the spring. Far down the sunlit road the stragglers could be seen, limping along bravely enough but making slow time. Most of them could do a full day's work in the fields and hardly notice it, but to march on a hard pike in the heat of the sun, with dust swirling about them, wearing heavy uniforms and carrying a mass of equipment, was quite another matter.

One by one the men came in, cast off their equipment, and headed for the stream. Lieutenant Mills had just finished his third cup of the clear cold water, when he suddenly jerked his head backward, clamped his thick arms across the lower part of his heavy belly, and fell over sideways. Seth Pomeroy knelt beside the officer. He looked up at the men. "Too much heat and too much cold water."

"He was riding in his buggy," said Jim Vickers. "Maybe it's some of us that should get sick."

"He's an older man than most of us," said the sergeant.

Corporal Derringer examined the officer, then looked at Sergeant Pomeroy. "We'd best get him back to town, Seth. We can't take him with us and we can't leave him here."

Seth nodded. He stood up and looked at the men. Elderly George Bruce was leaning against a tree, fully done in. "George," said Seth, "you'd better drive Lieutenant Mills back to Hinckley's Corners."

"Why me? I ain't going to leave the company now!"

"You're the oldest man in the company, George," Seth pointed out.

"I can outwalk and outfight most of these whippersnappers!"

Seth flushed. "It's an order, George."

The man stood up straight. "Listen, schoolmaster," he said angrily. "I got my rights. I stay here!"

A subtle change came over the quiet sergeant. "George Bruce," he said in a steady, clear voice, "you get to that buggy and get ready to drive Lieutenant Mills back to Hinckley's Corners."

Seth took one step toward Bruce. "Move," he said flatly.

George Bruce moved. They loaded the gasping officer into the buggy. He looked at Seth Pomeroy. "You're in charge, Pomeroy," he said weakly. "If Captain Waycross has returned to town, I'll tell him what happened, and he'll be out to join you. Stay here for an hour or so and if the rest of the militia does not show up, you must march north toward Gettysburg. Stay on the Taneytown Road so that Captain Waycross may find you."

"Are those all my orders, sir?" asked Seth.

Mills shrugged. "They were all I received. Good-by, Sergeant Pomeroy, and good luck. Good-by, boys!"

They silently watched the buggy move out of the shade and head toward Hinckley's Corners at a slow pace. Seth shoved back his forage cap and wiped the sweat from his forehead. "Lie down and rest, men," he said. "We've a long day ahead of us."

Ben Buell lay flat on the ground with his cap tilted so that the visor rested on his nose. He could see the rest of the company lying about on the ground. Bees hummed drowsily and some of the men were talking in low voices. Sergeant Pomeroy had walked to the western edge of the grove and stood there looking off across the rolling fields and low hills, as though listening and watching for the enemy.

B Company resumed the enervating march in the very heat of the day. Sergeant Pomeroy had left behind a full squad of his men, under charge of Corporal Sears, who suffered from an immense blister on his right heel. The squad was composed of those hardly able to continue the march. "The sick, the halt, and the blind," Sam Dennis had called them. Seth had made sure that none of them were shirkers. He could ill afford to lose at least a fifth of his small command, but there was nothing he could do about it. Captain Waycross would have to make arrangements to bring them on. Meanwhile "On to Gettysburg!" was the watchword of the men of Company B.

The afternoon sun was slanting down toward the distant mountains far to the west when Phil Abbott, who toiled along at the rear of the weary company, raised a dust-hoarse shout. "Sergeant Pomeroy! They's dust rising behind us, beyond them woods we passed through an hour ago!"

"Halt!" barked Seth Pomeroy. He hitched his musket from his left shoulder to his right and double timed down the length of the company. Shading his eyes with his hand, he spotted the thin spiral of yellow dust that was rising beyond the woods. The men leaned on their muskets, idly watching the dust.

"What do you think it is?" asked Jim Vickers of Sergeant Pomeroy.

Seth touched his dry lips with the tip of his tongue. "From the size of the dust cloud rising, it's more than just a few wagons or men moving along."

"Or cavalry," said Jim Vickers. "*Rebel* cavalry."

"This far north?" asked Harry Rinders nervously.

"Bosh," said Corporal Caxton.

Ben Buell sipped a little warm water from his canteen. The dust was getting thicker, and it had an ominous look to him. He looked at Seth Pomeroy. The young sergeant rubbed his dusty jaw. "The main force of the enemy *could* be in Chambersburg by now," he said quietly. "They don't call them 'foot cavalry ' for nothing."

"But that's almost due west of Gettysburg," said Dan Caxton. "Maybe a little further north though."

"Well then, what would their cavalry be doing around here?" demanded Sam Dennis.

Seth wet his lips again. The dust cloud was rising faster and higher. Someone was in an all-fired hurry this hot afternoon. "The Army of the Potomac is also moving north," he said thoughtfully. "If that's so, then there must be cavalry screens and scouts out between the two armies. Could be our cavalry as well as theirs."

Jim Vickers spat dryly. "Yeah," he said gloomily. "But if the Army of the Potomac is moving north, and the rebels are supposed to be in Chambersburg, how come we haven't seen hide nor hair of any of the Army of the

Potomac all this livelong day, Sergeant Pomeroy? Not even the rest of our *own* militia regiment?"

The long quiet that followed Jim's words was broken by Corporal Caxton. "You don't suppose, boys, that Company B is somewheres in between the Army of the Potomac and the Army of Northern Virginia, do you?"

By now all of the stragglers had caught up. Sergeant Pomeroy looked back over his shoulder. A tumbledown stone fence edged a shallow winding stream at the edge of a little grove of woods a quarter of a mile ahead of them on a gently rising ridge. "Company B! Fall in!" he commanded. He ran awkwardly to the head of the little column. "Forward march!" He started up the road, then looked back over his shoulder. "Double time! March!"

They started off at a weary, shambling run. "What's wrong with him?" demanded Jim Vickers. "He gone plumb out'a his mind?"

"You want to stand out here in the open and get cut down by some of Jeb Stuart's troopers?" demanded Dan Caxton.

Vickers stared at him openmouthed. "You mean Seth aims to *fight* 'em, Corporal?"

"Maybe you'd like to stay behind and weave daisy chains for their horses' necks?" asked Caxton sarcastically.

The noncom's words seemed to spur on the laggard militiamen. Seth reached the wall and climbed over it. He turned quickly. "Get that wagon along the road and into the woods, Barney!" he yelled at the driver. "Company B! Fall in!"

The harsh-breathing company lined up. "Load!" snapped out Sergeant Pomeroy. Paper cartridges were taken from cartridge pouches and the ends of the paper torn open with the teeth. The powder was poured down into the barrel, and the Minie bullet was driven down the barrel atop the powder and seated with a hard push of the ramrod, the rest of the paper cartridge acting as wadding. Then the heavy rifles were capped. "Take positions along the fence," commanded Seth. "Corporal Caxton, take charge of the right! Corporal Derringer, the left! I'll stay here in the center! Private Buell, plant the flag here!"

Ben thrust the spiked tip of the guidon staff into the soft ground. He thrust a hand inside his blouse and felt the butt of the pistol Walt had given him. The lone supply wagon was now at the far end of the woods, too far for him to run and get his rifle.

It was very quiet in the warm woods. Now and then a man moved, another coughed, still another nervously swallowed a mouthful of water from his canteen. At first they glanced back at the taut face of their young sergeant, but as the dust cloud continued to grow in size and get nearer and nearer, they could not take their eyes from it.

A pair of horsemen appeared at the edge of the woods beyond which arose the dust cloud. They moved forward slowly, riding easily. The heat shimmered up from the open ground and gave the two horsemen a curiously unreal appearance as though they were being viewed through water.

"Zack Pascoe," said Seth at last. "You've got good eyes. Can you make them out?"

Zack stood up. "They're soldiers all right," he said.

Now the dust was rising from within the other woods. Half a dozen horsemen appeared in the open, a hundred yards behind the first two mounted men.

"Zack?" asked Seth.

"More soldiers," said the fifer.

Seth paused. "What color uniforms?"

Zack shook his head.

Seth looked at Ben. "Skin up that tree there, Ben. Maybe you can make it out from there."

Ben climbed the tree, inched out on a thick branch,

parted the leaves, and eyed the oncoming troopers. He stared and swallowed hard.

"Ben?" called Seth.

Ben tried to speak but could not.

"Ben!" snapped Seth.

Now more horsemen had appeared. A platoon of them. Dust was still pouring up both from within and beyond the woods.

"Ben! What color uniforms?"

Ben looked down at the taut, dusty faces of the crouching men. "Gray," he said at last.

"This ain't no place for us," said Jim Vickers.

Ben slid down the tree and withdrew the heavy Colt pistol.

Jim spoke to Seth Pomeroy. "Maybe we'd better pull out, Sergeant Pomeroy. They's an all-fired bunch of them Graybacks in them woods. Too many for Company B."

"We stay," said Seth quietly.

"But, Sergeant!"

"We stay! The first man that runs I'll shoot down like a dog!"

Jim scowled and lay down flat again. "Just because he has three stripes," he growled.

They waited in the hot afternoon as the horsemen drew closer and closer. Beyond the platoon that had appeared, no other troopers could be seen, but the dust told of their presence. The men of Company B waited.

The first two men were a hundred and fifty yards away, with the squad fifty yards behind them, and as the men rode they turned their heads from side to side as though looking for the enemy. As yet they had not spotted the militiamen.

"Take down the guidon, Ben," said Seth Pomeroy out of the side of his mouth." Makes too good a target."

The horsemen slowed their pace as they eyed the quiet woods ahead of them.

"We'll fire by squads," said Seth hoarsely." Corporal

Caxton's squad will fire at the two scouts at my command. If the squad retires, we will hold our fire. If they advance, the middle squad will fire at them at my command while Caxton's squad reloads." His voice died away.

There was nothing more to do. If this was indeed the advance of Jeb Stuart's fabled cavalry, there was nothing to stop them but Company B of the Pennsylvania Volunteer Militia, the Hinckley's Corners Tiger Rifles.

The two horsemen had stopped and so had the squad. Dust drifted away on the vagrant wind. The troopers' eyes roved along the line of woods and then seemed to settle on the tumble-down stone fence. One of them pointed toward the fence. Company B had been spotted. The squad rode up. Carbines were un-snapped from slings. The sun glinted dully from the polished barrels and the brass trimmings. The platoon spread out in a line across the open field while a galloper rode hard for the other woods. He vanished, and in a few minutes more horsemen appeared.

"Look!" said Zack Pascoe. "Cannon!"

There was a seemingly confused movement at the edge of the woods. Horses appeared and disappeared. Dust billowed up. Then, almost as though by magic, there appeared a cannon, pointed toward the position of Company B.

"Salt, pepper, and gravel in the grease," said Sam Dennis. "And just whereat, Sergeant Pomeroy, is the Army of the Pot-o-mac?"

A tense silence like that which precedes the onslaught of a summer thunderstorm seemed to descend over the countryside. The cavalrymen had dismounted, spread out into a thin line, and were advancing with ready carbines toward the low stone fence.

"Those are *veterans*," said Jim Vickers. "They ain't no bushwhackers."

"What difference does it make?" demanded Phil

Abbott fiercely. "You want to run, Jim Vickers? Go on! Run! If you're scairt, you go run like a little bitty cottontail!"

"Sure I'm scairt! You are too! We all are!"

"Enough of that talk!" said Sergeant Pomeroy. He thumbed back his rifle hammer to full cock. It sounded very loud in the quietness.

Jim Vickers turned his head. "I said I was *scairt*, Sergeant Pomeroy. I didn't say I was going to *run*."

"Ready," said Sergeant Pomeroy.

The rifles came up and steadied.

"Aim!"

The rifles wavered a trifle and then steadied once more.

Seth Pomeroy swallowed hard. The advancing skirmishers were no more than fifty yards from the fence. He opened his mouth and closed it.

Ben Buell stared, then straightened up. He stared again at a bright spot of color that had just appeared at the edge of the woods. It was a swallow-tailed guidon. The wind shifted and the guidon rippled out. There was no doubt about it. It was the Stars and Stripes! "Wait, Seth!" he yelled. " They're our *own* men! Don't fire!"

The rifles shifted and the frightened militiamen swallowed hard. Ben snatched up the company guidon and waved it back and forth. "It's the Pennsylvania Volunteer Militia!" he screamed at the top of his dust-hoarse voice.

A carbine cracked flatly and the slug whipped through the folds of the company guidon. A cottony puff of smoke drifted off before the wind. Another carbine flatted off and the slug whispered evilly to Ben Buell as it whipped past his ear. "If you *hear* them, you're safe enough, Ben," Walt had once told them. "It's the one you *don't* hear that gets you."

"Wait! Wait! Wait!" yelled the men of Company B. They stood up and waved their arms.

Once more a carbine spat flame and smoke. There

was the sound of a stick being slapped into thick mud. Phil Abbott grunted and fell heavily against Jim Vickers. His musket clattered to the ground.

"Cease firing there!" an officer yelled as he galloped toward the wall. "Those are Pennsylvania Militia! Not the Johnnies! Cease firing!"

"How is he, Jim?" asked Seth Pomeroy.

Jim Vickers slid a hand inside Phil Abbott's coat and when he withdrew it the hand was coated with fresh blood that glistened brightly in the sunlight. "He's gone, Sergeant," he said brokenly. Tears began to cut tiny furrows through the dust on his lean face.

CHAPTER FOUR

They had buried Phil Abbott in the grove in a temporary grave, for there was no time to take him back for decent burial in Hinckley's Corners. The officers and men of the Seventeenth Pennsylvania Cavalry, Devin's Second Brigade of Buford's First Division, seemed duly sorry for the mix-up and the death of Phil Abbott, but those tough cavalrymen had seen too much death in their young lives to think overmuch about the accidental death of an unknown militiaman. They had other things to worry about. Other things such as the fact that the Army of Northern Virginia in full force was somewhere west of South Mountain in the Cumberland Valley, ready to consolidate their audacious invasion of the Keystone State. It was rumored too that Jeb Stuart, also in full force, was *east* of Gettysburg, somewhere between Westminster and Hanover. General Buford was concentrating at Gettysburg to guard the Chambersburg Road west of the town, in case Lee came that way from Chambersburg instead of continuing northeasterly through the Cumberland Valley to Carlisle, Kingston, and perhaps even to the state capital at Harrisburg.

It was the beginning of dusk when the Seventeenth

Pennsylvania pulled out of the grove and rode on toward Gettysburg. Colonel Kellogg, commanding officer of the regiment, paused long enough to talk with Sergeant Pomeroy. "I can't tell you what to do, Sergeant Pomeroy, but I can give you some good advice. *Stay away from Gettysburg.* In my opinion, if you march north as we are doing, you'll walk right into the toughest fighting you'll ever see. To the west is Lee and the Army of Northern Virginia. Rebel cavalry is far north, perhaps in Carlisle or even farther east. Jeb Stuart is raiding between us and Washington. Somewhere to the south of us are seven full corps of the Army of the Potomac, marching north to intercept Lee. The orchestra is tuning up for the overture to battle.

"Your men are green and tired. I know their hearts are in the right place, and they are as patriotic as any man in the Army of the Potomac, but if you lead them into the enemy, they'll be slaughtered like sheep."

"My orders were to proceed to Gettysburg, sir," said Seth quietly.

"Don't you see that all is confusion at this time? Telegraphic communications have been cut by Stuart's raiders. We are not sure of the exact positions of Lee's forces. The Army of the Potomac is widely scattered, marching toward Gettysburg to concentrate against Lee. These roads will soon be filled with rivers of marching men, horses, wagons, the whole of the Army of the Potomac, and your little unit of Emergency men would be shoved aside and lost in the mass of the army. Return to, where is it? Ah! Hinckley's Corners." He smiled whimsically. "I could hardly forget *that* name."

"My orders were to march to Gettysburg," said Seth again.

Kellogg shrugged. "As you will." He eyed the serious face of the young noncom. "You are a soldier, young man. Your disposition of your little company to receive our attack was admirable. Admirable indeed!" "He stripped a gauntlet from his hand and shook Seth's hand. "We of the Seventeenth are sorry about the death of your man. By God's grace none of my men or any more of yours were harmed. Fortunes of war, Sergeant Pomeroy. Fortunes of war. Goodbye!" He touched his horse with his spurs and rode alongside the long column of horsemen until he was lost to sight.

Ben Buell leaned on the guidon staff and watched the cavalrymen moving through the dusk light with a thudding of hoofs and a squeaking of leather and jingling of metal. The single artillery gun they had with them went by with a rumbling noise, gun and caisson each drawn by six horses, the cannoneers, and the rest of the battery personnel riding horses as well as the three drivers who rode the nigh horses of each team.

"Horse artillery," said Seth Pomeroy. "Regulars by the looks of them. The *corps d'elite* of the army. That's a 3-inch Ordnance Rifle with a lightweight carriage for fast movement and maneuvering. Can throw a shell about four thousand yards extreme range." There was almost a wistful note in his quiet voice.

"Why *corps d'elite?*" asked Ben.

Seth was following the gun with his eyes. "There is no more dashing command in the Army, Ben. The company of the guns sets them apart."

The heavy dust of the column began to settle in the dusky woods. The little group of men from Company B stood there leaning on their rifles, eying their young commander. In a little while the sound of the passage of a regiment of cavalry was muted by distance.

"Now what?" asked Jim Vickers.

"We march behind them," said Seth. "We'll give the dust a chance to settle."

"Ain't it about time to camp, Sergeant?" asked Charley Donaldson. "We've been marching most of the day. The war can wait. Let's camp, Sergeant."

Seth turned his head ever so slightly and looked at the

freshly mounded grave of Phil Abbott. *"Here?"* he asked softly.

There was no answer. Later, as the little command straggled along the hard pike in the darkness, Jim Vickers spoke up again. "It ain't as though the Hinckley's Corners Tiger Rifles was the *only* bunch in uniform in southern Pennsylvania."

"Yeah," said Jack Pierce. "What could we do if Robert E. Lee and his Army of Northern Virginia suddenly jumped out of the bushes between here and Gettysburg?"

Seth turned his head. "I know well enough we're only militia, boys. Emergency men. We couldn't stop *them*. But we can make ourselves useful one way or another. Our orders were to go to Gettysburg. We go to Gettysburg!"

They camped that night some miles short of Gettysburg. The men were too tired to eat or pitch their little shelter tents. It was hardly necessary to do so. The night was warm. It was the end of June and the coming July promised to be a hot one. The men stripped to their trousers and lay down on their blankets.

Ben Buell was on guard in the quiet hours before dawn. He had been too tired to sleep well, but the few hours he had slept had been enough, for there was a subdued excitement within him as he stood at the edge of the grove where the company had bivouacked and looked to the west to where the dim bulky line of South Mountain showed beyond the low hills. Somewhere over there was the Army of Northern Virginia, possibly even now marching up the Cumberland Valley toward Harrisburg, or perhaps already threading through the mountain gaps in an easterly direction. To the east beyond the Monocacy River were the seasoned cavalry of Jeb Stuart. To the south was the Army of the Potomac.

It was as though Company B, the Hinckley's Corners Tiger Rifles, was in a long and narrow corridor between the Army of North Virginia to the west, Jeb Stuart's cavalry to the east, and with rebel cavalry possibly closing the northern end of the corridor in the vicinity of Carlisle. All that was between Company B and the enemy were the two brigades of General Buford's First Cavalry Division, hardly enough to stop the rebels from taking Gettysburg or any other town they might fancy.

The watery light of dawn was beginning to show in the east when Seth Pomeroy aroused his weary command and started them again on the road toward Gettysburg after a hasty breakfast. The pace was slower this day. Aching muscles and blistered feet seemed worse than they had been the day before. When the sun came up and the first feeling of the forthcoming day's heat began to settle about the tired militiamen, Seth was forced to call one halt after another to get the stragglers caught up. Now and then dusty, hard-riding horsemen in blue hammered along the pike, glancing curiously at the tramping militiamen. Now and then small groups of cavalry clattered past, heading for Gettysburg.

By midmorning the Tiger Rifles were nearly done in. The town was not far ahead, but to the tired militiamen it might have been on another planet, the way they felt. They had hardly settled down to rest in a small copse when an officer courier hammered toward them from the direction of Gettysburg. He stared at the dusty men and then drew rein.

"The fighting has begun at Gettysburg!" he said. "The Johnnies have struck Buford's Cavalry Division just west of the town. Get on the move! Buford needs all the help he can get. What corps are you from?"

Seth Pomeroy had struggled to his feet. He opened his mouth to answer, but the officer had suddenly seen the dusty guidon. "Militia?" he said in a sneering tone. "I thought I was talking to men of the Army of the Potomac!" He raked his lathered horse with his spurs. "Militia!" he spat out as he raced to the south toward a fast-rising pillar of dust.

"Let 'em fight their own battle," said Jim Vickers in a sour voice.

Seth Pomeroy turned to the company. "Fall in," he said.

Jim Vickers stared at him. "You mean *we're* marching to Gettysburg?" he demanded.

"That's the idea," said Seth quietly.

"But we're militia! Like that officer said! We got no business fighting the Army of Northern Virginia!"

Seth eyed the older man. "You heard what the officer said, Jim. Buford needs all the help he can get. That means us too."

An older man looked up at Seth. "I can't go no farther, Sergeant. I ain't scared, but I can't walk another step."

"Me either," said Harry Rinders.

By the time Seth had the company on the move, it was hardly a company at all, but rather a handful of dusty and frightened men, shambling on toward the town through the bright sunlight, leaving behind many of their comrades, too tired to continue. Seth had told them to catch up when they could. At this rate, there wouldn't be many of the Tiger Rifles ready for battle. But if the will of Sergeant Seth Pomeroy had anything to do with it, the Hinckley's Corners Tiger Rifles would be in at the battle. Seth plodded on, with Ben Buell beside him, the once bright colors of the guidon now dull with dust. They did not look behind them, and it was well they did not, for man after man fell behind, straggling along until at last he gave up the struggle.

Early as it was in the day the sun was hard at work. A haze had begun to form over the low hills. Then the wind shifted a little and the dull, almost indistinct rolling of thunder came to them as they marched on.

"Goin' to rain maybe," said Dan Caxton hopefully. "Maybe it'll rain and cool us off."

The thunder rumbled again. Seth Pomeroy looked up.

"Halt!" he cried. The company came to a disorganized halt. "Quiet!" said Seth. Once more the thunder rumbled. There was an ominous sound to it. The wind shifted a little more and blew harder. There was another sound below the rumbling of the thunder, as though someone was popping corn in a gigantic skillet. "That isn't thunder," said Seth Pomeroy quietly. "That's artillery fire and the popping noise is musketry fire."

Ben swallowed hard. He glanced back at the silent men. There were so few of them now. The whites of their eyes showed against their dusty, sweat-streaked faces. Beyond the company, far down the pike, a moving cloud of dust showed, mingled with bright flashes and spots of brilliant color. Then Ben made out a group of mounted men followed by what looked like a river of dusty men, bluish gray in coloring, with their flags slanting forward as they marched steadily.

"Forward march!" ordered Seth Pomeroy.

The company slogged on, looking back curiously at the oncoming column. The faster Company B moved the faster the column seemed to move in long, steady strides, a mile-eating pace. In no time at all they were closing the gap between them and the slow-moving militiamen. An officer spurred forward, passed the company, and looked down at Seth Pomeroy. "What unit is this?" he asked.

"Company B, Pennsylvania Volunteer Militia, sir," said Seth smartly.

The officer stared at him. "What are you doing on this road?"

"Orders to report in Gettysburg, sir," said Seth.

The officer jerked his head toward the oncoming troops. "That's the Third Division, Eleventh Corps, Sergeant, and we have orders to get to Gettysburg as quickly as possible. Can you keep ahead of us?" There was a faint smile on his face.

Seth glanced back. Already the head of the column had pushed the stragglers of B Company off the road.

"We're probably going into battle," said the officer, not unkindly, "and, if you'll excuse me, it will be no place for a tired handful of Pennsylvania Volunteer Militia."

Seth nodded. There was a hurt look in his eyes. He saluted. "Off the road, men," he commanded. His voice broke a little.

The order came almost too late. The oncoming men of the Eleventh Corps pushed aside the little company as though it was chaff. The leading troops wore the blue crescent badge of the Third Division, Eleventh Corps. As the militiamen scrambled through the ditch and over the fence they looked back at the veteran troops. Instead of carrying heavy knapsacks, they had rolled their blankets, tied them in horseshoe shape, and had slung them over their shoulders. Their heavy white socks had been drawn up over the bottoms of their trousers and tied there to keep out the dust. They had shed their blouses, and they carried their heavy rifles every which way. There was a hard bronzed look about them as they flowed past, filling the road from ditch to ditch.

One company after another and one regiment after another. The watching militiamen could read their regimental designations on their flags. Eighty-Second Illinois, Forty-Fifth New York, One Hundred and Fifty-Seventh New York, Sixty-First Ohio, Seventy-Fourth Pennsylvania, all of the First Brigade. Fifty-Eighth New York, One Hundred and Nineteenth New York, Eighty-Second Ohio, Seventy-Fifth Pennsylvania, and the Twenty-Sixth Wisconsin of the Second Brigade. Five light artillery batteries rumbled past, forming the Artillery Brigade of the corps. Battery I of the First New York Light Artillery, the Thirteenth New York, Batteries I and K of the First Ohio, Battery G of the Fourth United States. Then wagon after wagon, heavily laden, with the corps badges painted on their sides.

The dust was a thickening pall as artillery and wagons ground past and the sound of the marching column filled the ears of the dispirited militiamen who watched them. Then there was a gap, filled now and then by knots of stragglers, lone horsemen, couriers, and other backwash of a marching unit.

Seth got to his feet. "We'll get rid of some of this equipment," he said. "Take out one blanket, roll it in your poncho, with extra clothing inside of it. We might not be veterans, but we can at least march the way they do."

The men felt a little better, now that they knew a combat division of the Army of the Potomac was between them and that rumbling, popping sound that seemed to be getting louder and louder. As they marched on they could see some of the buildings of Gettysburg and beyond them a curious cloud of smoke that thickened even as they watched. It took a moment or two for them to realize what it was — *powder smoke*.

"Say, Sergeant Pomeroy!" called out Sam Dennis. "You went to college in Gettysburg, didn't you?"

Seth nodded. "Pennsylvania College, Sam."

"Then you know the town and the country around it pretty well, eh?"

"Yes."

Sam looked up to his left. "What are them two hills there?"

Seth glanced at the two hills. "The south one is Round Top, and the north one is Little Round Top."

"And the ridge there, north of them?"

"Cemetery Ridge," said Seth.

Sam shivered a little. "A good name for a battlefield," he said, "Cemetery Ridge."

"It isn't likely they'll be any fighting there," said Seth seriously. "Our cavalry will hold back the Johnnies until the Eleventh Corps gets into position. An officer told me the whole First Corps is west of us, advancing to Gettysburg on the Emmetsburg Road. The two corps should contain the enemy west and north of the town until the rest of the Army of the Potomac gets here. No, Sam, there likely won't be any fighting on Cemetery Ridge."

As Seth finished speaking, the wind shifted, and the sustained and terrible roaring of a swiftly growing battle came to them. To Ben Buell it seemed almost as though the god of battles was laughing uproariously, and somewhat diabolically at Seth's profound prediction.

CHAPTER FIVE

The sun was beating down almost savagely on the town of Gettysburg, county seat of Adams County. Dust and battle smoke formed a thickening haze high over the town. Sunlight picked out the bright colors of the national and regimental flags of the many Northern units converging on Gettysburg from the south and southeast. They came trudging along the Baltimore Pike, the Taneytown Road, and the Emmetsburg Road. Men of the First Corps, veterans of Bull Run, the Seven Days, Antietam, Fredericksburg, Chancellorsville, and many other lesser known actions and engagements. Men of the Eleventh Corps, veterans of Bull Run, Second Bull Run, Chancellorsville, and other actions and engagements. They had been outflanked by Stonewall Jackson and his Second Corps of the Army of Northern Virginia at Chancellorsville, badly mauled, and routed, and they wanted blood in revenge this hot day of July 1. While the First Corps slogged up the Emmetsburg Road, advance units of the Eleventh Corps began to double time through the streets of Gettysburg to meet the enemy advancing south on the Carlisle Road.

Buford's dismounted troopers had met the first smash of battle, deployed across the Chambersburg Pike, and the troopers fought it out, dismounted cavalry armed with repeating carbines against a full infantry division of Johnny Rebs. The sullen roar of battle was rising higher and higher.

Company B, the Hinckley's Corners Tiger Rifles, was a dusty microcosm caught up in the veritable flood of blue-clad men who marched toward the sound of battle. A hard-riding company of cavalry smashed through the stragglers, scattering them as well as the men of Company B. When the dust settled a little, there was hardly more than a corporal's guard of the weary militiamen left marching behind Sergeant Seth Pomeroy toward the low hill just west of the town.

"What hill is that?" asked Sam Dennis as they slogged along past a halted string of ammunition wagons marked with the crescent badge of the Eleventh Corps.

"Cemetery Hill," called out a teamster. He grinned. "You boys are sure headed in the right direction."

Sam paled a little. "Cemetery Ridge and Cemetery Hill," he said gloomily. "Seems like the chief product of Gettysburg must be burials."

"You'll have your chance, soldier," said the teamster.

Seth halted the little unit when they reached the outlying houses of the town. Infantry tramped through the dusty streets. Cavalry thudded past. An artillery piece lay askew with a broken wheel while sweating drivers and gunners propped it up to replace the damaged wheel with the spare carried on the limber. A yelling driver was standing up in his ammunition wagon, lashing on the sweat-lathered team. The canvas wagon cover bore the red crescent badge of the First Division, Eleventh Corps. "Hurry up!" he yelled at the bystanders. "Reynolds needs every man he can get to hold back the Johnnies! "He swung his team expertly around a corner, narrowly missing an oncoming ambulance.

Seth smiled. "If General Reynolds is in command up there, the Johnnies will have a time with him."

Sam Dennis sipped at his canteen. "What do we do, Seth?"

Seth looked at his handful of men. There were but ten of them, counting Ben and himself. The rest of the Tiger Rifles were part of the flotsam and jetsam of the battle.

"Ain't hardly enough of us to act as pallbearers if one of us is killed," said Jim Vickers morosely.

"What do we do?" asked Dan Caxton.

Seth shouldered his rifle. "As a general rule," he said quietly, "the maxim of marching to the sound of the guns is a wise one."

"Brilliant," said Jim Vickers. "You make that one up, Seth?"

The young sergeant shook his head. "That's from *Precis Politique et Militaire de la Campagne de 1815*, by Jomini."

"Yeah," said Sam Dennis thoughtfully, "I *thought* I recognized it."

Seth Pomeroy did not speak again as he led the way along Washington Street, but now and then he looked up, first to the north, then to the west, as though trying to gauge where the battle was heaviest, but no man could do that, for the roar and crash of battle seemed to come in a great crescent of angry sound from a point due north of the town in a great curve to the west and then to the south almost to the Hagerstown Road.

It was about that time the plodding militiamen began to see some of the bloody debris of battle. Here and there wounded men sat on the curbing or lay quietly on the dusty grass of lawns, and beneath the harsh muttering of battle came yet another sound, the moaning of the wounded, rising now and then to shrieks of agony. Ambulances rattled past the militiamen with pale-faced men lying in them. Here and there civilians of the town were tending the wounded.

"General Reynolds has been killed, boys," a white-faced sergeant said as he staggered a little in his stride. He clenched his left shoulder. "Sharpshooter got him in McPherson's woods."

"Who is in command now?" asked Dan Caxton.

"General Howard, commander of the Eleventh Corps. The Johnnies have us badly outnumbered. I think we might have to fall back. One division of the Eleventh Corps is supposed to be fortifying Cemetery Hill." He passed on through the crowd.

"Cemetery Hill," said Jim Vickers quietly. "That's *behind* us, Sergeant Pomeroy."

The remnant of the Tiger Rifles had halted at the corner of Washington and Hanover Streets. They stood to one side as a regiment of infantry went by at the double quick, drums thumping steadily.

"Ain't no use, as I see it, walking right into the Johnnies," said Clem Briscoe.

Seth Pomeroy glanced after the hurrying regiment. "I wish I was with them," he said a little bitterly, "instead of with the Tiger Rifles."

Sam Dennis leaned on his rifle. "Maybe somebody ought to go up there and see what's going on before we walk into the rebel lines, Sergeant Pomeroy. Seems like everyone around here knows where to go. They got their orders. The only orders we got were to meet the rest of the militia here in town. We ain't seen nary a one of 'em."

Seth nodded. "All right," he said. "I'll scout ahead."

"I'll go too," said Ben quietly.

Seth looked at him, opened his mouth, and then closed it. The look on that earnest, though dusty face was enough to let him know that Ben Buell wasn't going to be left behind.

"Me too," said Zack Pascoe.

Ben glanced quickly at Zack. Zack hardly ever spoke. He let his fife do his speaking for him as a rule and that was enough for Company B. Zack smiled. "I've been getting a little sick of Hinckley's Corners," he said. "I like Gettysburg better."

"Like this?" asked Ben. "With the shooting going on?"

Zack nodded. "Like this." His eyes seemed to shine.

"Come on then," said Seth.

Ben handed the guidon to Clem Briscoe and followed Seth. When he looked back from the next corner there was no sign of the Hinckley's Corners boys. He followed Seth up a side street toward the loudest sound of battle, with little Zack Pascoe hard on his heels. "Look, Ben," said Zack. He pointed to a man who lay on a lawn, his dirty hands twisted tightly in his bloodstained shirt. His eyes were wide open, staring unseeingly at them, and the blue pallor of death was on his contorted face. Ben felt a little sick. He hurried on after Seth.

A team of horses had turned into the street, dragging a field gun after them. One of the swing horses was missing. A leader had blood coursing down his dusty flank. The drivers were lashing the frantic beasts. The gun careened from a curbing and almost capsized but somehow managed to right itself. The team and gun, with its limber, raced past them.

"Napoleon twelve pounder gun-howitzer," said Seth expertly. "The work horse of the war. Smoothbore. Short ranged but deadly, like a gigantic shotgun when they fire canister with it. That one has been in plenty of action."

"What I'd like to know," said Zack Pascoe in a small voice, "is how come it's going *that* way, and we're going *t'other*, Sergeant Pomeroy?"

Seth did not answer. He reached a house at the end of the street and paused. As he did so something hummed past Ben and Zack. "Mighty big bees," said the little fifer.

Ben paled. He swallowed hard. "That wasn't a bee, Zack. It was a spent bullet most likely."

"Fellow could get killed around here," said Zack wisely.

But they both followed Seth Pomeroy, who now kept

close to the shelter of the houses as he worked his way slowly to the west. Now they began to see more and more wounded men coming slowly down the street, most of them from the First Corps, although there was a strong leavening of men who wore the crossed sabers of the cavalry on their caps.

"How is it going?" asked Seth of a bearded infantryman who wore a black hat in contrast to the forage caps of the other wounded. He had rigged a sling about his neck and in the sling he supported his left arm, with the hand thickly bandaged and stained with blood.

"It looks bad," said the bearded man. "I'm from the Sixth Wisconsin, Meredith's 'Iron Brigade.' We smashed the rebel brigade of Davis'. We drove Archer's Brigade back through McPherson's woods and across Willoughby Run. Captured about a thousand of 'em, we did, including Archer himself! But the Johnnies are coming up by the thousands and we haven't got enough men to match 'em. At least not yet. I've never seen such hard fighting, boys, and I've been in since the start of the war. This looks like the beginning of a big battle. A big battle." He shook his head and hurried on.

"Big battle," said Zack. "He talks like it's hardly started."

Seth wiped the sweat from his sunburned face. "I think he's right. This isn't just a skirmish, boys. I think the whole Army of Northern Virginia is coming from the west and the whole Army of the Potomac is coming from the south and southeast."

"And we're in the middle," said Ben dryly.

Seth nodded. He glanced back toward the town. "The Tiger Rifles may get into this individually but never as a unit, boys. Both of you can go back if you want to."

"What about you, Seth?" asked Ben.

There was a curious smile on Seth's face. "I've been trying to get into this war since they fired upon Fort Sumter," he said. "They told me in the infantry I couldn't march, and they had no room for me in the cavalry; the artillery wanted the best men they could get. The best Seth Pomeroy could do was to drill militia on the village green in Hinckley's Corners! Well, Seth Pomeroy is right here in the middle of a battle, with a good rifle in his hands, and dressed in a blue suit! Militia, or no militia, I'm staying right here to give the Army of the Potomac a hand whether they like it or not!"

Almost as though in answer to Seth's spirited speech there was a rushing sound through the hot smoky air and then a bright flash followed by a sharp explosion as a shell burst almost directly over the three of them. Iron shards smashed against a frame building. A fragment tinkled on the street beside Ben. A wounded man who limped along aided by his musket, which he used as a crutch, staggered forward and fell heavily. Zack ran to his aid, took one look at the man, then turned back. There was no need for him to say anything.

Now the bullets whined through the street. Some of them slapped against trees or buildings. They were spent bullets, but they could still wound a man. Seth waved on the last of the Hinckley's Corners Tiger Rifles — all two of them — and dogtrotted steadily toward the end of the street where the open countryside, wreathed in drifting smoke, was to be seen. Seth kept on, but now his head was hunched between his shoulders, as though he was trying to protect it from invisible blows. Ben laughed wildly and then realized that he too, as well as little Zack, was running the same way, because of the constant whispering of spent bullets that sped past them.

Seth stopped at a fence row and peered across a field that was dotted with curiously shaped humps and clumps. It took a moment for Ben to realize that the humps and clumps were dead horses, seemingly from an artillery battery, for their harnesses had been cut from them. There were other smaller humps and clumps here and there amidst the dead horses, like bundles of dusty rags dropped by a junkman. Artillerymen who had died beside their guns.

Seth skirted the field, running lightly despite his weariness and his game leg, with his rifle at the ready. He did not look back but quested on as though the roaring of the savage battle ahead was meat and drink to him, meat and drink that he had craved all his life. For some men enjoy battle as others may enjoy good food and the peace and quiet of their own firesides.

"Look!" yelled Zack Pascoe as they worked their way up a ridge at the edge of town. Men moved through the drifting smoke, now and then turning, raising their muskets, and firing at something unseen beyond them. Ben's stomach seemed to moil uneasily, and he suddenly realized who those men were firing at. The Johnnies were that close! Ben gripped his Colt, then knew he could hardly hit anything with the unfamiliar weapon. A cavalry horse lay sprawled in the ditch and lying in the dust beside it was a heavy-breeched carbine. Ben snatched it up and recognized it immediately as a repeater such as those carried by Buford's cavalry division. There was no time to worry about whether it was loaded or not.

To their left was a large building with a cupolaed tower atop it. Seth flung out a hand toward it. "The Lutheran Theological Seminary!" he yelled back over his shoulder. "This is Seminary Ridge! The Johnnies are up ahead of us, boys!"

"Great, just great," murmured Zack with a sickly smile on his thin face.

The scattered wounded and dead, and those soldiers still fighting, were from the Third Division, First Corps. As the three members of Company B reached the rearmost ranks of the division, the battle seemed to slacken. Although there was still heavy firing to the right and to the left, there seemed to be a curious lull in the immediate front.

"Looks like these Johnnies have been fought out,"

said a redheaded sergeant as he replenished his cartridge box from a box of ammunition.

"They's plenty more where they come from," said a black-hatted corporal of the Iron Brigade.

An officer limped through the rifted smoke and eyed Seth Pomeroy. "What regiment?" he demanded of Seth.

"B Company, Pennsylvania Volunteer Militia, sir," said Seth smartly.

"*Militia?*" The officer stared. "These are the lines of the First Corps. You men had better rejoin your unit."

"We *are* the unit, sir," said Seth.

"You mean you have lost all the rest?"

Seth flushed. "Well, no, sir, it's like this: We had orders to march to Gettysburg and join the rest of the militia. By the time we got here most of the company had fallen behind or had gone back. We left the last of them in town. We figured the three of us, at least, could do some fighting."

The officer wiped the sweat from his face. "This is the hardest fighting I have ever seen. Hardly the place for three green militiamen, and two of them little more than boys."

"We've come to fight, sir," said Seth.

The officer shook his head. "I'm the provost, Sergeant. You get back out of these lines. Go back into town and make yourselves useful."

"We came to fight," insisted Seth a little angrily.

The officer turned. "Sergeant Cassidy," he called out. A huge sergeant came through the smoke followed by a squad of tough-looking men. "Disarm these men. Escort them to the edge of town. I don't want to see them in the lines again."

The three members of Company B were ignominiously escorted to the edge of town, below the ridge, after being relieved of their weapons, although Ben still had his heavy Colt concealed inside his blouse.

The provost sergeant smiled. "'Tis better for ye, lads.

'Tis no place out thayer for milishymen. Foind a hospital and make yereselves useful but stay away from the foightin'. It has really just begun. Ye'll thank the captain for what he did for ye before this day is over."

They watched the provost guard trudge back up the ridge. Almost immediately the heavy firing resumed. Seth Pomeroy looked away from Ben and Zack.

"Maybe we'd better do as he says, Seth," said Zack.

"No! If the First Corps doesn't want us, the Eleventh Corps might! Come on!"

Zack looked at Ben and shrugged. The two of them ran after Seth as he started north, trending along the very edge of the growing battle, through the wastage and backwash of the fighting, the dead, the dying, and the wounded, smashed wagons, dead horses, abandoned equipment, patches of clotted blood black against the dusty ground, broken rifles, smashed canteens, gaping haversacks — the signs of the passage of fighting men. And all the time, beneath the roaring of the battle to the left and in front of them, came the soft hissing of spent bullets looking for a mark before they fell to earth.

They had crossed the Mummasburg Road and suddenly noticed that the men about them wore the crescent badge of the Eleventh Corps. A low hill north of them seemed literally to belch flame and smoke, and a furious cannonading began, the shells smashing into the fighting ranks of blue, forcing them back. Then from the northwest came long lines of butternut and gray, decorated here and there by the bright colors of the Stars and Bars and with the reflection of sun on steel and brass.

The attack came on, seemingly unstoppable and invincible, while the crescendo of battle rose higher and higher.

"That must be Dick Ewell's Second Corps!" yelled an officer who was leading up a company at the double quick." The fat's in the fire now!"

"Our lines are awfully thin," said Zack Pascoe.

Seth nodded. "There's too much of a gap between the left flank of the Eleventh Corps and the right flank of the First," he said. "They need artillery here, boys! A battery *might* hold back the Johnnies!"

The three of them moved along behind the line of battle, eagerly watching the advance of the enemy, who were driven back, fighting desperately, only to reform and come on again.

"Oh, for a battery!" cried Seth.

Here and there were dismounted cavalrymen of Buford's Division, fighting along with the infantrymen of the Eleventh Corps. But there were only a few Union guns firing, not enough to stop the reforming lines of the enemy. It was only a matter of time before the Confederates would press on again, and this time, without additional artillery support, the Union lines could not hold.

Ben heard hoarse yelling behind him. He turned. Men were waving their rifles and throwing their hats into the smoky air. For up the road, at full gallop, came a battery of artillery, heading straight for the dangerous gap in the lines. They had arrived in the nick of time!

"Horse artillery!" yelled Seth Pomeroy. "And regulars to boot, I'll bet! Look at the way they handle those teams!"

There were but four guns, two less than the usual six-gun battery, but still enough power was in them to stop the Confederate charge, if the guns could get into firing position in time. Ben found himself yelling at the top of his lungs as he watched the gun teams, drawing gun and limber, slamming pell-mell down the slope, each of them followed by a caisson team. At the front of the battery rode an officer, and close behind him a trumpeter, while the guidon bearer raced along on the opposite side of the lead team, carrying his guidon thrust into its socket at his right stirrup. Ben could not take his eyes from that guidon. It was swallow-tailed, with the red and white stripes of the national colors, having a blue field emblazoned with a double circle of white stars, with additional white stars, one in each corner. It was the most beautiful thing he had ever seen!

Dust swirled up behind the rolling guns and caissons. The battery was a thing of grace and precision as it hurtled down the gentle slope toward the field of battle.

"They can't beat us now!" screamed Zack Pascoe.

"No?" yelled a wounded cavalryman. "Look there!"

CHAPTER SIX

The rebel guns on Oak Hill had found the range. Four shells burst directly in front of the leading gun of the Union horse artillery battery. The team was flung aside as though by a giant and invisible hand, the limber and gun slamming forward to ride up over the fallen bodies of the kicking, thrashing team. The limber slewed sideways and jackknifed, and the second gun team drove full tilt into it, ending up in a wild snarl of rearing horses and yelling drivers, who plied their whips and fought to get the excited team free of the wreckage.

The third gun team missed the tangle in the roadway, slammed down into the ditch, careened through a gap in the fence and swung to the right to follow the fence line, while the fourth gun was halted in a welter of dust and maddening confusion. The third gun seemed as though it would make it all right, but before it reached the end of the field it was drawn to a halt and men ran forward with axes in their hands to clear a way through the stake-and-rider fence. The last team followed the third team into the field and drew up behind it to wait for the way to be cleared. The caisson teams had been halted on the road.

Ben looked back toward the rebel lines. They were

moving forward again, but sustained musketry fire from a thin line of Union infantry was slowing their advance. If that battery could only get into action!

The fence had been leveled. The battery commander punched his right hand forward and the trumpeter sounded off. The gun team slammed into their collars. The gun began to move. But the rebel guns again found the range, this time along the fence line. Shell bursts flashed and roared, scattering death and destruction. Men fell from their horses or leaped free when their horses went down. The small lead horses started through the fence gap, followed by the bigger swing horses.

"They'll make it!" yelled Seth Pomeroy.

"Look at that off wheeler!" cried out Zack Pascoe.

The big wheelhorses had reached the gap and the driver on the nigh horse was frenziedly lashing the off wheeler with his whip. The off wheeler had obviously panicked. He threw himself sideways, dragging the nigh wheeler with him and holding back the lead and swing pairs.

The rebel lines were reforming once more. Officers yelled orders and pointed their swords toward the thin Union lines. The Union infantrymen were slowly withdrawing, slapping their cartridge boxes to indicate to their mates that they were out of ammunition. There was nothing to stop the rebels now except a scattered sprinkling of dismounted cavalrymen pumping shots from their Spencer repeating carbines, certainly not enough to hold back the enemy.

Ben was staring at the maddened wheeler. Then slowly, ignoring the whining bullets and the bursting shells, he walked toward the fence. The off wheeler was a big bay. A big bay with dark points! "Dandy!" yelled Ben. He ran forward. He vaulted the fence and landed lightly in the field, close to the bay.

"Get out av there, bhoy!" yelled a red-faced sergeant,

with a musical Irish lilt to his voice. "That crazy baste will kill ye!"

Dandy was swinging his upper body back and forth, smashing against the fence on one side and striking hard against his team mate on the other. The driver plied his whip, then screamed in agony as Dandy smashed his leg against the horse the driver rode. He fell sideways from his saddle.

"Kill that bay and cut him loose, Dolan!" ordered a bearded officer.

The big Irish sergeant drew his Colt and started for the bay.

"Wait!" cried Ben. He darted in front of Dandy. "Dandy boy! Dandy! It's me! It's Ben!"

The great hoofs came thrashing down, and Ben jumped to one side. "Dandy! Dandy!" he screamed.

The bay stopped his frenzied neighing and dropped his forefeet to the ground. Ben wasted no time. He ducked behind the bay and swung up into the saddle of the nigh wheeler. "Come on, Dandy!" he called out. He reached over and gripped the bay's thick and dusty mane.

"Forward hoooo!" cried Dolan.

The nimble leaders had already cleared the ditch and the swing horses followed them. The gun moved forward as the big wheelers threw their weight into the collars. A shell exploded on the far side of the road, scattering retreating infantrymen like chaff. The blast of the shell almost flipped Ben's forage cap from his head. He hung on for dear life as the gun was pulled swiftly toward an open area beyond the road. The rebel infantry were no more than two hundred yards away now.

"Action Front!" screamed the bearded officer.

There was nothing for Ben to do but hang on as the drivers of the lead and swing teams lashed their mounts. The leaders swung in a great arc to lead the swing and wheel horses to the left, with gun and limber bouncing and careening behind them. Ben dared a glance to the rear. The fourth gun was close behind them now and the gun that had run into the first gun and team in the roadway had managed to get free and was now slamming full tilt across the torn-up field to follow the other two guns. In a moment it had come through the fence gap and drew up close behind the fourth gun to fit neatly into the beautiful maneuver of Action Front.

The guns were swung around to face the oncoming Confederates. The teams were released from the limber and driven back. The gun crews swung down from their mounts and clustered about gun and limber. Ammunition chests were flung open, and Ben looked back to see a gunner quickly lift a small spotted dog from one of the chests and place him on the ground. By the time the team had reached the rear of the three remaining guns of the battery, the trumpeter's brassy notes seemed to file across the uproar of battle.

"Load—canister — double!" came the command.

Rammer heads thumped solidly into the gun as they were loaded. "Ready!" shouted each section chief.

"Ready — by piece — fire!" came the command from the bearded officer.

There was no need to designate the target. The rebels were trotting swiftly toward the half-strength gun battery, crimson battle flags slanting forward, bayonets flashing in the afternoon sun and then suddenly a high, piercing yelling began. It sent a cold chill throughout Ben Buell as he stroked Dandy's face and looked toward the oncoming battle line. His brother Walt had told him of the rebel yell and its effect on troops waiting the spirited onslaught of the Confederates. Ben glanced to right and left, and suddenly, despite the presence of the artillerymen of the battery he seemingly had joined, as well as the thin lines of Union infantrymen and cavalrymen still disputing that shot torn and smoky acre or so of ground, he felt an intense loneliness.

But the artillerymen went about their business like

dusty automatons. The first gun to the right suddenly roared in savage defiance, spitting out flame and smoke, to be immediately followed by the second gun. The two guns slammed back on their trails as the third gun spoke thickly. Dense smoke swirled about the three cannon.

The command came clearly through the noise and the rifted battle smoke. "Load — canister — double!"

Ben held tightly to Dandy and looked at the calm bearded man who had given the command. At first Ben had thought he was an older man, but he could hardly be more than in his middle or late twenties.

The powder charges were thrust into the freshly swabbed bores of the guns. The rammers slammed them home. The canister charges were placed in the muzzles and pushed home. Meanwhile friction primers had been inserted in the cannon vents. It was swiftly done, the mark of well-trained gunners working at their deadly trade.

Ben peered through the smoke, and his heart sank. The rebel lines had been thinned considerably, for behind the oncoming infantrymen lay the dead and wounded, in windrows it seemed, right in the path of the heavy charges of canister, musket balls, or perhaps iron balls packed almost solidly in tin cylinders, like gigantic shotgun charges. But the butternut-and-gray lines still came on, and now they were covering the ground in long strides, with their powder-blackened mouths squared as they drew up the fierce rebel yell from their diaphragms and spat it out into the smoky air.

"Hurry! *Hurry!*" screamed Ben at the calm battery commander.

"Ready! Ready! Ready!" barked the section chiefs each in turn.

"Ready—by piece—fire!" came the command.

This time each friction primer ignited the powder charge almost in unison with the others. A blast of smoke and flame came from the three rifled guns, practically at point-blank range. Before the effect of the firing was seen through the dense wall of smoke, the commands came again, seemingly in a confused welter, but really the disciplined stamp of a battery of skilled artillerymen. "Sponge — thumb the vent—ram—trail left!"

Ben talked constantly to Dandy. "See the little dog, Dandy? *He* isn't afraid!"

The big bay seemed to understand as he pressed hard against the boy master he had lost and then miraculously had found again in this strange place of noise, smoke, confusion, and sudden death, far away from the quiet meadow on the Buell farm where he had spent his whole life. The little dog stood between two of the smoking guns, barking and yapping his defiance at the enemy, who, broken by the smashing charges of canister, were milling in confusion on that field of death.

"F-o-o-o-o-r-r-r-r-w-a-a-a-r-r-d! Guide c-e-n-t-e-r-r-r-r!" came the clear cry of the rebel officers as they tried to reform their decimated regiment.

The command came once more from the bearded battery commander. "Ready—by piece — fire!"

The battery was swathed in smoke and flame as the guns slammed back in recoil and the combined effect of the canister was terrible to see. The enemy ranks were blasted. No troops in the world could have faced such a fire. One by one, then in twos, threes, and fours, the rebels began to retire, but sullenly, loading, aiming, and firing at the Union battery even as they fell back toward their own guns.

Now the counterbattery fire began, and this time the weight of metal was with the Confederates, and their target the closely bunched men and guns of the horse artillery battery that had driven back the rebel infantry. The gun and caisson teams had been taken to the rear of the caisson positions, along with the horseholders who had ridden back when the battery had been emplaced, leading two riderless horses on either hand, the mounts of the cannoneers and other mounted personnel of a horse artillery battery. Ben Buell was with this detail, still wondering how he had gotten mixed up in it. He looked through the smoke for a sight of Seth Pomeroy or Zack Pascoe, but neither one of them was to be seen. There were so many dead and wounded on that field. Perhaps Seth and Zack had fallen.

His mind was instantly ripped away from thoughts of his two comrades by a shattering explosion to the left of one of the guns. The heavy piece seemed to rise and fall as though on an invisible wave. Men fell to right and left of the gun, leaving but two men standing on their feet, dazed and shaking from the explosion of the enemy shell.

Sergeant Dolan ran toward the gun to give a hand. Bullets whispered past or slammed into gun carriages, limbers and caissons. Some of them sang thinly and eerily from the metal gun carriage fittings or from the guns themselves. Over the strident voices of the bullets came the sound of the artillery projectiles, shrieking, whining, or whistling demoniacally.

There was a crashing discharge fifty feet from Ben Buell, followed by a great blast of air. He was smashed to the ground, still clinging to the harness of Dandy. He looked underneath the belly of the big bay in time to see a heavy caisson wheel come down through the smoke and strike a man to death. Bits and fragments of wood and metal sailed through the air from the shattered caisson to strike and maim. Two horses were down, their legs thrashing in agony. Another horse was galloping madly right past the guns into the rifted battle smoke that hung over the field.

Ben got to his feet and hung onto the bay; it was the only thing that kept his mind from cracking in that havoc. Now the battery was surely licked. The rebel infantry would reform and charge across the field once more and this time they would not be stopped. As though to agree with Ben, the missiles came thicker and thicker and the exploding shells seemed to come one right atop of another. Now and then two projectiles would strike in mid-air with snakelike flashes as they exploded, showering hot and jagged metal on Yankee and rebel alike.

"Ready—by piece—fire!" The clear and calm command came over the badly shaken men and horses like oil over stormy waters.

Ben peered toward the gun that had been all but unmanned by the shell that had exploded right next to it. Sergeant Dolan was there at the muzzle, swabbing out the hot bore. A slight figure moved through the smoke carrying a powder charge. A slim man who moved with a limp was at the breech of the gun, inserting a friction primer. The powder charge was slammed in and rammed home. A man staggered up with two canister shot and handed each of them in turn to the slight man at the left of the gun. He placed both projectiles into the muzzle, and they were rammed home by Sergeant Dolan. The man at the breech stepped clear after he had hooked the lanyard hook into the ring of the primer. Sergeant Dolan looked at him and nodded. "Ready!" snapped out the man at the breech, and the clear, steady voice was that of Sergeant Seth Pomeroy of Company B, the Hinckley's Corners Tiger Rifles, and the slight man to the left of the gun muzzle was quiet Zack Pascoe of the same command!

The guns to right and left of Seth's gun roared and flashed, but Seth's gun had led the way. The three doses of double canister swept all the scattered rebels from the field.

"Suspend firing!" came the command.

The bearded officer crouched and fanned impatiently at the smoking air as though trying to clear it so he could see the enemy.

A curious lull came over the field, broken only by the

scattering musketry fire and the cries of the wounded men thickly dotting the ground.

It was then that Ben Buell saw the bright Confederate battle flags moving in the woods beyond the enemy guns on Oak Hill. "Surely they're not going to charge again?" he said aloud.

The driver of the lead pair of the gun team of which Dandy was a wheeler, turned and looked at Ben. "I'm almost sure those Johnnies are Gordon's Georgians, younker. If they are, they'll keep a-comin' until we wipe them out or they overrun us. They play for keeps." He grinned a little weakly. "But then, so do Crispin's Bulldogs."

Ben stared at him. "Crispin's Bulldogs? Who are they?"

It was the lead driver's turn to stare. "Who are *they?* Who are *you?*" He shook his head. "You come out'a nowheres and get that big bay there to mind his manners as though you was a horse artillery driver from the year one, and you don't even know what *battery* you're fighting' with? This is *Crispin's Bulldogs,* boy!" He swung out an arm to encompass the shattered caissons, the three smoking guns, the dirty, tired, battered men who manned the guns, the dead, dying, and wounded horses, as well as those still on their feet, ready for duty no matter what befell them. "Battery B, Eighth United States Horse Artillery, greenie! Crispin's Bulldogs! First Bull Run! The Seven Days! Antietam! Fredericksburg! Chancellorsville! Brandy Station! I tell you, boy! This war is just a little difference between the *whole* Confederacy and *Battery B, Eighth United States,* and we ain't about to give an inch, here or anywheres else! *Now* do you know who we are?"

Ben grinned weakly. "I think I have the general idea."

"Good! You just stay with that big bay and make him mind his manners!"

"Yes, sir!"

The driver casually waved a hand. "Don't 'sir' me, boy.

I'm Private Jonas Whitlow, driver of the best lead team, in the best gun section, in the best gun battery, in the best horse artillery regiment, in the best Army in the world! Outside of that, I ain't nothing."

"Who is that bearded officer, Jonas?" asked Ben.

The driver turned. "Him? That's Captain Carter Crispin, our battery commander; West Pointer, gunner, and a *man!*"

There was a rapid tattoo of hoofbeats on the road and a horseman turned his mount into the field where Battery B held its ground. Lathered foam flew from the horse as the horseman reined in sharply. The horse reared, but the horseman held his seat magnificently. "Crispin!" he called.

Captain Crispin turned. "Yes, Colonel York?"

"Under these conditions you had better limber up and pull out, Crispin! Barlow's division is shattered! We can't give you infantry support! Limber up and get out! Save your guns!"

Crispin waved a hand to indicate his battered command. "We'd hardly have time to hitch up, sir. The Johnnies would be upon us before we got out of the field."

"Then spike those guns and abandon them!"

There was a moment's hesitation and then Crispin said quietly: "I will not forsake my guns, Colonel York. We have not lost a gun in nine battles, and *we will not lose one now!*"

The colonel leaned forward in his saddle. "I repeat, Captain Crispin, that I cannot give you infantry support! We are outgunned and outnumbered. The First Corps is already retiring, and it is only a matter of a half an hour or so before the Eleventh Corps will be unable to hold *its* ground. This is a major battle, sir, perhaps the beginning of the greatest battle of the war. Either limber up and get out of here or spike those guns!"

"Is that an order, sir?"

York impatiently cut his hand sideways. "You are under command of the commanding officer of the Cavalry Corps, Crispin. I have no real jurisdiction over you. You can do what you like! But you will lose those guns one way or another! That is all I have to say. Goodby and good luck, sir!" York wheeled his horse and galloped away to his own command.

A line of skirmishers and sharpshooters had drifted out from the woods near Oak Hill. Minie bullets began to sing through the air or slap into wood or metal. Now and then a man went down at his post.

"Artillery against skirmishers is like shooting at mosquitoes with a rifle," said Driver Whitlow sourly.

"Attention!" called out Captain Crispin. "Men of Battery B! We will *not* lose these guns! Retire by prolonge! Gun Number Two, then Number Three, then Number Five, in that order!"

Ben held onto Dandy as the battery moved swiftly in a movement he had never heard of before. There were thick ropes wound in a figure eight about hooks atop the gun trails of the battery. These were removed. A hook at one end of each of the ropes was attached to the lunette at the very rear of the trail and the men tailed onto the ropes.

Crispin turned. "Hitch up those limbers, men! You've got about enough horsepower to draw those limbers through the field and back onto the road! Sergeant Fox! Dump out a dozen rounds of canister for each gun, then get those limbers out of here! March order there! *March order, Battery B!*"

The skirmish lines had thickened and become bolder. Bullets began to take their toll. It was then that Gun Number Five blasted off a double round of canister to hold back the enemy. Meanwhile Guns Number Two and Three had been hauled back twenty feet. Number Three, the gun manned by Sergeant Dolan, Seth Pomeroy, and Zack Pascoe, as well as three other men from the battery, was ready to fire. As soon as Five had fired it had bucked back into recoil, and with that impetus, the understrength crew managed to get it rolling back, pulled by the prolonge rope. No sooner had it passed Number Three when that gun was fired at point-blank range into the skirmishers. Then Number Three was hauled back past Number Two, and the instant it had cleared the muzzle, the gun roared at the halted enemy skirmishers.

But there was little time for Ben to see the rest of the retirement, other than the part in which he was a bit player. The team was hitched to the limber and driven across the road and through the ditch. For a moment the limber hung in the ditch, just about to turn over. If it did, it would block the retirement of the other limbers and the three guns. "Dandy!" shrieked Ben. The other drivers were plying their whips, almost viciously, but Ben had none, nor would he have used it if he did have one. He slapped the big bay on the withers, leaning over from the saddle of the nigh wheeler, which he bestrode. "Dandy! Pull, Dandy! *Pull! Pull! Pull!*"

Dandy slammed into the collar, leaned his great shoulders forward, scrabbled with his strong hind legs, and almost immediately the limber seemed to move up out of the ditch easily, through the gap in the shattered fence, and into the shot-torn field.

Whitlow turned in his saddle. "Good driving, there, soldier!"

Ben felt as though President Lincoln had personally congratulated him. He turned in his saddle and looked back. The guns had reached the road and were being dragged back. Now infantrymen had rushed up the road to help drag the guns to safety. There was hardly time to spare, for the skirmishers had parted to each side to let another battle line of rebel infantry cross the field in long, steady strides, with their almost fiendish yelling rising above the turmoil of the battle. The few Union infantrymen were running now, trying to reach the town.

The Eleventh Corps had been broken again, as it had been on the Plank Road when it had been surprised and smashed by Stonewall Jackson at Chancellorsville.

There was no time now for Crispin's Bulldogs to emplace and open fire. The hot guns were attached to the limbers and the understrength teams pulled limbers and guns, limbers and caissons, to the road beyond where the fourth gun of the battery had been righted and made ready to roll. The other three guns were hauled into the road.

Captain Crispin peered back through the battle smoke. He spoke quickly to his wounded trumpeter. The trumpeter raised his trumpet and blew it. Instantly the battery started forward toward Gettysburg, on the Mummasburg Road, past groups of sullen-faced infantrymen of the shattered Eleventh Corps. Captain Crispin had been as good as his word. *We have not lost a gun in nine battles, and we will not lose one now!*

Three newcomers rode with Crispin's Bulldogs. A capless blond sergeant who clung to a limber seat ahead of the gun he had served so well; a small, slightly built fifer who rode on a bouncing, jouncing caisson; a dark-haired boy who rode the nigh wheeler of a gun team, holding onto the mane of a magnificent bay off wheeler, who pulled as though he was drawing the limber and gun all by himself. The boy driver looked back and saw a wide grin on the face of Seth Pomeroy and a wider grin on the dusty, powder-blackened face of little Zack Pascoe. Another statement seemed to come back to Ben Buell above the drumming of the hoofs and the grating of the wheels on the hard road. "Militia, or no militia," Seth Pomeroy had said stoutly, "I'm staying right here to give the Army of the Potomac a hand whether they like it or not!" He, and his two comrades from Company B, Pennsylvania Volunteer Militia, the erstwhile Hinckley's Corners Tiger Rifles, had been as good as his word.

CHAPTER SEVEN

Ben Buell walked with Seth Pomeroy and Zack Pascoe through the hot and humid night of the first day's fighting at Gettysburg. The Baltimore Pike was somewhere to their left. They had stayed with Battery B after the pell-mell retreat of the Eleventh Corps through the streets of Gettysburg, where thousands of Union soldiers, confused in their directions, had fallen captive to the victorious Confederates. Despite the stubborn fighting of Buford's Cavalry Division in covering the retreat, the losses of the Federals, in captives alone, was staggering.

General Winfield Hancock, commander of the Second Corps of the Army of the Potomac, had arrived on the field of battle in time to help reorganize the Federal defense of Cemetery Hill. The pursuing rebels had been stopped by the fire of some of the Reserve Artillery and the sharpshooters in the houses and barns on the slopes of the hill.

Battery B had not been in action again after its close call on the Mummasburg Road. By a miracle, the gun section that had not been in the fighting there, had managed to rejoin the battery in its bivouac between

Cemetery Hill and Culp's Hill, not far from the Spangler farm. They had been detached on the march to Gettysburg, under the command of First Lieutenant James Pike, second in command of the battery, and the only other officer on duty with it. Second Lieutenant Vincent Barry was home in Connecticut still recovering from wounds received at Chancellorsville. Second Lieutenant George Pettit had been mortally wounded at Brandy Station, and no replacement had as yet been assigned to the battery.

"Where do you suppose the Tiger Rifles are?" asked Zack thoughtfully.

"Where are the snows of yester-year?" asked Seth. "I hope they're all safe."

"What happens to us now?" asked Ben. He looked at the dim lantern that shone through the dark woods. It marked the simple headquarters of the battery—a cracker box for a desk, a log for a seat, a lantern for light, and the sky for a roof.

Seth shrugged. "I'd like to stay with the battery, boys."

Zack spat. "Fat chance of that, Sergeant. They don't want a cripple, a boy, and an undersized punk like me in Crispin's Battery, and I don't mean any offense to either one of you."

Seth nodded. "All the same, they're shorthanded. Sergeant Dolan said the Johnnies are bringing up their full army and that General Meade is going to concentrate our forces here. Battery B may be able to use us for a little while yet."

They paused beyond the circle of light cast by the lantern. Captain Crispin was in low and earnest conversation with Lieutenant Pike, a six-and-a-half-foot giant of a man, as broad as the side of a barn, with thick red hair and mustache.

Ben looked off through the darkness. There were thousands of men literally within shouting distance and yet it was curiously quiet despite the presence of such a host. Lanterns dotted the darkness with their dim yellow glow. A steady and low groaning sound came from the many wounded of the day's battle. Now and then a rifle shot cracked flatly in the distance. There was a constant and restless stirring of men and beasts, and a curious and eerie foreboding seemed to have descended with the dusk. The night air was thick with the lingering fumes of powder smoke, mingled with the miasma of horse and mule droppings, sweat-soaked clothing, and blood.

Wagons grated past on the unseen road in a constant stream, mingled with artillery pieces and caissons, the sound of thudding hoofs, grinding wheels, jingling trace chains, squeaking of dry axles, all mingled with tired voices of men hurrying to get those all-important supplies of ammunition and cannon into position before daylight.

The vast restless movements of thousands of men and animals in the tense darkness of the night would prevent sound sleep for Johnny and Yank as well. Beyond the scrap of woods where Battery B was bivouacked came the sounds of ammunition chests being replenished from wagons of the ammunition train. The big traveling forge had been lighted and the artificers of the battery were hard at work repairing some of the worst damage to guns, wheels, limbers, and caissons.

Drivers moved up and down the long picket line of horses, examining each of them, talking quietly to them, while other men spread forage taken from the battery wagon for the horses.

Battery cooks worked about their fires brewing coffee and frying crumbled hardtack in deep bacon grease. A detail of men tramped off into the darkness, with strings of canteens hung about their necks, carrying water buckets in each hand, looking for a well, stream, or spring. There would be many such details hunting throughout the night for the precious fluid, and many of them would be bitterly disappointed.

"Pomeroy, Pascoe, Buell!" called out Sergeant Dolan as he came through the darkness from near the battery headquarters.

"Here, Sergeant!" called out Seth. "The Captain will see ye now, boys."

Seth led the way to the headquarters. Giant Lieutenant Pike leaned against a tree, filling his pipe, and his steady blue eyes thoughtfully studied the three dusty, powder-blackened militiamen who stood at attention before the battery commander.

"At ease, men," said Captain Crispin. "Sit down if you like — on that log there."

"Thanks, sir," said Seth with a faint smile.

Crispin leaned back against a tree and eyed the three of them. "First I want to thank the three of you for your work with Battery B this day," he said. He looked at Ben. "If it hadn't been for your handling of that big bay wheeler, young man, the battery might not have been able to get into action at all. We received a new draft of horses on the march here to Gettysburg, and he was one of them. A fine horse, but no one seemed able to handle him. I understand he was your horse, Buell, before he was bought by a Government contractor."

"That is right, sir," said Ben. "He always was hard for anyone else to handle. He was mine since the day he was a colt."

"And yet you sold him?"

Ben eyed the officer. "I didn't sell him, sir. There was a family difficulty, and the horse was sold. I never thought I would see him again."

"Lucky for Battery B that you did."

Ben smiled. "Someone had to get him under control, sir."

Crispin nodded. He looked at Seth and Zack. "And you two: Your work on that gun today was well done. I am confused in a sense. I know you are members of the Pennsylvania Volunteer Militia, and probably well qualified as infantrymen, but to find two such cannoneers in the heat of a battle, when we needed them the most, as we did young Buell here, seems almost miraculous."

Ben spoke up. "Sergeant Pomeroy has been studying gunnery as far back as I can remember. My father taught Seth and me about such matters."

"Your father?"

"Captain Maynard Buell, sir."

Lieutenant Pike stared at Ben. "There was a Pennsylvania battery in action not far from us at Gaines' Mill. Buell's Battery, I think it was called. Would that have been your father's battery?"

Ben nodded proudly. "Battery A, First Pennsylvania Independent Artillery, sir!"

Pike tugged at his mustache. "As I recall, they kept firing, without infantry supports, until they were overrun by the Johnnies. There wasn't much left of the battery when the battle was over."

Seth Pomeroy spoke up. "They made a last stand, sir. They took all the ammunition from the chests and stacked it beside the guns. They loaded their Napoleons to the muzzle and fought them until the rebels overran the battery. Captain Buell suffered wounds that eventually caused his death. There was no better artillery man in the Army of the Potomac, sir!"

Crispin looked at Ben. "Today Battery B saved their guns, in a fighting retirement. I will not call it a *retreat*. We are still on the field and ready to fight despite our losses. But guns *can* be lost with honor, young Buell, as your father's guns were lost at Gaines' Mill."

"Thank you, sir," said Ben. Right at that moment he would gladly have charged, singlehanded, against the rebel guns that had fought them from Oak Hill that day.

Crispin fiddled with a pencil. "I called you here to thank you while I had the chance. I might not see you again. We are in reserve because of our condition after today's fight, but that does not mean that we will be left out of tomorrow's fighting. As long as we have a gun and a crew to serve it, we can be called upon. There is nothing more to keep you here. I have written out a statement regarding your service with this battery for you to show to your commanding officer in the militia. I hope it will repay you, in some small measure, for what you did today with Battery B."

"Thank you, sir," said Seth as he stood up. He glanced at Zack and Ben. "I know that the three of us considered it an honor to serve with Crispin's Bulldogs, sir. Inasmuch as your battery is still shorthanded, we feel that we might be of some use until this crisis is over. We may be but militia, Captain Crispin, but not one of us would want to leave the field of battle before the issue is decided. On that basis, sir, we request permission to stay here and serve as temporary volunteers with the battery, sir."

Lieutenant Pike stared at Seth, then shoved back his forage cap and wiped his brow in mock amazement. "Listen to him, sir," he said. "I could swear it was my old schoolmaster speaking."

"He is a schoolmaster," said Ben. "And a good one."

"As good as he is at serving a gun, Buell?" asked Captain Crispin.

"After today, I am not sure, sir."

Crispin stood up. "It is all right with me. We can use you. Since Chancellorsville, and through Brandy Station, we have lost many good soldiers. Up until Antietam this battery was composed mostly of Regulars. Since then we have taken in many volunteers, all fine men I am happy to say. I think that before the war is over, we may be composed for the most part of volunteers. Men such as you three."

Zack Pascoe seemed to grow several inches over his full five feet two inches.

Seth smiled. "We will be proud to serve with the battery, sir."

"Report to Sergeant Dolan then." Crispin looked out

into the lantern- and campfire-spangled darkness." "I hate having to bivouac on a battlefield," he said, almost to himself. "The heat and death of battle are as nothing compared to nights such as this, when the wounded cry out."

They reported to Sergeant Dolan, and despite the fact that they had, in a sense, been more or less heroes that day, it made little difference to that hard-driving Irishman, a Regular for twenty-five years and in the artillery every day of it. Seth and Zack, as members pro tem of the Gun Detachment, went to the guns and to work, while Ben Buell went to the horse picket lines. There was little time to spend with Dandy. The big bay was only another horse along the picket line. The horses trembled with weariness. Some of them stood lock-legged and asleep, while others lay flat on the hard ground. Here and there a detail of men under the command of the battery veterinarian noncom doctored minor wounds, and there were many of them.

After an hour's work Ben went to mess beside one of the campfires. He was bone tired, and it was hard to eat, but he knew he would need his strength. None of the eating men spoke. They chewed their hardtack and coosh, a mess of hardtack fried in bacon grease. They sipped their hot black issue coffee and looked off into the velvety darkness with eyes that did not see. Many comrades had been lost to them that day—killed, wounded, or perhaps captured. Favorite horses, too, were missed, and some of the men sitting there had been forced to fire the mercy shot to put a hopelessly wounded or crippled horse out of his misery.

Ben looked up to see a man drift through the darkness from the road, with his rifle carried under his arm like that of a squirrel hunter. He stopped and eyed the fire and the food on the battered tin plates. His forage cap was tilted far to one side, broken visored, and on the top of it, above the bugle insignia of the infantry, was his corps badge, the white circle of the Second Division, First Corps. His eyes were a startling light gray against the bronze of his tanned face. "You boys want the news?" he asked.

Sergeant Fox looked up. "Sit down, 'news-walker,'" he said. "What's the latest?"

The man turned. "Wait till my partner gets here." He cupped his free hand about his mouth. "Danny! Danny!"

A short man with a bandaged wrist came out of the darkness and squatted beside the first man. "Coffee smells good, Lem," he said.

Sergeant Fox jerked his head at one of the cooks. The cook filled two plates and poured two cups of coffee, which he passed to the strangers. They ate rapidly, then filled their pipes, lighting them with sticks from the fire. "Meade is concentrating here at Gettysburg," said Lem. He drew in on his pipe. "General Meade had figured on fighting at Pipe Creek before this ruckus started. General Slocum has brought up the Twelfth Corps. They're getting in position along Rock Creek and around Culp's Hill. Sickles' Third Corps is here too, come from Emmetsburg. Seems like most of the Army of Northern Virginia is already here though."

Danny coughed. Lem glanced at him and nodded. Danny took his pipe from his mouth and sipped his coffee. "Our officers can't figure out why Lee didn't press his attack late this afternoon. Could have probably taken Cemetery Hill. They can't figure out why the Reb's Second Corps didn't occupy Culp's Hill either. Lucky for us they didn't. We got men flooding the roads south and southeast of Gettysburg, coming on as fast as they can."

Lem emptied his coffee cup. "Our boys of the First Corps are still in position on Cemetery Hill. I heard the Fifth and Sixth Corps are on the way. Figure they might get here tomorrow or maybe tonight. I ain't sure about that news."

"What about the Cavalry Corps?" asked Sergeant Fox.

Lem rubbed his bristly jaws. "Of course you know Buford's First Division was fighting here today."

"We ought to," said Fox dryly.

"I heard Gregg's Division is out along the Hanover Road," said Danny.

"Kilpatrick's Division is somewheres south of here, I think," said Lem.

"Anything else?" asked a bearded corporal.

Lem shook his head. "Nothing more than that Meade aims to give battle here, boys. The whole Army of the Potomac is coming up, like I said."

Danny eyed Sergeant Fox. "What news you got, Sergeant?"

Fox quickly told him of the work Battery B had done that day and of the activities of the Eleventh Corps along the Mummasburg and Carlisle Roads, the troops they had faced, and the results of the fighting.

Danny nodded. He stood up. "Come on, Lem," he said. "Good night, boys." The two of them vanished into the darkness as quietly and as mysteriously as they had appeared from the road.

Sergeant Fox looked at Ben. "Those were 'news-walkers'" he said. "Self-appointed reporters, you might call them. They gather information from each unit, pass it on, gather more information and so on, until they have a good picture of how the battle went. It's a sort of a point of honor to tell them the truth."

Driver Whitlow appeared at the edge of the firelight. "Yeah, but don't leave anything around loose," he said. "Particularly a full haversack, for they'll be gone with it before you know it."

"Them boys know more about the battle than the generals do," said a cannoneer.

"Hear, hear," agreed the bearded corporal.

Sergeant Fox emptied his pipe. "The old Cavalry Corps is scattered all over. Buford near Gettysburg. Gregg out on the Hanover Road. Kilpatrick probably on the Taneytown or Emmetsburg Roads. And Battery B all alone, fighting with the infantry."

"Well, I always said this war was a little difference between Battery B and the whole Confederate States Army," said Jonas Whitlow. He looked at Ben. "You still here?"

"Captain Crispin said my two friends and I could stay a while. The battery's shorthanded and he thought we could be of use."

"You sure were of use today, boy," said Sergeant Fox. "When you came out of nowhere and walked right up to that big bay and talked to him like a Dutch uncle I thought you'd be stomped to death. I was hoping Dolan would get a bullet into him before he did any damage. Thank God he didn't."

"Aye," said Jonas Whitlow. He eyed Ben closely. "Best get some sleep. Won't be easy. It never is on the night of a battle."

"I'm pretty tired," said Ben. "We marched most of the morning to get here. Funny thing: tired as I was before the real shooting started, I seemed to forget about it. Then, when we got here, after dusk, I felt as though I was made of wood."

Fox nodded. "That's the way of it. Get some sleep, boy. Never know when we have to move out. Might not be for a day or so, and might be in five minutes. You never know."

Ben walked to where Seth and Zack lay beside the battery wagon on loose forage that had been dropped there. Zack was sound asleep, but Seth lay with his hands behind his head, staring up at the star-spangled sky.

"How do you feel, Seth?" asked Ben.

The schoolmaster turned to look at him. "All right, Ben. It's a strange thing, but I feel as though I have come home here. This is *my* battery, Ben. *My* guns and *my* horses. *My* comrades."

Ben dropped beside him and rose up on one elbow. "Until they don't need us any longer, Seth."

Seth shook his head. "They'll need us. They'll surely need us! You mark my words, Ben Buell."

Ben lay flat again and looked up at the sky. He could hear the restless stirring of the vast forces gathering at this place of sudden death, yet he would not have been any other place by choice. Maybe it was his home too. *His* battery. He closed his eyes and instantly attained the deep oblivion of exhausted sleep.

CHAPTER EIGHT

The harsh voice ripped at the veil of sleep that hung about Ben Buell. "Arise, ye terriers! Arise and shine, ye cannoneers and drivers! Harness and hitch! Harness and hitch! Saddle up! Boots and saddles there, I say! Rise and shine, Battery B!" Ben sat bolt upright and stared into the red face of Sergeant Dolan. Dolan looked as fresh as the dew-wet shamrocks of his native Ireland. "What is it, Sergeant?" Ben gasped out.

"March order! Seems like we are to let the infantry and the artillery fight it out here, whilst we av the harse artillery march to join our own Cavalry Corps, boy. Now up wid ye!"

"You heard the sergeant," said Zack Pascoe. He yawned prodigiously, so that Seth Pomeroy reached over and tenderly assisted him in closing the gap.

They staggered to their feet. Ben buckled on his belt and placed his cap on his head. He waved groggily to his two friends and walked off into the lantern-washed night to find the picket line. The battery area was a swirling maelstrom of organized confusion as the members of the battery went about their business in sour silence.

In a matter of half an hour the drivers had harnessed

the teams and hitched them up to gun limbers and caisson limbers, battery wagon, and the traveling forge. The cannoneers and other battery personnel, other than the team drivers, had saddled up and now stood to horse, holding their bridle reins near the bit, booted and spurred, for horse artillerymen other than the drivers rode individually, it being impossible to ride on limbers and caissons traveling at speed across rough country as horse artillery quite often had to do.

Ben worked quickly with Dandy and Big Barney, the nigh wheeler teamed with Dandy. He had smoothed down the manes beneath the collars as Jonas Whitlow had told him to after smoothing down the hair beneath the saddle blankets. Jonas came quickly down the line of the team, checking each horse. Lanky "Mexico" Bates, the swing team driver, grinned at Ben. "You aim to handle those wheelers, boy?"

Ben straightened up. "I don't think I'm supposed to, Mexico."

"Then who is?" asked Jonas. "You're serving with Battery B, boy. Good time for you to get the feeling of a team. You can handle Big Barney if you can handle that bay. Big Barney is steady and knows what to do. You just follow the leader, boy. Just follow the leader."

Ben nodded. He examined the saddle on Big Barney. It was a Jennifer, such as his father had used in his battery; much more of a padded seat than that of the standard McClellan used by the cavalry and other mounted personnel of the Army. The padded seat was heavily stitched. The saddle was high and curving, almost like a wishbone effect, with brass-trimmed pommel and cantle.

"You carry your valise on the off wheeler," said Mexico as he examined a hoof of his nigh swing horse.

Ben couldn't help but grin, tired and excited as he was. "All I have is on me, Mexico."

"A good way to go to war. Anything you need, you ask

Old Father Jonas up there, being as how he has adopted you. Kindly old fellow, boy."

"One of these days, Mexico," warned Jonas.

Mexico yawned. "One of these days you'll fall off that leader, Jonas, and maybe me and Ben here can get a *real* lead driver up there."

"It's a cinch it won't be *you,* Mexico! All you can do is sit on that nigh swing horse and have me pull you and Ben push you. And *you* call yourself a *driver!*"

"Now, Jonas!"

"Now, Mexico!"

"Now the *both* av ye!" roared a harsh Hibernian voice like the brassy clap of doom. "Quiet thayer or by all the saints I'll put that boy up on that lead team to teach ye both how to drive!"

Dolan stalked on with his hard blue eyes striking out right and left almost like blows of an invisible whip, and there was nothing that he missed.

"With all the *good* Yankee-born sergeants in the United States Army, why did they have to import him from Ireland?" growled Mexico.

Jonas peered over his saddle and made sure Dolan was out of earshot. "For two cents I'd ask him out beyond the horse lines tonight."

Mexico grinned. "I'd like to see *that.*"

"You don't think I can whip him?"

"I don't *think,* I *know!*"

"Well, I can take *you, Mister* Bates!"

"Maybe you'd like to try?"

"Bates! Whitlow!" roared Dolan. "So help me! Ye kape quiet, or I'll have the both av ye out beyond the harse lines this noight! Ye hear me!"

"He can do it too," said a quiet voice.

Ben turned to see Sergeant Fox, the section chief. Fox eyed the two red-faced drivers. He spoke out of the side of his mouth to Ben. "They've been feuding since '61, and they'd die for each other." He walked up and down the team line, then went back to check the wheels of the limber and the gun. He then opened the ammunition chest and checked the tow packing that had been thrust down between the rounds of ammunition to keep them from striking against one another. He took out a smooth stick and carefully packed down the wadding here and there to check it against looseness. He looked up at Ben. "I've seen ammunition chests blow up on a rough road because of careless packing."

Ben leaned against Big Barney. There were so many things to remember in an artillery battery — things that might make the difference between life and death.

Hughie MacLean, the battery trumpeter, was mounted, and single-footing toward the head of the battery column. "Voice commands only, boys!" he called out. "We don't want to wake up any of the sleeping men around here."

"Drivers mount!" came the command.

Ben swung up into the saddle on Big Barney and settled himself. He was more used to riding bareback on Dandy than in using a saddle, but it was a right comfortable seat.

"Cannoneers mount!"

There was a smashing of leather as the cannoneers swung up into their saddles.

"Forward, ho! March! Trot!"

Ben looked ahead through the graying dimness, suddenly realizing with a start that it must be just before the true dawn. There was a spot of color where the guidon bearer rode at the side of the lead team of the first gun. Then the head of the column turned right onto the Baltimore Pike, and in a matter of minutes there came the steady clattering of hoofs on the hard road, the grinding of the heavy wheels, the jingling of trace chains, the creaking of leather, and the snorting of the horses, as Battery B marched south to join part of the Cavalry Corps wherever that might be.

They kept to the right as they rode steadily on through the slowly growing light of dawn, passing thick columns of steady marching infantry. The columns stretched as far as the eye could see in the dim light, marked here and there by the cased regimental colors. Very little was said by these tired men who had been marching for days, and now, tired and footsore, dusty and thirsty, they were moving up into what promised to be another day similar to that which had just passed at Gettysburg, and in all likelihood it would be worse. It was the dawn of July 2, 1863.

The sun was fully up when some of the light artillery batteries of the Artillery Reserve came into sight, riding toward Gettysburg. The leading drivers looked curiously at Battery B, which was battle-scarred and shorthanded. "Hey, horse artillery!" called out a gunner marching beside a limber. "You're heading the wrong way!"

"We've been softening the Johnnies up for you," retorted Jonas Whitlow.

"Whoever saw a dead horse artilleryman?" jeered a rival driver.

"Ye'll see a dead light artilleryman in a minute!" roared Sergeant Dolan.

They rode on as the sun came up, and still they passed mile after mile of marching infantry, artillery, ambulances, wagon trains, and units of all the arms and services of the Army of the Potomac.

At the noon halt the word was passed along the battery column that they were to join Buford's First Division somewhere near Westminster. Jeb Stuart was still on the loose somewhere east of the Army of the Potomac, perhaps northeast, and the Cavalry Corps was feeling for him to cut him off from Lee.

Even as they moved on again, the wind shifted, and the muted roaring of battle came to them. Now and then a driver or cannoneer would turn in his saddle and look back through the hazy light to where thick battle smoke was again arising over Gettysburg. It was a big one, there was no doubt of that.

Mexico turned in his saddle. "Well, maybe it is so that we are going in the wrong direction for the rest of the battle. But it was Buford's boys who blunted Lee's advance on Gettysburg and gave the First and Eleventh Corps time to come up. And it was Crispin's Bulldogs who slowed the Georgians from smashing the Eleventh Corps. It'll be another inscription on the battery guidon, boy, for they can't say we missed any of the first day's fighting."

"Will we be fighting with the Cavalry Corps now, Mexico?" called Ben.

"Who knows? But if we are looking for Jeb Stuart, you can bet your boots we'll find him. Jeb isn't the boy to run away from a fight, and we're the boys to give him one."

Jeb Stuart! The fighting leader of Lee's cavalry! The general who had led his command in a daring raid completely around the Northern forces when General McClellan had been fighting almost on the doorstep of Richmond, Virginia in June of 1862. From the information gained from that raid, General Lee had confidently sent Stonewall Jackson to fall on McClellan's flank and rear during the Seven Days, eventually causing McClellan, with a much larger force than Lee's, to retreat ignominiously, crying for help from Washington. Again, in August of the same year, Stuart had again ridden around behind the Northern lines and attacked the rear of General Pope's Army of Virginia, inflicting a great deal of damage, and even capturing Pope's private and official correspondence. From the information gained, Lee had again sent Jackson on a vast turning movement, which had resulted in the smashing defeat of Pope at Second Manassas, or Second Bull Run, as the Federals called it.

In October of 1862, Stuart had led his hard-riding cavalry in yet another raid, this time deep into Pennsylvania. Ben remembered that incident very well, for at that time the Pennsylvania Volunteer Militia had been called out, but by the time they had mobilized, Stuart had struck and run. He had raided Mercersburg and Chambersburg, fully in the rear of the Federal Army, and ninety miles from the protection of the Army of Northern Virginia. In thirty-six hours his command had ridden ninety miles, and his entire loss was one wounded and two missing.

There was something legendary about Jeb Stuart, and the man seemed invincible, no less than the troops which he commanded, men born and bred to the saddle, for which, until the beginning of the third year of the war, the Federal cavalry had hardly been a match.

But the odds were that Ben Buell, Seth Pomeroy, and Zack Pascoe would not be with Battery B when the Cavalry Corps tangled with Jeb Stuart. A boy, a cripple, and a runt would hardly pass muster in Crispin's Bulldogs. As soon as the battery was up to full strength, it would be back to Hinckley's Corners and the weekly evening drill in the quiet town square, far from the eager roar of battle, for the three of them.

They bivouacked that night many miles from Gettysburg, not far from a small town that was a way station for the local telegraph line. Sergeant Dolan, with Captain Crispin's permission, rode into the town and got the news of the second day's battle at Gettysburg from the telegraph office. He repeated it to the tired artillerymen who had gathered together near battery headquarters.

"Lee is said to be at Gettysburg and in command," said Dolan. "Our lines extended from Cemetery Hill south along Cemetery Ridge — that was the Second and Eleventh Corps — wid the Twelfth holding Culp's Hill, to the northeast av the line. Sickles brought up his Third Corps and moved out to the Emmetsburg Road, beyont the main army, lavin' a wide gap between his corps and the Second Corps.

"In the afternoon the ribil First Corps av Longstreet attacked Sickles' Third Corps. T'was touch and go and the losses were terrible, Sickles' left being cut to paces, until some av our Second Corps boys came up at the double and fought the ribils in a wheat field thayer, but it was still in the balance, boys.

"Warren was sent by Ginral Meade to reconnoiter on the left, and he saw that the key to the battle was Little Round Top, ye mind we passed it whin we left the area? So re-enforcements was sint there quickly from the Fifth Corps. The Fifth Corps boys threw back the ribils and held Little Round Top. That's all the news at present."

Two hard days of battle! The thought ran through Ben Buell's mind that night after he had finished his work on the horse lines. Yet it seemed as though the fighting at Gettysburg was not over. The fighting for Richmond, the Peninsula Campaign, had been done in seven days, which had been one of the names given to the fighting in general. The Seven Days! Mechanicsville, Beaver Dam Creek, Gaines' Mill, Savage Station, White Oak Swamp, and Malvern Hill. Second Bull Run or Second Manassas had been fought for two days. Antietam, bloodiest of all battles in the eastern theater, had been fought for one day. The futile assault of the Union forces at Fredericksburg had taken two days. Chancellorsville had been a two-day battle. But now it seemed as though Gettysburg would continue on, and if the second and third day's fighting had been as hard as it had been the first day, Gettysburg might well be the biggest battle of the war.

Ben dropped atop his borrowed blanket. It was too warm that night for covering. Seth Pomeroy came through the darkness and squatted beside Ben. "Sergeant Dolan told me that we would get filled up to strength once we reached the Cavalry Corps, Ben."

"Yes?"

"You know what that will mean."

Ben nodded. He had been thinking of nothing else all

day long. They wouldn't need the three Hinckley's Corners boys then.

Zack Pascoe drifted through the darkness and sat down beside his two comrades. Silently he opened his haversack and began to remove the contents, which he piled up on Ben's blanket. A loaf of fresh-baked bread, which filled the air with its fresh and tantalizing odor, a crock of butter and one of jam, a dozen big, hard-boiled eggs, several thick slices of ham, two fried chicken legs, and a large pound cake.

Seth whistled softly. "Where did you get all this?"

"Farmhouse," said Zack laconically.

"You don't have any money," said Ben.

Zack casually waved a hand. "Didn't need any."

"So how did you do it?" asked Seth suspiciously.

Zack grinned. "You remember me finding that busted wooden reb canteen and that old slouch hat?"

"Yes."

Zack smiled. "Tole the ol' farmer they was battlefield relics, full of shot holes."

"They didn't have any shot holes in them," said Ben.

Zack tenderly patted the loaf of fresh bread, then he slid a hand inside his shirt and brought out a sharpened tent peg. "Surprising how a hole punched in a hat or a canteen with this thing can look like a bullet hole."

"Wouldn't fool me," said Seth quickly.

Zack sniffed at the jam crock. "Well, maybe and maybe not, but if there was one or two flattened bullets *inside* that ol' canteen and that ol' hat, it just might fool you, mightn't it?"

"Possibly," said Seth. "Particularly if someone had picked out a few *unflattened* bullets first, and had given them a good lick or two with a hammer or a rock."

Zack closed one eye, placed a dirty finger alongside his nose and nodded. "Exactly," he said mysteriously. "Dive in, Tiger Rifles!"

"Wait!" said Ben. He peered about. "I've heard it said

that the first sergeant really runs a battery or a company. We've got enough for ourselves and a guest. *One* guest."

"Such as?" asked Seth and Zack together.

"Guess," said Ben smugly.

"Sergeant Dolan?" they chorused.

"Exactly," said Ben, imitating Zack's gesture of placing his finger beside his nose.

"Tricky, that boy," said Zack.

"But clever," said Seth.

So it was. Sergeant Dolan said little, but he ate well. When he was done he filled his old dudeen pipe and accepted a light from Seth. He drew in on the pipe and expelled a ring of pungent smoke. "Who was the forager?" he asked.

"Zack," said Ben.

Dolan nodded in appreciation. "Some boys wud starve in a sutler's tent, and him away at the toime, whilst others, such as Zack here, could find manna in the desert. I congratulate ye, Private Pascoe."

"It was nothing," murmured Zack. "Nothing at all, Sergeant."

Dolan placed his back against a limber wheel and half closed his eyes. "A foine night," he said. "Reminds me a bit av Ireland."

Zack Pascoe reached inside his shirt and withdrew his fife of pale-brown wood, placed it to his lips, and blew softly into it. Then he began to play, his tapered fingers moving swiftly over the six holes. Ben recognized the tune. It was "Haste to the Wedding."

Dolan's eyes seemed to snap open. He stared at the little fifer.

Zack swept from "Haste to the Wedding" into the "Turkey Gobbler" and from there into "Charlie Over the Water."

"For the love av hiven!" said Dolan. "The lad is a fifer indade! He plays the gob-stick like a master! Do ye know 'The Road to Boston'!"

Zack nodded, finished "Charlie Over the Water," then swung at once into "The Road to Boston." As he played, one member of the battery after another came through the darkness from their low campfires and sat or squatted in a ring about Zack Pascoe. He finished "The Road to Boston" with a flourish.

"You know 'The Old Seventy-six'?" asked Sergeant Fox.

"'The Tattered Jack'?" called out Jonas Whitlow.

"'Biddy Oats'?" asked Mexico Bates.

They could not stump Zack Pascoe. He knew them all—"All Take Tea," "Corn Cob," "Paul Revere's Ride," "Jaybird and Gilderoy."

Ben looked up to see Captain Crispin leaning against a tree, idly beating time with a finger, while Lieutenant Pike puffed at his pipe, his eyes glistening with delight as the wild notes of the fife rang through the darkened woods.

Zack was no fool. He played "Sergeant O'Leary" for Sergeant Dolan, then finished up with "The Battle Hymn of the Republic," and every man of Battery B sang along with him.

Later, when the three comrades were alone, Seth Pomeroy spoke in a low voice. "Ben, you did well in thinking of inviting Sergeant Dolan here. Zack, your foraging and your fifing have set us in solid with Dolan and the battery as a whole. Now, it's up to me. By the time we reach Buford's Division, we'll either be enlisted in this battery, or my name isn't Seth Pomeroy."

The soft notes of "Tattoo" drifted through the woods from an infantry regiment camped farther down the road, to be followed some time later by the new tune of "Taps," sweet and lingering, but by that time, the three Hinckley's Corners boys were deep in sleep.

CHAPTER NINE

It was late in the afternoon of the second day of marching from Gettysburg when the tired and dusty men and horses of Battery B turned into a large field where the smoke of many cooking fires drifted up through the treetops and hung in a rifted layer in the clear air. As far as the eye could see, from one fenced field to the next, and through the groves and meadows, there were horses and men, white-tilted wagons, limbers, guns, caissons, and battery wagons, traveling forges and ambulances, with tents scattered here and there amidst the encampment. Metal rang against metal from the vicinity of half a dozen traveling forges. Troopers and artillerymen walked to and fro about their business or sat by their cooking fires. A guard detail tramped past through the dust.

Mexico Bates turned in his saddle. "Part of Buford's First Division," he said. "Gamble's First Brigade and Devin's Second Brigade. I can't see any of Merritt's Reserve Brigade."

But Ben's eyes were on the horse artillery park that ran along a winding stream. "How many horse artillery batteries are there in the Cavalry Corps, Mexico?"

Mexico rubbed his jaw. "The First Brigade is Robertson's: Ninth Michigan, Sixth New York, B combined with L and M Batteries of the Second United States, and E Battery of the Fourth United States. The Second Brigade is Tidball's: Batteries E, G, and K of the First United States, Battery A of the Second United States, and Battery C of the Third United States. Plus B Battery, Eighth United States, Crispin's Bulldogs"!

"Trouble is," called back Jonas Whitlow, "that Ol' Battery B is the fire department of the Cavalry Corps, seems like. When there's trouble it's Battery B that goes to the fire."

"The willing horse," agreed Mexico. He flushed. "By George! I finally agreed with ol' Jonas there! Must be getting soft in my old age."

"I have to agree with you there," said Jonas. "Soft in the head anyways."

"Now, Jonas!"

"Now, Mexico!"

"Quiet thayer!" roared Sergeant Dolan as he cantered past.

"Never fails," said Mexico. "Me and Jonas get into a quiet difference and ol' Dolan comes past every time!"

"He always hears that big mouth of yours," said Jonas.

The trumpet sounded off, and the battery came to a dust-shrouded halt. In a few minutes they filed into an area at one end of the horse artillery park and from then on there was hardly time to talk or do anything but unhitch, picket the horses, wipe them off and rub them down, bring them forage, and do all the hundred and one things that must be done before the artillerymen could sit down and eat in the dusky woods.

Ben emptied his plate and looked across the wide bivouac. Not all of the units of the First Division were there, and some of the horse artillery batteries had not yet arrived at this rendezvous. This night, or perhaps the next day, he and his two friends from Hinckley's Corners would know their fate. At a time when conscription was the order of the day to fill up the depleted Union ranks, and when many able-bodied men were trying every trick and device they knew of to get out of military service, here were three militiamen — a boy, an undersized fifer, and a lame sergeant schoolteacher — on tenterhooks, worried sick for fear they would not be accepted into Battery B, Eighth United States Horse Artillery.

Sergeant Fox came through the dusk and stopped beside Ben. "Your two friends are waiting for you outside of the battery commander's tent," he said.

Ben got to his feet. "How does it look, Sergeant?" he asked.

Fox tugged at his short dark beard. "I can't say, boy. You are all more than welcome in this battery from what I have seen and heard, but the battery itself doesn't make the decision in that respect, Ben. Go and see for yourself and my best wishes go with you."

"Thanks, Sergeant Fox."

Ben dusted off his bedraggled uniform and rubbed his forlorn-looking forage cap and its infantry insignia with an elbow. It didn't do much for either one of them. He hurried toward the battery commander's tent. Seth Pomeroy and Zack stood nearby.

"Well?" asked Ben.

Seth shrugged. "Sergeant Dolan has made out the enlistment papers," he said. "Left out a couple of things though."

Ben thought he already knew what had been left out.

Seth took a deep breath. "Your age; Zack's height; my physical condition."

Zack nodded. "Now, if we was to take your physical condition, Ben, Seth's height, and my age, the three of us might make one 'harse' artilleryman, as Sergeant Dolan would say."

"What can we do?" asked Ben in a low voice.

Seth wet his lips. "Lie," he said.

"That'll be easy for me," said Zack. "But I can't lie

myself into a couple of more inches. You can't lie about that short leg of yours, Seth. Only one who could lie, and maybe get away with it would be Ben. He's big enough to look eighteen. He certainly can *act* eighteen."

They could see figures moving about in the tent. Then a tall soldier came out and walked toward them. His cap had the infantry insignia on it, and there was a wide grin on his tanned face. "Made it, boys," he said cheerfully. "Served with Calef's Battery A at Brandy Station as a volunteer. Liked being with the guns. Applied for a transfer and got leave to hitch a ride here. Got accepted too."

"In what battery?" asked Ben.

"This one! Hope you boys make it." He whistled cheerfully as he walked off into the darkness.

"Makes one less they need," said Zack dolefully.

Seth leaned against a tree. "Dolan said we were short twelve men."

"That still leaves eleven to go, after him," said Ben, jerking his head toward the ex-infantryman.

Seth shook his head. "Five men were transferred from the First Brigade to this brigade some time before we got here. *All* of them were assigned to Battery B."

"Still leaves six," said Zack. "Never say die!"

Seth shook his head again. "Three more men arrived from sick leave. They had been with the brigade headquarters, but their places had been filled. They were sent here."

"Still leaves three," said Zack in a low voice.

"Look," said Ben.

Three men came through the darkness, and it was obvious that they were heading for the tent of the battery commander. One of them glanced at the three militiamen. "This headquarters, Battery B, Eighth U.S.?" he asked.

"It is," said Seth. "But Captain Crispin is pretty busy, friends."

"He ain't too busy to see *us,*" said a broad-shouldered bearded man.

"How so?"

"Seems like Battery B is shorthanded. Need some real men, it's said. Well, we're here."

"Who be you?" asked Zack.

"We're from the wagon train. Sick of driving miles and plowing through gumbo mud whilst the artillerymen get all the glory."

"Oh, we get the glory all right," said Ben carelessly.

"You fellas in Battery B?"

"Sure are. Just got in from Gettysburg."

"How was it?"

Ben glanced at his two comrades. "He wants to know how it was, fellows."

Zack leaned against a tree. "You're looking at all that's left of our entire gun section. 'Course, we didn't get it as bad as some of the *other* batteries, that's why there's *all* of us still alive."

"All of you?" asked a thin man in a small voice.

"Yup," said Ben. "All three of us. Pretty good, hey? At Brandy Station it got hot and heavy and when the shooting was over we looked around and thought the rest of the boys were all asleep on the ground."

"In the middle of the battle?" asked the shortest of the three teamsters.

Seth smiled. "Well, they sure fooled us! They weren't asleep at all!"

"No?"

Ben shook his head. "Dead," he said soberly. "One shell hit a limber. Poof! 'Bout twenty of them were gone."

"Just like that?"

"Just like that," agreed Zack. "Some joke on us, hey?"

"Yeah," said the bearded man. "Some joke."

"All recruits too," said Seth.

"Recruits?" asked the thin man nervously.

"Yup," said Zack. "Fact is, most of the battery was

recruits." He grinned. "That was because of Chancellorsville."

"What happened there?"

"Poof!" said all three of the militiamen. "Just like that!"

"Bloody B Battery," said Ben. He smiled. "Of course, we kinda like the nickname, *Bloody* B!"

Seth nodded. "We're the fire department of the brigade. Ol' Cap Crispin, when he rides up to a fight he cocks his head, figures out where the heaviest shooting is going on, then B Battery heads into the flames. Hot and heavy — that's the way we men like it in ol' Battery B."

The thin man rubbed his jaw. "Come to think of it, boys," he said, "I'm a trained teamster. They need teamsters. Ain't right for me to leave the old wagon train."

The short man nodded his head vigorously. "We got to put our duty ahead of our wishes," he agreed.

The bearded man scratched in his beard. "Well, I'd rather be in the artillery, but you fellows are the majority. Good night, boys."

The three teamsters vanished into the darkness.

Zack inspected his fingernails. "Still leaves three," he said.

"Pomeroy, Pascoe, and Buell!" yelled Sergeant Dolan from the battery commander's tent. "On the double!"

They doubled over to the tent and entered it. Captain Crispin was seated at a folding table, with Sergeant Dolan standing behind him. There was another officer there, wearing the silver bars of a first lieutenant. He sat beside Captain Crispin, with a number of enlistment forms and other papers before him. His gray eyes studied the three militiamen.

"This is Lieutenant Chapel, acting brigade adjutant," said Captain Crispin. "He has the authority to enlist you three men, if you are so willing."

"We are," chorused the three militiamen.

Crispin turned. "Sergeant Dolan," he said. "Were

there not three teamsters who wanted to transfer into this battery?"

"Yis, sorr."

"Where are they?"

"They were due here twenty minutes ago, sorr."

"We should take them before we consider these three men."

"I have not seen them, sorr."

Seth Pomeroy spoke up. "There were three teamsters outside, a while back, sir. They decided they did not want to leave the wagon train."

Crispin's steady eyes fixed themselves on each of the three enlisted men in turn. "I understood they were quite anxious to join."

"Well, sir, they did ask about Gettysburg."

"And you made quite a story of it, is that it?"

"Well, sir, it was quite a story, wasn't it, Captain Crispin?" answered Seth with a smile.

Chapel leaned back in his chair. "You need three men to bring you up to full strength, Captain Crispin."

"That is right, Chapel."

Chapel eyed the three enlisted men. "How tall are you?" he asked Zack Pascoe.

"Five feet four, sir."

Chapel rubbed his jaw. "Are you sure?"

"Maybe a mite below, sir," admitted Zack.

"About two inches of mite, eh?"

"Maybe, sir."

Chapel looked at Seth. "You have a limp, Sergeant. From a wound perhaps?"

"I was born with it, sir."

Chapel nodded. He looked at Ben. "How old are you?"

"Eighteen, sir," lied Ben easily.

Dolan coughed. Crispin smiled a little. Chapel rubbed his jaw again. He looked at Crispin. "From what you have told me, Captain Crispin, these three men have already proved themselves in battle. If they proved themselves in Battery B, they would certainly have enough qualities to overcome any of their shortcomings."

"I agree."

Chapel looked at Seth, Zack, and Ben in turn. "I have the authority to enlist you. I do not have the authority to pass on any of your deficiencies. If I were to do such a thing, and your deficiencies interfered with your performance of your duties, I would find myself in considerable trouble."

"My limp is only on one side, sir," said Seth quickly.

Zack pulled himself to his full height. "I can reach a cannon muzzle without any trouble, sir."

"I helped drive a team at Gettysburg," said Ben quietly, "and I drove from Gettysburg to this place as part of a gun team."

Chapel smiled. "I'll take my chances," he said.

Half an hour later the three friends walked from the tent, full-fledged horse artillerymen of Battery B or so they thought.

Sergeant Dolan came through the darkness to their simple bivouac. He placed his hands on his hips. "Do not, for wan moment, think ye are *really* harse artillerymen," he said coldly. "Not yet, at any rate. 'Tis my job as top soldier in this battery to see that ye toe the mark and learn yere duties. And the first thing ye will do, right this moment, is to get thim horns off av yere caps!"

The three of them hastily removed the bugle insignia of the infantry from their forage caps.

"It is a custom in Battery B, that a recruit does not wear the crossed cannon av the artillery until he has proven himself worthy av wearing thim." Dolan felt in his pocket and took out something. "But Captain Crispin and meself agreed that ye three had already done so at Gettysburg, even though ye were not members av the battery at the toime. At my request, yere enlistment dates have been changed to July 1, 1863, so that ye will get credit for the battle. This is a personal gift from the captain and meself." He held out his hand and in it were three insignia—the crossed cannon of the artillery. They each took one and looked again at the hard bronzed face of the big top soldier. "Pin them on," he said shortly. "See that ye wear them from now on with *honor*. The company av the guns sets ye apart, boys. We av the harse artillery are a *corps d'elite,* and nivir ye forget it! Battery B is a Regular Army battery. The duty here is strict and the discipline tough and if ye do not measure up, ye will have me to deal with! "

"Yes, Sergeant," they chorused.

Dolan nodded grimly. "The Captain has wan rule, which ye had best remember. *There must never be anything to explain in Battery B.* Good night, boys!"

Dolan stalked off into the darkness like an avenging spirit.

"Whoooeee," said Zack. "I'm beginning to think he hates us."

"It's just his way," said Ben weakly.

"He knows his business," said Seth with a slightly superior air. "As a noncom myself, I can vouch for his every word. I agree with him, and no matter how hard he is, you must remember he is doing his duty, as he sees it. Don't dislike him for it. Now I—"

Seth's last profound sentence was shattered before it got into being by the blasting of a Hibernian voice out of the dimness near the picket lines. "Pomeroy! Take ye thim three stripes off yere arms! Do ye think this is a *milishy* outfit? Take thim off this instant, *Private* Pomeroy!"

Seth hastily ripped at his chevrons. "Big bully," he said angrily. "The man hates me."

Zack grinned. "He knows his business. As a noncom yourself, you can vouch for his every word, *Private* Pomeroy."

"You agree with him, no matter how hard he is,"

chimed in Ben, "and you must remember he's doing his duty as he sees it. Don't dislike him for it, *Private* Pomeroy."

Seth grinned a little shamefacedly. "Yes," he said. "I guess I had better take it. Well, I wanted to be a Regular. I'm thankful that we all made it."

"All *four* of us," said Ben. "Dandy is here too."

Later, as they lay on their blankets, Ben could hear the steady breathing from Zack and Seth, but sleep came slowly to him as he looked up through the leafy treetops to the star-studded night sky. He was thinking of his mother. She had lost one of her three men in the war and had had another one come home, embittered by the loss of an arm. Now her third and last man was on the march, whose ending no one could foresee.

Ben was roused out of a sound sleep by hoarse shouting from near the road that passed the bivouac. "Lee has been defeated at Gettysburg! He sent fifteen thousand of his men against Cemetery Ridge, and they were smashed by our boys! Lee's invasion of Pennsylvania has been blocked! Already his army is retreating to the south!"

Pandemonium broke loose in the bivouac. Men yelled and screamed. Lamps and fires were lighted. Blank charges were fired. A vast snake dance was formed and in the lead was little Zack Pascoe, playing his fife for all he was worth.

When the noise and excitement died away, it was an hour before dawn, and the weary cavalrymen and artillerymen went to their beds.

Ben had just dropped off again when trumpets rang throughout the bivouac, echoed by the harsh voice of Sergeant Dolan as he stalked through the battery. "Arise ye terriers! Arise and shine, ye cannoneers and drivers! Harness and hitch! Harness and hitch! Saddle up! Boots and saddles there, I say! Rise and shine, Battery B, for the First Cavalry Division is after Robert E. Lee! Rise and shine! March order! March order!"

Ben stumbled wearily toward the horse lines. There was a faint suspicion of the dawn in the eastern sky, and a hint of forthcoming rain in the air. This time, with Jonas Whitlow's permission, he placed the Jennifer saddle on Dandy and hitched him up as nigh wheeler, using Big Barney as the off wheeler.

The first drops of rain sifted down through the trees as Battery B moved out of the bivouac area and turned south on the road. Already the cavalry units of the First Division were on the march. Somewhere ahead of them in the gathering grayness was Lee's Army of Northern Virginia in full retreat, but those lean Johnnies could turn on a pursuer with a snap and a snarl. They had lost a battle, but they had not yet lost the war.

Sergeant Dolan cantered along the line of the battery on his fast-pacing gray. "Sit up thayer in that saddle, Buell, or get down and walk! Ye'll wear a sore on that bay's back!"

Ben straightened up as though he had been jabbed with a red-hot bayonet.

Mexico Bates turned and grinned. "Bet you wish you'd a been born a girl baby, but, come to think of it, you're a *volunteer!* Hawww!"

On they went through the increasing drizzle, with a jingling of trace chains, squelching of hoofs in the pasty mud of the road, grinding of wheels, and squeak of wet leather. Horse artillery on the march to overtake Lee and his tough and sullen Army of Northern Virginia. Ben Buell hunched his shoulders to raise his damp collar higher about his neck. Up and down the column cannoneers were taking their rubber talmas from their cantle rolls, while drivers were removing theirs from the valises carried on the off horses. Ben had had no time to draw equipment. He rode in the same uniform he had donned the morning they had left Hinckley's Corners on the road to glory.

Sergeant Dolan appeared again, this time on the side of the nigh horses, the rain glistening slickly on his talma. His hard blue eyes fell on Ben. Then suddenly he took off his talma and tossed it to Ben as he passed. "Mind ye return it, boy," he said harshly, and he was gone.

Ben put on the talma. Mexico turned in his saddle. "Now you know why we'd rather have Dolan, tough as he is, for a top soldier, than any other three-striper in the brigade!"

The rain slanted down harder than ever. But Ben Buell didn't mind. He was a driver in Battery B, Eighth United States! *Crispin's Bulldogs!*

CHAPTER TEN

MUD, MUD, and yet more mud; quagmires and tenacious morasses of the stuff; wide sheets of it glistening in the late winter rain, deceptively smooth as to surface, but a clinging, sucking trap to man or animal who wandered into it. The cold rain turned at times to wet flakes of snow that swirled down, beautiful to see until they landed atop the mud and melted, adding to the seemingly bottomless pits of gumbo. Sleet that slanted down and froze to the windward side of the scrub pines and glazed them as well as the myriad labyrinths of corduroyed roads that lay across the bogs like a vast grid and had to be constantly maintained. Log hut after log hut with old pork and beef barrels for chimneys. Piles and piles of supplies for men and horses, covered by soaked tarpaulins, black beneath the watery sunlight that sometimes managed to seep through the low-hanging gray clouds of winter. Horse and mule lines, seemingly stretching on into infinity, the patient animals standing with their rumps against the cold wind. Above it all the drifting smoke of fires that mingled with the cold mists. The sounds of impatiently whistling supply locomotives dragging heavily laden freight cars along the Orange and Alexandria railroad.

The ringing of axes against the wet trees and logs of the sparse woodlands. The whinnying of horses and the braying of mules. The brazen voices of trumpets and bugles mingled now and then with the soggy drumbeatings. The murmuring voices of many men, and over all these mingled sounds, and below it, like a lone thread woven through a vast pattern of other sounds, the constant coughing and hacking of men weathering a Virginia winter in the open. Brandy Station, Culpeper County, Virginia, now Headquarters of the Cavalry Corps, Army of the Potomac, and of the Second Corps as well; winter of 1863-1864.

The encampment was almost like some of the drawings and pictures of the settlements of pioneers in the early days of Pennsylvania, Ohio, and Kentucky. The thought was Driver Ben Buell's as he shrugged his talma higher on his shoulders and plodded through the greasy, clinging mud, toward the horse lines of Battery B, Eighth United States. To right and left were blacksmith and wheelwright shops, always smoky and always busy. Sheds and stalls, veterinary hospitals, as well as a field hospital for the men, warehouses and storage sheds, a prisoners' stockade, sutlers' shops, officers' quarters and the long lines of enlisted men's quarters, with their muddy streets and the thick-rifted layers of bittersweet smelling smoke hanging over the wet treetops.

The gun park was not far from the horse lines, for if Stuart had the temerity to raid Brandy Station that winter, there would be little time to harness and hitch. There had been sporadic fighting in the general area around Brandy Station in September, October, and November of '63, but it had definitely become Union Territory in the end.

Ben had plenty of time to report to the horse lines. Five of the cannon of Battery B were swathed in their tarps, but the sixth had been uncovered and was sheltered beneath a roof held upright on saplings, and clustered around the gun was a group of new recruits to Battery B. They were being given basic instructions on the piece, and the instructor wore the two stripes of a corporal of artillery. Ben stopped and watched them. He knew that corporal, and he knew that when Corporal Seth Pomeroy taught a class, they would be the best instructed class in the brigade.

Seth smiled at Ben. A change had come over the schoolmaster of Hinckley's Corners. The faint and rather shy smile had given way to the smile of a man who was much more sure of himself. Seth Pomeroy had proved himself in the first day of fighting at Gettysburg. In the subsequent cavalry clashes of the fall of he had substantiated his standing in Battery B. When Corporal Danish had died of pneumonia in the early part of the winter, it had been Sergeant Dolan who had recommended that the rating be kept open until such men as were interested in those stripes could prove themselves. There hadn't been any doubt in Dolan's mind as to who it would be. He had been right. Seth Pomeroy had been promoted, and there had been no griping from any of the other men. They knew that would be the decisive year of the war and that their chances of surviving that year, and perhaps the year after that, would depend on the skill and abilities of their noncoms and officers.

"Battery B is equipped with six of these guns," said Corporal Pomeroy. "It is a fine gun for fast-moving horse artillery. It is the three-inch Ordnance Rifle, a lightweight gun, averaging about 815 pounds, pulled by a six-horse team so that it may be kept up with the cavalry. The gun can fire all types of rifled ammunition. Range with shell, about two and a half miles. They are excellent guns for their purpose. In fact, so excellent are they, that the Johnnies prize them highly as trophies for their own use. I might add that Battery B, of which you are now members, has never yet lost a gun in battle."

Ben looked at the faces of the recruits. About half of

them looked big enough and strong enough to serve in a horse artillery battery, but this was the third winter of the war, and the splendid volunteers of 1861 and 1862 were now hard to come by. The conscripts and bounty men, as a class, were pretty low in the human scale. Then, too, there was no bounty offered for men enlisting in the Regulars, of which Battery B was composed. A number of famous gun batteries had been consolidated for just such a reason. Still, there were men who wanted to serve with the Long Arm, as the artillery was known. Men to whom the red stripe and crossed guns of the artillery, and particularly a battery of Regular horse artillery, transcended every other consideration.

Seth placed his hand upon a brass plate affixed to the breech of the gun. "You all know this is Battery B, Eighth United States Artillery, nicknamed with good reason, 'Crispin's Bulldogs,' men. Up until Antietam this battery was mostly composed of Regulars, and there are still many of them in the battery. There are no finer soldiers and artillerymen. But, since Gettysburg, it has been difficult to get men such as yourselves to enlist in the Regulars. Many of you are volunteers, transferees from infantry and other units, for the duration of the war.

"Because of that, Captain Crispin received permission from the Corps Commander to affix a brass plate to each gun. Each gun has been named after a different state — the six states who have the larger majority of men in this battery.

"The other guns, Two through Six, are named respectively, New York, Ohio, Massachusetts, Illinois, and Michigan." Here Seth paused. He removed his hand from the brass breech plate. "This is Gun Number One, named Pennsylvania, but more commonly called 'Keystone' by the members of its crew." He smiled. "I think you know now why I serve on her crew and selected her as my demonstration piece for my classes."

"Stable Call" ripped stridently through the damp air.

Ben waved a hand to Seth and then trudged toward the battery horse lines. The improvised lyrics of "Stable Call" ran through his mind as he listened to it.

"Go to the stable, as quick as you're able, And groom off your horses and give them some corn; For if you don't do it, the captain will know it, And then you will rue it, as sure as you're born."

The lyrics were no joke in Battery B, as Ben Buell and the rest of the members of the Drivers Detachment knew. The trails of the fighting armies could be followed by the dead and dying horses and mules cast aside as of no further use. Crowbait and carrion, usually undernourished, and many of them diseased and uncared for, lining the roadsides, lying in the fields, stinking to high heaven and breaking the heart of every horseman who passed them, until he too became inured to the waste and suffering that was one of the many curses of wars. To some men it was harder for them to see the sick, starving, or mutilated horses of war than it was to see men in the same conditions. But most of the men were there because they had wanted to be there, while the poor beasts had had no choice but still served as faithfully and as long as they could.

A horse artilleryman and a cavalryman were like slaves to the horses of their units. It was a high price that they paid for being in a so-called glamour unit. After all, the infantryman took care of his sidearms and his feet and belly, and that was it; but a cavalryman took care of his horse first, and then himself; while the horse artilleryman, a *corps d'elite* man if there ever was one, took care of his horses and guns first, and then himself, if there was time, and in the Regulars there *was* time, for the men had to look as spic and span as the horses and the guns, or meet the boiling wrath of Sergeant Dolan.

Battery B had done itself proud in providing dry footing for its horses. A brick house had been shattered by gunfire at the battle of Brandy Station in June of 1863.

The bricks had been hauled almost piecemeal by battery members to the horse lines, and placed on a corduroying of saplings. Atop this was placed hay or straw, and this was replaced as often as possible, for the condition known as "greased heel" would start to flourish if the horses and mules stood in mud or snow. The skin around the fetlocks and pasterns would grow hot and then crack. A wart-like growth would appear and then the legs would swell until the horse or mule became lame. Rubbing with oil was a hit-or-miss preventative. It was thoroughly acknowledged that dry footing was the only sure way to combat the disease.

Ben got his nosebags and filled them with forage and took the bags to Big Barney and Dandy. Dandy whinnied, almost cheerfully, thought Ben as he hung the nosebag on the big bay. He took out curry comb and brush and set to work on Big Barney first. It was a job he always liked to do, although he would have preferred doing it to one horse, rather than two. At times, when the battery was shorthanded, the drivers had to take care of as many as six to eight horses.

There were so many things to think of in the care of horses in the field: glanders—or farcy as it was sometimes called—grease-heel, hoof rot, sore mouth, and many other ills. The horses had to be groomed and rubbed down, their hoofs picked out and cleaned, manes and coats cleaned and smoothed. The nostrils had to be inspected and sponged out, and looked at carefully for the telltale running mucous that might mean glanders. Such a horse would be reported and immediately isolated, for glanders was highly contagious, usually spread by horses using the same watering bucket. Glanders could all but immobilize cavalry and artillery if it was allowed to spread. The running sores were highly infectious. The only known treatment was isolation of the infected animal or animals, or in extreme cases, they had to be destroyed. Under good conditions it was possible for a horse to recover. If the disease was incurable, the animal would die in a matter of days.

Jonas Whitlow came down the line and paused to look down at Ben. "I'll expect new respect, Buell," he said archly. "No more will you get away with calling me 'Jonah' rather than my given name of Jonas."

"Why not?"

"Look up, my boy. Look up!"

Ben crawled underneath Dandy and stared at Jonas. The twin stripes of a corporal were on his blouse sleeves. Ben blinked and covered his eyes with curry comb and brush. "Blinding," he said. "Congratulations, Corporal."

"Well, now I *know* we're losing the war," said a dry, sad voice.

"Is that so, Mexico?" snapped Jonas.

Mexico Bates nodded dolefully. "Well, maybe it ain't so bad." He brightened. "Maybe they'll move you into another gun section!"

"I stay in *this* section, Bates! Someone has to keep your long nose against the grindstone. Captain Crispin said to me: 'Whitlow, you keep that Mexico Bates straightened out. I don't care about the rest of them. They are soldiers and drivers! But that Mexico Bates —aaahhh!"

"That's all he said? *'Aaahhh?'*"

"Aaahhh!" Jonas nodded. "Like that. Full of disgust it was. Almost made one of the ration wagon mules bolt when he heard it. Aaahhh!"

Mexico carefully placed his curry comb on a keg. He wiped his hands on his thighs and tilted his head to one side. "Now, Corporal Whitlow," he said in low, measured tones, "if you're half the man you *think* you are, you'll meet me behind the horse lines after 'Taps' tonight, minus them outsized stripes, to see who is the better man."

Jonas leaned forward until the visor of his cap was almost touching the nose of the taller Mexico. "I'll be there, Bates! See that you are! And if you are *not,* I'll come and *get* you!"

"Ye'll get to work, ye will, both av ye! By holy Saint Pathrick! By *all* the saints! By the name of me blessed mither! Get to worruk!"

Jonas scooted off. Mexico swung about and began to brush his team. Ben grinned.

"Buell!" roared Sergeant Dolan. "Do not ye sit there loike a pagan idol! Get to worruk!"

Ben bent to his work and listened until he heard Dolan's boot squelches fade away. "Get to worruk!" he said sourly. "One of these days!"

"Aye," growled Mexico. "Aye! I can hardly wait!"

"We might get another noncom officer twice as bad."

Mexico nodded sadly. "Oh, well," he said. "We might get used to Dolan in the next thirty years or so."

Ben groaned, then brightened as "Recall" blew. He hurried back toward the battery street after washing up. The pungent odor of beans drifted from the cook shack. The doors and windows had been opened because of the heat of the stoves. A short but slightly plump cook stood at the doorway, a white cap on his head, and he held a huge ladle in his hand like the scepter of an ancient Egyptian monarch. His cold eyes were on a lean recruit who was peeling potatoes. "More skin and less potatoes when you peel, sonny," he growled.

Ben grinned. "Hello, Zack," he said.

Zack looked up. "Come in and have some Java," he said. "Mess sergeant's gone to get some supplies. Left me in charge."

"Couldn't find a better man, Zack."

Zack filled two tin cups with coffee and pushed the sugar can toward Ben. "What's the news from the *harse* lines?" he asked.

"Nothing much. Same old thing. Comb and brush. Clean, water, and feed. It'll be a great day for me when we can harness and hitch and pull out of this gumbo heading south to Richmond."

"Oh, I don't know," said Zack leisurely. He looked about. "Me and Mess-Sergeant Freitag get along fine. Food is good. Hours ain't bad. Beats working on a gun, my boy."

"All the same, I think you'll miss it, Zack."

"Not me."

Ben shrugged. He emptied his cup. "I have just time to get twenty minutes' sleep before next call," he said. "I need it. I was hardly able to sleep last night because of all the coughing in our shebang."

"Buell! Buell!" roared Sergeant Fox from outside. "Get to the harness shack! There is harness to be treated! Get going there!"

Ben jumped to the door. "See you later," he said.

Zack's laughter still rang in his ears when he entered the pungent-smelling harness shack. There were three other men there rubbing neat's-foot oil into various pieces of harness to keep them soft and supple, for dry leather would crack and break under strain, and on the march or in the heat of battle, it might mean the loss of a gun when it was most needed.

"You think we'll ever use these things again?" growled Mike Woolsey. "Seems like all we ever do is oil them. By the time spring comes and the ground dries out, there won't be much harness left from all this rubbing. It will be more oil than harness. Do you think we'll ever move, Sage?"

Sage Pennycook, the battery oracle, took his pipe from his mouth and relighted it. He looked over the flare of the Lucifer at Mike. "I heard a rumor we were to be transferred west," he said wisely.

"No!"

Sage nodded. "It's said that the Army of Tennessee will march down to Texas, where it is warm and sunny all the time. A good place for Battery B."

"Sure, sure," said a sarcastic voice from the door of the shed. "Wait until you feel a blue norther sweeping across Texas. You'll wish by then you had stayed here in Virginia." It was Mexico Bates.

"You've been there, have ye not, Mexico?" asked little Pat Shayhan, a countryman of Sergeant Dolan's.

Mexico picked up a can containing neat's-foot oil and set to work on a stirrup leather. "Aye. A fine country for men and dogs but hard on women and horses."

"They say all it needs to become a first-rate state is more water and better citizens," said Mike Woolsey.

"Ye can say the same thing about hell," said Pat Shayhan.

"What else did you hear, Sage?" asked Ben.

Sage puffed at his pipe. "It is said, on good authority, that General U. S. Grant, victor at Vicksburg, will soon arrive here in Virginia to take charge of the advance on Richmond. He'll be in command of all the armies of the Union but will come here to oversee the Army of the Potomac in the spring campaign."

"Fat chance of that," growled Mexico.

"No," said Pat Shayhan quickly. "It is true! I was clerking in battery headquarters the ither day whin the brigade commander came in and told the very same thing to Captain Crispin and the ither battery officers."

Ben rubbed steadily at a collar. Grant! The very name was magic. The victor of Forts Henry and Donelson and of Vicksburg, as well as other battles. Grant the bulldog who had taken Vicksburg in one of the great campaigns of military history. Lee had defeated McClellan, Pope, Burnside, and Hooker, almost with ease. Meade had defeated him, but Meade had fought on the defensive and had let Lee come to him, while Lee had, perhaps, relied too much on his magnificent infantry of the Army of Northern Virginia, of which there was no better. But Meade had allowed Lee to slip away from Gettysburg and get back across the Potomac practically unscathed, to fight on.

"If Grant comes here," said Mexico Bates quietly, "we'll march when the dogwood blooms. South against Lee. There'll be no turning back, boys, if Grant is in charge. No turning back even if we *are* defeated in battle. We'll go on and on until we win or they do. U. S. Grant knows no other way."

"Well, we cannot move in this weather," said Pat Shayhan to break the silence that had followed Mexico's quiet and foreboding words.

"No," said Mike Woolsey. "Look!"

They turned. The wind had driven off the clouds. A watery-looking sun peered down. It was only the beginning. Enough sunny days and the ground would dry and firm. Battery B would start foot and mounted drill. The horses would be exercised. The weak, unfit, and unwanted men would be ruthlessly pruned from the battery roster. Worn and weak equipment would be replaced. Time was running out for the 1863-1864 winter bivouac of the Cavalry Corps of the Army of the Potomac at Brandy Station.

When the dogwood bloomed . . .

CHAPTER ELEVEN

The warm spring air was filled with the mingled fragrances of dogwood blossoms, violets, and bush honeysuckle. The bright sunlight glinted from polished steel and brass, from shining leather and white-tilted wagons. Throughout the greening woodland on the shade-dappled roads, now long dried out from the winter rains and snows, there was a vast movement of thousands of men in blue, of wagons and of horses, of artillery, of fluttering guidons and flags. Somewhere off in the woods, a band was playing "John Brown's Body" accompanied by hundreds of young voices. The Army of the Potomac was on the march south. The dogwood was indeed in full bloom.

As the Union troops crossed the Rapidan River, they knew that Richmond itself was no longer the goal that it had been for the first three years of the war. The goal now was Robert E. Lee and the Army of Northern Virginia. Richmond was nothing now; the Army of Northern Virginia was everything. As long as the lean, hard-fighting Johnnies were in the field with full cartridge boxes the war would continue. The solution then was simple enough. The complete defeat of Lee's forces.

The solution itself was simple; the way and effort of doing it was quite another thing. The Army of Northern Virginia hadn't the slightest intention of making the problem any easier for the Army of the Potomac.

South of the Rapidan was a vast area of thickly tangled second-growth timber, with few good roads, and not many cleared areas, and through it all ran crooked little streams that sometimes flowed into low areas and created bogs and tangled swamps. It was certainly no place for battle, but in the paradoxical ways of wars throughout history, that was where the Army of the Potomac ran full tilt into the Army of Northern Virginia, and the dark woods bloomed with the short-lived and deadly blossoms of gunfire. The area had been well named by the locals — The Wilderness.

May 5, 1864, the lean and fierce infantry of the Army of Northern Virginia ran full tilt into the right center of the Army of the Potomac shortly after daybreak. The dawn had come up with the thunder of gunfire, and battle smoke swirled thickly and rose to hang in an ominous rifted layer above the tangled Wilderness.

Battery B, Eighth United States, rode south along a winding and rutted road that was hardly more than an enclosed lane, and a man could hardly tell which direction he was going unless he had a compass. It was no place for infantry to fight, least of all an arena for the clash of arms between cavalry and horse artillery.

Ben Buell, wheel horse driver, Gun Number One, ducked his head to avoid low-hanging branches. The growling thunder of gunfire came across the woodland, but there was nothing to see except an occasional tendril of smoke far across the low treetops as the vagrant wind shifted a little now and then. A man could hardly see with clarity for fifty yards in any direction.

"No place for horse artillery," growled Mexico Bates. He turned in his saddle and looked at Ben. "I'd like to know what we're doing in this jungle."

"I have a feeling they don't figure on using us in here," said Ben. "Maybe it's wishful thinking, but we didn't, train all spring with the cavalry to end up fighting in this tangle. They say Phil Sheridan isn't the type of commander who will use cavalry the way it has been used around Virginia since the start of the war, separated and scattered in squads, platoons, and companies all over the army as escorts for generals, to guard outposts and act as pickets. Corporal Pomeroy says that even General Meade thinks cavalry is hardly fit for more than guard and picket duty."

"So what does that do to your idea that we weren't trained all spring to fight in here? Meade *still* commands the Army of the Potomac."

Seth Pomeroy drew alongside and kneed his horse closer to Dandy. He smiled at Ben. "I heard what you two have been saying. Certainly Meade commands this army, but Grant commands *all* the armies. Phil Sheridan is one of his boys too, Mexico, and don't you forget it. Meade may want to hold Sheridan back, but Grant knows a good hound when he sees one, and if he gets a chance to loose Sheridan, you can bet your bottom dollar he'll do just that."

"I heard Captain Crispin say we have over ten thousand troopers in the Cavalry Corps on the march," said Mexico.

The battery had moved out from the dappled shade of the trees into a rather open area, one of the few they had passed through that morning.

"Looks familiar around here," said Mexico Bates.

"It ought to," said Sergeant Fox. "We're not far from Chancellorsville."

Mexico turned quickly and swallowed hard. "You don't think we'll fight here again, do you, Sergeant?"

Fox shrugged. "All I know is this: We'll fight Lee wherever he may be."

The distant roaring of battle seemed to get louder.

But it was not the fate of Battery B to fight the Johnnies in the wild tangle of The Wilderness. They went into bivouac late that afternoon, although there was little sleep for them that ominous night. News came that there had been hard and vicious fighting all that day around the Orange Plank Road. Then, too, the smell of smoke from the burning woods near the fighting lines drifted across The Wilderness, and fires cast a lurid glow against the dark sky.

The men of Battery B sat up late that night, watching the firelight against the sky, talking quietly. They had been saved from wounds or death that day; they were not big enough fools to think they would be saved in the days to come. There had been some cavalry fighting, but the rumors were vague, and in a place like The Wilderness it was hard to find the truth of such matters.

Mexico Bates was leaning against a tree, eying something at the edge of the thick tangle of brush and woods that ran along the edge of the bivouac like a wall. He walked slowly to the edge and looked down at something.

"What is it, Mexico?" called Jonas Whitlow. "A fat chicken?"

Mexico did not answer.

"Mexico!" called Jonas.

They all turned to look at the lanky driver. He had gone down on one knee and was touching something white and rounded.

"What is it, Mexico?" repeated Jonas.

Mexico picked up the white object and walked slowly back toward the campfire. He held out the object wordlessly. It was a grinning skull, with a gaping hole in the forehead. Mexico's eyes were wide in his head. "I swear it was looking right at me, boys," he said in a low voice. His face was almost as pale as the bones of the skull.

"It's an omen," said Sage Pennycook wisely.

"It's nothing but the skull of a poor unburied fellow

from the fighting about here last May," said Sergeant Fox. "Get rid of it, Mexico."

But Mexico Bates stared at the thing as though fascinated by it. "Sage is right," he said hoarsely. "It's an omen. It marks my death sentence."

"Enough of that!" snapped Fox. "Get rid of it! It means nothing. We can *all* see it. I don't think it means *my* death sentence."

"Nor mine," said Jonas Whitlow.

Mike Woolsey nodded. "Pitch it into the woods, Mexico, or make a tobacco jar out of it." He laughed harshly.

Ben Buell watched Mexico. The lean driver was obviously troubled. "None of you saw it first," he said. "Only me." He looked at the men about him. "I won't survive this campaign, boys. Mark my words. This is my last march with Battery B." He walked slowly away, looking down at the skull.

"Can ye beat that?" asked Pat Shayhan. "Shure and he means it, boys."

Sage Pennycook refilled his pipe. "*He* knows," he said.

The group slowly broke up. Ben walked to where he had placed his blanket beside the limber of Gun Number One. Seth Pomeroy had his back against the left wheel of the gun and his arms folded across his chest. His blue eyes were fixed on the thick smoke that was arising from the woods and the lurid glare of the flames dancing and obscenely posturing against the backdrop of the smoke and the dark sky.

"What do you think, Seth?" asked Ben quietly.

For a moment the corporal did not speak and then he turned to look at Ben. "This time we will not fight and then retreat," he said. "Grant's a bulldog, tenacious and a hard hitter. He'll hang on and keep hitting until we end this war."

"But Lee is a hard and good fighter too," said Ben.

"Maybe a better one than Grant. You heard the fighting today. Does that sound like we are winning?"

"Who can tell? But we have more men than Lee; more and better supplies. The blockade off the Southern coasts is getting tighter and tighter. It doesn't look as though any of the European countries will aid the Confederacy. Grant will keep on hammering along this line. Sherman is a hard fighter too, perhaps, in a sense, a better all-around general than any of them. Old Cump Sherman probably understands modern warfare better than any general, North *or* South."

"If Grant's such a fighter," said Ben, "why does he leave most of the Cavalry Corps sitting idly in the woods? The North has lost more than one battle by not taking advantage of superior numbers. You've told me that yourself."

"Yes, Ben, but this time Grant will hit with all he has. One way or another. The Wilderness is no place for the effective use of cavalry and horse artillery, but I have a feeling that Grant won't keep Phil Sheridan and the Cavalry Corps on the leash very long."

Later, as Ben tried to sleep, the words of Seth Pomeroy kept running through his mind. He had been with Battery B long enough to know the old Army game. Hurry up and wait! They had hurried to cross the Rapidan; now they were waiting south of that dark river of spilled blood. Waiting for what?

———

GRANT the Bulldog was still hanging on with all his strength, but the Army of Northern Virginia was giving as much as it was taking, and when the odds are tallied, it is always the attacking force that has the higher losses from the very nature of their task. From May 5, when the battle had opened on the Orange Plank Road, through the bloody sixth of May, and again on the eighth, it had been the battle-hardened Federals who had been the aggressors. On the seventh the Army of the Potomac had sidled to the left flank and had met the enemy in the vicinity of Spotsylvania Courthouse. There had been spirited cavalry fighting there on the eighth of May, but as yet Battery B of the Eighth United States had not fired a gun.

March, march, and march again, had been the fate of Battery B until a good knock down and drag 'em out scrap would have suited the battery personnel just fine.

Late on the evening of the eighth, Battery B was on the march again, until they reached a great bivouac near a place called Aldrich, hardly more than a wide place along the tree-walled road. The battery members thought at first that it would be another of those monotonous and cheerless bivouacs, with the sullen muttering of hard-fought battles going on in the distance while Battery B waited in the wings. But there was a different feeling in this bivouac, for artillerymen and cavalrymen were not sitting or lying about their fires, sipping their coffee, with one ear cocked to the sound of the guns in the thick woods to the west and south.

This bivouac was a veritable beehive of activity. Troopers were leading crippled and worn-out horses to the rear while others brought up fresh strings of remounts and new teams. By the light of lanterns, ammunition chests and caissons were being replenished. The ringing of metal against metal came from traveling forges. Ration wagons had drawn up to each unit, and quartermasters were issuing three days' rations while forage masters were doling out half rations of grain for one day for the horses and mules.

A column of dismounted men tramped past in the darkness, intermingled with loaded ambulances. Couriers trotted past the column, turning in here and there to the various regiments and batteries to deliver written orders to the various commanding officers. "Officers' Call" sounded through the busy darkness, and the officers gathered at Corps Headquarters. The rumor came swiftly down the line that the entire Corps was in the area, three full cavalry divisions, led by Generals Torbert, Gregg, and Wilson. To each division would be attached two batteries of horse artillery, with the same number in the reserve.

The corps was being stripped of all impediments, such as unserviceable equipment and wagons, tents and other unnecessary gear. The ammunition train had been fully supplied and would accompany the corps wherever it was going. Two ambulances were to be allowed for each division and a few pack mules for baggage. All dismounted men were to be sent to the rear.

Canister, the little dog who served as battery mascot, was the very picture of excitement. He darted here and there, yapping insistently with a strange knowledge of his own, at the heels of the men who were slow in their preparations.

"He knows," said Sage Pennycook. "We are heading into battle, boys. Canister knows."

Ben examined the legs and hoofs of Big Barney and then those of Dandy. He pried loose a small pebble from the bay's left rear hoof and looked up to see Mexico Bates repacking his valise. The lean driver was mumbling something to himself. His face was pale and drawn, glistening with cold sweat as he worked. Ben stood up and eyed the man. Mexico was fitting something into the valise. A fire flared up and the light glowed pinkly on the white object. A chill chased down Ben's spine as he recognized the bullet-punctured skull Mexico had found and had insisted was an omen of his death.

A hand touched Ben's shoulder, and he turned to see the serious face of Corporal Jonas Whitlow. "I am worried about him, Ben," he said, jerking a thumb toward Mexico.

"It's all foolishness, isn't it, Jonas?"

Jonas shrugged. "I've seen such things before. At

Antietam I saw one of the gunners die with a bullet through his throat. For two days before the battle he had said his throat had been hurting, and he was sure he'd not survive the battle."

Sage Pennycook poked his head around the limber where he was repacking the tow about the ammunition. "Aye," he said. "And just before Gettysburg it was Cass Raymen who came to me and gave me all his letters, his watch, and personals to send home to his wife. I told him it might be that I wouldn't survive the battle, but he said I would. He also knew he *wouldn't*. You mind the caisson that blew up, Ben? Cass was right next to it. Never saw hide nor hair of him again."

Ben wiped the cold sweat from his face. He turned to see a cavalryman walking toward them. It was easy enough to recognize a "news-walker." The three artillerymen walked to meet him.

"Norris, is the name," he said easily. "Sixth Ohio, First Brigade, Second Division. Where have you boys been?"

"All over The Wilderness," said Jonas, "and ain't fired a shot."

"You will," said the Ohioan.

"What's the latest?" asked Sage.

"General Torbert was disabled. General Merritt has taken over command of the First Division. Merritt is young but keen. We have three divisions here, composed of seven brigades in all, plus you horse batteries. 'Bout thirteen thousand men in all."

"Closer to fifteen thousand," said Jonas.

"Paper strength," said the cavalryman. "Lot of dismounted men, sick, wounded, and disabled being sent to the rear."

"That's probably right," said Seth Pomeroy as he joined the group along with Sergeant Fox and Corporal Goodroy.

"Where we headed for?" asked Sage.

"It's said that Stuart has been trying to get into our

rear, but the Cavalry Corps took care of that. Some hot fighting here and there. Guess you boys missed most of that."

"All of it," said Ben, "but we've covered every road, lane, and path in the rear of the Army of the Potomac."

"Well, from what I've heard up and down the line," said Norris, "you won't have to worry."

"Go on," said Seth eagerly.

Norris looked about as though confiding a vast secret. He lowered his voice as he spoke. "Seems like Phil Sheridan and General Meade had an argument. Something about the Cavalry Corps blocking off the Fifth Corps from getting on a road to Spotsylvania. Sheridan was pretty hot about it. He claimed he could draw Stuart after him and whip him if he was permitted to break loose from the army. Grant told him to go ahead. That's it."

"That all?" asked Sage.

"What more do you want?" demanded Seth. "You wanted action, you fellows! Well, if we go south toward Richmond, Stuart will chase us, and he won't hold back from any fighting we might have in mind."

Norris nodded. "The rumor is that we'll pull out of here tomorrow morning, trying to get around Lee's right flank."

Jonas whistled softly. "Fighting aplenty then, boys."

Norris waved good-by to them and vanished into the darkness toward the road.

"What is this?" roared Sergeant Dolan. "A bloomin' tay party, is it? Get busy thayer, or ye'll rue the day ye wuz born, ye will! Harse artillerymen ye call yereselves? More like old ladies having a bit av a gossip in the parlor it is! Jump thayer! Get to worruk!"

They jumped. There was indeed *worruk* to be done aplenty.

There were a few hours of exhausted, yet restless sleep, before the trumpets of the corps sounded "The

General" throughout the great cavalry bivouac. In Battery B the drivers harnessed and hitched while the cannoneers saddled up. The guns and caissons were aligned in column, and chains rasped as limber pole props were let down to take the weight from the necks of the wheel pairs of each team. Dirt was kicked over the still smoldering fires that had brewed coffee and fried bacon for a hasty field breakfast.

The battery was almost at full strength that early May morning. In addition to Captain Carter Crispin and his second-in-command First Lieutenant James Pike, the battery had two other officers. One was Second Lieutenant Vincent Barry, a Volunteer officer who had been severely wounded at Gettysburg, and who had rejoined the battery just before its crossing of the Rapidan. The other officer was Second Lieutenant Archer McLeod, who had been graduated from West Point the year before and had served with a battery in the defenses of Washington until Grant had called for all the men he could get to fight against Lee. The battery called for one more officer, but it was hard to get officers to serve in Regular Army artillery batteries because of the slow promotions.

Battery B was still short a few men, but Captain Crispin had made certain during the long winter that every man in the battery, cooks, artificers, trumpeters, orderlies, and clerks could serve on the guns as well as the cannoneers. It was an axiom in an artillery battery whether heavy, light, or horse artillery, that in addition to each man's knowing his own duties thoroughly, he must also be drilled in the duties of other men, particularly those who served the guns, for if the guns fell silent the battery would have failed its purpose. Thus Ben, along with the rest of the battery personnel had learned the routine of loading and firing, the ability to estimate distances and ranges with fair accuracy, how to cut fuzes and to take any part in the dismounting of the piece and carriage, the transfer of limber chests, the insertion of a spare pole, the mounting of a spare wheel, and the method of slinging a gun under its limber in case a piece wheel should be disabled.

Over and over again, day after day, in clear weather and in foul, the artillerymen of Battery B, as well as those members of other batteries had learned to perform these duties until it was almost mechanical with them. The piece and carriage had to be dismounted and remounted, sometimes against time and other times in matches against other gun sections. The men of Gun Number One, nicknamed Keystone, the gun on which Ben served as driver, had managed to take the gun apart, reassemble it, load, and fire it in less than a minute.

Ben had liked the field maneuvers best of all. It required plenty of room, and there was no more thrilling sight than to see a six-gun battery, with their accompanying caissons and each cannoneer mounted, pelting full tilt across a field until the trumpeter, at a command from the battery commander, blew "In Battery," with the thrilling spectacle that followed, only to limber up again, race back across the field, and perform the maneuver over again.

The sun was beginning to throw its warming rays into the scrub timber when "Boots and Saddles" sounded throughout the area. In a few minutes Battery B moved out onto the Old Turnpike Road and turned east. Already the dust was rising in filmy clouds from thousands of hoofs and hundreds of wheels.

Sergeant Dolan posted past on his big gray Killarney. His hard eyes swept the battery as it rolled along.

"What division are we attached to, Sergeant Dolan?" called out Mike Woolsey.

"None," said the big Irishman." Battery B is part av the Reserve it is, and ye all know what that means, do ye not?"

Jonas Whitlow nodded. "The ol' Fire Department of the Corps," he said dryly. "Wherever the fighting is heaviest and the trouble is thickest, you can look for Old Battery B."

Ben turned in his saddle. Seth Pomeroy was riding a sprightly Canuck he had named Hardtack. There was a smile on Seth's face. He raised a clenched hand and punched it forward, a battery commander's signal for Action Front! There was no need for him to say anything. *"Wherever the fighting is heaviest and the trouble is thickest, you can look for Old Battery B,"* Jonas Whitlow had said.

Thirteen miles of mounted troops in column. Hard-bitten cavalrymen and artillerymen; Volunteers and Regulars for the most part. Regiments from Michigan, New York, Pennsylvania, Massachusetts, New Jersey, Ohio, Maine, Illinois, Connecticut, Indiana, and Vermont, as well as those from the Regular Army. Horse Artillery batteries from New York and the Regular Army. Almost thirteen thousand men in blue, looking for trouble and knowing full well they'd find it, or they had badly underestimated Jeb Stuart and his regiments of Virginians, Georgians, Mississippians, South Carolinians, and North Carolinians. They would oblige as they had always done so.

CHAPTER TWELVE

There was a new headquarters flag snapping in the breeze as the Cavalry Corps of the Army of the Potomac began their raid into rebel territory. It was a red-and-white flag with twin stars upon it, the flag of Phil Sheridan, and if the yellowlegs and redlegs of the Cavalry Corps hadn't fully learned it as yet, the realization that they were being led by a different kind of fighting man was beginning to grow rapidly.

The Corps were led at a steady mile-eating walk. Most of the men in the Corps knew about the cavalry raid toward Richmond in February of the same year, for indeed many of them had been on it. Led by General Judson Kilpatrick, four thousand cavalrymen had ridden south on an audacious plan, proposed by Kilpatrick himself, to attack the Belle Isle prisoner-of-war camp in the James River at Richmond, release the Federal prisoners, and also distribute the President's amnesty proclamation to the Confederates. It was a daring and audacious plan, but Judson Kilpatrick had earned a nickname from his veteran troopers of the Third Cavalry Division. "Kill Cavalry" they called him, and none can fit a nickname to a commanding officer better than the men who serve under him. He had earned the nickname by his recklessness in the manner in which he wore out both men and horses.

Kilpatrick's Raid had almost been a military fiasco. The advance had been led by one-legged Colonel Ulric Dahlgren, with orders to seize the main bridge over the James River into Richmond. Kilpatrick had run into superior forces and had been driven back. Meanwhile Dahlgren, with five hundred troopers, had managed to destroy some grist mills and other rebel property but could not find a way across the James. He retreated, fighting most of the way, had been ambushed and killed. There had been bitter recriminations against Kilpatrick because of the losses of men and horses.

The Corps had left Aldrich and had headed first toward Fredericksburg, with Merritt's First Division in the lead, reached Tabernacle Church, then headed almost due east to reach the Telegraph Road, thence down that highway to Thornburg, and from that point through Chilesburg toward Anderson's Crossing of the North Anna.

There was a feeling of excitement and determination in the immensely long column. The sound of gunfire came from the rear on the Chilesburg Road. The word passed swiftly up the column. "It's 'Fitz' Lee and his Virginians attacking our rear!"

The part of the column that contained Battery B slowed and then halted in swirling dust. Corporal Jonas Whitlow stood up in his stirrups and scowled. "Here it is again," he said sourly. "We get news the Johnnies are in our rear and the whole thing falls to pieces."

The gunfiring was louder now and then suddenly the column moved *forward* again to the *south*. Dusty grins appeared on the faces of the men. On and on, at the steady mile-eating walk, until word came along the column again, this time from the van. When Sheridan had been told of the attack on his rear he had simply said: "They can't hurt us by hitting our tail. Stuart is probably trying to delay us by diversionary tactics in our rear while he tries to get in front of us. Well, he'll have to move fast!"

They were well beyond the right flank of the Army of Northern Virginia by now, heading for the crossing of the North Anna at Anderson's Ford. Battery B was ordered forward from the rear of the First Division into the interval between the First and Second Brigades of the division. There was a sustained feeling of excitement in the battery now.

Ben had noted that the bronzed troopers of the First Brigade all wore red scarves about their necks, bright splashes of coloring against the dusty blue of their jackets. "What brigade is this?" he asked Sergeant Fox.

"The Michigan Brigade," said Sergeant Fox. "First, Fifth, Sixth, and Seventh Michigan. Led by the Boy General."

"Boy General?" asked Ben curiously.

Fox grinned. "Custer," he said. "George Armstrong Custer. A fire-eating, fire-breathing dragon for all his youth. Graduated from West Point in June of '61, at the bottom of his class and commissioned a second lieutenant; a temporary captain on McClellan's staff in '62; again a first lieutenant in late '62; in June of '63 he was suddenly promoted to brigadier-general and given command of the Michigan Brigade. I can tell you one thing, Buell: If we ride this day with Custer, you'll see action if there is any to see!"

But the greater part of that day was spent in column, riding steadily mile after mile, while pack mules brayed, trace chains jingled, thousands of hoofs thudded on the Telegraph Road, and dust swirled thickly. This was no secret raid. Rumor had it that Kilpatrick's Raid, earlier that year, had been known in Richmond shortly after it was planned. Phil Sheridan, now that he had his fast and unexpected start well under way, didn't care how much the rebels knew about his raid, for he'd welcome the chance to break lances with Jeb Stuart to see who would win the prize.

As yet there had been no sight nor sound of Jeb Stuart. The column had crossed the Ny, Po, and Ta Rivers, any one of which would have provided the enemy with a fine defensive position, but the Johnnies were strangely missing. Dusk was in the offing when the Michigan Brigade splashed across Anderson's Ford on the North Anna and headed for Beaver Dam Station on the Virginia Central Railroad.

A ripple of excitement came down the column to Battery B. The dust pall rose higher and thicker, and the battery moved from a walk to a trot. Ben Buell raised his scarf about his nose and mouth. Smoke was rising somewhere ahead of them. Then the battery was in the clear, pounding down a long straight road while above the thudding of the hoofs, grinding of the wheels, and the myriad sounds of a passage of horse artillery came dust-hoarse yelling from the galloping Michigan Brigade.

Ben suddenly saw a cluster of buildings and near them a locomotive with steam up and a long train of cars behind it. By now the leaders of the brigade were in a headlong race toward the waiting locomotive.

"First Gun Section — Action Front!" came the command.

Battery B, like a well-oiled automaton, went into action. The first gun section composed of two guns, Numbers One and Two, nicknamed Pennsylvania and New York, raced ahead of the remainder of the battery, swinging wide to come to a dust-shrouded halt while the guns were released from the limbers, the limbers drawn to the rear, the teams unhitched and led even further to the rear, all in a matter of minutes. The remaining two gun sections, four more guns, remained in mounted column alongside the road.

Carbine and pistol fire popped through the gathering dusk, their vivid flashes like giant fireflies. Here and there through the shifting veils of dust and smoke could be seen rebel cavalry and infantry putting up a resistance, but in a matter of minutes they had been driven off and the whooping, yelling troopers of the Michigan Brigade surrounded the train, some of them holding pistols on the locomotive crew. Others threw back the doors of box cars and released hundreds of blue-clad men, prisoners of the Confederates.

Captain Crispin focused his field glasses on the activity about the station, then lowered them. "I don't think they'll be needing us, Jim," he said to Lieutenant Pike.

"Look at those piles of supplies, sir," said the giant officer.

Ben Buell stood up on a caisson and looked toward the station. There were piles of barrels, boxes, crates, bags, and loose materials. There were about a hundred railroad cars in the area, and another locomotive beside that which had been at the station. In a matter of minutes the well-trained Michiganders went into destructive action. Fires were started amidst the piles of supplies and within the railroad cars. Already parties of troopers were riding both ways along the right of way to destroy tracks and other facilities. Troopers had scaled the telegraph poles to cut the lines.

That night there were high jinks about Beaver Dam Station while Battery B remained about their guns, ready for action, moodily watching the yelling, laughing troopers as they completed their work of destruction. It was a blow to Lee and his hungry Army of Northern Virginia. The railroad station went up in flames as well as three full trains of cars, ninety wagons, and some two thousand pounds of bacon and other supplies, about a million and a half rations, as well as the entire medical stores slated for the Army of Northern Virginia. All through the night, troopers of the Michigan Brigade worked up and down the railroad tracks for miles in both directions from the station, ripping up track, cutting telegraph wires, destroying anything and everything of even the slightest value to the Confederacy.

The tantalizing odor of burning bacon mingled with that of burning leather, wood, frying paint, hay and straw, corn and oats, quinine and iodine, bandages, blankets, bread, and meats of many kinds. Now and then there was a sharp explosion, a glaring of orange-red light and a puff ball of black smoke as powder barrels or cases of ammunition blew up.

Prisoners told the Northerners that Lee had planned to fall back from his positions farther north, and therefore had his supplies moved from Orange Court House to have them directly in his rear, or else had planned falling back to the line of the North Anna.

Firelight leaped and postured against the lowering clouds and now and then a spit of silvery rain came down but hardly enough to bother the roaring fires that seemed to laugh in demoniacal glee as they consumed the Confederate supplies that night. Men of the Army of Northern Virginia would go hungry for many days because of the work of Union cavalrymen the night of May 9, 1864.

The van of the raid pulled out before dawn that night, with a slight rain falling, leaving behind them the still roaring fires. Still *forward* and still *south*, heading for the crossings of the South Anna, while Jeb Stuart drove his men on to get in front of Sheridan's hard-riding troopers. When daylight appeared the sound of gunfire could again be heard from far to the rear as the wind shifted, but still the van moved on.

This rainy day Ben Buell began to realize really for the first time, the true functioning of cavalry and horse artillery. No more the scattered little units of cavalry guarding wagon trains, serving as pickets beyond infantry lines, escorting generals and all the other myriad of pettifogging details that had mired down the Cavalry Corps of the Army of the Potomac since the start of the war. Now it was a toughened lance, tipped by the hardened steel of the First Cavalry Division, driving deep into the vitals of the Confederacy, and as yet nothing the Johnnies could do would stop those blue-clad troopers in their tracks.

Past Zion Church and Negro Foot to Ground-Squirrel Bridge on the South Anna, an easy day's march compared to that of the first day. The Corps crossed the South Anna and bivouacked on the south bank after a fifteen-mile ride and although some of Stuart's cavalry had struck at Gregg's Division while they had been crossing the North Anna, it had had but little effect. The Union troopers were too strong and too many. The news that night was that Stuart was driving on south too, still trying to get ahead of Sheridan. So Sheridan had accomplished one of the objectives of his raid — to draw Jeb Stuart away from the fighting armies up north around Spotsylvania.

Davies' Brigade of Gregg's Division pulled out at three o'clock the morning of the eleventh of May, driving east toward Ashland to cut the Richmond, Fredericksburg, and Potomac Railroad. Later the rest of the Cavalry Corps marched before the light of day, with Merritt's First Division still in the lead, later in the day joining with Davies' Brigade at Glen Allen Station on the R. F. & P. Railroad, to hear the news that they had reached Ashland ahead of the enemy, had driven out a small force occupying the town, had burned a locomotive and a train of cars, cut the railroad, then had marched on to meet the rest of the corps.

Merritt's First Division pulled out from Glen Allen Station, leading the way for the rest of the command. South, south, always south!

The roads were muddy as they forged on, for the rain had fallen steadily all during the tenth. News passed up and down the column. Stuart was somewhere ahead at last, along the line of the railroad and the Telegraph

Road, between the Federals and the capital. But there was no stopping the long, talma-coated column as it marched on; no hemming and hawing, no backing and filling this time. Jeb Stuart, as always, wanted a fight. Good! The Cavalry Corps led by Fightin' Phil Sheridan would give him one.

"Just where are we?" called out Jonas Whitlow as a courier cantered past the battery.

"Not far from the Brook Turnpike," said the courier.

"And where is that?"

"Runs into Richmond," said the courier over his shoulder.

"How *far* from Richmond?"

The courier turned in his saddle and grinned. "About eight miles, as far as I know, Redleg!"

Jonas thrust a fisted hand upward. "Any more signs of Jeb Stuart?" he yelled.

"Some of his boys are in our rear," called back the courier. "Not enough to bother with. A prisoner told us Stuart is killing his horses, trying to get ahead of us. Might be ahead of us right now for all we know."

It was a fertile countryside through which the column rode, gently rolling, with cultivated gardens, well-tended farms, and green fields, freshened by the rain. They were following the Mountain Road, which would join the Telegraph Road from Fredericksburg to form the Brook Turnpike, which led into Richmond itself.

Conversation and laughter had died along the marching line. Troopers and artillerymen loosened sabers in their sheaths and revolvers in their holsters. They began to look ahead, then quickly to right and to left, as the column moved on at a steady pace through the lush countryside. Now and then as the wind shifted, the distant popping of gunfire came to them but nothing to indicate a pitched fight.

Richmond was less than ten miles away. The Johnnies, least of all Jeb Stuart, would hardly let the Yankees ride right up to the city. The country began to become more wooded and rough. It was almost *too* quiet. It was getting warmer, and the road was drying quickly. The sun was rising toward its zenith.

Suddenly heavy gunfire broke out, this time *ahead* of the column, to the south. Smoke drifted up from the woodland. The horse artillerymen of Battery B glanced quickly at one another. The firing was steadily increasing.

There would be no turning back now. Battle had been joined at last. Steadily onward went the column of men and horses toward the sound of the guns. Seth Pomeroy's maxim came back to Ben Buell. "As a general rule the maxim of marching to the sound of the guns is a wise one."

"*Precis Politique et Militaire de la Campagne de 1815* by Jomini," said a quiet and amused voice from Ben's left.

Ben flushed and turned quickly to see the smiling face of Corporal Seth Pomeroy. Ben had not realized he had spoken aloud. "What's up ahead, corporal?" he asked to cover his confusion.

"Wide place in the road. I think it's called Yellow Tavern, Ben."

"It is," said Captain Crispin as he cantered past the column, his gray eyes taking in everything, missing nothing.

"An odd name for a possible battlefield," said Sergeant Fox.

"No odder than Brandy Station," said Seth Pomeroy.

Yellow Tavern, Virginia, May 11, 1864. It was a day never to be forgotten by the Confederacy.

CHAPTER THIRTEEN

The barking of the dogs of war was getting louder. Gunsmoke drifted up from beyond the thinning woods. Battery B hammered over a creaking wooden bridge spanning a sluggish stream. A trooper galloped toward the head of the battery and drew up his horse in a foam-splattering halt. He saluted Captain Crispin. "Bring your battery forward, sir!" he said. "Captain MacInnes will show you where to go! The shooting gallery is up ahead, sir!"

"Who is there, soldier?" asked Crispin.

The man grinned. "Jeb Stuart *himself,* sir!"

There was no time for Ben Buell or any of the others to think as Battery B moved forward at a trot, then into a steady gallop to where a staff captain sat his mount by the side of the road. He waved Captain Crispin on. The sound of the firing was turning into the sustained roar of a major fight. Captain Crispin whipped out his saber and swept it forward, jerking it up and down to increase the pace of the battery. He seemed to lift his mount in a clean leap over a mossy log. There was no time for Gun Number One to slow down or bypass the log. Jonas Whitlow's whip rose and fell like the sledge of a blacksmith pounding his anvil, and Mexico Bates was following suit. Ben leaned forward. "Faster! Faster! Faster!" He leaned over and gripped Big Barney's mane. "Come on, Barney!" he screamed.

The leaders cleared the log, followed by the swing team and then the big wheelers were over. The limber hit the log and bounced crazily into the air and came down heavily. If those limbers and caissons had not been properly packed—The gun rose like a startled partridge as it hit the log and daylight showed clearly beneath it. The mounted gunners were low in the saddle now, crouched forward, talking to their racing horses as one after the other of them cleared the log just ahead of the leaders of Gun Number Two.

Gun Number One was racing toward a pair of tall pines, and Ben Buell knew in his heart of hearts that it was too narrow for the limber and gun. He screamed as he saw Jonas take the leaders between those trees. "Come on, Dandy! Come on, Barney!" One of the tree trunks seemed to flash past him, and he could have sworn he saw every crack and crevice in the rough bark. The off wheel of the limber struck a tree and gouged the bark deeply. The gun careened crazily from side to side, avoiding striking either trunk by some miracle.

Ben was hoarse from yelling. The battery commander led the way down a stump-littered slope and the wheels of limber and gun rebounded from them. Then Ben saw the shallow ditch at the bottom of the slope. Crispin leaped his horse over. Jonas Whitlow was shrieking like a berserker, and Mexico Bates was howling like a banshee. The leaders went in and out, the swing team followed them, then the big wheelers hit hard, and Ben saw Captain Crispin turn in his saddle to watch.

Dandy and Big Barney squatted and drove their powerful hind legs at the lip of the ditch, clawing like cats for a foothold. Then they were up the side of the ditch slope, and the limber and gun were clear. One after the other the rest of the battery came through, five more guns, six caissons drawn by their six lathered horse teams.

Ben looked ahead. The sun shone on the bright starred-and-striped guidon of Battery B as Crispin crossed a road and raced across a stubbled field. Battle smoke was swirling across the field from the woods beyond it. The grayish-black smoke was brightly stippled with gun flashes. Something shrieked through the smoky air, and a shell burst in the center of the field, casting whining iron fragments about.

The trumpeter raised his trumpet and the sun glinted from the polished brass. "Forward Into Battery" sounded. The battery fanned out from column into line as "Action Front" sounded. Pioneers ran forward from behind the guns being swung about, to tear down a line of fence for a clearer field of fire.

Ben drew in Dandy and Big Barney to let the dismounted gunners unhook the gun from the limber. Then the team moved forward to drop the limber. The team was unhitched and driven to the rear. A shell screamed overhead, and Dandy trembled violently at the sound. The horseholders were leading the cannoneers' horses back behind the limbers. The gunners were flinging open their ammunition chests while the guns were being sighted. Another shell whined overhead and burst just short of the horses. A dun went down and lay still while a gray broke loose and raced back toward the distant road with blood staining its flank.

"Steady, boy, steady!" said Ben. He drew Dandy's head close and spoke quietly to him. The big bay leaned closer to his teammate Big Barney.

"Load — shell!" came the command.

Number Six had prepared the shell with his fuze gouge. He handed the projectile to Number Five who ran toward the gun, handing the powder cartridge to Number

Two who placed it in the gun muzzle to have it rammed home by Number One, who then stepped back, waited for the shell to be placed in the muzzle, then rammed it down hard against the powder charge. Meanwhile the Gunner had sighted the piece and had stepped to one side to observe the effect of firing. Number Three had pricked the cartridge with his priming wire through the vent. Number Four had inserted a lanyard hook into the ring of a friction primer. "Ready!" snapped the Gunner. Number Four stepped in close to the gun, dropped the tube into the vent as Number Three removed his hand, then moved to the rear to keep the lanyard slack.

"Fire!" came the harsh command.

The six guns of the battery roared and flashed almost simultaneously. Acrid black smoke blew back over the limbers and the gun teams. Dandy reared and whinnied. Ben Buell hung desperately to the big bay, talking all the time.

"Watch that bay, Buell!" snapped Jonas Whitlow. "He's going to stampede! Bates! Look alive!"

Mexico Bates smiled thinly. "I'll not survive the battle, corporal," he said. "The skull you know. I —"

"Shut up! Act like a man!" "I'll not survive I tell you!"

A shell shrieked and burst between Gun Number One and Gun Number Two, shattering a limber wheel, dropping two men, and killing one of the Number Two Gun's team. Big Barney reared and plunged. The harness snapped. He drew back and raised his forelegs, pawing at the smoky air, and it was then that Ben Buell saw the ugly gash on the wheeler's flank. Big Barney flung himself to one side and began to gallop jerkily toward the front of the battery. Dandy whimpered and tore loose from Ben. He smashed aside some of the gunners clustered around the limber of Gun Number One and raced after his wheelmate. In a moment the two big horses were lost to sight in the wreathing smoke.

"Should have killed that big bay back at Gettysburg!" yelled the Number Six of Gun Number One as he gripped a shattered arm received when Dandy had driven him back against the limber.

Ben whirled toward the held horses. He thrust a foot into the stirrup of the nearest gunner's mount and swung up into the saddle. "Get off that horse!" yelled the angry horseholder. Ben ripped the bridle reins from the man's hands and rammed his spurs into the horse. It buck-jumped and tried to throw Ben, but Ben had spent too many hours riding bareback to be thrown. He drove the spurs in again and brought his free hand down hard atop the horse's head. The horse seemed to leap forward toward the guns, which had just fired again. Through the dense smoke and into the stubble field flew horse and rider.

"Buell!" roared Sergeant Dolan. "Come back here, ye young scut! Come back here I say!"

A column of blue-clad cavalry was coming from the woods to the left. A trickle of dismounted and wounded men was coming from the smoky woods to the front. Gun flashes sparkled from the rebel positions farther to the right in the thickest of the woods.

Ben saw the two wheelers going through a clearing ahead of him. A road could be seen beyond the woods, with a fence running alongside it. Beyond the road was a swirling mass of mounted men, blue and gray, fighting it out, and even as he watched the blue were driven back. The two wheelers halted at the fence line where curious dismounted Federal cavalrymen looked up at them as they reloaded.

Ben spurred on until he was fifty yards from the team and suddenly felt a falter in the striding of the horse. He spurred it again and felt the horse lurch. He had time only to kick the stirrups free when the horse went down. Ben hit the ground running, heading for the fence line. It was then that he saw the enemy gun battery on a slope, pumping fire against the blue lines, tearing gaps in them, scattering the Federals.

Ben glanced to his right. Mounted Federals were forming, and he could see the bright splashes of red about their bronzed necks. It was Custer's Michigan Brigade. Through the smoke he could see the flashes of enemy artillery and the guns of the Federals. Dandy and Big Barney turned and trotted along the fence line with Ben hot after them.

"Get down, boy!" yelled a red-faced sergeant. "This ain't no mock battle! That's Jeb Stuart's boys over there!"

A mad swirling of horses and men took place near the road, and this time the Johnnies fell back. Dismounted Federals were pumping lead from their repeating carbines and dropping Confederate after Confederate.

There was a bluff to the east behind a thin line of woods, with a strong battery concealed in the woods, revealed only by the smoke and flashes of its firing. Along the edge of the woods was a long line of dismounted Johnnies firing as fast as they could at the Michigan Brigade. In front of the Federal brigade was a familiar figure, a slim man with long yellow hair, wearing a velveteen jacket and the red scarf about his throat. Custer!

As Ben watched he saw two regiments of the brigade go forward on foot, firing as they advanced until they drove back the enemy and occupied part of the woods, where they held on. Ben followed Dandy and Big Barney, but he could not catch up with them. Now and then a bullet whispered past him.

Custer was forming another regiment beneath the cover of the woods. Ben saw the flag of the First Michigan. Enemy artillery fire crashed out, tearing gaps in the forming lines, but the veteran Michiganders calmly went about their business as though on parade, forming into column of squadrons. Then the Seventh Michigan formed into column of squadrons behind the First

Michigan. There was another regiment in the distance preparing to join them. The two wheel horses were now trotting toward company of their own kind, for there must have been several thousand horses being formed for what was evidently going to be a charge.

Suddenly the sun flashed from thousands of sabers that were whipped from scabbards with a harsh metallic clanging. Ben began to run after his team.

The trumpet commands sang out above the noise of battle. "Attention to Charge—Forward—March." The masses of horsemen moved steadily forward, guidons and flags slanted, sun sparkling from brass and steel. Big Barney was at the rear of a company, but Dandy had held back. Ben drove himself forward and as Dandy turned to follow Big Barney, Ben reached the bay.

The trumpets sang again. "Trot — March!"

The massed regiments began to trot, dust swirling up from beneath thousands of hoofs to mingle with the smoke. Ben gripped Dandy by the reins, but the big bay had begun to follow his teammate. Ben swung up into the Jennifer and tried to turn Dandy aside.

Once more the strident voices of the trumpets. "Gallop — March!"

The horsemen moved ponderously on and the earth had begun to shake beneath the hoofs in a compelling yet frightful rhythm. Dandy was galloping on close to the flank of a company. No one looked at Ben. They had enough to keep them busy; a single-mindedness that brooked no other thoughts. It was like a mighty freshet of blue-clad men and thundering horseflesh. Ben knew now he was going along with the Michigan Brigade whether he liked it or not. He reached down to where his issue saber hung at the left side of his saddle and drew it, pointing it forward as he saw the others do.

The trumpets ripped out again, loudly and clearly in the most thrilling of all calls. "Charge!"

Not instantly, but almost slowly, the pace of the

masses of troopers increased until Ben's whole world was a thundering, clashing, dust-and-smoke-ridden maelstrom of sound and fury. Guns smashed ahead and the pict of bullets sounded close to him. *If you hear them, you're safe; it's the one you don't hear that gets you.* It was poor comfort to Ben Buell.

From somewhere ahead the shrill, inspiring notes of "Yankee Doodle" rose even above the din as Custer's musicians played the brigade into battle. There was a smashing, crashing noise ahead, mingled with the cracking of guns and the clashing of steel against steel, and Ben suddenly found himself racing past two cannon about which were men in butternut and gray, fighting desperately with pistols, rammers, and handspikes to hold off that avalanche of blue horsemen.

The gray line was shattered. Rebel troopers went down beneath saber blows and pistol shots or were hurled aside by the charging horses. A grinning trooper rode past Ben, shaking a faded rebel guidon. Ben saw Big Barney trotting back through the smoky press. He sheathed his saber and gripped the harness of the wounded wheeler, spurring Dandy to get him out of the press of mounted and dismounted men, riderless horses, the dead, the dying, and the wounded. He was clear of the melee at last, but the bullets still whizzed past and here and there were rebel cavalrymen still fighting as though the fate of the battle depended on them individually.

Ben rode behind the line of battle, saw a knot of charging Johnnies to his right, and rode farther south, away from them and away from his shortest route to the battery. He led Big Barney into a patch of woods, comparatively quiet as against the rest of the area, and dismounted to look at Big Barney's wound. It was an ugly gash, but it had been caused by a piece of shell cutting through hide and into flesh, and there was no evidence that the fragment was still embedded in the flesh.

When he looked up it seemed as though the battle had reached a temporary stalemate, for dismounted troopers were drifting back from the lines and officers and noncoms were forming their units. Ben led both horses through the woods toward the battery, but when he could see clearly through the dissipating smoke his heart sank. The battery was not there! He knew it was the place, for the debris of war — material, animal and human — still lay scattered on the torn-up ground.

He rested the horses and walked about trying to find where the battery had gone, but no one was sure. Some said to the rear, others to the right flank, still others to the left flank. Finally, he tethered Big Barney to a tree and rode slowly along the rear of the lines until he saw a squadron forming amidst the trees. Gunfire was rising. The battle was bubbling and boiling again. He asked a bearded sergeant-major if he had seen Battery B. "To the right flank, boy," the man answered. "Best stay with us until after this charge. The Johnnies are all over the place."

"What regiment is this?"

"Fifth Michigan."

Ben wiped the sweat from his face. This was a fine mess, indeed. "How does it look?" he asked the Michigander.

"All right. We have Stuart where we want him. Some of our boys are astride the Brook Turnpike between here and Richmond. If the Johnnies don't bring up infantry, we've got Stuart in a trap. The Johnnies are in a sort of a *V* position and we're going to hit them where it will hurt the most, right at the bottom of the *V*. Break 'em! Smash 'em! This is *our* day!"

Then the cavalrymen moved forward again to the sound of the trumpets as they had done during the charge in which Ben had been an unwilling participant. Dandy trotted after the last of the horses. Ben let him have his way. Ben drew his saber and stood up in his stirrups. Gunflashes were stippling thick wreathing smoke at the edge of some woods that crossed the Telegraph Road. A small stream was between the Michiganders and the enemy. But there was no time to worry about that.

He was in at the rear of the charge, felt the smash of battle, saw the Michiganders driven back, saw them drive forward in turn. A small group of the enemy along a fence line was firing industriously at dismounted Federal troopers who were streaming back out of the press. Dandy bucked and reared. Ben slid from the saddle and tried to quiet the bay. He saw an outstanding figure among the men at the fence line. A heavily bearded man with a large nose and the light of battle in his eyes. He wore a slouch hat pinned up at one side. It flaunted a black plume. He was mounted on a fine gray horse and was just behind the line of shooting Confederates.

Ben thought he knew that man. The sun shone on the gold stars that ornamented the standing collar of his jacket. A blue-clad trooper, running along the fence line, raised his pistol and fired almost casually at the rebel officer. The officer pressed a hand to his side. His head fell forward and his hat dropped from it.

"Get out of here!" yelled a trooper at Ben. "The Johnnies are going to charge!"

Ben led Dandy back, fighting him all the way. He saw the trooper who had shot the general, an older man with the look of a veteran about him. The trooper looked at Ben. "Who was that officer I shot?" he asked.

Ben looked back. Troopers were helping the wounded man from the field, beyond the shock and smash of the fighting. "I'm not absolutely positive," he said slowly. "But I think it was Jeb Stuart."

"You're joshing!"

A wounded officer rode past holding a bullet-shattered wrist. "That was Jeb all right," he said. "I knew him before the war. Hit hard too. We won't have to face him for quite a while, or I miss my guess."

Ben led Dandy back to where he had left Big Barney. He led the wounded animal to the nearest road and began to follow the road to the south, toward Richmond. There was little need to worry about the Confederate cavalry now, for they had been broken and driven off. Already some units were forming in line of column along the road ready to continue the advance on Richmond, now but six miles away. A courier told Ben that Battery B was farther south on the road, close to the head of the column.

He rode on, taking it easy with the tired horses. Now and then he looked back. Jeb Stuart was badly, perhaps mortally, wounded. He was one of the greatest cavalry leaders of all time, and certainly the best in this mad war, North *or* South. The Confederacy was losing many men, far too many men. They were not defeated yet. That would take more time. But in the gathering dusk of that day, Ben Buell seemed to know that ultimate and total victory would come to the United States rather than to the Confederacy.

Lightning suddenly crackled and snapped across the darkening skies, illuminating the area with an eerie bluish light. There was a sudden silence and rain began to fall slowly and steadily on the battlefield.

The lightning lanced again, and Ben Buell saw something up ahead that made his heart leap. A guidon bearer was getting ready to fold his guidon to place it in its waterproof covering. It was a fork-tailed guidon, with red and white stripes and a little field of blue stippled with white stars. Battery B!

He spurred Dandy on, while a wide grin wreathed his dirty face. First-Sergeant Dolan was putting on his talma. The hard blue eyes of the veteran noncom seemed to shoot brighter lightning than the heavens. "Buell," he snapped, "dismount!"

Ben slid from the saddle.

"Give me yere arms!"

Ben stared at the sergeant but handed him pistol and saber. "What's up, Sergeant Dolan?" he asked.

"What's up, is it? Ye left the battery on the field av battle, me foine boyo! Under arrest ye are! The Captain wants to see ye now! On the double, ye miserable thing, ye!"

CHAPTER FOURTEEN

A brooding quietness hung over the wet scrub woodlands. Even the sound of the pattering rain seemed subdued. Now and then the lightning would flicker. When the wind shifted the barking of dogs could be heard in the distance. Earlier in the evening there had been other sounds from the distance. The ringing of alarm bells. Both bells and dogs were in Richmond. The Cavalry Corps of the Army of the Potomac was that close.

Ben Buell hunched on the wet and hard seat of the battery wagon. After his interview with Captain Crispin he had been transferred from the Driver's Detachment to the "Spare Men" Detachment. It was a heartfelt disgrace to Ben Buell. Even though Captain Crispin had believed his story about chasing after Dandy and Big Barney, the fact still remained that he *had* left the battery on the field of battle. Further than that, he had been ordered back by First-Sergeant Dolan and had disregarded that order. So Ben had been ordered to drive the battery wagon instead of the wheel team of Gun Number One. His team on the battery wagon was his own team from Gun Number One: Big Barney because he had been wounded, Dandy because he too was in disgrace after his instability on the battlefield. The rest of Battery B, officers, enlisted men, and horses had acquitted themselves with honor. There would be another battle honor emblazoned on the battery guidon — Yellow Tavern. The bitter part of it to Ben Buell was that he had probably seen more of the battle than the whole battery put together. But he had left his post of duty without permission. The past words of Sergeant Dolan had seemed to din in his mind as Captain Crispin had talked quietly with Ben after his return to the battery. "The Captain has one rule, which ye had best remember. *There must never be anything to explain in Battery B.*"

The column moved on. Scouts had found a road that would lead toward Mechanicsville, thence to Fair Oaks, both well-remembered scenes of fighting during the Seven Days, and onward to reach General B. F. Butler's Army of the James, on the south side of the James, four miles south of Richmond. Phil Sheridan was convinced he could capture Richmond, but he was also well aware of the fact that he could not hold it. He had accomplished his mission. He had drawn Jeb Stuart away from Lee, and indeed, had put Jeb out of action; he had destroyed Lee's massed supplies at Beaver Dam Station; he had defeated the rebel cavalry at Yellow Tavern. Now his objective was to join Butler's Army of the James.

It was a good enough road despite the fact that the steady cold rain would eventually turn it into mire, if not gumbo. There was one thing wrong with the road. Just *one* thing: It ran between the outer and inner lines of the fortifications that girdled Richmond, manned mostly by Home Guards, but they had plenty of artillery, and they could shoot well enough from behind fortifications to stop even veteran cavalry.

A muffled shot rang out through the dripping woods and was immediately echoed by other shots. The column moved on through the wet darkness with a rustling of wet talmas, squelching of hoofs, and grinding of wheels.

A few minutes passed and up ahead there was a series of muffled explosions and brilliant orange-red flashes of light. Then the acrid odor of burned powder drifted back through the rain and the column came to a halt. A man screamed in pain. A horse whinnied shrilly.

"Pass the word back to bring up some of the prisoners," called a trooper just ahead of Battery B.

The word was passed along from one unit to another and in twenty minutes a bedraggled file of prisoners slogged by under mounted guard.

"What's going on?" asked Zack Pascoe from inside Ben's battery wagon where he had been sleeping for an hour snug and dry.

Ben shrugged. Sergeant Goodroy reined in beside the wagon. "The Johnnies have planted torpedoes in the road," he said grimly. "They attached trip wires to friction tubes in the torpedoes. Several of our horses were killed and some men wounded. General Sheridan had the prisoners brought up to feel for those torpedoes before any more of our boys got hurt."

"It's getting to be a dirty war," said Zack Pascoe.

Sergeant Goodroy rode on. "I've never heard of a clean one yet," he said back over his shoulder.

Ben looked to the south. There was a weird reddish glow on the low hanging clouds — reflection of the Richmond lights. So near and yet so far. A bell was ringing at intervals.

"I'll bet the Johnnies are excited," said Zack.

Ben nodded.

Zack eyed Ben. "None of the boys think you did wrong, Ben."

"Captain Crispin does."

"You came back, didn't you?"

"Yes, but Sergeant Dolan said he had ordered me back and I ignored him."

"Yeah," said Zack. He coughed. "They going to bring charges against you?"

"I don't know. They might not in the Volunteers. We're Regulars, you know."

Zack nodded soberly. "Yeah. How well I know. Listen!"

There was more gunfiring in the darkness. The column moved on at a snail's pace, stopping, starting, moving a few hundred yards, stopping again, while all the time the bells could be heard ringing in the city and the sound of gunfiring grew and grew. Still, most of the shooting was high. Home Guards were not exactly skilled artillerymen.

The rain slashed down heavily. The battery came to a halt. "Big gap between us and the next unit," said Farrier-Corporal DuCroix. He stood up in his stirrups and looked back. "Can't see anyone back there either."

The battery moved slowly on until the lightning flashed to reveal a shabby farmhouse at the side of the road. A man wearing a caped blue overcoat with sergeant's chevrons on the sleeves stood beside a horse. He pointed to the road beyond the farm, and the battery turned up it, guns and caissons ahead, then forge wagon and finally in the ignominious position at the very rear, the battery wagon. Ben glanced at the guide. There was an odd smile on the man's wet face. As Ben turned his team up the road, he saw the man mounting his horse, revealed by the flickering lightning. Ben stared. It almost seemed as though the guide was wearing trousers of gray tucked into boots, but the light was too vague and indefinite for Ben to be sure. Darkness fell and when the lightning flashed again the man was gone. The road behind the battery was empty of troops.

Twenty minutes passed and then Zack Pascoe thrust out his head. "Bumpy road, Ben," he growled. "Fellow can't sleep."

Ben nodded. That mysterious guide had been bothering him. There was no sight nor sound of troops ahead of Battery B, nor any behind them. It was almost as though they were riding in a dripping and black world all their own. A right *lonely* world.

"Halt!" the command was passed from man to man down the column. In the silence that followed the rain pattered down steadily. There was a faint flickering of lightning, and it reflected from a leaden-looking irregular surface. Ben suddenly realized that it was a large pond of some sort. The leaders of the battery had halted beside it, and the road ahead seemed to fade out into nothingness.

A horseman came back along the battery line. It was Lieutenant Pike. "We're going to turn back," he said.

"Have to turn hard left here and back to the road we came in on. Take it easy. The mud is deeper than it looks."

Zack Pascoe crawled out onto the seat beside Ben. "I don't like this," he said. "Where's the rest of the Corps?"

The lead gun began to move, swinging wide for the turn, but Jonas Whitlow, for once, miscalculated and one of the gun wheels struck a stump and rebounded heavily. The team slogged through the mud. Lightning flashed, and the battery was clearly revealed. Something else was revealed as well. A strange-looking humped shape across the pond, and there was a man atop it, wearing a slouched hat on his head, staring at them. "Halt!" he yelled. "Who goes theah?"

"Those are rebel fortifications!" Zack cried.

The guns were being turned one after the other and already Number One was almost even with the battery wagon, forming the battery in a large circle.

"Halt! Who goes theah? Halt or we fiah!" yelled the sentry.

Whips rose and fell as the drivers urged on their teams. Cannoneers, officers, and every man who could be spared leaped to the guns and thrust shoulders against anything they could find or gripped the muddy spokes of the wheels.

"Fiah!" The command cracked through the darkness, which instantly vanished as heavy guns blasted forth flame and smoke followed by a whirring, rushing sound through the air just over the trapped battery, like the passage of a covey of giant partridges as they rose into sudden flight. Men staggered here and there

from the concussion of shells that burst high over the battery and just beyond it.

"Load! Canister — Double!" came the command from the fort.

Number One was even with the battery wagon now, and one of the gun wheels was wobbling a little. Number Two passed and then Number Three. There was a gap between Number Three and Number Four when the enemy command ripped through the dripping darkness. *"Fiah!"*

"Jump!" said Zack Pascoe to Ben. He gripped Ben by the shoulder and dragged him from the wagon as the guns blasted the night. The two of them hit the mud as something struck the battery wagon and smashed it into flinders, casting the contents high in the air. Bits of wood, metal, and leather pattered down on the two boys lying in the mud. When Ben looked up the battery wagon seemed to have vanished. There was nothing left but the running gear and that was shattered. He jumped to his feet and ran to the team. Both horses had been untouched, but they were rearing and plunging from the shock. Zack helped Ben quiet them down as the rest of the guns passed by, followed by the heavy caissons and the forge wagon.

"Cut that team loose!" said Sergeant Dolan to Ben.

They cut loose the team and led them through the mud. They could plainly hear the enemy guns being reloaded. Ben thanked the Lord that those men were not trained artillerists such as Lee had in his Army of Northern Virginia, for they would have been firing almost constantly and with greater accuracy.

Then the guns flamed once more, and the double charges of deadly canister ripped clean through the air where Battery B had been, pocking the mud, cutting down the scrub trees, and geysering the muddy pools of water.

The battery slogged on until they reached the road where they had been turned off by that mysterious guide. Ben knew now that the man had been a Johnny wearing a Federal overcoat. He looked at Zack. "How did you know we should jump when we did?" he asked.

Zack shrugged. "I don't know. Something told me to."

"Thanks, Zack."

Zack's pale and muddy face wrinkled into a faint smile. "You know sometimes, Ben, I almost wish we were back in Hinckley's Corners, drilling on the village green with the Tiger Rifles."

"Strangely enough," mused Ben, "I had exactly the same thought back there when that wagon was blown to pieces."

The battery was being formed on the road in a downpour of cold rain. Captain Crispin was looking at the damaged wheel of Gun Number One. "She'll hold for a while," he said. "Bring up the rear with this piece. March order, Sergeant Dolan."

Gun Number Two led the way this time, while Number One trailed along behind the forge wagon, but behind that humble vehicle trotted Dandy and Big Barney, bestrode by a couple of the boys from the Hinckley's Corners Tiger Rifles. The lightning seemed to have died away, but the rain was heavier. Battery B had never lost a gun in battle to the enemy yet; but to run into Home Guards and to lose the *entire* battery without firing a shot from those six Ordnance Rifles was unthinkable. Yet . . .

Lieutenant Barry led a scouting party ahead through the night. Several miles from where the battery had almost been trapped, the sound of gunfire came from ahead, and Sergeant Fox led back the remainder of the party to report that the rebels held a bridge in force up ahead and that Lieutenant Barry had been killed, while two other men had been badly wounded and captured by the rebels.

Lieutenant Pike led out another party, threading its way through the wild second growth timber on a road that wasn't quite as bad as the one that led into the dead end near the pond beneath the guns of the city's fortifications. The going became harder and harder until at last Gun Number One's damaged wheel snapped, the gun carriage lurched and slewed sideways into a water-filled ditch, and the gun's great weight began to sink until the carriage was beneath the mud and the barrel of the gun seemed to be resting on it.

Captain Crispin came back and stood at the edge of the ditch, looking down on the mired gun. "I should have had you replace that wheel, Fox," he said quietly.

"We can get her out, sir!" said Seth Pomeroy.

Crispin bit his lower lip. Lieutenant Pike came through the darkness and saluted. "We've found a way, sir. Ran into a rear guard of the Third Division. They said to hurry up, and they'd cover us. The Corps has found the road to Mechanicsville."

"Thank God for that anyway," said Crispin.

Pike looked at the gun. "We won't have time to get enough teams back here to pull that out," he said soberly.

Crispin hesitated. "No," he said at last.

Seth Pomeroy's face was desperate in the darkness. "We can't leave the gun here, sir!" he said.

Crispin looked at the earnest face of the young non-com. "A gun can be lost with honor, Pomeroy," he said quietly. "I can't jeopardize five other guns and the rest of the battery for *one* gun."

Sergeant Dolan saluted. "I'll stay and get her out, sorr."

"No. I can't spare you, nor Sergeant Fox for that matter."

The rain slashed down, and the lightning flickered.

Seth Pomeroy raised his head. "Let *me* stay, sir."

"I can't spare too many men," said Crispin.

"Volunteers, sir," said Seth quickly.

Crispin tugged at his beard and looked about.

"The rear guard won't wait much longer," said Pike,

Crispin turned. "Who will stay?"

Every man within hearing cried out for the chance.

Crispin shrugged. "Pomeroy, I'll allow you eight men. With yourself, a full crew of nine. Pick them out now."

Seth looked about. "Corporal Whitlow, Privates Bates, Woolsey, Pennycook, Shayhan and Schmidt!"

"That leaves two more," said Crispin.

Seth's eyes fell on the pale, taut face of Ben Buell. He looked away.

"Pascoe!" cried out Zack.

Seth nodded.

"One more," said the battery commander briskly.

"Sergeant Dolan! March order!"

"Yis, sorr!"

Again, Seth looked at Ben and the two big wheelers standing on each side of him, three battery members in temporary disgrace. Ben swallowed hard. His pride would not let him cry out for the chance again.

"One more!" snapped Crispin.

"Buell!" said Seth. "He can handle that team, and they are of no use to you now, sir, without the battery wagon."

Crispin started to shake his head, and then he turned to look at Ben Buell, and he remembered then the boy clad in dusty and ill-fitting blue who had appeared out of thin air that hot and heavy first day of battle at Gettysburg, to handle a huge bay like a veteran driver. "All right, Sergeant Pomeroy," he said at last.

"It's *Corporal* Pomeroy, sir," said Seth.

Crispin smiled. "Acting *Sergeant,* Pomeroy. It's the

least I can do for you now. Good-by, men. Good luck!" Then he was gone.

The nine of them stood there in the mud, with the rain drifting down and the distant flashing of the lightning revealing the mired gun and tired team. They listened to the grinding of the battery wheels through the muck and the muffled plodding of many hoofs, and then Battery B was gone, perhaps forever.

"Move!" said Sergeant Pomeroy. "The Johnnies may be trailing us!"

They waded into the cold, clinging mud and heaved at the mired gun, but it would hardly move. Jonas Whitlow, Mexico Bates, and Mike Woolsey mounted their horses, nigh lead, swing, and wheel, and at a word from Seth they plied whips and spurs, while the six other volunteers heaved at the gun, now sinking deeper and deeper into the gumbo. They stopped, breathing harshly.

"No use," said Sage Pennycook. "She ain't even hit bottom."

"Still sinking," agreed Pat Shayhan.

"Impossible to get it oudt," said Artificer Fritz Schmidt in his thick German accent.

In the silence that followed, they heard distant gunfire borne on the wind. Seth Pomeroy looked about." "Sergeant Dolan always says: 'Never say a cliff's inaccessible; just say *difficult* for harse artillery,'" he said quietly.

"We can do it," said Ben Buell.

They all looked quickly at him, the youngest of the lot.

"Vhat vould you do, poy?" asked Schmidt.

Ben looked at the blown team. They had been worked hard for days on short forage. "Unhitch that team first," he said.

"You loco?" asked Mexico Bates.

"Can *you* get the gun out?" retorted Ben.

"No."

"Then unhitch that team!"

Ben knelt in the mud of the road and studied the gun. "Cut saplings and brush. Corduroy the road for twenty yards," he said over his shoulder.

Seth nodded. The men set to work with hatchets and sabers. They spread brush and saplings atop the thick mud.

Ben looked at the limber. "Unhitch the limber from the gun," he said. He watched them unhook the gun and haul the limber up the road. One of them placed his ear against an ammunition chest, then laughed. He opened the chest and lifted out little Canister, the battery mascot, then slipped him inside his jacket so that the little head stuck out. "We've got luck with us now, boys!" he called out.

Ben led up Dandy and Big Barney. They were tired too but pulling the battery wagon hadn't been as tiring as hauling gun or caisson. Besides, the battery wagon carried the spare forage and Ben had seen to it that both horses had gotten more than their share, although that was against strict orders.

Ben looked up at Seth. "We'll have to rig a set of tackles on the axles and the gun barrel for a straight pull."

"What's wrong with using the lunette hook?" asked Mike Woolsey.

Ben shook his head. "Take a gun out of the mud the same way she went in," he said.

"Smart kid," said Mike in admiration.

Ben shook his head. "Thank Captain Maynard Buell, Battery A, First Pennsylvania Independent Artillery. He taught me a lot about artillery, Mike."

"He's not here," said Mike.

Ben turned slowly, and the lightning illuminated his muddy face. "Yes, he is," he said. "You can't see him, Mike, but he's here all right."

They were ready now. The two big wheelers stood patiently in the driving rain. Ben had removed a Jennifer saddle from one of the other wheel horses and had saddled Dandy. He swung up into the saddle, and Mike Woolsey held out a whip toward him. Ben shook his head. He looked about. The narrow corduroy road. The leaden-colored rain. The dripping trees. The water-filled ditches. The pale and tired faces of the mud-coated artillerymen. Finally he leaned forward to speak to Dandy. "Remember the farm, Dandy," he said in a low voice. "Remember how you led all the other horses. You were a leader then and you're a leader now! Big Barney is ready and willing. You've got to show him the way."

Dandy nickered. Ben looked back at the mired gun and at the brass plate affixed to the breech, etched with the name of his state. Pennsylvania. The Keystone State! "Now, boys," he cried out to the team. "Now!" They surged forward and the traces tightened. "Pull, Dandy! Pull, Barney! Pull! Pull! *Pull!*"

Their great legs began to sink into the mud as they threw their weight into the collars, and for a moment it seemed to the bystanders that it was a tableau, or a set of lifelike statuary, horse, boy, and gun, poised there in the dripping night. The lightning snapped and crackled, and the gun seemed to move.

"Pull, Dandy! Pull, Barney! Pull, boys! Pull! Pull! *Pull!*"

There was a grinding and a squelching, a thudding of great hoofs against the snapping corduroying of the road and then Gun Number One rose steadily until the gunners could slam shoulders against it, or grip the mud-coated spokes to help move the gun out onto firmer ground, such as it was.

"Replace that broken wheel!" snapped Seth Pomeroy. "Unhitch that team! Hook up to the limber! Hitch on a full team! Jump, ye terriers! March order! March order! Ye're in the *harse* artillery now!"

They moved swiftly like the well-trained men they were. The wheel was changed, gun hooked to limber, limber hitched to team, with Dandy and Big Barney as wheelers. Canister was dumped into the ammunition chest and just as the lid was being closed the little mascot barked and then snarled. Sage Pennycook looked at him in surprise. Then he turned to look back along the road. His face blanched. "Sergeant!" he yelled. "The Johnnies!"

Every man turned. A group of gray-clad cavalry was plowing through the mud, plainly revealed by the lightning.

"Forward, ho! Walk! March!" cracked out Sergeant Pomeroy. "Gunners to the rear! Trot! March!"

The few mounted gunners fell in at the rear of the slowly moving gun, drawing pistols as they did so. The lightning flickered out as they moved on, with the unseen enemy closing in behind them. It was a long muddy way to the rest of Battery B and the Cavalry Corps of the Army of the Potomac, and Battery B, Eighth United States, "Crispin's Bulldogs" hadn't lost a gun in this war yet.

CHAPTER FIFTEEN

The muddy river was almost above its banks, rushing along in a brown flood, carrying debris on its surface. The buttresses of the bridge and the main timbers were still in place, but the decking had been removed leaving only the stringers. In the fitful illumination of the lightning the rain could be seen slanting down in silvery veils to strike the surface of the river.

Nine men stood silently at the edge of the flood, looking down at the impassable barrier. "We can swim the horses across, Sergeant," said Jonas Whitlow.

"We can't swim the gun across," said Seth quietly. He looked back. "See anything, Woolsey?"

"Nothing, Sergeant!"

"Maybe they kept on going along that road we got mired on," said Zack Pascoe hopefully.

"When they reach the river farther down they'll figure that we're up here," said Seth.

They all looked at one another. The odds were that they might safely cross the river, or at the least lose perhaps one man. But the gun . . . Ben Buell looked at the dull steel of the barrel, glistening wet in the rain, and at the thick mud daubing the wheels. It would be an ignominious disgrace to leave it sitting there in the road, cold and wet, instead of hot and dry, smoking with the angry breath of battle, the way a gun should be lost, if it *had* to be lost.

Schmidt eyed the bridge. "The stringers are goodt," he said. "Midt blanking for a deck, ve couldt maybe make idt over midt the gun."

"There's a shack over there," said Sage Pennycook.

In two minutes those who were not on guard at the road were tearing at the walls of the rain-sodden shack with handspikes, rammer, hatchets, sabers, and bare hands, and the shack seemed to collapse almost magically from the furious onslaught. Horses were hitched to the stouter timbers by means of picket lines, dragging them free from the tangle of wood and moving them down to the bridge where Artificer Schmidt took over the makeshift construction of the decking. The bridge was planked halfway across when Mike Woolsey whistled sharply. It was the signal for the approach of the enemy.

Fritz Schmidt kept on working, helped by Pat Shayhan, Zack Pascoe, and Sage Pennycook, while Jonas Whitlow, Mexico Bates, and Ben Buell followed Sergeant Pomeroy to where Mike Woolsey stood behind a tree, cocked pistol in his hand.

"What did you see?" asked Seth.

"Looked like a rebel scout, Sergeant."

Ben looked back over his shoulder. Schmidt was working steadily. The planking seemed to be inching across the naked stringers. The distant shooting they had heard some time ago had been the last of it. It was very quiet now except for the pattering of the rain and the rustling of talmas as the artillerymen took up positions behind trees. Colt pistols were fine weapons for close-up use, but in a fight such as they could expect, the rebels could stand off and pick them off one after another with rifles or carbines, without chance of any return firing from the artillerymen.

ACTION FRONT! 169

Minutes ticked past and then suddenly Zack Pascoe was there in the road. "All done, Sergeant," he said breathlessly. "Looks like it will hold the horses. We ain't sure about the gun and limber."

"Keep the wheelers hitched to the gun. Tell Schmidt to get the rest of the horses across. Hurry!"

Slowly and carefully the three men at the bridge led the leaders and swing horses across, then the other horses, until only Dandy and Big Barney were on the dangerous side of the river.

"Ben?" said Seth.

Ben looked at him. There was no need for Seth to say anything further.

"Jonas or Mexico can do it," said Seth.

Ben shook his head. "It's my team," he said simply.

"Go on then."

"Give me a hand, Mexico," said Ben.

They took the ammunition chests from the limber. The spare wheel had already been taken off to use on the gun. Ben mounted Dandy and touched him with his spurs. The big bay moved forward until Ben halted him at the end of the bridge. It had looked solid enough from a distance.

"Walk them across," said Mexico. "Lead 'em, boy."

Ben was tempted, but he knew both horses would respond better if he rode Dandy across. But if the bridge collapsed there would be little chance for him to escape. But he could not move the team forward; something was blocking his will.

Something cracked sharply back in the woods. The Johnnies had opened fire.

"Go on!" said Seth.

Ben swallowed hard. He touched Dandy with his spurs. They moved forward. On the far bank were Schmidt, Pascoe, and Shayhan, holding the rest of the horses, while their dirty faces stared at Ben and the big team. The team was fully on the bridge now and the limber creaked down the slope and out onto the makeshift decking. Ben drew rein and then spurred on again. If he stopped, the weight might collapse the bridge. It was better to move on. Then the gun rumbled out onto the bridge. A shot sounded. Ben turned before he realized it was not a gun shot, but rather a breaking or cracking plank.

There was nothing else he could do. He gripped Big Barney by the mane. "It's just a little way, boys," he said earnestly. "The bridge will hold. It *has* to hold!"

Now the cracking of the timbers was mingled with the crackling of gunfire from across the bridge as the rebels moved in on the handful of men who stood guard. "Fall back!" yelled Seth. "Grab one of those ammunition chests!"

The team was on the bank of the river now and the limber was being pulled up the slope when, with a report like that of the cannon itself, a stringer snapped. The gun lurched to one side. Ben's reaction was instantaneous. He rammed his spurs into Dandy and yelled fiercely. "Pull! Pull! Pull!" The big wheelers

squatted on the slope, driving with their hind legs, bellies almost touching the mud, as they slowly pulled the gun free from the shattered timbers and up the slope.

Something struck the gun and sang thinly off into space. Another bullet slapped into the limber. Ben drove his tired team up the slope and into the shelter of the trees before he turned to look back. The rest of the gun crew were running across that crazy bridge, two of them carrying an ammunition chest. Gray-clad figures flitted through the dripping woods, firing now and then. There were a lot of them.

The artillerymen were all across now. Mexico Bates was the last. He turned and yelled derisively, "Yaaaa-aaah!" At that instant a Johnny fired. Mexico clapped his hand to his heart and dropped like a stone. His mates hooked hands under his armpits and dragged him up the slope and to the shelter of the trees. Seth and some of the others were firing their pistols, hardly effective at that range but enough to keep the Johnnies from attempting to cross the bridge.

Mexico lay on his back, staring up at the sky. "I knew it," he said faintly. "It was that skull."

"Where did it hit you, Mexico?" asked Zack.

"In the heart, comrade."

"Are ye kilt entirely, Mexico?" asked Pat Shayhan with tears in his eyes.

Jonas Whitlow eyed the wounded man. Then he knelt beside him and began to unbutton his muddy jacket.

Sage Pennycook blew the smoke from the muzzle of his pistol. "Aye, lads, 'twas the skull all right," he said wisely. "An omen it was. A death sentence."

Mexico groaned and his eyes were wide in his head. "I knew this was my last campaign, boys."

Jonas Whitlow took out something from the jacket. He eyed it. "Get up, Mexico," he said quietly.

"I'm dying, old friend."

"Get up!"

"A foine way that is to talk to a man, and him on his death bed," said Pat Shayhan.

Jonas laughed. He laughed harder. Tears began to run from his eyes.

"Such a hard-hearted man I haf never seen," growled Schmidt.

Jonas held out his hand. There was a small black book in it and embedded in the book was a Minie bullet. "He isn't dying at all," he said in a choked voice. "He was only wounded in the Testament! I ain't laughing at the narrow escape, boys, but at him and that skull he's been carting all the way from Chancellorsville!" Up until that time the Johnnies had figured they might be able to rush the bridge. After all there was only a handful of tired artillerymen over there, and they wouldn't have time to get their deadly gun into action. But now the Johnnies wondered, for the sound of continuous laughing was coming to them on the wind from the other side of the river, and if the Yanks were laughing that hard, they certainly weren't worried about an attack by the Confederates. The Confederates stayed in their positions, full of wonder, and watched the gun being dragged out of sight and they allowed half an hour's time before they cautiously approached the bridge and crossed it, leading their horses one by one.

There was something else that made them pause as they started up the long slope from the river. The lightning lanced coldly across the gray skies. The eerie light showed something in the middle of the road. A skull, glistening wet with rain, placed upon a stick thrust into the mud. The vacant eyes stared at the wet and shivering Johnnies, and the bullet hole in the center of the forehead seemed a forecasting of doom to the more superstitious among them, as it had to Mexico Bates.

———

THERE WAS a faint suggestion of dawn in the eastern sky. The rain had stopped, and a cold wind blew through the wet woods. The lone horse artillery gun, and its lonely crew drew rein at the far end of a wide clearing and turned to look back. The clearing was two hundred yards in width, and in the woods beyond it, dim figures moved about. Confederate infantry with a company of cavalry was forming over there. As yet the artillerymen had seen no signs of the rest of the Cavalry Corps. They were still on their own. Twice they had almost reached disaster, only to be saved at the last possible moment by a tired boy and two big wheel horses.

"What do we do, Sergeant?" asked Mike Woolsey. "Cut and run?"

Seth did not answer. His eyes were on those men across the clearing, more plainly to be seen now in the slowly growing light. "This is the Mechanicsville Road," he said. "This is the route the Corps took to reach the James."

The nine of them stood there in the cold mud, watching the Johnnies. Then they all looked at the muddy gun.

"Well," said Jonas Whitlow, "we haven't lost it yet!"

"Action Front!" snapped Seth Pomeroy.

In a matter of minutes the gun had been unhitched from the limber. The lid of the ammunition chest had been thrown up and Canister taken out. The men took their positions. Ben was Number Two, loader at the muzzle of the gun, while Mike Woolsey was Number One, rammer and sponger. Sage Pennycook was Number Three, ready to serve the vent, and opposite him was Jonas Whitlow, Number Four, who would fire the gun. Seth Pomeroy was Gunner, while Fritz Schmidt would cut fuzes as Number Six. Pat Shayhan was Number Five, who would carry powder charge and projectile to Ben for loading into the gun. In reserve, if one could call it that, were Mexico Bates and Zack Pascoe.

"Load! Shell!" commanded Seth.

There was a moment's hesitation.

Seth turned and looked blackly at Pat Shayhan.

Pat swallowed hard. "Sergeant," he said in a small voice, "we picked up the wrong ammunition chist, we did. The *full* wan is back thayer in the swamp. This wan has but half a dozen powder charges."

"Then bring them as needed!"

Pat swallowed again. "But this chist has but six rounds in it, Sergeant. Three solid shot. Three defective shell."

"The rebels are forming at the edge of the woods!" yelled Mexico.

Seth raised his head. "Zack Pascoe! Do you have your fife?"

"Yes, Sergeant!"

"Then play us a tune and keep on playing!"

Zack whipped out his fife and climbed atop the limber. The shrill notes rose in the quiet dawn air and carried clearly across the field to the Johnnies.

"We'll load alternately, solid shot and shell," said Seth. "Shell first! Range two hundred yards!"

Pat carried powder charge and shell to Ben. He placed the charge into the muzzle and Mike rammed it home, then rammed home the defective shell.

"Trail left!" commanded Seth.

Number Three, Sage Pennycook gripped the handspike and moved the trail as commanded.

"Fire!" snapped Seth.

Jonas Whitlow stepped clear, holding the lanyard, gave it a steady straight pull and the gun flashed and roared, driving back on the trail. The shell made it halfway across the field before it prematurely exploded.

"Sponge! Thumb the vent! Load! Ram! Trail right!"

Seth sighted along the gun barrel. He stepped back. "Fire!"

Zack Pascoe had shifted into "Granny, Will Your Dog Bite?" He took the fife from his mouth as the solid shot skipped along the muddy road and spun out of sight into the woods.

The next shell plunged into the woods and did not explode. The second solid shot struck a tree and it fell along the forming rebel lines. The enemy scattered. Some of them opened fire with their rifles. The cavalry company cantered out along the road. Sabers shone in the cold gray light.

The Johnnies began to move forward.

Seth wiped the cold sweat from his face. "Load — Double — Solid shot and shell!"

The men's faces paled as they looked at him. It was downright dangerous, for the double charge might explode in the gun.

Seth shook his fist at his crew. "Load! It's all we have! If they keep coming we'll have to wreck the gun anyway to keep it out of their hands!" He whirled. "I told you to play, Pascoe!"

"Yes, sir!"

"Don't 'sir' a noncommissioned officer!"

"No, sir!"

Zack began to play "Adam Bell's March."

"Fire!" commanded Seth.

The crew scattered as Jonas Whitlow stepped clear of the trail and took the slack from his lanyard. He pulled it steadily and deliberately. "Keystone" roared and spat flame and smoke from the heavy charge. The gun slammed back in recoil. The shell burst in the air just over the cavalry company and scattered them back against the infantry whose lines broke. The solid shot hit a tree and shattered it, casting deadly splinters through the air.

The smoke began to clear. The eastern sky was beginning to lighten with a rose-and-gold color as the sun came up. The gun breathed a final ring of smoke. The last shot from the chest had done its job. The gun crew was defenseless now except for their pistols, and the rammer and handspikes, traditional weapons of an overrun gun crew for the last stand.

The rebels were reforming. Officers shouted and waved their swords.

Zack Pascoe began to play "The Battle Hymn of the Republic."

The rebels moved forward across the wide muddy field.

Suddenly a trumpet sounded in the wet woods behind

the lone gun. The gunners turned. Brass and steel flashed in the woods and a flag could be seen. A flag of glorious red and white stripes, with a star sprinkled canton of blue. An officer came forward. "We heard you firing, men. We're the rear guard. Captain Crispin said he had been forced to leave a gun behind. In a few minutes we would have been across the river and had planned to burn the bridge behind us. Your firing brought us back."

A cavalry regiment was behind the gun now. Tough veteran troopers, with Spencer repeating carbines. Men like Buford's troops at Gettysburg who had held up the advance of a rebel division while fighting on foot.

"The Johnnies are falling back, sir," said a sergeant.

As the sun came up the Confederates faded away into the woods, leaving a few scattered dead men and horses in the road and the field.

"Let's move out, Sergeant," said the officer.

"March order!" commanded Sergeant Pomeroy.

The cavalrymen moved their horses out of the road to watch the lone, mud-splattered gun and its muddy and weary crew pass between their lines. Suddenly one of the troopers began to cheer until every trooper and officer was cheering at the top of his voice for Gun Number One, Battery B, Eighth United States, and its crew who had kept up the tradition of "Crispin's Bulldogs" by not losing a gun that had had the odds stacked high against its ever joining Battery B again.

They reached the battery bivouac late in the afternoon. Guns Number Two through Number Six sparkled in the late sunlight. The horses were groomed. The swallow-tailed battery guidon snapped in the breeze in front of the little headquarters tent. The widely grinning men of Battery B stood in a ring about Gun Number One, back from the wars.

"And what do ye think this is?" roared a well-known Hibernian voice. "A blessed tay party, is it! There is brass to be polished and harses to be fed. There is worruk to be done! Ye're in the *harse* artillery!"

"No glory here," said Mexico Bates.

"Did you expect any?" asked Jonas Whitlow.

"Ye're in the *harse* artillery," said Zack Pascoe blackly.

"Get that Number Wan gun cleaned up thayer! 'Tis about toime ye boys brought her back where she belongs!"

"Maybe we should have left her in the swamp," said Mike Woolsey.

They all looked at Sergeant Dolan. There was a broad grin on his red Irish face. "Boys, 'tis not *ye* who will clean that gun. The rest av the battery, including Sergeant Dolan *himself,* will see to that! Now get ye some slum! Sergeant Freitag fought a desperate rear guard action against a ribil pig and stabbed him to death wid his saber, he did! Roast pig, boys! Action Front!"

When the sun had slid down behind the western hills, the men of Gun Number One lay about the ground, full of roast pig and contentment, while the firelight glinted from the polished surfaces of "Keystone."

"What is this place, Seth?" asked Ben.

Sergeant Pomeroy looked about. "A place your father knew well not so long ago, Ben. It's called Gaines' Mill."

Ben stood up and walked into the woods. It was almost as though he knew his father was about there in spirit, in the place where he had fought his battery in a last stand, sustaining the wound that had caused his eventual death. But in a sense his father had been with Battery B since that hard-fought day at Gettysburg, in spirit if not in flesh. Ben took off his forage cap and prayed for the first time since he had left home.

There would be another year of war. Battery B would fight at Hawes' Shop and Trevilian Station, and later in the Shenandoah Valley at Winchester, Strasburg, and Cedar Creek, and they would not lose a gun. All six guns and caissons would be driven in the Grand Review held in Washington in May of 1865 participated in by a hundred thousand men in blue. A newly commissioned second lieutenant of artillery would ride in that parade — Second Lieutenant Seth Pomeroy. Two great wheel horses would pull in the harness of Gun Number One, and they would be driven by Corporal Ben Buell, as Battery B, Eighth United States, "Crispin's Bulldogs," rode on into the pages of history behind their swallow-tailed and battle-stained guidon.

GLOSSARY

Artificer: In military life, a carpenter, blacksmith, or other mechanic attached to a unit; a modern-day mechanic.

Battery wagon: A wagon, sometimes with limber attached, to carry tools, various supplies, and forage for the battery horses.

Caisson: Technically an ammunition wagon, two wheeled, with limber attached, for carrying extra ammunition. Each gun in a battery has its own caisson.

Canister: A metal case containing many bullets or balls of cast iron, which when fired, scatters the contents much in the manner of a shotgun shell; a deadly projectile at close range.

Corduroy road: A muddy road paved by placing tree trunks, saplings, and brush atop the mud, crossways to afford better footing.

Foot cavalry: A nickname originally given to Stonewall Jackson's infantry in the Valley Campaign because of the long and swift marches that they performed, later applied in general to the infantry of the Army of Northern Virginia, C.S.A.

Friction primer: A device, inserted in the vent of a muzzle-loading cannon, which ignites by friction to detonate the powder charge in the chamber of the cannon.

Fuze gouge: A tool used to prepare artillery shells of the Civil War period by cutting away a composition, so that the flight of the projectile can be timed to explode.

Horse artillery: Light artillery that serves with cavalry. It differs from the usual light artillery battery in that its gunners, rather than riding on the limbers, or walking behind the guns, are all mounted — cannoneers and other battery members, other than drivers, ride behind the guns.

Iron Brigade: One of the famous fighting units of the Army of the Potomac, composed of Indiana, Michigan, and Wisconsin troops. They wore a distinctive black hat as compared to the forage cap worn by most other units. Their heroic fighting at Gettysburg caused them terrible losses.

Johnny or Johnnies: One of the nicknames given to the Confederates by the Federals, originally Johnny Rebel, as opposed to the Confederates calling the Federals "Yanks" or "Yankee."

Lead, swing, and wheel teams: Three pairs of horses used to pull the guns and caissons in light and horse artillery. One horse in each pair is ridden by a driver. The lead team was usually the smallest pair, nimble and fast; the swing horses were a little larger; while the wheel horses were the largest and strongest, for the heavy work usually fell to them in both pulling and braking.

LIMBER: The forepart of the carriage of a field artillery gun, consisting of an ammunition chest or chests set on a frame supported by two wheels and an axle, with a shaft for the horses.

LUNETTE: The after part of the gun trail, of heavy forged iron or steel, in a half-moon shape, used to pull the gun muzzle to the rear.

MILITIA: A body of citizens regularly enrolled and trained to do military exercises but not permanently organized in times of peace, or, in general, liable to serve out of the country or with regularly organized armies.

MINIE BULLET: The invention of Captain Minie of the French Army prior to the American Civil War. A conical lead bullet of large caliber used largely by both the North and the South.

NAPOLEON GUN: Bronze fieldpieces, smooth-bored, developed during the reign of Napoleon Third of France. The foremost fieldpiece of the Civil War, used by both North and South; although it lacked accuracy it was a fearsome weapon at shorter ranges, the favorite charge being canister. It was usually issued to light artillery batteries, being too heavy, as a rule, for the use of horse artillery.

NEAT'S-FOOT OIL: A preservative oil made from the hoofs of cattle, used to preserve leather and waterproof it.

NEWS-WALKER: Self-appointed reporters of the armies of Civil War times; men who would wander from unit to unit, gathering bits of information, passing it on to other units, etc., until they had formed a fairly clear picture of the day's activities in battle.

NIGH, OR NEAR HORSE: The left-hand horse in a pair, as opposed to the right-hand horse, known as the off horse. In light and horse artillery the nigh horse was ridden by the pair driver; in a six-horse team there were three drivers, lead, swing, and wheel.

ORDNANCE RIFLE: Three-inch caliber rifled cannon, formed of wrought-iron sheets wrapped about a mandrel, welded and turned to shape, weight between 815 and 850 pounds, usually issued to horse artillery. Extremely accurate and prized as war trophies by the Confederates.

PENNSYLVANIA BUCKTAILS: Famous infantry regiment of the Army of the Potomac, so-called because the members, mostly recruited from the deer-hunting country of Pennsylvania, wore a buck's tail on their forage caps.

PRIMING WIRE: A wire used to thrust clown into the vent of a muzzle-loading cannon to pierce the cover of the powder charge so that the friction primer could ignite the charge.

PROLONGS: A twenty-seven-foot rope, with a hook spliced into one end, used to hook onto the lunette of a gun so that the gun could be pulled by hand. The prolonge rope was carried atop the gun trail wound in a figure-eight pattern about two prolonge hooks.

PROVOST: A police detail of soldiers used to keep order in army camps or areas, used in battle to turn back skulkers, etc.

REDLEG: Army nickname given to artillerymen because of the red stripe on their breeches.

Seven Days, the: General name given to the series of battles fought in a period of seven days during McClellan's attempt to capture Richmond in 1862. Included in the Seven Days were the battles or engagements of Mechanicsville, Gaines' Mill, Savage Station, White Oak Swamp, and Malvern Hill.

Shebang: Nickname used by soldiers of the Civil War period to designate the crude shacks or buildings they erected during winter quarters.

Talma: A rubberized cape used by mounted troops during and for some time after the Civil War.

Torpedoes: A general term used during Civil War times to name fixed explosive charges, either in water or on land, the forerunners of water mines and land mines of later times.

Traveling forge: A vehicle containing a small but efficient forge, which was part of the equipment of a battery of artillery, used to heat horseshoes and do other blacksmithing work, so that fieldwork could be done in that medium.

Valise: A sort of pack used by drivers of horse and light artillery teams to carry their personal articles and equipment and carried on the back of the off horse.

Vent: An aperture atop the breech of a muzzle-loading cannon through which the priming wire could be thrust to pierce the powder charge in the chamber, after which the friction tube was inserted to detonate the charge. "Thumbing the vent" was performed by the Number Three. He wore a leather-padded thumb-stall, which he pressed down atop the vent to prevent the inrush of air, which might possibly ignite a new powder charge prematurely. In times of intense firing, a gun could be discharged by merely removing the thumbstall and quite often the thumbstall was burned to a crisp. Woe to the Number Three who would carelessly remove the thumb-stall from the vent while Number One was ramming home a charge. It was considered quite correct for the Number One to withdraw his rammer and lay it down across the skull of Number Three, for a premature discharge might easily kill Number One, or at the very least, cost him the loss of an arm.

Yellowleg: Army nickname given to cavalrymen because of the yellow stripe on their breeches. Hardly ever used in modern mechanized times.

AUTHOR'S NOTE

Ben Buell, Seth Pomeroy, Zack Pascoe, and the other members of Battery B, Eighth United States Horse Artillery, are fictitious, as is, indeed, Battery B itself, for though in the years after the Civil War there was an Eighth United States Field Artillery with honorable service in other wars, it did not exist during the Civil War. B Company, Pennsylvania Volunteer Militia, is also a fictitious unit, but such units did exist during the Civil War and some of them did see action. Some of them also bore such glamorous names as "Tiger Rifles." While the story of "Crispin's Bulldogs" is fiction, it closely follows the chronology of events leading to the Battle of Gettysburg, thence through the hard winter of 1863-1864 and the campaign of The Wilderness. Sheridan's raid toward Richmond, the destruction of the Confederate stores, the fight at Yellow Taverns, and the ride within the outer defenses of Richmond are historically true, as are many of the military units and commanders mentioned in the book.

The organization, drill, and service of the horse artillery batteries such as Battery B are based on accurate research through many accounts and histories of the times. The author, some years ago, covered much of the ground described in the movements and battles mentioned in the book with the exception of the battleground of Yellow Tavern.

As an ex-artilleryman, the author was struck by the lack of fictional works about the famed horse artillery of both the Union and Confederate Armies. There was nothing else to do but write such a book as ACTION FRONT!

BIBLIOGRAPHY

Battles and Leaders of the Civil War (Century, 1887). Thomas Yoseloff Reprint Edition, 1957. Volumes 1, 2, 3, and 4.
Photographic History of the Civil War, 1910. Thomas Yoseloff Reprint Edition, 1957. Volumes 2, 3, 4, 5, 8, and 10.
Official Records of the Union and Confederate Armies in the War of the Rebellion. Sound of the Guns, Fairfax Downey. David McKay Company, Inc., 1955, 1956.
Clash of Cavalry: The Battle of Brandy Station, Fairfax Downey. David McKay Company, Inc., 1959.
The Guns at Gettysburg, Fairfax Downey. David McKay Company, Inc., 1958.
Pickett's Charge, George R. Stewart. Houghton Mifflin Company, 1959.
The Great Invasion, Jacob Hoke. Thomas Yoseloff New Edition, 1959.
Lee's Lieutenants, Douglas Southall Freeman. Charles Scribner's Sons, 1944, Volume 3.
Horsemen, Blue and Gray, Pictures by Hirst Dillon Milhollen; text by James Ralph Johnson and Alfred Hoyt Bill. Oxford University Press, 1960.
The Story of the U.S. Cavalry, Major General John K. Herr and Edward S. Wallace. Little, Brown and Co., 1953.
Personal Memoirs of P. H. Sheridan, P. H. Sheridan. Charles L. Webster 8c Company, 1888.
The Battle of Gettysburg, W. C. Storrick. J. Horace McFarland Company, 1938.
Gettysburg, What They Did Here, L. W. Minnich. Tipton & Blocher, 1924.
A Stillness at Appomattox, Bruce Catton. Doubleday & Co., Inc., 1953.
This Hallowed Ground, Bruce Catton. Doubleday & Co., Inc., 1956.
Soldier Life in the Union and Confederate Armies, edited by Philip Van Doren Stern. Premier Books, Fawcett Publications, Inc., 1961.

Many others far too numerous to mention.

THE GRAY SEA RAIDERS

*Dedicated to my only son, BRIAN ALLEN SHIRREFFS,
in the hope that he will love the sea
as much as his father
and his Scottish ancestors
have loved it*

CHAPTER ONE
John Newland Maffitt

A damp breeze swept across Wilmington, North Carolina, rustling the trees and carrying with it a faint tang of salt sea air from the Atlantic Ocean miles to the east. It was very dark just before the rising of the new moon but the river front was stirring and humming with life. Across the Cape Fear River on the marshy flats near the Market Street Ferry the big steam cotton press rumbled steadily as it did practically twenty-four hours a day, packing cotton as tightly as possible in bales so that the Confederacy's "white gold" could be stowed into the holds and on the decks of the fast, slim-hulled blockade-runners that lined the wharves of Wilmington.

The sky-colored vessels would slip down the Cape Fear River, wait for their chance to run the alert Federal naval blockade at the river mouth, then head out to sea for the "Nassau Track." At Nassau in the Bahamas the cotton would be unloaded, and in exchange the runners would take on cargoes of artillery pieces, ammunition, saltpeter, lead, musket caps, rifles, pistols, blankets, food stores, quinine and other medicaments, as well as French perfume and bonnets, Belgian lace and Irish linen, for business in fripperies was better than in munitions. The trade was good; the Confederate armies were winning victories; and the rest of the world's great powers, for reasons of their own, seemed to favor the South over the North in the fratricidal struggle just entering its second year in May of 1862.

But to Acting Midshipman Clinton Wallace, Confederate States Navy, the world was not too bright nor inviting that damp May night as he walked through the muddy alleyways toward the river front. The Confederate armies were winning glory, while the Confederate Navy was hardly more than a name on official papers, consisting principally of a handful of men and officers, a few obsolete sailing ships, a few beat-up revenue cutters, some homemade ironclads of dubious value, and the rest of the "fleet" was made up of river double-enders, ferryboats, barges and leaking tugs, armed with a few field artillery pieces. Clint Wallace *knew* he had picked the wrong service.

Clint was tired, fed up, and far from home. He had lost his ship at the Naval Battle of New Orleans, which had taken place just eight days before. His commander had died of his wounds, and the gallant *McRae* lay at the bottom of the muddy Mississippi; her smoke-blackened and shot-torn ensign was probably hanging in the wardroom of some Yankee man-of-war riding easily to anchor in front of New Orleans, the Crescent City, holding that proud place in subjection beneath the muzzles of great guns.

Clint staggered a little in his weariness. He had escaped from New Orleans with a handwritten order releasing him from further service there, had managed to get aboard a creaking, dilapidated train heading eastward at the strictly enforced ten-miles-per-hour speed of all trains in the Confederacy, and had arrived in Wilmington just at dusk to report for duty to the naval establishment. It was then he had found out that they knew nothing about him, had no quarters or rations for him. They had advised him to head for Richmond and Naval Headquarters there for further orders.

He felt in his pockets again, hoping to find at least a small coin. His new gray "reefer" uniform was a ruin. Soaked in battle smoke and river water and later in sweat and train smoke and dust, it was hardly imposing enough for him to bluff his way into the meanest of all rooms for a night's rest.

Clint stopped at a corner and rested a hand on the guard of the short sword he had worn all the way from New Orleans. He might be able to sell it. But it was government property entrusted to him. He shook his head. He too was government property in a sense, but no one seemed much concerned about him.

There was always the river front and the slim-hulled runners, and if a seaman couldn't find help on a ship, then times had changed since Clint had sailed on his uncle's graceful *Creole Queen* to various Caribbean and West Indies ports. There was bitterness in Clint. He had no desire to serve on a runner, although he had heard that the government itself had entered the business through its agency of Fraser, Trenholm and Company, by borrowing six swift steamers and manning them with naval officers and crews to get in munitions and necessary military supplies with which to pursue the war. It had been the only way to get in sufficient quantities, for the private corporations, financed mostly by British interests, and in some cases Northern interests, were more interested in personal gain than in the winning or the losing of the war. It had been a bitter lesson to the government.

It was the intense darkness just before the rising of the moon, and there were few fights in the houses, for the hour was late. In the distance he could see the faint flickering light from the furnaces that heated the boilers for the steam press. The light danced against a small mountain of tightly packed bales, a veritable fortune in cotton. It also revealed movement in the narrow street just ahead of Clint—a cloaked figure, wearing a top hat at a rakish angle, twirling a heavy walking stick. The man was whistling "Lorena" as he paced steadily along.

Probably a gambler, thought Clint. The town was alive with them and with speculators and other parasites who preyed on the Confederacy. The smell of the river was stronger now, and he could see the graceful silhouette of a runner anchored in midstream, tugging at her moorings as though anxious to get to sea. It was the way Clint felt, too. He wanted a slanted deck beneath his feet and white wings high overhead and the sound of the sea breeze in the taut rigging.

He looked at the man again and was startled, for now he saw a quartet where there had been one man striding along. Then the whistling stopped, and the man turned quickly, raising his stick as the other three shadowy figures closed in on him. He leaped to one side and brought the cane down hard upon the head of the closest man. The man grunted and went down on one knee. The man in the cloak stepped in, thrust the cane like a rapier, and drove the shod tip against the throat of the second man. He gagged and dropped the club he had been carrying in his right hand. "Provost Guard!" cried out the cloaked man in a musical voice.

Clint ran forward. He had heard that the town was full of footpads and sneak thieves, drawn there by the flowing of gold into everyone's hands and pockets.

Now the three men were closing in slowly and deliberately, while the lone cloaked figure thrust and slashed with his stick, parrying short vicious club blows. Then the cane snapped and the man was driven down on one knee by a blow.

"Provost!" yelled the fallen man.

A gray-clad figure struck from behind. Clint had ripped his short sword from its sheath. He struck with the bell guard against the back of a head, driving a shoulder against another of the attackers. The third man slashed his club at Clint and caught him on top of his left shoulder. It was no time for niceties. Clint swung his blade and slashed viciously. The man screamed and fell heavily, rolling from beneath the feet of the fighters.

Clint went battling back to the wall of a warehouse. He was almost exhausted from his long journey and from lack of food. A blow crashed down on his left forearm and he winced with the savage pain of it. "Provost Guard!" he screamed.

He lunged and parried, slashed and thrust, hot and heavy, steel against wood and courage against weight and numbers. He poised himself and thrust hard, being rewarded with a shrill cry from the wounded man. He whirled, dropped the point to thrust again, and met nothing but air. A club hit him across the shoulder blades. He slipped on the slick ground and reeled against the wall.

"I'm with you, lad!" yelled the cloaked man. He was on his feet, pitching in with fists and feet, driving two of the footpads back by the sheer ferocity and brilliance of his attack.

Then suddenly the footpads were gone, pounding up the dark alleyway. A door opened and a flood of yellow light fell across Clint and the man he had rescued. Or had he been rescued himself?

"Are you all right out there?" called out a man from the house.

The cloaked man turned. "Aye, mate!" He turned and saluted Clint with the shattered stub of his cane. "Companion at arms!" he said sonorously, "I salute you! A fine fight! An epic! We repelled the boarders, sailor!"

Clint nodded wearily. "I hope you are all right, sir."

"Slightly ruffled, but sound between wind and water. But you, you've been hurt, son!"

Clint straightened. "I am Acting Midshipman Clinton Wallace, sir. Allow me to escort you safely to your quarters, Mister ..."

The man saluted again. "John Newland Maffitt, at your service, reefer!" he said, with a merry twinkle in his fine eyes.

The name was familiar somehow to Clint but he was too weary to think upon it. John Maffitt was of medium build and well knit, with a neatly trimmed imperial beard and bushy black hair shot with gray. But it was his deep-set lively eyes and smiling face that took Clint's fancy. Here was a man who had served most of his life outdoors. Perhaps a seaman at one time.

The nearby door closed, plunging the street into darkness again, but there was a faint, vague light in the east, predicting the rising of the moon.

"My quarters are at the Bailey Hotel," said Mister Maffitt, "but I was on the way to check the manifests of the *Nassau*. She is almost ready for sea. I suggest you accompany me, sir, to freshen up and have a steaming cup of ambrosia, to wit, the finest Brazilian coffee."

"Coffee?" said Clint faintly. *"Real* coffee?"

"The very best, my boy."

Clint flushed. "I'm an officer of the Confederate States Navy, sir," he said a little shortly.

The man smiled broadly. "I *am* sorry, sir. But will you accompany me, Acting Midshipman Wallace?"

"There may be other footpads on the street."

"No match for a pair of blades like us!"

Clint couldn't help but laugh. The man thrust out an arm, linked it through Clint's arm, and the two of them walked toward the river like old comrades. He had mentioned a ship, the *Nassau,* so he must be a blockade-runner, one of the Brotherhood. Probably a clerk or supercargo, if he was going to check the manifests. Clint couldn't help but feel a little distaste. Many of the runners had little use for the struggling Confederacy beyond the immense profits they could glean from her. The profits were fantastic, the risks legion, and the rewards magnificent. Cotton bought for six cents a pound in Wilmington could be sold for sixty cents a pound in Liverpool, or for a dollar a pound in New York, if, by some devious means, it could be gotten there.

Blockade-runner captains averaged five thousand dollars a month in gold; pilots two thousand per round trip; while ordinary seamen received one hundred dollars in gold plus another fifty dollar bonus for a successful roundabout trip between Wilmington and the Bahamas or the Bermudas. It was a well-known axiom that if a runner got through twice with merchandise and twice with cotton, the Yankees were welcome to her, for her owners could retire on the fortune she had made for them. The profits averaged two hundred per cent on some voyages. Human greed had taken precedence over patriotism. The runners were out for the profits and cared not a whit about bringing in materials so desperately needed by the Confederacy, which was already beginning to feel the strangling hold of the great Federal naval blockade.

"There she is," said Maffitt proudly. He gestured with the stub of his cane. "The *Nassau*."

She was moored to the sagging wharf, swaying gently with the motion of the river, a long, slim shape painted a neutral bluish white, with huge outsized paddle wheels and two towering, telescoping funnels. She had stubby masts, a curved turtle deck extending from her bows almost to the low superstructure. She had a curious humped appearance amidships, not only from the huge paddle boxes but also from the ranks and ranks of compressed cotton bales that seemed to occupy every free inch of space on the slim ocean racer.

"Clyde-built in Glasgow, Scotland," said Maffitt. "She can make fourteen knots on good anthracite. Few of them can keep up with her."

He ushered Clint aboard and guided him down a companionway lined with cotton bales to a tiny cubicle of a cabin lighted by an oil lamp hanging in gimbals. "Jim!" he cried out, "coffee for two here!"

"Aye, suh," a muffled voice answered from somewhere nearby.

Maffitt took off his faded, well-worn naval cloak and hung it up, almost tenderly. "You're a North Carolinian, Midshipman Wallace?" he asked over his shoulder.

"My mother is from Raleigh, North Carolina, and my father was from Florida, while I was raised in Mississippi and in Louisiana, sir."

Maffitt turned. "I am North Carolinian myself, having spent my early years in Fayetteville, although that is not my birthplace." He smiled mischievously. "I was born at sea, my birthplace being longitude 40 west and latitude 50 north, but of Irish descent. A sort of Irish-American merman."

A colored man brought in a tray with a coffeepot and cups. He looked at Clint's disreputable uniform. "Let me have that coat, suh, to bresh up a bit. No *naval* officer should have to look like that, beggin' your pardon, suh."

Maffitt nodded as he poured the coffee.

Clint hesitated. "A Confederate naval officer must wear his uniform at all times. It isn't regulation to appear in public out of uniform."

"Sho!" said Jim in surprise. He glanced at Mister Maffitt. "That right, Lieutenant?"

Maffitt nodded.

Clint looked quickly at him. That name was still in his mind. Maffitt...John Newland Maffitt. It should make some sense to him. "*Lieutenant* Maffitt, sir?" he said. "I thought you were the supercargo aboard this ship?"

Jim smiled and shook his head. "Lieutenant John Maffitt, Confederate States Navy, commanding the government blockade-runner *Nassau!*"

Clint flushed deeply. Now he knew! John Newland Maffitt, the elusive ghost of the runners. The Rider of the Moon, who time and time again, by strategy or speed, had outwitted the Federal blockaders and had made a laughingstock of their blockade. Maffitt, of the old United States Navy, who had charted the coasts from Nantucket to the mouths of the Mississippi for fourteen years. No man knew the Atlantic or Gulf Coast better than he did!

Maffitt smiled. "Your coffee will get cold, Midshipman Wallace."

"Sir, I ..." Clint's voice trailed off. He remembered all too well his grandiloquent words. *"I'm an officer of the Confederate States Navy, sir. A Confederate naval officer must wear his uniform at all times. It isn't regulation to appear in public out of uniform."*

"Suh?" said Jim, holding out his hand for the coat.

Clint reached for the top buttons, and then remembered he had no shirt beneath the coat.

Maffitt sipped his coffee. "I wonder if midshipmen of these days wear shirts beneath their coats?" he said quietly.

Clint couldn't help but grin. "They do if they have them, sir."

They all laughed until the tears ran out of their eyes.

Later, as Maffitt showed him over the ship, Clint wondered why such a skilled naval officer as this had been assigned to such a duty instead of to a fighting ship.

Captain Maffitt seemed to read Clint's mind as they stood at the low rail and watched the moon rise slowly. "We haven't much of a navy, reefer," he said quietly. "A few decaying naval vessels and revenue cutters. A handful of ironclads being built. Odds and ends at best. The South has an abundancy of resources to the casual eye, but these cannot be used to build a navy. The timber is too soft and green; iron that has not yet been taken from the earth; no rolling mills for sheet metal; no ropewalks to make needed cordage; not one real builder of marine engines in the entire South; no powder factories; no generations of skilled seafaring men such as the New Englanders." He sighed.

"What can we do then, sir?"

Maffitt gripped the rail hard. "There is only one way to destroy the Federal naval blockade. A process of dilution, so to speak. Use fast steamers to destroy Yankee shipping, thus causing Northern vessels of war to be detached from blockading duty to run down the commerce destroyers."

"But we haven't any such vessels, sir."

Maffitt smiled mysteriously. "No," he said quietly, but it seemed almost like a probing question the way he said it.

"I'll have to find quarters, sir," said Clint. He could hardly keep his eyes open.

"You have no quarters? What is your duty?"

Clint explained his predicament. Maffitt took him by the arm. "There are cabins not being used aboard this ship. I'll take charge of you, reefer, until you know where you are to report."

"Probably to land duty somewhere with a naval battery, and there is nothing that can be done about it, sir."

Maffitt shrugged. "No," he said in the same tone he had used when Clint had said that the South had no fast commerce destroyers with which to attack Yankee high seas shipping.

Clint looked at him quickly and saw the same mysterious and elusive glint in the merry eyes of the officer. Maffitt showed him the way to a tiny but comfortable cabin. "Good night, reefer," he said.

"Good night, sir."

"Don't worry about the future, reefer."

"I'll try not to, sir."

The door closed behind the officer, and Clint looked up at the moonlit ceiling above him flickering with reflected light from the water. He had but vague orders, no money, no ship and a uniform that was hardly more than a covering for his nakedness, and he wasn't supposed to worry about it.

Still, there had almost been a silent message sent winging to him by John Newland Maffitt. He was on a ship. Not a line of battle craft of the Confederate States Navy, but still a government-owned vessel commanded by a naval officer. The easy motion of the slim-hulled craft began to lull him to sleep, and in a little while he forgot his sense of being tired, fed up, and far from home.

CHAPTER TWO
Running the Blockade

The soft rain pattered down upon Wilmington and the ranked cotton bales. It glistened on the painted sides and the wooden decks of the blockade-runners. It dimpled the surface of the Cape Fear River and slanted down through the trees. It was welcomed by the local farmers and by the blockade-runners, for the rain would bring mist, and in mist they could more easily evade the Federal watchdogs off New Inlet or the Western Bar Channel.

But the same rain brought nothing but gloom to Acting Midshipman Clinton Wallace. The *Nassau* still tugged restlessly at her moorings as she had been doing in the two days since Clint had been aboard her waiting for new orders. He had pitched in to help wherever he could, and had been put to work making forms and filling them out, while sitting in the cramped supercargo's office on the wharf.

Clint fiddled with his pen. He had learned plenty about smiling John Maffitt in the past few days. Born at sea of Irish parentage as the officer had so proudly stated, he had spent his earlier years in North Carolina and had formed a permanent attachment to that state. He had been appointed midshipman at the age of thirteen aboard the old *Saint Louis,* and later, at fifteen years of age, he had been assigned to the United States Ship *Constitution,* "Old Ironsides," for duty in the Mediterranean. In 1842, at his own request, he had been assigned to the Coast Survey and had served there for fourteen years. Hydrography had fascinated the man. Charleston Harbor had a Maffitt Channel named after him. For some years he had been billeted at Smithville at the mouth of the Cape Fear River.

Maffitt had later served aboard vessels chasing slavers, and just before the present war, while the Southern States were seceding one by one, he had been in command of the United States Ship *Crusader.* While at anchor in Mobile Bay, he had been approached by the Mobile Defense Committee to surrender the vessel for the use of the navy of Alabama. But John Maffitt, despite his Southern sympathies, was a man of trust and honor. He had said, "My vessel belongs to the United States. I'll shoot the first man that touches her!"

He had returned the vessel to New York and then had resigned at the start of hostilities to offer his sword to the Confederacy. Stephen Russell Mallory, Confederate Secretary of the Navy, had commissioned Maffitt a lieutenant. He had served with Commodore Tattnall's "battle fleet" at Savannah, Georgia, a scarecrow collection of a side-wheel steamer with two guns, three old tugs, and a decaying cattle barge mounting ten guns in all. Later he had served as naval aide to General Robert E. Lee, before taking command of the first of the Confederate Government blockade-runners, the swift *Cecile,* which had become well known for its successful runs, through the skill and daring of John Maffitt.

The rain sluiced down. Clint set to work on another form. There were rumors of ironclads of great power being built, and perhaps he could be assigned to one of them, although his heart was set on going to sea. He had served as cabin boy and later as apprentice seaman and ordinary aboard his uncle's fast steamer *Creole Queen*. He knew the Gulf ports and other places on the fast runs. Pensacola and Havana; Pensacola and New Orleans; New Orleans and Matamoras. His greatest pleasure had been when the *Creole Queen,* spreading the white wings of her barkentine rig, had sped before the wind without using her paddle wheels. The war had started, and he had lied about his age and had joined the little *McRae* on the Mississippi just some months before the fatal Battle of New Orleans.

The *McRae,* under command of Lieutenant Thomas B. Huger, had been waiting upstream of Confederate forts St. Phillip and Jackson, when the Yankees had attempted to force the passage of the Mississippi. In the hard fighting that had followed the *McRae* had been almost battered to pieces, her armament blasted from their carriages, her commander mortally wounded. A young Mississippian, Lieutenant Charles W. "Savez" Read, had promised Lieutenant Huger he would not lower the Confederate flag, and when Admiral Farragut had asked why the helpless vessel's flag was still flying he had been told why, and he had allowed it to proceed upstream to New Orleans, where she had gone to the bottom just as the last of her wounded had been removed. But "Savez" Read had escaped to the shore, and with him had been a powder-blackened boy by the name of Clinton Wallace. It had been Lieutenant Read who had written out Clint's orders to report to the nearest naval establishment for orders and reassignment.

"Bah!" said Clint. He hurled the pen at the ink-splattered desk and watched it quiver as the point struck into the wood. Better it would have been if he had stayed with the Confederate forces on the Mississippi to fight the Yankees from a cattle barge than to be sitting in a damp wharf office in Wilmington doing a clerk's monotonous work.

"Acting Midshipman Wallace?" a quiet voice asked.

Clint was startled. He looked toward the door. A one-armed soldier stood there at hand salute, with a fold of paper thrust through the upper part of his wet coat. "Yes," he said.

"I'm from the office of the military telegraph. This message is for you."

"For *me?*"

There was a sarcastic glint in the veteran's eyes. "Yes, *suh.*" It was hard for a nineteen-year-old battle veteran of a North Carolina fighting regiment to say "suh" to a wet-nosed sixteen-year-old naval "reefer." "From Richmond, *suh.*"

Clint took the paper and unfolded it. He read it three times before the whole thing made any sense. It was a message from Naval Headquarters at Richmond, Virginia, stating that Acting Midshipman Clinton Wallace, Confederate States Navy, at the request of Lieutenant John N. Maffitt, had been assigned aboard the Confederate Government Vessel *Nassau,* under command of Lieutenant John N. Maffitt, Confederate States Navy, for duty as required aboard that vessel, pursuant to the further orders of the Confederate States Naval Headquarters at Richmond, Virginia.

It wasn't exactly what he had wanted but it was better than sitting in Wilmington like a stray cat wondering where he would end up next. At least he would be at sea!

"Any reply, *suh?*"

Clint shook his head.

"Nothing, *suh?* Nothin' at all?"

Clint grinned. "One word, soldier."

"Yes, suh?"

"Yaaaaaah!" The thrilling rebel yell seemed to slam back and forth in the narrow confines of the office.

The soldier smiled wistfully. "Orders for active duty?"

Clint nodded.

His eyes dropped to the empty gray sleeve, and then the soldier saluted and was gone into the slanting rain.

Clint grabbed his hat and ran to the door. He stopped to look through the rain toward the graceful *Nassau,* then started for the gangplank.

"In *civilian* clothing, reefer," said someone close at hand.

Clint turned to look at the smiling face of John Maffitt. "Aye, aye, sir! And, sir?"

"Yes?"

"Thanks!"

Maffitt nodded. He tilted his hat lower over his eyes. "I wonder if you'll thank me for the duty some months from now."

"What does the lieutenant mean, sir?"

Maffitt shrugged. "I don't really know. Get out of that uniform. Get some civilian clothing. Tell no one who you are or where you're going."

"When do we leave, sir?"

Maffitt twirled his new walking stick. "As soon as you get aboard, reefer. Jump and make it so!" He tapped the brim of his top hat with his stick and walked quickly toward his ship. Then he turned, reached inside his coat, and held out some bills to Clint. "Here," he said. "You can repay me out of your first prize money."

"Yes, sir!"

Clint watched Maffitt board the loaded *Nassau,* now low in the water with her cargo of "white gold." "Prize money?" he said in a puzzled tone. There was no prize money on runners, and officers and men aboard her did not share in the profits as the crews of the commercial runners did. Clint himself got forty dollars a month Confederate, when and if he got it.

"Prize money?" he said again as he headed for a clothing store. Maybe it had been a slip of Maffitt's tongue. Maybe...

The wind had shifted during the twenty-eight-mile run from Wilmington to the mouth of the Cape Fear River, and the rain was hardly a spit in the misty air. A crewman on the wet deck of the *Nassau* could hardly make out the rail on the opposite side of the narrow hull. There was a feeling of protection in the drifting, nebulous mist, but every man-jack aboard knew it was a betraying quality, for the slightest sound seemed to be carried a great distance.

The crewmen padded about in soft slippers or bare feet, and wore white duck uniforms for minimum visibility once they crossed the bar into the open sea. There wasn't a pin point of light to be seen aboard the runner. The only lights were in the already stifling stokehold and engine room, and the binnacle light which had been shielded by a large cone of thick paper, with only a narrow slot-like opening for the helmsman to peer through to see the compass. Tarpaulins covered every opening and sealed off the engine room, and as the stokers heaved in good anthracite to get up steam, the heat became almost intolerable below decks.

The lookouts stood at their stations, waiting for the *Nassau* to start her run. Theirs was one of the most important jobs aboard the runner, for failure to see a blockader in time would possibly be failure for the *Nassau,* which in turn meant the loss of thousands of dollars' worth of ship and cargo, while the officers and pilots would be shipped away to Fort Warren, and there wasn't any exchange for pilots. A lookout was paid a dollar for every sail he sighted, but fined five dollars if a deck hand saw it first.

Steady-nerved seamen uncoiled and recoiled their lead fines to make sure they payed out freely. Their stations were on each quarter of the ship to give correct bottom soundings, and the difference of a few feet, aye, even a few inches given by an excited or careless leadsman might take the thin metal bottom clean off the

Nassau, in the same manner as a lid being peeled from a tin of sardines.

The muted roaring of the surf came through the mist, like the moaning of a great giant in pain. Somewhere off there in the drifting mist the Yankees had a triple cordon of ships waiting like vultures for incoming and outgoing runners. Small-boat patrols laden with armed seamen plugged the gaps between the blockade ships.

There were two outlets to the sea from the Cape Fear River: the Eastern or New Inlet, and the Western Bar, or main channel. Barely six miles separated these two channels, and between them was Smith's Island, a delta that steadily tapered south until it rose to the high dune known to coast-wise seamen as Cape Fear. Beyond the cape, Frying Pan Shoals creamed breakers for another ten miles. To a runner lying off Smithville, a village on the river's west bank, equidistant from either bar, the offshore blockading squadrons were plainly visible.

The Yankees blocked both entrances, and their blockading squadron numbered about thirty vessels of various types. One division patrolled the Eastern Inlet and the other the Western Bar Channel. They had only to keep out of range of the guns of powerful Fort Fisher, on the great tongue of land north of New Inlet, known rather incongruously for the times as Federal Point. Fisher was big and Fisher was dangerous, a low-lying monster of sandbags, pine and palmetto logs, armed with heavy guns and trained artillerymen. There were twenty-four big guns in the fortifications, and there were British Whitworth guns that could be moved about, and those breechloaders could hurl a shell five miles at a $25°$ elevation.

Clint Wallace had been drafted as an extra lookout, and he stood atop the port paddle box, trying to pierce the cottony mist with his eyes. A seaman stood beside the rail just below him. "How far out are the Yankee ships?" asked Clint in a low voice.

The man laughed softly. "Practically just beyond the surf. They cruise offshore in three crescent lines, one beyond the other, during the day. At night they close in and anchor, with shotted guns and crews lying beside them just waiting for fools like us."

"What are the odds of getting through?"

The seaman shrugged. "They say it's a one-in-four chance during the day and eight-to-one at night. Maffitt knows his business though. There ain't a better man in the business."

The tug of the current and the shifting of the wind had moved the runner a little. She had a full head of steam by now.

"High water soon," said the seaman. "Plenty of mist."

"Makes it easier, eh?"

The man looked up at Clint. "The shoals are always there as well as the Yankees. It's a cat-and-mouse game and it's played for keeps. Some of them Yankees out there will make fortunes in prize money before this war is over, one way or another."

Prize money! There it was again. The elusive words of John Maffitt came back to Clint. They couldn't get prize money on a runner.

The thought was driven to the winds by the quiet commands that came from the bridge. Smoke drifted from the twin funnels and the tang of anthracite filled the misty air. The anchor was hove up short, then catted, and the paddle wheels began to turn slowly, making a yeasty foam alongside the slim hull of the runner. The faint coughing of the exhausts started and the *Nassau* began to come to life.

Dim blue lights showed from ashore as the runner met a stronger play of the dark waters and her slender hull seemed to twist and turn like an eel, while a faint rushing noise came from beneath her keel, the sound of the sand bottom sucking at the runner. The wind had shifted again, tattering the mist, making grotesque shapes of it, and Clint peered through the tatters. Try as he could, he was not able to see any of the blockaders. The surf was roaring louder now, and it was matched by the steady, rhythmic beating of the great paddle wheels.

Then he saw something looming in the mist. A great dark hull and tall masts. A man-of-war for certain! He opened his mouth to make a report but one of the keen-eyed lookouts had already seen the craft. The runner altered her course and swayed back and forth, up and down, in a wild fashion as the stronger currents snatched at her speeding hull. A faint hail drifted through the mist.

Then the bottom of the hull hit hard and the runner rang and reverberated like a dropped tin pan. Clint's heart crept up into his throat as he saw a thrashing fine of surf so close that it seemed as though the runner would beach herself.

The wind moaned through the rigging and it seemed as though it had developed a voice. "What ship is that? Ahoy there! What ship is that? Heave to or we fire!" the harsh voice came through the misty night.

Something flashed, and in the bright orange-red glow Clint saw the black side of a warship illuminated by the light. Something whispered overhead. The runner shifted in its racing stride. It was then that Clint saw the second ship, dead ahead, looming up through the tatters of mist. "Heave to there!" The sentence was punctuated by the bursting of a Coston flare high overhead, followed by the crashing discharge of half a dozen guns.

It was too late to turn. The helmsman held his course. The *Nassau* shot alongside the Federal blockader and there was a scraping and tearing noise as the channels of the Yankee craft struck the paddle boxes of the runner. Clint stared with widening eyes right down onto the decks of the blockader and clearly saw the glistening wet broadside guns, with their yawning muzzles not more than a yard or two from the thin metal plating of the *Nassau*. *Why didn't they fire?*

Then he knew why! The gun crews had run in their guns and were loading them swiftly with the precision of Yankee gunners, but a little too late to shatter the thin hull of the *Nassau*. A great yard on the blockader's foremast scraped the top from the *Nassau's* stubby foremast as she sped past, and then the runner veered to port in her course, cutting at a sharp angle across the bows of the Federal vessel, then straightened out again to sheer away from a possible port broadside.

But a forward pivot gun cracked flatly and the projectile seemed to pick its way delicately through the rigging of the runner, and the wind of its passing had the smell of death in it to Clint.

Light after light flared up bathing the angry blockaders in an eerie glow dotted by the staccato flashing of the guns, but all of the projectiles searched the air in vain over the *Nassau* as she shifted her racing course again, wallowed heavily in a ground swell, and shot into a patch of mist that folded itself about her graceful hull like an old and familiar cloak.

"It's all over now, lad," said a veteran seaman as he grinned up at Clint. "Close, eh?"

Clint tried to speak but his throat was too dry.

"Well soon be on the Nassau Track," said the seaman. "Five hundred and seventy miles of open seas, with Federal cruisers waiting for us to run the gantlet. They won't catch the *Nassau* though."

The runner steadied on a new course to meet the open seas, racking and rolling as she pitched and swung about.

"Start the pumps!" came the command from the bridge.

The runners had thin hulls, easily racked, and quite often the pumps were kept going a good part of the way to Nassau, or in turn, to Wilmington.

"How did you like it, reefer?" a quiet voice asked.

Clint turned to see Captain Maffitt draped in his old naval cloak. "A little close, wasn't it, sir?"

"Aye."

Then somehow Clint knew that John Maffitt had taken the calculated risks so necessary in his dangerous profession. He had handled his fast ship like a toy between the Federal lines. He had known that the ship with which they had almost collided had fired her starboard broadside, and that was why he had shaved past her, then driven straight ahead to avoid the port battery, chancing the risk of a hit from the bow pivot gun.

"Those last shells of the Yankees were almighty close," said Clint at last.

"But high, reefer."

"I thought the Yankees were better gunners than that, sir."

"There are none better," said Maffitt quietly as he looked astern through the tattered mist. "But you see, reefer, those Coston flares and Drummond lights of the Federals radiated the mist so that the *Nassau* seemed higher than she really is. An optical illusion, so to speak. That is why they fired high."

Clint looked at the smiling, assured naval officer beside him, and knew now why he was one of the best in the business. The runners were unarmed and could not fire back if they had been armed, for to do so would be to lay themselves open to charges of piracy. There are many men who are brave under enemy fire if they can fire back. It takes the coolest men of all to do their duty under fire when they cannot fire back. This eventful night would come back to Clint Wallace one day, in a different place and under different circumstances.

The *Nassau* rolled heavily and a graybeard of a wave rose alongside of her, close enough for Maffitt to reach out a hand and touch it before it vanished swiftly astern. He smiled and spoke in his musical voice:

"And I have loved thee, Ocean! and my joy Of youthful sports was on thy breast to be

Borne, like thy bubbles, onward: from a boy I wanton'd with thy breakers...

And laid my hand upon thy mane—as I do here."

He waved a graceful hand forward. "The Nassau Track, reefer!"

CHAPTER THREE

Nassau and the Mystery Ship "Oreto"

Nassau, on New Providence Island in the Bahamas group, was like a vivid dream come true to Acting Midshipman Clinton Wallace, as he walked beside Lieutenant Maffitt toward the Royal Victoria Hotel, while a colored boy carried their bags behind them. The wide blue sky and the warm air, coupled with the soft wind, was quite a contrast to the days at sea aboard the wallowing *Nassau*.

It was the sea about the islands that fascinated Clint. He had never seen such clear water, shimmering and transparent, brilliantly crystalline and shot with incredible shades of green and blue. As the *Nassau* had come slowly toward the promised land, it had been almost impossible to tell where the water ended and the land began.

John Maffitt had said little to Clint other than that they would not return aboard the *Nassau* for the return trip to Wilmington, or anywhere else for that matter. They were still in civilian clothing, although Clint's faded uniform was in the slim bag carried by the colored boy.

Clint looked about at the narrow streets, brilliant in the clear sunshine, and at the white and pastel buildings with the ever-present hibiscus blooming profusely. The streets were filled with swaggering seamen from the runners, some of them with gold earrings in their ears and brilliant scarfs about their necks. Many of them were English, Scots, and Irish, the well-known Liverpool "Packet Rats," who had sailed the fast ships between Liverpool and New York or Boston until the high pay and ample rewards of blockade-running had drawn them like magnets to Nassau.

There was a crowd of shrieking colored boys blocking the street ahead of them. On a hotel balcony sat several men with canvas bags on their laps into which they dipped their hands at regular intervals and then cast out handfuls of bright shillings that reflected the sunlight as these fell to the street, while the boys snatched at them and fought over them.

Maffitt reached up with his cane and shoved back his hat. "Look at them," he said quietly. "Rich as Croesus today and as poor as Job's turkey tomorrow."

"Runners, sir?"

"Aye. Some of them trash, who couldn't keep a command in the old days, and now they make fortunes with each trip, hauling in laces, perfumes, silks and satins, while the Confederacy is hard put because of lack of weapons and ammunition."

They worked their way through the crowd to the hotel. It was a crowded and exciting place, filled with seamen, British naval and army officers, Confederate officers in uniform, and even a Union officer or two in their blue uniforms, but the latter didn't seem too welcome in the gathering, and Maffitt nodded when Clint mentioned it. "Aye, they have every right to be here, but the people are against them. The working people of the great mills in England are starving because of lack of cotton for their looms, and they blame the Yankees for the trouble. The Confederacy has many friends in England, reefer." He winked as he said the last. "Many friends."

It was evening when Clint returned to the room he

shared with his commanding officer. Lieutenant Maffitt was standing at the window with a paper in his hand, deep in thought. He nodded as Clint came into the room.

"Bad news, sir?" asked Clint.

The officer shook his head. "Quite the contrary. We have a new ship, reefer."

"Sir?"

Maffitt smiled. "The *Oreto*. She lies at anchor in Cochrane's Anchorage nine miles east of here, and has been there a week awaiting us."

"Another blockade-runner, sir?"

Maffitt shook his head. "No, reefer." He smiled again. "We'll go to see her tomorrow. How did you like Nassau?"

"An incredible place, sir."

"I knew you'd like to look around."

"Thanks, sir." Clint shook his head. "It doesn't seem possible, but I actually saw crates, boxes, and bales plainly addressed to the Confederate States Government being carted through the streets to the wharves from British warehouses. I even saw some drays loading cases of rifles from a private home. The wharves are packed with runners, three abreast, unloading cotton or taking aboard rifles, artillery pieces, food supplies, and many other items we need so badly at home."

"I said we had many friends in England," said Maffitt. "Some of the runners are even captained by Royal Navy officers on special leave from their duties on Her Majesty's ships."

"But the United States Government! Don't they protest?"

"Aye, they do, but precious little good it is doing them now. However, if they get rough, things might turn out differently."

"Tell me more about the *Oreto,* sir."

"Not now. We'll dine in style this evening. You shall

see the *Oreto* soon enough, and then you can form your own opinion of her."

"Thank you, sir." Clint watched his commanding officer get ready for dinner. It was all so mysterious. The *Oreto!* An odd name, perhaps of Italian or Spanish origin. It seemed to promise adventure to Acting Midshipman Clinton Wallace. At least he hoped it did!

"I must inform Adderly and Company, to whom the *Oreto* is consigned, that, as a Southern officer, it is my duty to become custodian of the lone Confederate waif upon the waters until the pleasure of the Navy Department shall be expressed," said Maffitt softly, almost to himself.

Nothing more was vouchsafed Clint about his future ship that evening, but he did dine in a style to which he had never been accustomed, with a man whose wit and charm were even more pleasurable than the excellent seafood of the Royal Victoria Hotel.

She floated upon the clear, translucent waters like a graceful sea bird, and the instant Clint Wallace saw her he lost his seaman's heart to her. The *Oreto* was of about seven hundred tons burthen, almost two hundred feet long, three-masted and bark rigged, that is to say square-rigged on the fore and mainmasts and fore and aft rigged on the mizzenmast. Two slim funnels arose between the fore and mainmasts. Her cutwater was gracefully curved and her bowsprit and jib boom seemed to soar from her bows.

The small boat that carried Clint and Lieutenant Maffitt toward the anchored *Oreto* was manned by several colored sailors and skippered by a half-caste who spoke the purest King's English. He eyed the *Oreto*. "British built," he said casually, but with the tone of an expert.

"So?" said Maffitt softly.

"Aye, and not from her British colors either, sir. Her lines, her very rigging. I'd say ..." His voice trailed off.

"What is it?" asked Maffitt.

The man looked curiously at him. "I served in Her Majesty's Navy, sir. She is the very model of one of Her Majesty's gunboats!"

Clint looked at Lieutenant Maffitt but the man's face was expressionless to what the half-caste had said. In a moment, though, a new look came across it, the look of a man who has seen a ship and has instantly fallen in love with her.

They came alongside, watched curiously by members of the crew, and they were all British without doubt. Then, as Maffitt preceded Clint onto the deck he did a very curious thing. He saluted the quarter-deck, the act of a naval officer or seaman as he sets foot upon the deck of a man-of-war.

Maffitt disappeared below to consult with Master John Low and left Clint to his own devices. He walked back and forth on the decks and looked aloft, absorbing every detail of the fine new craft, for she was new, as new as a ship could be.

"Take a look below, matey," said a British tar as he flaked down a line. "She's a beauty alow and aloft."

He did not exaggerate. The *Oreto* was built of wood and had engines to deliver seven hundred horsepower, with a top speed of twelve knots, or so one of the engineers told Clint. "She can do better than that though," he said wisely.

Clint was inclined to agree. With steam and sail power she would be very fast.

"Her propeller can be drawn up into a well to eliminate drag when she is under sail alone," said the engineer. "Takes but fifteen minutes."

There were other fascinating mysteries about the ship. Her funnels were hinged, one to be lowered forward and the other aft. There were many specially built rooms and features in her. Rooms and features that did not belong aboard a peaceful merchant ship or even a blockade-runner. Clint's suspicions were more than confirmed when he noticed the gun ports cut into her stout bulwarks.

"How do you like her?" asked Lieutenant Maffitt when he came up on deck.

"Beautiful, sir."

"I'm glad you think so, reefer, for if all goes well, this will be the ship upon which you will serve under me for some time to come."

Clint stared at John Maffitt. The officer beckoned him to a deserted part of the deck. "In my official capacity as an officer of the Confederate States Navy I have been ordered by Secretary of the Navy Mallory to take command of this vessel at once and get her to sea quickly before the Royal Governor of the Bahamas becomes too interested in her. That is to say, her character and ultimate occupation. I have officially accepted her for the Confederate States Navy. Let us hope we can get the *Manassas* to sea before we are stopped by the involved red tape tangled between the Government of the United States, the colonial government here, and the Confederate States of America."

Clint was more than bewildered. She was the *Oreto,* and now his commanding officer had called her the *Manassas,* and was talking forcefully of taking her to sea as a vessel of the Confederate States Navy.

Maffitt seemed to read his mind. "She was known as the *Oreto* in England where she was built," he said. "I have renamed her the *Manassas* in honor of the great victory won by our land forces there."

"A fine choice, sir."

Maffitt nodded and the elusive, mysterious smile flitted over his face. "I thought so. Yet she might have another name before too long. It depends on the Fates."

The hull seemed to sway a little in the freshening wind. She was lively and would handle easily under sail and steam, or under either one. Clint was stunned, knowing that he was to serve aboard her. "But what is her character and ultimate occupation, sir?"

There were sailors lounging about on the deck, obviously interested in the conversation between the two Americans.

"Come with me to my cabin," said Lieutenant Maffitt. "There are too many ears to catch our conversation here."

Maffitt waved expansively as they entered the fine cabin. "Quite different from my old quarters aboard the *Cecile* and the *Nassau* with tiers of cotton usurping every spare inch of the deck and sometimes even my quarters, small as they were."

It was sumptuous and well furnished with the best of everything. The sunlight sparkled on the clear waters and reflected light into the airy cabin.

There was a rap at the door and a sturdy-looking man entered. Seaman was written all over him, and there was an unmistakable British cut to his jib.

Maffitt smiled. "Master John Low, meet Acting Midshipman Clinton Wallace who will serve with us aboard the *Manassas.*"

Low extended a hand and gripped Clint's warmly. "Glad to have you aboard, reefer." His accent was definitely English.

Maffitt sat down at his desk. "Mister Low is a Georgian, reefer."

Clint was startled. The man was English to the core.

"Born in England," said Low.

"And now a warrant officer in the Confederate States Navy," said Maffitt with a grin. He looked at Clint. "Trustworthy and prudent and a fine navigator. We shall have need of his services."

Low flushed a little. "Sir!"

"Take credit where it is due, Mister Low." Maffitt leaned back in his chair. "Midshipman Wallace is utterly confused about our *Oreto.*"

"Begging the Lieutenant's pardon, sir," said Clint quickly, "but this ship is the *Manassas.*"

Maffitt tugged at his beard. "So it is! Seems like I'm a little confused myself."

"What is it you would like to know?" asked Low of Clint.

Clint widened his eyes and threw out his hands. "Everything!"

"Small order," said Maffitt dryly.

Low paced back and forth. "She was built in Liverpool at the yards of William C. Miller and Sons, shipbuilders, while Fawcett, Preston and Company, engine builders, contracted for the whole ship. The Millers built hull, masts, rigging, and general sea equipment.

"They used a scale drawing of one of Her Majesty's newest and fastest gunboats as a base. The ship, labeled a 'merchant ship,' had been ordered by Mister James Dunwoody Bulloch for a firm in Palermo, Italy, and called the *Oreto.*"

"*Mister* James Dunwoody Bulloch happens to be *Commander* James Dunwoody Bulloch, Confederate States Navy, our secret naval emissary to Great Britain," interrupted Maffitt.

Low nodded. "It was tricky business, because Bulloch had been commissioned to purchase six steam-propelled vessels suitable for cruisers, with armament and munitions, for the express purpose of destroying Yankee highseas shipping."

Clint's heart flipped over. He looked at Maffitt. "Prize money!" he said.

Low laughed heartily along with Maffitt. "He learns quickly, does the lad," he said. He leaned against the bulkhead. "The *Oreto* was built of wood, because Bulloch figured iron would be too brittle to bear the recoil of heavy guns; then too, on an extended cruise, in faraway ports, it would be extremely difficult to find skilled ironworkers to repair her if need be, while wooden shipbuilders could be found all over the world."

All over the world! Visions began to dance through Clint's befuddled head.

"She is seven hundred tons, one hundred- and ninety-two-feet length, and her engines can deliver seven hundred horsepower, with an estimated top speed of twelve knots, or perhaps more."

"And she cost our government 45,000 pounds," said Maffitt dryly.

"She has a spare suit of sails and boatswain's stores for twelve months," said Low. "It is too involved to tell you now about how Bulloch managed to get her out of Liverpool without getting entangled in Britain's Foreign Enlistment Act. But he did it!"

"But the guns," said Clint. "She is unarmed."

"Spoken like a true navy man," said Maffitt. He glanced at Low. "Tell him, John."

"Blakelys, the finest made in England! Two rifled seven-inch pivot guns and eight smoothbore broadside 32-pound-ers. Two hundred British Enfield Navy Model rifles with issue cutlasses to match."

"But they can't be in the ship," said Clint.

"No," said Low. "We are to meet a ship at a secret rendezvous. The *Bahama,* a merchantman, cleared West Hartlepool in Scotland, laden with our guns and ammunition, outwardly bound for Hamburg in Germany."

"She'll never get there," said Maffitt with a smile.

Low paced back and forth. "In short the *Oreto,* or *Manassas,* as we call her now, is registered as an English ship, in the name of an Englishman, first commanded by a Scot, Captain James Duguid, then turned over to another Englishman, a citizen of Georgia, myself namely, for delivery to Henry Adderly and Company, the Nassau branch of Fraser, Trenholm and Company, which you might know is none other than the secret fiscal agency of the Confederate States of America.

"She has a regular British official number, and her tonnage is marked upon the combing of her main hatch, under the direction of the Board of Trade, which, up until this time, makes her perfectly secure against capture by Yankee men-of-war, or interference with her, until an attempt is made to arm her, or to change the flag."

"Which, under the circumstances, can only be effected at sea," said Lieutenant Maffitt.

"Then she is a commerce destroyer in disguise," said Clint excitedly.

"Precisely," said Maffitt. "Remember our first meeting? Our talk aboard the *Nassau* that night?"

"Yes, sir. The Lieutenant said that there was only one way to destroy the Federal naval blockade. A process of dilution. Using fast steamers to destroy Yankee shipping, thus causing Northern vessels of war to be detached from blockading duty to run down the commerce destroyers."

"Yes," said Maffitt quietly. He stood up and walked to the center of the cabin. "You are now standing in the captain's cabin of such a vessel, reefer."

The impact of his commanding officer's words helped to clear up the confusion in his teeming mind.

Maffitt's face was serious now. "We will stay here in the Bahamas until such time as we can get together officers and crew, arrange a rendezvous with the *Bahama,* or any other that can bring us our guns and munitions. After that, God willing, we shall raise the Confederate ensign and attack enemy shipping whenever and wherever we can find it. *We shall seek out and destroy!*"

"Hear, hear," said Low politely.

"But the Yankees, sir," said Clint. "Will they not suspect what we are up to? They have fast screw steamers, heavily armed, that can seek *us* out and destroy us."

"They haven't found us yet," said Maffitt.

Low was now standing at one of the stern ports. He spoke over his shoulder. "No. Look out to sea, sir."

Maffitt and Clint walked to portholes and looked out to sea, beyond a low coral islet dotted with bent palms. Beyond the islet, etched against the clear sky and the brilliant sea, was a black-hulled vessel moving slowly across its lovely backdrop. Her sails were as white as snow, and her whole shape and rigging had an inordinately neat and trim appearance. The United States flag fluttered in the easy wind, and a long pennant flew from the mainmast.

"Man-o'-war," said Low.

"Yankee man-o'-war," said Maffitt softly. He reached for a brass telescope and drew it out, resting it on the edge of the port. He studied the trim craft for a long time.

"She's coming about," said Low. He shook his head in admiration. "Like a machine!"

Maffitt nodded as he replaced the telescope in its rack. "I think she is the *Adirondack,* gentlemen."

"Can she come in after us?" asked Clint.

"Not in these waters," said Low, "but she can wait out there for us until we do try to get out."

"Maybe she'll leave before then," said Clint.

Maffitt laughed dryly. "Not her. She's a Yankee bulldog. Never fear, she, or other Yankee men-o'-war will be waiting for us the day we weigh anchor and head for sea."

A cold feeling crept over Clint as he watched the *Adirondack* come about easily. Her sails filled and she bore off on her new course. Back and forth she would prowl like a cat watching for an elusive mouse until her time came.

"Get acquainted with your ship," said Lieutenant Maffitt to Clint. "One thing: Everything you have heard in this cabin is of the strictest confidence. The day will come when we can proclaim our mission to the world and fly the flag of our newborn republic at the peak. Until that time we must observe secrecy."

"When will that be, sir?" asked Clint.

"Some weeks," said the officer quietly. "It will not be easy to wait, but as officers of the Confederate States Navy we must do our duty, no matter how tedious it may be. Be patient, reefer. Our day will come!"

Clint made his way to. the deck. The *Manassas, ex-Oreto,* swayed a little in the breeze, as though anxious herself to get to sea. Some weeks, *Manassas,* thought Clint. No time at all. Your day will come!

The ship seemed to bow and dip a little in response.

CHAPTER FOUR
The Confederate States Ship "Florida"

The burning August sun beat down upon the anchored *Manassas,* bubbling the pitch in her deck seams and making the deck so hot that the veteran jack-tars, with their horny-soled bare feet could hardly stand the touch of the teak planking. There was no breeze and the ship seemed listless in the hot air. Heat waves shimmered and danced from the brilliant white and pastel buildings of Nassau. The only activity was at the wharves, where the slim blockade-runners were either discharging cotton or picking up their valuable cargoes to run into Savannah, Charleston, or Wilmington.

Beyond the *Manassas* was the trim *Greyhound,* of Her Majesty's Royal Navy, at anchor, with the *Manassas* under her guns, while beyond the *Greyhound* was the British gunboat *Petrel,* getting ready for sea. There were other men-of-war in sight too. They were under way, cruising slowly back and forth with their snow-white sails reflecting the intense sunlight. The United States Ships *Adirondack* and *R. R. Cuyler* were there. Still waiting, as Lieutenant Maffitt had said they would. There were other Yankee men-of-war prowling about the Bahamas and particularly off Nassau. Ten of them it was said, enough to blow the *Manassas* into fine matchwood if she dared poke her pretty nose out of Nassau Harbor.

Clinton Wallace, Acting Midshipman, Confederate States Navy, and acting officer of the deck aboard the *Manassas* in the absence of her other officers, lounged on the quarter-deck beneath the awning, watching the two Yankees move back and forth like picture ships upon a painted ocean. "A few weeks," he said sourly. It had been about three months since he had first boarded the *Manassas*. Since that time the graceful craft had never been out of sight of land. Three more officers had joined her, though. Lieutenant John M. Stribling, who had served on the Confederate raider *Sumter* under the redoubtable Raphael Semmes, and who had been on his way home to South Carolina, had offered his services to Lieutenant Maffitt and had been accepted. Then there was Lieutenant J. Laurens Read, Maffitt's stepson, and Midshipman Sinclair, who had had little experience at sea but seemed able and willing.

The *Bahama* had indeed showed up with the guns for the *Manassas* and had been promptly seized by a British naval ship as a lawful prize for infringement of the Queen's neutrality proclamation, but the Crown's Attorney had promptly released her. Two days later she had been seized again and just as promptly released.

The *Manassas, ex-Oreto,* had become a storm center. The American Consul at Nassau, Samuel Whiting, fought tooth and nail against any thought of the colonial government allowing the vessel to leave the harbor. The ship had been libeled and hauled before the Queen's Prize Court for possible seizure as a violator of the Foreign Enlistment Act. Maffitt had not shown his hand as yet. Officers of H.M.S. *Greyhound* had inspected the ship and had testified what was quite manifest, that she was in all respects quite adaptable to war purposes, although unarmed and weaponless. In their professional opinion she could be equipped for battle in twenty-four hours. The Chief Justice had refused to condemn her for the prize court and had ordered her released, to the cheers of the people in the packed courtroom. Consul Whiting had said bitterly, "A person landing at Nassau, ignorant of the facts, would certainly think this was England's war!"

Maffitt himself had never ceased working. Seamen, engineers, and firemen were hard to find. As late as August 2, 1862, the fate of the craft was still in doubt. There had been times when Clint and the other officers had been forced to leave her and stay in a hotel. But strangely enough, their presence on board at times had never been questioned as it would have been by a nation anxious to prove both its friendship and its neutrality to the United States.

The sun was at its zenith. From ships all over the busy, crowded harbor eight bells was struck. A small boat drifted alongside the *Manassas* and a young seaman skipped nimbly aboard, saluted the quarter-deck, then hurried to Clint. He saluted again and handed Clint a fold of paper.

Clint opened it and scanned it quickly. It was from John Maffitt. The *Manassas* was free to go when and where she pleased, as far as the Queen's Prize Court and the Crown Attorney were concerned. Clint's heart leaped.

"Any answer, sir?" asked the seaman.

"None...wait a minute! Just say to Captain Maffitt that the falcon is free and the hood stripped from her eyes."

"Yes, sir. The captain will be aboard at eight bells this afternoon, sir."

Clint watched the boat return to shore. They had hardly enough men aboard the *Manassas* to take her to sea — maybe a score of seamen and engineers, most of them dredged up from the water front and representing three or four nationalities, mostly British. Hardly enough to work ship, let alone handle a gun battery. But they were going to sea!

The captain was as good as his word. Just as eight bells struck that afternoon he came up the side of the ship, saluted the quarter-deck, and took over command of the ship from Lieutenant Stribling who had preceded him aboard. There was little for Captain Maffitt to do to get ready for sea. He had been ready for sea for many weeks.

Maffitt stood on his quarter-deck and looked at his officers, still clad in civilian clothing. "The Sovereign Queen's Court of the Bahamas has released us, gentlemen. Our destination is St. John's, or any Confederate port. Due to secrecy I am not listed as captain. My stepson Lieutenant J. Laurens Read shall have that honor."

The officers looked at each other with wide grins splitting their tanned faces.

Maffitt unfolded an official-looking paper. "These are our sea orders from the Secretary of the Navy. I quote: 'You will cruise at discretion, the department being unwilling to circumscribe your movements in this regard by specific instructions. Should your judgment at any time hesitate in seeking the solution of any doubt on that point, it may be guided by the reflection that you are to do the enemy's commerce the greatest injury in the shortest time. The strictest regards for the rights of neutrals cannot be too sedulously observed, nor should an opportunity be lost of cultivating friendly relations with their naval and merchant service, and placing the true character of the contest in which we are engaged in its proper light.'"

As the officer's voice died away, Lieutenant Stribling touched his cap and then pointed beyond the commanding officer. "Look, sir!" he said tensely.

The officers stared toward the mouth of the anchorage. A trim and fast sloop of war was moving swiftly toward them with a fine bone of foam in her teeth, every sail drawing nicely and a whisker of smoke drifting from her funnel. She was heading directly toward the anchored *Manassas*.

"The U.S.S. *R. R. Cuyler*," said Maffitt quietly.

The sloop was moving faster now.

"Her gun ports open and her guns run out," said Stribling.

"She means business," said Laurens Read.

"In here?" asked Master Low.

"She's a Yankee," said Maffitt.

But another vessel was closing in swiftly, too, the British gunboat *Petrel*, and her guns were also run out. But she was quite a distance from the two American vessels.

The *R. R. Cuyler* came on, footing nicely, a beautiful and dangerous-looking machine of war.

"She means to ram us!" said Sinclair excitedly.

"Or blow us out of the water!" said Low.

Maffitt shifted a little. "There is nothing we can do, gentlemen, except stand here like officers and gentlemen and smile like crocodiles. Come on now! Smile!"

It wasn't easy to smile. Not with that deadly craft driving down on them at a fast clip.

"Stand by to come about!" the command came from the quarter-deck of the *R. R. Cuyler*.

Dangerously close as she was to the *Manassas*, the Confederate officers could not help but admire the way the Federal craft came about, only to veer close to the *Manassas* again until it seemed as though she would cut the would-be raider in half.

"Which shall it be?" asked Maffitt thoughtfully, "her guns or her cutwater tearing us to pieces?"

They could hear the crisp commands as the fast sloop of war was maneuvered with hairlike precision. Closer and closer.

"*Smile*," said John Maffitt.

There wasn't anything else they could do.

Now the British *Petrel,* as trim and as well-handled a craft as the *R. R. Cuyler,* maneuvered close to the speeding Federal craft. "Ahoy there!" came a hail from the commanding officer of the British ship. "What are you up to, sir?"

There was some indistinguishable reply from the quarter-deck of the *R. R. Cuyler,* while the vessel came about again to the crackling of sails and the slapping of lines in the freshening breeze.

But the Britisher wasn't fooling. "These are neutral waters, sir! I cannot permit you to maneuver in here with guns run out. Nor can I allow you to endanger other peaceful craft."

"That's good," said Laurens Read with a wide grin.

Now the Yankee hesitated, beating back and forth.

"Leave this anchorage at once, sir!" roared the angry Britisher.

The Yankee didn't want to go. The eagle wanted to fight but the bulldog was in his way. Oh, how that Yankee hated to leave!

The *R. R. Cuyler* came about once more and shot past the starboard side of the anchored *Manassas,* and a chin-whiskered old gunner patted the fat breech of his forward pivot gun. "Our day will come, you rebels!" he promised. The sloop sped past and the rebel officers could see right down into the yawning black muzzles of the broadside guns one by one until the Federal craft was past them, surging a little in the swell, heading for the open sea. She would be waiting out there.

Maffitt's face relaxed from its set beaming smile. "I couldn't have kept it up much longer. Mister Stribling, you will go ashore at once, sir! The *Manassas* sails about midnight."

"There will be a bright moon, sir," said Clint.

"We can't stay here, Mister Wallace!"

And so it was. At midnight under a full moon the

Manassas went to sea for the first time under the command of her famous skipper, John Newland Maffitt.

It was then that the officers and crew of the raider knew what kind of man commanded the swift vessel. She slipped from the harbor under steam power, then turned sharply so as to get the shadow of the land, while the Federal craft could be plainly seen at sea, hovering back and forth, patiently waiting for their prey.

"There is a steamer aft of us, sir," said Laurens Read.

Maffitt lowered his telescope. "Aye," he said. "The *Prince Alfred.*"

"She seems to be following us, sir."

"So? That's odd!"

Clint was on his way to the forecastle watch, and he eyed the fast steamer as it parted the waves at a slight angle forging away from the brilliant wake of the raider. She was probably bound for Charleston, Savannah, or Wilmington, for she was heavily laden.

"Maybe she'll draw the Yankees away from us," said Read. "If they capture her they'll be too busy counting up their prize money to bother with us."

"I hope not, Mister Read!"

They eyed the commanding officer.

Maffitt tugged at his whiskers. "Mister Stribling happens, by a strange coincidence, to be aboard the *Prince Alfred.*"

"Yes, sir?" said Read.

"And," continued Maffitt, "so are our guns, ammunition and supplies, transferred from the *Bahama.*"

Read grinned. Clint slapped his hands together. John Maffitt looked down at Clint. "Where is your watch, sir?" he said harshly.

"Forecastle watch, sir!"

"Then jump and make it so, sir, or it will be masthead for you!"

Clint moved. Maffitt was a friend and a jovial companion, but Maffitt was also a seaman and a commanding officer. John Maffitt liked discipline and a smart ship.

They took the *Prince Alfred* in tow at the break of day. By full daylight they anchored side by side off Green Key, ninety miles from New Providence on the edge of the Great Bahama Bank, within the marine league, which placed them within British colonial waters in case of interference. Green Key was a desolate coral islet with a shining beach. Below the keels of the two vessels, eight fathoms below in the astoundingly clear waters, were fantastic coral gardens, but there was no time to enjoy them. The business of converting the *Manassas* into a full-fledged raider must be done first, and there would be no rest until that was done.

"Rig ship for loading, Mister Read!" snapped John Maffitt. Thereupon he shucked his white duck coat and pitched in to work with the others.

The main lift fall was rigged for hoisting. The sun was now beating down in full fury and the sea was like glass. It was the first day of six exhausting days which were branded forever into the minds of Clint Wallace and the officers and crews of both vessels. There was no time for rest. Nothing but a few hours of restless sleep away from the hauling at the stay tackles, while guns and carriages weighing several thousands of pounds apiece came aboard and were lowered gently to the burning decks and then painfully levered and rolled into positions.

Net load after net load of shells, round shot, canister, grape, and the charges to propel them came aboard and were carried down to magazines and shot lockers. Barrels of salt pork and beef, boxes, crates and bales of boatswain's stores came aboard. The best Cardiff coal came aboard and was dumped down the coal chutes into the bunkers to top them off.

On the evening of the second day the wardroom steward sickened and died and was carried ashore at night and buried, while Lieutenant Stribling read the burial service over the body. But there was no time to mourn. He had come aboard at his choice and had died from exhaustion doing his duty, or so Lieutenant Maffitt had said. Exhaustion...?

The guns were mounted first. Two seven-inch rifled pivots and a battery of six six-inchers, not the eight smoothbores that had originally been intended for the broadside batteries. John Maffitt himself traced out the pivot tracks on the baking deck. When the guns were in position at last, ready for action, Lieutenant Stribling cautiously approached his tired and perspiring commanding officer and whispered something into his ear. Maffitt looked as though the world had come to an end. In ten minutes the story was all over the ship. The rammers, sights, sponges, quoins, and locks, which were absolutely necessary to load, fire, and clean the guns, had been left behind at Nassau. The eight-gun battery was absolutely useless. A pall of gloom settled over the quiet ship.

The crew of the *Manassas* watched the *Prince Alfred* stand out for Nassau, and the faint cheers of her crew drifted back across the crystal waters to a quietly apprehensive group of thin and exhausted men standing on the raider's filthy decks.

"Stand by to clean ship!" cracked Lieutenant Maffitt.

"All hands! All hands! Rig for cleaning ship!" said Lieutenant Stribling.

And so it was. John Maffitt loved a clean ship. Everything was neatly stored. The decks were washed and holystoned.

"Six days shalt thou labor and do all thou art able, and on the seventh day holystone the decks and scrape the cable," groaned an old salt as he leaned hard on his holystone. Clint wiped the sweat from his face and nodded in grim agreement.

A spick-and-span *Manassas* stood out for sea that afternoon of the seventh day. As she entered the Queen's

Channel, the boatswain's pipe twittered. "All hands aft to the quarter-deck! Jump and make it so!" cried out Clint Wallace.

Lieutenant Maffitt stood on his spotless quarter-deck with his small coterie of officers behind him and his minimum of a crew standing before him. Clint knew that the commanding officer had planned an elaborate ceremony and impressive formalities in commissioning the Confederate States of America's first foreign-built warship, but because of the circumstances he had decided to forego it. There were cases of natty blue and white duck uniforms for the crew stored below, but there was no time to break them out and put them on. There was more important business at sea.

The quartermaster stood by the halyards that kept the flapping British ensign aloft. At a glance from Lieutenant Maffitt, Clint walked to the mainmast and took a cloth ball from the hands of an old seaman. It was attached to a halyard. Aft, the quartermaster had snapped a similar ball to a set of halyards beside that of the British ensign. Four seamen stood at the ready on the weather side of the ship with primed and loaded muskets in their hands.

The *Manassas* moved steadily along under all plain sail, dipping her clean cutwater into the clear waters. It was quiet; it was very quiet except for the sighing of the wind through the rigging and the steady rushing of the water along the sides of the raider.

John Maffitt cleared his throat and read his orders: his commission as captain of the ship from President Jefferson Davis and Secretary of the Navy Mallory, and also his orders to take command. He raised his head and looked at his proud ship. "I now christen thee *Florida!*" he said, and then waved his hand.

The two cloth balls wriggled aloft on their halyards. Maffitt waved his hand again. Clint and the quartermaster jerked on their halyards, and the British ensign came down at a run from the peak, while the cloth balls seemed to explode in the clear air. The commissioning pennant fluttered out from the ball Clint had raised, but none of them looked at it. Their eyes were glued on the beautiful new ensign that fluttered bravely at the peak in place of the British ensign. A brilliant red field, crossed by a blue, white-bordered St. Andrew's cross, stippled evenly with thirteen white stars. The Stars and Bars!

The four muskets roared as one in salute to the colors of the new republic, and the smoke drifted across the decks, raveled by the rigging, and the *Florida* dipped gently in salute to her masters.

Clint looked back toward Green Key, slowly dropping astern. He could not see the single white cross planted there on the coral over the first of the C.S.S. *Florida's* crew to die. He wondered how many more there would be. A soft trade wind blew as the *Florida* sailed on a southern course for Cuba. The gray sea falcon was loose at last!

CHAPTER FIVE

Yellow Jack!

Bare feet slapped on the deck beside Clint Wallace's bunk. He opened his eyes and saw the dim form of a seaman standing beside him. "Yes?" he said.

The seaman knuckled his forehead. "Sir," he said hoarsely, "they's two men sick for'd. Taken bad they are."

Clint sat up. It was one of his duties, that of master's mate of the berth deck, as well as small-boat duty, gun captain of the after pivot gun, and regular watch on the forecastle. "What is it, Simmons?" he asked. He shrugged into loose shirt and trousers. The man did not answer. Clint looked up. "Well?" he asked sharply.

"They are shiverin', sir. Sweatin', glassy eyed and ravin' wi' fever."

Clint's feet hit the deck. "Dysentery?" he said hopefully.

Simmons shook his head. "You mind the steward we buried at Green Key? Poor 'Arry?"

"Yes. It was exhaustion."

"So? Ye mind how *yellow* he was?"

A cold feeling swept over Clint as he stood up. "It was exhaustion," he said stubbornly.

"No, sir! Ye know the fever struck Nassau hard last

July. Aye, even Lieutenant Brown of the Fourth West India Regiment, Captain Maffitt's fine little friend, died of it!"

"You talk like a fool!" said Clint fiercely.

The man leaned close. "No, sir, beggin' yere pardon! The reason I came, at the request of me mates, was because the two sick men are vomiting black!"

Clint felt sick himself. He looked away from the man, but the hoarse voice reached him plainly enough. "Aye, 'tis Yellow Jack!"

Clint walked forward. Yellow fever had been rampant in Nassau, although it had not touched the crew of the *Florida,* safe enough out at anchorage. But somehow it had been brought aboard by God alone knew what means. Maybe by those of the crew who had had shore leave in Nassau, perhaps by the crew of the *Prince Alfred.*

Clint walked into the forecastle. Those of the men who were not on watch had fled from the place. He walked to the first of the two men and looked down upon him in the faint light from a porthole. His face was pale and dewed with cold sweat, and he shivered in paroxysms at regular intervals. His eyes were wide and glassy and there was a black froth upon his dry lips. The foul, acrid stench of vomit assailed Clint's nostrils. He looked at the other shivering wretch and the man's symptoms were the same.

"Ye see, sir?" asked Simmons from the doorway.

Clint nodded. He had seen yellow fever cases in Cuba and in Mexico, as well as in New Orleans. It was deadly, the dreaded scourge of the tropics.

Clint unconsciously backed toward the doorway, and when his back touched one side of it he looked for Simmons. The man was gone. Clint stepped outside and padded aft until he reached the door to Maffitt's cabin. He raised his hand twice to knock and twice he let it drop. How could he tell the captain, who already had more than enough troubles besetting him, that Yellow

Jack was aboard and vying for command? Shorthanded at best, hunted by Yankee men-of-war, with guns and no means to shoot them, and now Yellow Jack to add to the list.

He rapped twice on the door and heard Maffitt's cheery voice. "Aye?"

"It's Midshipman Wallace, sir."

"Yes."

"I'd like to see the captain, sir."

"Come in, Mister Wallace."

Clint entered the big cabin. Maffitt was sitting up in his bunk. "Yes?"

Clint quickly told his commanding officer his dreadful message, hoping Maffitt would say it was not so. But John Maffitt got dressed as quickly as possible. "It's Yellow Jack without a doubt," he said. "Have an awning rigged on the quarter-deck for a quarantine ward. I'll need steaming hot water, mustard plasters, piles of blankets, and a strong laxative for those men. Jump and make it so!"

Clint jumped and made it so. By full daylight the two sick men were ensconced on the quarter-deck under layers of thick issue blankets to bring on sweating. John Maffitt, with the skill of a professional nurse, had bathed their feet and backs in hot water, given them a strong laxative, applied mustard plasters to their stomachs, and had finished off with a hot draught before piling on the blankets. It was the routine treatment of the "Old Navy," and Clint knew that John Maffitt had been an active nurse in July, helping the many patients in the Royal Victoria Hotel at Nassau. Even so, three of his close friends had died of the scourge.

The after guard attempted to conceal it from the crew, but it was a hopeless effort, for every man-jack aboard had already experienced the sight of the stricken. As the long day wore on, the trade winds freshened. Lieutenant Maffitt stood by the weather rail with his face to the breeze. "Perhaps the wind will bring disinfection," he said to Clint Wallace as Clint bathed the tortured face of one of the men.

It did not happen so.

By sundown half of the crew were down with Yellow Jack.

It was a horrifying dilemma, much worse than that which faced landsmen in time of plague. For on a ship there is no place to hide, nor can one run away from the scourge, or at least free himself from the ever-visible and terrifying presence of the disease. As the shadows fell over the gently heaving waters and the breeze died away to cat's-paws, the moaning of the sick and their delirious ravings echoed throughout the stricken ship. Worst of all to Clint Wallace as he tried to battle the epidemic were the pinched and resigned faces of the dying with their yellow hues and bloodshot eyes.

At dawn the sailmaker was busy lashing the dead into their hammocks with a heavy shot tied to the bottom. One after the other the shrouded forms slid from the boards into the clear waters and vanished with a swirling of bubbles into a seaman's unmarked grave.

At sunup three quarters of the crew were too ill to work ship. Off to port was a hazy island which Maffitt said was Aguilla. Cuba, the Pearl of the Antilles, was just to the south, a pastel blur on the horizon, crowned by fleecy white clouds.

Clint had little rest. One engine-room fireman and two seamen had answered for duty that morning, and as the lowest ranker aboard, Clint was drafted to work and help them. There was no question now of the *Florida* cruising for prizes, nor could she turn back to Nassau. There was nothing else to do but head for Cardenas in Cuba and hope for the best. Yellow Jack was now in command and he rattled his skeleton bones in macabre glee on the quarter-deck.

They seemed to drift across Nicholas Channel toward

the great island dreaming on the blue seas. "The loveliest land that human eyes have beheld," said John Maffitt to Clint. He smiled sadly. "Christopher Columbus said that. I wonder if *he* had Yellow Jack aboard at the time?"

The *Florida* slowly moved toward the harbor on the great bay in front of Cardenas. Clint stood watch at the helm of the raider, trying not to hear the cries of the sick and dying men.

Master John Low was standing at the after rail and he turned to speak to Lieutenant Maffitt. "Look aft here, sir."

Maffitt and Clint looked aft. White topsails were showing in two directions. Men-of-war probably. They were still hounding down the *Florida*.

The raider crept into the harbor. "Let go!" commanded Master Low, and the anchor dropped to plunge into the clear harbor waters, and the raider slowly rounded into the wind as her sails were furled slowly by the handful of men able to handle them.

A small boat came out toward them, flying the red and yellow flag of Spain. Maffitt glanced at Clint. "Do you speak their lingo, reefer?"

"After a fashion, sir."

"Then take over."

"Aye, aye, sir."

The quarantine officer refused to come aboard. *"Vomito! Vomito!"* he said expressively. It was the grisly, repellent name for Yellow Jack in Spanish.

The yellow quarantine flag was hoisted aboard the *Florida*. There could be no help from the shore, said the Spanish officer, for the *vomito* raged in Cardenas. No physicians or nurses were available. Furthermore, he reminded *Capitan* Maffitt of the Spanish Queen's proclamation of neutrality. The *Florida* must leave Cardenas within twenty-four hours.

Maffitt looked down into the bobbing boat. "Tell him," he said to Clint, "that I refuse to leave. That I will send Lieutenant Stribling to Havana for aid. He cannot, and he will not, by the powers, refuse me!"

The officer shrugged and motioned to his crew to take him ashore. Lieutenant Stribling was taken ashore by a bumboat for his mission to Havana, and evening began to settle over Cardenas. Offshore, pacing back and forth, were two Yankee men-of-war.

"What can we do now, sir?" asked Acting Master Wyman of Maffitt.

The officer took off his cap and looked aloft. "There is one power left to ask aid from, Mister Wyman! I suggest we all pray to that power."

That night a swift and violent thundershower swept across Cardenas and wetted the decks of the *Florida,* cooling the air for her delirious patients, and thoroughly soaking Captain Maffitt as he paced his quarter-deck.

At dawn of August 22, Clint was aroused and told that the commanding officer wanted to see him and the other officers aboard who were still on their feet. They gathered in the dim cabin and eyed their leader. Lieutenant Maffitt looked at them. "I have it too now," he said quietly. "I have had it before and know how it affects me. It invariably affects my brain, and I will be unable to stay in command. Therefore, before I am helpless, I will instruct you gentlemen in the care of the sick as well as giving orders for the *Florida.*"

Clint went on deck to feel the dawn wind across his heated face. His beautiful ship had ugly death in charge.

But he had his duty. He had suffered a mild case of the disease when he had been very small and perhaps it somehow made him immune. He did not know. He could remember how he had felt in his own case. His brain had throbbed, and he had had a dizzying blindness, with shooting pains of excruciating agony, while his bones had seemingly converted to red-hot tubes of iron. His tongue and throat had blistered, and it had brought on an unquenchable thirst that nothing could alleviate, accompanied by violent nausea. Burning fever had been succeeded by icy chills, and then the fever had returned again. Delirium had ebbed and flowed like the tides.

Yellow Jack began to strike more swiftly now that he had the *Florida* on full defensive. An engineer and three sailors died quickly, followed by young Lieutenant J. Laurens Bead, Maffitt's stepson, who had stayed at his stepfather's side until too ill to remain there.

In the light of a dreary dawn several days after Lieutenant Maffitt had been stricken, a boat pulled swiftly out to the *Florida* and the cheery voice of Lieutenant Stribling hailed the ship. Stribling came aboard with a man in civilian clothing who carried a doctor's case in his hand, followed by fourteen newly recruited seamen and engineers for the stricken *Florida*.

Stribling turned toward the doctor. "Young Wallace," he said, "this is Dr. Barrett, a Georgian."

"Pleased it is indeed I am to meet ye," said Dr. Barrett in rich Irish tones.

Clint gripped the doctor's hand. "Georgia?" he said with a smile.

"By way av Ireland," said the doctor. "Now where is me countryman, Captain Maffitt?"

"In his cabin, sir. And, sir, please do not tell him that Mister Bead has died."

Stribling paled a little. "No!" he said in horror. He gripped Clint by the shoulder. "You've had a thin time of it, reefer, but we'll all pull the *Florida* through!"

It did seem as though the *Florida* would pull through now. Dr. Gilliard, a Spanish gunboat surgeon, came aboard, joined by another Spanish doctor from Cardenas, and the three men of medicine fought a hard battle against Yellow Jack with all the skill they possessed.

The bright sunlight brightened the holystoned deck of the raider and sparkled from her brasses. Clint looked about the deck once and then went below to the captain's cabin. Lieutenant Stribling and Acting Master Wyman were there with Dr. Barrett. The doctor took Maffitt's pulse, then stood up and glanced at the chronometer that hung on the bulkhead. "Gentlemen," he said quietly as he looked down upon the unconscious captain, "I am convinced, from careful investigation, that the captain cannot survive beyond the meridian."

In the silence that followed, John Newland Maffitt opened his eyes. "You are a liar, sir. I have too much to do. I haven't time to die!"

When Clint returned to deck, he found that the effusive Spanish boarding officer was alongside again. "It is the suggestion of Governor-General Serrano that the *Florida* be steamed to Havana, Senior Midshipman, where she can be made more secure under the great guns of Morro Castle. Cardenas is undefended, as you can see, and there are a number of Federal cruisers just offshore. It is said in Havana that the Federals plan a 'cutting out' party. Please convey this information to your commanding officer with my compliments!"

Clint hurried below and conveyed the news to Lieutenant Maffitt. The sick officer closed his bloodshot eyes. "Tell the officer that I will sail to Havana, and that I will take no prizes on the way. Tell him to telegraph that information to Governor-General Serrano, whom I know well."

Clint passed the information on to the officer and in a surprisingly short time the message came back to the waiting *Florida:* "Let the *Florida* sail. The word of a Southern gentleman must be taken! Signed, Serrano."

The night of the last day of August was overcast as the *Florida* slipped her cable and eased out toward the mouth of Cardenas a short distance behind the local mail steamer. No sails were set, steam alone being the propulsion. The *Florida* edged toward shore without showing any lights, while the little mail steamer forged off in another direction, quite unaware she was a decoy for the darkened raider.

Suddenly, off in the distance, flashes of gunfire showed, followed by the dull, thudding noise of big guns.

Lieutenant Stribling looked at Clint who had the helm. "Rather a dirty trick. The Feds will catch the very devil for firing on the mail steamer."

The *Florida* slipped through the dark night and at dawn steamed slowly into Havana Harbor and dropped her hook under the looming walls and threatening guns of Morro Castle.

Just as full daylight came, the boats began to come out to view the raider. *"Viva la Confederation del Sud!"* the cheering people cried. Flowers and fruit were tossed up to the grinning seamen. A local band valiantly played "Dixie," with a Latin beat to it, and definitely not unpleasing.

The welcome was tumultuous from the local populace, but not from local officialdom. Despite the fact that the Confederacy was far more popular in Cuba than was the United States, the officials knew it would not do to bait Uncle Jonathan's powerful men-of-war. Nothing could be purchased. The officials were excessively polite and just as excessively adamant. "Nothing, Senior Capitan Maffitt, nothing whatsoever!" And so it was. Not even a piece of wood that could be shaped into a rammer for a gun was allowed aboard the raider.

News came aboard the waiting ship. The telegraph had been clicking all day, summoning Yankee ships to Havana, and by dusk a half dozen of them hovered just beyond the legal limits, waiting, waiting, waiting...

They carried Captain Maffitt up to his quarter-deck, sick as he was, and he held a short council of war with his officers. "There is nothing we can do here, gentlemen. Refitment and re-enforcement are outlawed. The ship is doomed if we delay. We will be forced to leave this harbor when the fever abates or suffer being interned for the duration of the war, and that is not why we have taken this fine vessel to sea!

"We cannot handle our guns. We do not have the equipment to fight them. It is my intention to run that blockade out there this very night. Lieutenant Stribling, you will lay a fuse to the magazines, long enough if capture is imminent, to blow up this ship if capture looms, and allow the crew to reach safety. We will either blow her up or run her aground and fire her before one Yankee can set foot on this deck!"

It would be a moonless night. Coal scoops rattled below as steam was gotten up in the boilers to the required pressures. The fuse to the magazines had been laid. The cable was slipped and the slim-hulled *Florida* crept out beneath the lowering bulk of Morro Castle to the open sea.

Clint Wallace stood on the gently heaving forecastle, holding onto a line, straining his eyes to look for Yankee patrol ships. Three times and out. Twice already John Newland Maffitt had slipped beneath the very noses of the enemy. From Nassau and then from Cardenas.

The waves washed softly against the sides of the raider as she met the surge of the open seas, and yet there was no sign of the enemy. No quick rattling challenge; no sudden deadly crashing of gunfire; no sight of sail or black hull. Nothing but the heaving waters of the sea and the cloudy skies.

The men lay quietly on the decks. No one could sleep that night. Now and then Clint could hear the muted grating of the scoops against the iron deck of the stokehold as the sweating stokers fed the good anthracite to the hungry fires. The funnels breathed the acrid fumes of the hard coal, but did not betray the presence of the raider by a telltale flare-up of smoke.

Then Clint saw a ship ghosting along a quarter of a mile away, moving in the opposite direction. Beyond that ship was yet another, moving in the same direction as the *Florida*. They seemed like great prowling black leopards. A deathwatch for the beautiful and helpless steamer that was moving out almost as though to meet them.

He looked aft along the decks and saw the men at the bulwarks staring out to sea. Beyond was the dim quarterdeck with Captain Maffitt sitting weakly in his chair, and the steady hand of John Low at the helm.

The *Florida* swayed and dipped, slipping through the seas with as little fuss as a porpoise.

The Federal ships were still on the move, straining sight and hearing for the rebel raider they knew could not escape them this time.

Second after second, minute after minute, and still nothing to break the quiet of the dark tropical night.

Stribling stood at his post with ready matches, and men stood by the seacocks to open them at the word. The small boats had been slung out ready to drop into the sea to receive the crew if they were ordered to abandon ship.

Nothing. The *Florida* moved on as through a vague, drifting dream world, peopled at a distance by white-sailed, black-hulled Yankee killers who did not seem to know of the approach of their prey.

Closer and closer, then the *Florida* sheared off a little and very gently to point her long jib boom a little more to the west.

A man coughed on the deck of the raider and was instantly struck by two other hands who lay beside him on the heaving deck. A block creaked somewhere aloft. The flag rustled in the dry wind.

Nothing.

Minute after minute until the Federal ships were now behind the *Florida* and it seemed as though the sea was free of them.

Then somehow, without a spoken word, every manjack aboard knew Maffitt had incredibly done it again! Three times! The third time was again the charm.

Clint walked aft in time to hear Captain Maffitt say

quietly, "Mister Stribling, you may shape course for Mobile Bay. I think we have given them the slip."

"Aye, aye, sir! I think we have an invisible ship, sir!"

Maffitt shook his head and looked up at the overcast sky. "Say rather we have a guiding power, Mister Stribling. Give me a hand, young reefer, for I want to go below."

Clint helped him from his chair. He looked out over the gently heaving waters. He smiled and began to speak softly:

> "Far as the breeze can bear, the billows foam, Survey our empire, and behold our home!"

The water chuckled beneath the dipping cutwater of the *Florida,* as though in appreciation.

CHAPTER SIX
Old Salamander

They had been three days at sea. The fever had abated but five men still swung in their hammocks beneath the quarter-deck awning. The afternoon of September 4 was bright and clear, with visibility thirty miles from the mastheads. The *Florida* was running at top speed with her steam engine making all of fourteen knots, standing toward Mobile Bay and safety.

Clint stood high on the ratlines of the main starboard shrouds and watched the distant ships passing back and forth before the bay, in great slow ellipses. He had been watching them for some time now. They were Yankees.

A young seaman clambered up beneath him. "Sir, do we have a chance of getting in?"

"Certainly," said Clint, but he hadn't convinced himself as yet.

"You've been here before?"

"Yes. In and out any number of times on my uncle's ship."

"What's it like?"

Clint didn't want to talk for he was too tense and excited, but he didn't have the heart to tell the apprentice to keep quiet. After all, the boy was in the same state as Clint himself.

"The entrance is narrow, Brinker," said Clint slowly, "and across the main channel, facing each other, are two forts. Pentagon-shaped Fort Morgan and smaller Fort Gaines, both armed with heavy guns. Inside the bay is Fort Powell guarding the inlets from Mississippi Sound, and protecting the fairway into the city itself, thirty miles up the bay.

"There are numbers of channels into the bay, some of them too shallow for deepwater vessels such as the *Florida*. Most of the channels are shoal-ridden and dangerous, navigable only by skilled pilots. There are a number of islands off the bay entrance. It's a tricky place to get into and out of, but it's one of the prime cotton ports of the Confederacy, with runners trying for Havana or Matamoras.

"The Yankee Western Gulf Blockading Squadron holds the gates. That is them waiting for us."

"Seems as though they're always waiting for us," said Brinker gloomily. He looked down at the useless guns on the deck of the *Florida*.

"We'll get through."

"Sure, sure! But then we have to get out again, don't we, sir?"

There wasn't any answer from Clint. The boy was right. It seemed to be the fate of the graceful *Florida* always to be on the run and never able to fight back.

The *Florida* was flying British colors and a British pennant, and with her unmistakable British build there might be a chance.

"Ahoy there!" hailed Stribling. "Mister Wallace! How many Yankee ships can you make out?"

"Three, sir. There are two smaller steamers close to the bay entrance, but I don't think they are Yankees. More likely blockade-runners jockeying back and forth for a chance to slip out."

"What do the Yankees look like?"

Clint eyed the three distant vessels. "One of them is a gunboat, sir! Two masts. Schooner-rigged. Tall funnel just abaft amidships. She reminds me of the *Winona*. I saw her at New Orleans. She only carried two guns at that time."

"And the others?"

Clint squinted his eyes. "The smallest of the two is another schooner, smaller than the *Winona*." He hesitated.

"Go on!" cried Stribling.

"The other one is fairly big, Lieutenant. Three-masted. A steamer. She looks familiar. Like the *Oneida*."

Glancing at Maffitt, Stribling opened his mouth, then closed it as Maffitt shook his head.

"What's wrong, sir?" asked Brinker in a low voice.

Clint looked down at him. "She's new and has a lot of power. Ten guns of big caliber."

The *Florida* forged on. Clint descended to the deck and went aft. Stribling was talking quickly to Maffitt, in an almost argumentative tone. "But, sir! We can't take a chance! That's the *Oneida*! She can blow us out of the water and we can't fire a shot in return. Half of our crew are still weak from fever, and you yourself are not well as yet! We are crippled, sir! We can't fight the smallest and weakest of them!"

"What do you suggest, sir?" asked Maffitt quietly.

"I suggest we haul off and approach after dark."

"No. Our draft is too great to poke about among those shoals after dark."

"Then what can we do, sir?"

Maffitt hesitated a moment. "Take the sick men to the berth deck. All men below but the officers. They might mistake us for an English vessel, and they'll be cautious after the Trent Affair."

Clint eyed his commanding officer. The Trent Affair. A Federal man-of-war had stopped a British vessel on the high seas and had taken off two Confederate foreign emissaries by the names of Mason and Slidell, and there had been a terrible furor about it in international circles. The British seemed to have a short memory of the War of 1812—the United States had gone to war for practically the same thing, when British ships had stopped American ships to look for British citizens to impress into the British Navy. Nations have short memories, he thought.

"It might work," said Stribling dubiously.

"It will, Mister Stribling. And, Mister Stribling, kindly lash me to the rail. It might get a little rough ere we make Mobile Bay."

The *Florida* tore on with a wraith of smoke pouring from her twin funnels. The *Winona* ranged in closer. Fifty yards from the speeding raider she hailed her. "What ship is that?"

Stribling cupped his hands about his mouth. "Her Britannic Majesty's steamer *Vixen!*"

The *Winona* sheared off and signals crept up her halyards.

"She seems satisfied," said Stribling.

"Smile," said Maffitt.

The *Oneida* slowly changed her course to cut across the bows of the *Florida*. Maffitt spoke over his shoulder to Quartermaster Billups. "Steer directly for her, Quartermaster!"

"Aye, aye, sir!"

On she went, and suddenly the *Oneida* was reversed to avoid collision. "Heave to! What ship are you?" hailed her captain through a tin trumpet.

Maffitt smiled. "That's George Preble," he said. "He was once a reefer aboard the old *Constitution* with me."

The *Oneida's* gunners were at their stations and the big, ugly 11-inch guns seemed to leer at the *Florida*. Then a bow gun cracked flatly, sending up a spurt of water across the bows of the raider. She did not stop. A second gun spat flame and smoke, but the shell passed harmlessly ahead of her.

Stribling looked up toward the clear sky. "For what we are to receive, let us be thankful," he said.

The broadside battery of the *Oneida* seemed to blast as one gun. The wave of smoke and flame seemed to reach out to touch the *Florida,* and Clint Wallace fell flat on the deck while there was a smashing chaos of smoke, metal, and splinters just above his head. The *Florida's* small boats were crushed to kindling; the hammock nettings were cut through as though by invisible shears; rigging snapped and spars splintered.

"Too high!" screamed Stribling.

"Run up our true colors, Mister Wallace," said Maffitt.

Clint sprang to the halyards, swiftly hauled down the British Cross and George, and snapped the Stars and Bars onto the halyard. He ran it up with mighty pulls on the line, and the wind picked it up and snapped it flauntingly through the rising smoke.

A gun roared and the halyards fluttered to the deck while the flag fell gracefully right into Clint's arms. He was scared but he forced himself to snap the flag onto a spare set of halyards and run it up despite a sharp pain in his left forefinger.

He couldn't help but salute his country's flag, and it was then that he felt the pain again in his left forefinger. He looked curiously at it. The tip of his left forefinger was gone cleanly. He stared at it incredulously.

"Well done, Mister Wallace," said Captain Maffitt.

Now the *Oneida's* consorts moved steadily in, the *Winona* off the port beam and the *Rachel Seaman* off the port bow, and their small batteries barked steadily, slamming shot at the speeding raider enveloped in smoke like an old familiar cloak.

They raced past the roaring *Oneida.* "Starboard your helm, Quartermaster," said Maffitt steadily.

"Aye, aye, sir!"

Clint finished tying his scarf about his bloody hand,

wondering what was happening now. Then he saw that Maffitt had maneuvered to place the three Union ships in line and thus escape the fire of at least one of them.

Then the savage battering began as one 11-inch shell after the other smashed into the wooden hull of the helpless *Florida*, shaking her and splintering her. She shuddered violently as a shell smashed through the starboard side several inches above the water line, tore through the hull, and emerged from the port side to explode harmlessly just beyond the ship.

"If that had exploded inside," said Stribling with a pale face.

"Smile, Mister Stribling. Smile," said Captain Maffitt.

A shell crashed through the pantry, shattering the fine English crockery marked with the rebel flag that had been ordered by Bulloch in England. Nothing but the best for the *Florida*. She was getting the best right now, thought Clint grimly. The best the Yankees had to offer.

A shell shattered the port gangway. Then a sparkle of firing opened from the rigging of the *Oneida* and musket balls began to rip into the *Florida*. The Marines had taken a hand in the bloody game of give, but not take.

It was not a fight, but a beating. The cannonading was steady and precise and it never let up, until it seemed as though the *Florida* would be torn to pieces before she could sink.

Captain Maffitt raised his head. "We had better make sail, Mister Stribling," he said.

"All hands make sail!" roared Stribling. "Aloft ye terriers!"

The men came up from below and raced up the shrouds. Clint was up with them, making for the maintop.

"Lay out and loose!" came the command.

Meanwhile the fore and aft sails were being hauled slowly up by the weak men on deck.

"Let fall!" cracked the next command above the roaring of the guns.

Now the gunners were loading with deadly canister and grape. Canister was composed of many musket balls contained in a tin case that shattered when fired and spewed lead balls like buckshot, while grape was heavier balls of cast iron, contained in a wire framework that performed practically the same havoc when it struck except that it was heavier. And the Marines never stopped their deadly practice with their sharpshooting muskets. A seaman pitched from the yardarm next to Clint. Another slid down the shrouds with blood pouring from a severed foot. One after the other men were hit. It was hardly worth the effort to raise the sails for the wind was very light, and now the clean canvas was spattered with blood.

"Lay down from aloft!" commanded Stribling.

But the gallant *Florida* was gaining. The smoke from the funnels of the Federal vessels was thicker as they fed rosin to the fires for more heat.

"Four points to starboard, Quartermaster," said Maffitt.

The *Florida* did not slow her pace, but her change of course brought the *Winona* and the *Rachel Seaman* into fine, defilading the *Rachel Seaman* so that she could not fire for fear of hitting the *Winona*. It also caused the big *Oneida* to yaw to bring her belching guns to bear on the fleeing raider.

On and on went the *Florida,* gaining inch by inch, foot by foot, and yard by yard as the afternoon began to wane. But shot and shell were falling shorter and shorter now as the Yankees dropped behind, furiously firing and elevating, elevating higher and higher, to no effect.

"Fort Morgan!" cried Clint.

The pentagon-shaped brick structure was plain to be seen, and even as they looked she opened fire on the three Yankees. The sun was almost gone now.

John Maffitt loosened the ropes that had held him to the rail throughout the ordeal. "Quartermaster, take her in slowly. We will anchor off Melrose, above Fort Morgan. Half speed, Mister Stribling, if you please."

She limped in past Fort Morgan, and the soldiers lined the ramparts and cheered until they were hoarse, as the *Florida* passed slowly beneath them. A twenty-one gun salute roared.

The shaken crew wandered about the littered decks looking at the gaping wounds and the blood splotches on the deck. No ship could have taken that beating and lived to stay afloat, but the *Florida* had.

"She's a lucky ship," said Seaman Simmons.

"Aye, that she is," said another jack-tar. He looked aft toward the erect figure of John Newland Maffitt still standing at his post. "And 'Old Salamander' got her through that hell fire. No one else could have done it."

"Three cheers and a tiger for 'Old Salamander,' mates!" yelled Simmons.

The cheering echoed from the shore.

Old Salamander! It was a good name for John Newland Maffitt, for the salamander is an amphibious reptile that supposedly has the ability to live in, and sometimes extinguish, fire.

The *Florida* too had her share of glory. She had slipped away from England under the name *Oreto;* from Nassau under the name *Manassas;* and from Cardenas and Havana under her proper and final name, *Florida*. Now she had slipped past the Yankees for the fourth time. It would not be the last time.

Although the yellow quarantine flag flew above her, hundreds of people came out by boat to look at her, and they did not come empty handed. Flowers, gifts, and delicacies of all kinds flowed aboard her.

A message came from Secretary Mallory. "The escape of your defenseless vessel from an overwhelming force with liberty to choose its own ground and mode of attack, was due to the handsome manner in which she was handled, and I do not remember the union of thorough professional skill, coolness, and daring have ever been better exhibited in a naval dash of a single ship."

She was taken into a dock after quarantine of two weeks. Fourteen hundred wounds, by actual count, scarred her hull and spars. News came that the second Confederate commerce destroyer named the *Enrica* while building, had also escaped to sea and had been christened the *Alabama,* while a third ship, to be christened the *Georgia,* was about to be launched in England.

With all the good news, there was also some bitter news. John Stribling of the stout heart had died of yellow fever a few days after the *Florida* had made Mobile Bay. Robert E. Lee and his tough veterans of the Army of Northern Virginia had suffered a defeat at Antietam Creek at Sharpsburg, Maryland, although they had inflicted bloody losses on the Army of the Potomac. But Lee had fallen back south across the Potomac. Then, too, although everyone aboard the battered *Florida* had confidently expected their captain to be promoted, such was not the case. Congratulations and hero worship, but no promotion. He said nothing, but he had been hurt.

Two new rifled pivot guns, firing 110-pound shells, arrived for the *Florida,* this time with full accessories and equipment. Slowly but surely new faces arrived aboard her. Men from all over the Confederacy arrived, until one hundred men berthed aboard her, four-fifths of them Southerners born and bred, and the remainder composed of a dozen different nationalities.

Clint's work was cut out for him in the busy weeks of getting ready for sea, although he managed to get home to see his mother, his father being with his regiment on active service in Virginia.

But it had been Christmas leave and he had his new reefer uniform to wear. A long-skirted coat of field gray over darker gray blue-striped trousers. A double row of brass buttons embossed with a fouled anchor, crossed cannon, and the letters C.S.N. A leather belt with a brass buckle and a flat-topped gray cap with leather visor. There was only one thing missing. He had never had a sword since he had left his first issue weapon back in Nassau by mistake.

It was a cold, windy day when he walked through the streets of Mobile toward his ship. He was eager for a sight of her and he wasn't displeased at what he saw. She was trim and neat, spick-and-span aloft and alow, and she sparkled in the cold sunshine.

He wanted to run up the gangplank but he had to conduct himself with decorum. He returned the salute of the sentry at the foot of the gangplank and ascended, saluting the quarter-deck as his foot touched the deck.

"Well done, reefer," a quiet voice said.

Clint whirled to look into the smiling face of Lieutenant Charles William Read. Old "Savez" whom he had known aboard the doomed *McRae!* "Mister Read!" he said with a face-splitting grin. He surveyed the cool and courageous officer of his old ship. He was slight of build, with an alert, boyish face, close-clipped brown mustache and whiskers, and despite his whiskers he looked hardly older than he was, twenty-two years of age.

"I had an idea we would serve together again, reefer," said the officer.

"You said that last April, sir."

The eyes seemed far away. "Fate perhaps. I've heard a lot about you, Clint."

Clint flushed. "I didn't do much, sir."

"Perhaps you think you didn't. Captain Maffitt has a different opinion. He said he wanted to see you as soon as you came aboard."

Clint saluted and then hurried to the commanding officer's cabin to tap on the door.

"Come in," said a familiar voice.

Clint entered and saw John Maffitt standing by a

stern porthole. The officer extended his hand after he returned Clint's salute. "Glad to have you aboard, Mister Wallace."

"Glad to be aboard, sir."

"You've come back just in time."

"Do we have orders for sea, sir?"

Maffitt nodded. He glanced quickly at Clint. "You're eager to go, of course?"

"Yes, sir!"

A faint cloud seemed to pass across Maffitt's usually smiling face. "I knew it." He paced back and forth. "But a complication has come up regarding you, Mister Wallace."

Clint stared at his commanding officer. "Something I've done, sir?"

"In a sense." The quick smile came. "You've done your work aboard the *Florida,* reefer, if that's what you mean. That's what makes it so difficult for me to tell you what I have to tell you."

The ship swayed a little in the water as the wind shifted. Clint could hear the voices of seamen on the deck above the cabin and the sound of feet moving about.

Maffitt looked up. "Yes," he said, "it won't be long before we head out to sea to do what we were originally intended to do...raid Yankee commerce."

"What is it the Lieutenant has to tell me, sir?"

Maffitt hesitated. "You know we have been filling our complement of officers. Our gallant and tragic Mister Stribling has been replaced by Lieutenant S. W. Averett. Lieutenant Charles Read, who has spoken very highly of you, as indeed we all do, reefer, is with us. We have two surgeons. Thirteen officers in all. Lieutenant Hoole, Mister Low, of course, Midshipman R. S. Floyd, Engineer Brown, and others whom you will meet, as well as those you well know."

"Yes, sir?"

Maffitt looked out of the porthole. "We have a new midshipman aboard. A Mister Robert Lester. A fine young man."

A curious feeling came over Clint. He stared at his commanding officer's back. Could it be that he was not to sail aboard his beloved *Florida* after all?

Maffitt turned. "It seems as though our officer complement is now complete as far as our requirements go for midshipmen, Mister Wallace."

"Does that mean, sir, that I am no longer part of the ship's complement?"

Maffitt waved a hand. "Not necessarily. There is a choice. Mister Lester is rated as a Passed Midshipman, while you, sir, are still rated as an Acting Midshipman."

"That doesn't really matter, sir," said Clint desperately.

"I want you to know that I recommended you to stand before a board to rate your Passed Midshipman examination. I know you can do so. Every officer and man who knows you is sure of that, sir. But they say there is not time for such a board. There is a war on, it seems." He smiled bitterly. John Maffitt himself had cause to be bitter. His expected promotion had not come through either.

"Does that mean I cannot sail with the *Florida,* sir?"

Maffitt slapped a hand against a bulkhead. "No. But you will rate as the lowest officer aboard, even amongst the 'steerage officers,' reefer. I wanted you for my aide, sir. But *Mister* Lester comes highly recommended." There was a slightly sarcastic tone to the officer's voice. He looked squarely at Clint. "You may stay aboard as Acting Midshipman, the lowest ranking officer aboard, to get all the dirty work and take the guff of your superiors, including *Mister* Lester. It will not be easy. *Mister* Lester is rather a superior young man."

"I'll stay, sir." Clint's voice caught a little in his throat. "May I have permission to leave now, sir?"

"Yes."

Clint saluted and walked toward the door.

"Wait, reefer," said John Maffitt.

Clint turned.

The officer reached behind his desk and took out something about three feet long in a chamois wrapper. "Here is something you should have, sir." He handed it to Clint.

Clint stripped the cover from a sheathed sword. He stared at it unbelievingly.

"Draw it, reefer."

He drew it from the sheath. It was beautifully engraved with the cotton plant chased into the steel on one side of the blade, and the leaves of the tobacco plant chased on the other side. Engraved also, on both sides, were the Stars and Bars, and the Confederate naval coat of arms, two crossed cannon and a fouled anchor. The fine steel glinted in the soft lamplight. Clint looked up at his commanding officer but he could not speak.

"May you always carry it in honor, reefer. Remember the fight we had in the alleyway in Wilmington so long ago?

Maffitt took a new sword belt from a drawer and buckled it about Clint's waist. He hooked the sheath to the belt and Clint let the fine sword drop into it with a ringing of steel. "Thank you, sir."

Maffitt waved a hand. "I could not get you a rating as Passed Midshipman, but something had to be done for the reefer who may have saved my life in Wilmington; who worked like a Trojan aboard the *Manassas,* and stood firm and loyal on the *Florida* through all her trials and tribulations. You owe me no thanks, young sir. It is I who owe thanks to you."

Later, Clint walked to his quarters aboard the raider. It was dark now and a cold wind whispered about the ship, but he did not feel it. The weight and feeling of the sword at his side was sufficient to keep him warm enough. He entered the steerage. It was well lighted with oil lamps in gimbals. A young man, about nineteen, sat at a table poring over books, while another, lean and lanky, lay listlessly in Clint's own bunk, with a slim leg almost reaching the deck overhead.

The midshipman at the table turned. He smiled easily. "I'm Floyd, reefer. You must be Wallace."

"Yes, I am. Pleased to meet you."

Floyd turned a little. "That, over there, is Lester."

Clint turned and held out a hand. He saw a handsome face and the clearest gray eyes he had ever seen. Midshipman Lester yawned. "Pleased, I'm shuah. Please close the door, Acting. It's a habit you'll have to get into if you stay here."

Clint eyed the elegant young man. He was hardly older than Clint. Then Clint looked forward to the most cramped bunk in the steerage. Not only were his duffel and gear dumped carelessly on the deck near it, but there were other items piled on the bunk. Odds and ends of this and that. Things that should have been neatly stowed away in the spaces provided for them.

Clint walked to his bunk and began to remove the things.

"See that you stow them away properly, Acting," said Lester.

Clint turned a little. "My bunk isn't a storage place, Mister."

"Hear *him*," yawned Lester. He draped his long legs over the side of Clint's old bunk and tilted his head to one side. "Jump and make it so, *Mister*."

Floyd was watching both of them but he didn't open his mouth. He was the senior, but he knew better than to get into a thing like this.

Clint remembered Maffitt's words. "You may stay aboard as Acting Midshipman, the lowest ranking officer aboard, to get all the dirty work and take the guff of your superiors, including Mister Lester. It will not be easy. Mister Lester is rather a superior young man."

So it was beginning already.

Clint slowly began to stow the things away.

"You're due on anchor watch, Lester," said Floyd.

Lester yawned. "So I am. Boring. Who's going to steal the filthy old thing?" He shrugged into his long-skirted frock coat and buttoned it. It was made of the finest material and fitted like a glove. He placed his cap atop his dark curls with a slightly rakish tilt to it, then reached for his sword belt. "Say, Acting, that's a fine sword you have there. Be a sport and let me wear it on watch."

Clint could hear a slight pattering of rain against the sides of the raider. That sword wasn't going to get wet. Not just yet. Not the first day he was wearing it.

"Youah heah me!" snapped Lester.

Clint turned and found the midshipman standing a few feet from him with his hand out. He was almost a head taller than Clint but wasn't as broad through the shoulders nor as big boned. "I heard you," said Clint quietly. "The sword stays here."

In the quiet that followed eight bells rang sweetly.

"Your watch, Lester," said Floyd.

"I'll need that sword."

"Take mine."

"No."

Floyd stood up. "Mister," he said quietly and very plainly, "it's your watch! Jump and make it so!"

Lester stepped back and a red flush filled his handsome face. "I'll remember this, Acting!"

"Do," said Clint politely.

Lester turned on a heel, calmly appropriated Clint's oilskins from a hook and left the steerage, with the door gaping wide behind him.

"Lester!" roared Floyd. "Close the door! It's a habit you'll have to get into if you stay here!"

A slim hand reached in, gripped the door, and slammed it shut.

Clint leaned against a bulkhead. "Nice fellow," he said dryly.

"You could have let him have the sword."

"No."

Floyd's calm eyes studied Clint. "I see." He turned to his books, then he turned again. "It looks like this might be a long and interesting voyage, Mister Wallace."

"Aye, aye, Mister Floyd."

Clint stowed away the mess on his bunk, then found a pair of dirty socks and a rumpled shirt among the mess. There wasn't much doubt whence they came. He pitched them carelessly onto Lester's bunk.

Floyd looked up and his eyes met Clint's. "Mister," he said quietly, "I've heard the *Florida* is a happy ship. Let's try to keep it that way."

The raider moved up and down a little as though to agree.

CHAPTER SEVEN

Seek Out and Destroy!

A hard gale was blowing offshore in wild gusts; there was no moon and the January night was bitter cold, with the dark surface of the Gulf lashed with foam and wind-driven spume. The *Florida* plunged back and forth, fighting and dragging at her anchor as though to be free of Mobile Bay once and for all. She was ready for sea.

They had daubed her lovely black sides with a hideous mixture of lampblack and whitewash at the suggestion of Admiral Buchanan, Mobile's naval commandant, and it had gone hard with her crew to do so, but it would make her less visible to the Federal watchdogs off Mobile Bay. Captain John Maffitt had been studying the Federal blockaders for four days from the wind-swept ramparts of Fort Morgan. He was anxious to get to sea, too, for a strong rumor had come to him that the editor of Mobile's leading newspaper, a man with great political powers, had suggested that the *Florida* be kept at Mobile Bay to hold the thirteen Union blockading vessels bottled up watching her, when they should be busy elsewhere; a sort of reverse blockade. He didn't know John Newland Maffitt very well.

The channel ran seaward for four miles beyond Fort Morgan, just about far enough for the Union vessels to take anchor close to the channel bar and yet be out of range of Morgan's big guns. The *Florida* had already been through two false starts. The crew had been praying for a northeast gale. This time they had it.

The crew had been alerted at dusk. The raider was ready for a fight, this time with ready guns. The hammock nettings had been taken down, and the men crouched at quarters. Steam was up and hissing and whistling at the safety valves. Every man-jack knew they were going out that night. They lay down in their hammocks in full clothing and pea jackets, after a double watch had been set.

At 2:20 A.M. general quarters shrilled throughout the waiting ship and the men raced to their posts while officers had been stationed every twenty feet along the main deck aft to the helm, where Maffitt, wrapped in his old naval cloak, stood beside the helmsman. "Mister Averett," he said quietly. "Weigh and cat the anchor, sir!"

The hook came up with a steady clicking of capstan pawls, was hove short, and then broken free as the *Florida* moved slowly ahead to take the strain off the cable. The gun crews crouched beside their cold charges, and the seamen went aloft in the shrieking windy darkness to loose sail if need be. It would be a wild night on the Gulf.

The *Florida's* anchor broke water and was quickly catted. The raider moved out, heading to sea up the channel beneath dark Fort Morgan. Clint Wallace shivered in the searching wind. He glanced at Captain Maffitt who stood easily on the swaying deck with his speaking trumpet in his hand.

Now they were almost at the bar.

"Sail dead ahead, sir!" called out Clint.

"Starboard your helm, Quartermaster," said Maffitt.

"Sail dead ahead, sir!" called out a lookout.

"Port your helm, Quartermaster," responded Maffitt.

One after the other five ominous shapes were passed in the howling darkness. Now they headed to pass between two more. Big ships these were; big enough to blow the *Florida* to pieces. It was dark and the cloak of darkness would conceal the raider. Suddenly, just as they passed between the two Yankees, there was a bright flare-up of flame from both lean funnels of the *Florida* and it revealed her like a sitting duck.

"That did it!" said Mister Read.

A flare arced up through the darkness and burst in an eerie glow, followed by half a dozen more, splattering flame and color against the dull sky. The wind shifted a little, and the thudding of drums beating general quarters aboard the Yankee vessels could be plainly heard.

"All hands make sail," said Captain Maffitt.

"Aloft there!" roared Averett. "Lay out and loose!"

The seamen worked out on the footropes and cast off the sail gaskets.

"Let fall!"

The sails snapped out in the wind.

"Sheet home!"

The sails were sheeted after a hard struggle. The *Florida* began to plunge like a pilot boat.

"Lay in! Lay down from aloft!"

Yankee guns dotted the darkness with hot orange-red flame. But the wind and darkness were with the speedy raider as she tore along with her sails set like white marble and a streamer of smoke trailing from her funnels to be torn to pieces by the wild, shrieking wind.

No man went below. Gunners and seamen crouched behind the protection of the bulwarks, staring into the darkness.

"Ship dead ahead, sir!" yelled a lookout.

She was a big one. Familiar enough, thought Clint.

"The *Brooklyn*," said Lieutenant Read.

One broadside from her could send the *Florida* to the bottom, but somehow the big Yankee did not see the slim raider slipping past.

Then suddenly a man could see things more clearly, and with a start the officers and crew realized it was breaking daylight.

"Fast ship astern," said Mister Averett.

"The *Cuyler*," said Read. "She's *fast!*"

"As fast as the *Florida?*"

Read shrugged. "Maybe faster," he said quietly.

"Can she make fourteen knots?"

"Yes."

The officers looked at each other. The *Florida* had made about that speed coming into Mobile Bay but she had been full out, with rosin on the fires.

The *Cuyler* was indeed fast. All that day she hung on, three miles astern, gaining slowly but perceptibly as dusk crept across the heaving seas.

John Maffitt rubbed his reddened eyes. He had not left his post all day. He glanced at the *Cuyler* and then at the darkening sky. "Mister Averett," he said quietly. "All hands shorten sail!"

Averett's commands crackled out and the men went aloft like monkeys to secure the canvas in long neat bunts to the yards.

"Stop the engines," said Maffitt.

The propeller stopped turning. The *Florida* pitched and heaved in the long steep swells, mostly hidden from the sight of the pursuing *Cuyler*. Every man-jack aboard the *Florida* was praying as he had not done for years. Then a man laughed, followed by another one and then another, until officers and crew, tired as they were, were roaring delightedly. The speedy *Cuyler* was speedy all right; speedy enough to be vanishing from sight in a direction where the *Florida* definitely was not!

John Maffitt handed his speaking trumpet to Mister Averett. "All full sail, Mister Averett. Shape a course to the north until we have surely lost yonder Yankee."

The *Florida* turned slowly in the plunging seas and then steadied on her new course.

"Pipe all hands aft, Boatswain," said Captain Maffitt.

The silent crew watched him as he took out his orders and read them. "We are to avoid a fight. We are to fight if forced to, but we cannot risk losing the ship." He glanced at the crew, then read on. "You are armed for defense, not offense. Your weapon is the torch. Cruise at discretion. You are on your own. Live on the enemy if you can. Burn, sink, and destroy enemy merchantmen wherever you find them save in neutral waters. Hit the enemy in his pocketbook. The North would gladly sacrifice fifty vessels to rid the seas of the *Florida* and the *Alabama.* Destroy enough Northern shipping and the merchant princes of New York and Boston would gladly cry 'Peace! Peace!' And the Washington politicians would be glad to comply."

The crew were dismissed and as Clint started forward he heard Maffitt, who was looking at the lowering sky, distinctly say, "Oh, Lord! who hast delivered us from the fury of the storm, send us fair winds and take the helm if we go wrong."

The *Florida* was soon steered for the coast of Cuba, the great highway for Northern merchant vessels that traded in the West Indies, and also for Federal warships, stationed there to protect them. Officers and men, less those still on watch, went to their bunks and hammocks, after having gone thirty-six hours without sleep. The *Florida* was loose at last!

It was six bells of the afternoon watch when the lookout on the mainmast called out, "Sail ho!" "Where away?" called out Mister Read.

"Broad on the port beam, sir!"

Clint Wallace looked eagerly to the east toward the faint western tip of Cuba and the Florida Strait. Sure enough! A two-masted ship was moving slowly along under all plain sail. The *Florida's* course was changed and she sped after the stranger. "Hoist the Stars and Stripes, reefer," said Read quietly.

The United States flag crept up to the peak. The *Florida* rapidly closed the gap. Mister Maffitt was up on deck now, studying the stranger through his brass telescope. "She's a Yankee," he said. "A new ship from the looks of her. Deep laden. Mister Wallace, have the bow gun fired across her bows if you will."

The strange brig moved on, rounding into Florida Strait. The *Florida* was within a mile of her when Maffitt signaled to Clint. Clint stepped back and jerked the lock string of the gun. She slammed back, spitting out smoke and flames. In an instant the ball struck the water fair across the bows of the brig, sending up a spout of clear water. The *Florida* moved closer. Then the brig let fly all her sheets.

"Mister Hoole," said Maffitt. "Take away a cutter to her."

Hoole glanced at Clint. "Come along, reefer," he said. "Cutter away!" he called out.

The laden cutter hit the water with a splash as the *Florida* lost way. The cutter swung easily up and down on the smooth swells, being driven by the stout ash blades toward the brig. They rounded her bows and saw the freshly carved and painted figurehead of a girl on the vessel. Hoole whistled softly. "I'd like to see the model for that, reefer."

They came alongside and Clint followed Mister

Hoole up the Jacob's ladder. A bearded Yankee stared at them in their natty uniforms. "Who are ye?" he asked.

"What ship is this?" asked Hoole.

"The *Estelle* of Boston, sir. Who be ye?"

"You are a prize of the Confederate States Ship *Florida,* Lieutenant Maffitt commanding. I am Lieutenant Hoole, sir.

"I am Captain John Brown. This ship is Spanish property!"

Hoole smiled. "So? Let me see your manifests, Captain Brown."

That was all there was to the *Florida's* first capture. The *Estelle* was spanking new, two days out of Santa Cruz, homeward bound, laden deep with honey and molasses. Value, ship and cargo, one hundred thousand dollars. Her flag, chronometer, and charts were placed in the cutter with part of the *Estelle's* crew in irons, and ferried to the raider. It was getting dusk when the last of the captured crew was carried to the *Florida* along with a few barrels of molasses and honey for the messes of the raider.

The cutter was swiftly pulled back, loaded with some spare sails and cordage. Lieutenant Hoole looked about the empty decks of the gently rolling brig. "Well, reefer," he said quietly, "it's about that time."

"Yes, sir," said Clint in a puzzled tone.

"Come on and I'll show you the latest improved methods."

"Yes, sir." Clint followed the officer into the captain's cabin. A keg of lard was already lying there. Hoole calmly pulled out the drawers beneath the captain's bunk, smashed them with his foot, then piled old newspapers atop the wreckage. He dumped the lard atop the whole pile and felt in his trousers. Then he grinned. "Give me a match, reefer."

Clint stared at him. "You're not going to fire this ship, are you, sir?"

Hoole tilted his head to one side. "What did you

think we were going to do with it? Slide it into a bottle and keep it on the mantelpiece back home?"

"But she's so pretty! A lovely ship, sir!"

"The matches!"

Clint handed him a block of matches. Hoole whistled softly as he set fire to the mess on the clean deck. The fire snapped and crackled, ran up the varnished side of the bunk, then licked hungrily at the neat chintz curtains over the portholes. "Time to leave, reefer," said Hoole.

They hurried up on deck. The sound of axes came from the forecastle and the galley, and in a few minutes tendrils of smoke writhed from them, and grinning seamen hurried to the side of the ship and dropped into the cutter one by one. One of them held a squawking parrot in a cage.

Hoole and Clint got into the boat and started back for the *Florida*. Fire was already licking up the lower rigging of the brig. By the time the cutter had been made fast to the falls and hoisted to the davits of the *Florida*, a great puff of smoke and flame came from the main hatch followed by the savory odor of stewing honey and molasses. The smoke twisted upward toward the darkening sky. As the *Florida* got under way, the men on deck watched the blazing brig. That smoke and flame could be seen thirty miles or more. Even as they watched, the masts toppled over into the sea with a great upsurge of smoke and steam.

John Maffitt closed his telescope with a snap. "Mister Read," he said quietly. "Set our course for Bahia Honda."

"Yes, sir."

"And, Mister Read, no fights tonight."

"Aye, aye, sir."

Clint Wallace stood by the starboard rail for a long time staring back at the blazing mass that had once been a fine, seaworthy brig. Seek out and destroy. That's what they had to do. The *Estelle* would be only the first of many.

IN THE BUSY, flaming weeks that followed the sinking of the lovely *Estelle,* the officers and crew of the *Florida* were driven hard by their captain and their mission. Day after day was filled with activity. Drill at the guns, cutlass exercises, pistol practice, musketry, loosing, reefing and furling sail. For the midshipman there was recitation under various senior officers, and navigation under the master of them all, John Newland Maffitt.

The *Florida* slid into Havana Harbor to the blaring of bands playing a Latin version of "Dixie" and hoarse cries of: *"Viva la Confederation del Sud"* And gifts of fruit, flowers, and cigars came aboard for "Pirata Maffitt" and his grinning crew. The crew of the *Estelle* was released, the bunkers were topped with coal, and the *Florida* slipped out again within the twenty-four-hour time limit in a neutral harbor. She had broken only two rules: she had entered after sundown, and she had failed to obtain a health clearance.

Then the raider set about her fiery business. First the fine brig *Windward,* laden with molasses, out of Matanzas, was set ablaze. Then the *Corris Anne,* another brig, laden with hogshead shooks, was set ablaze, and she drifted luridly into Cardenas Harbor. But the coal bought at robber's prices in Havana was poor stuff and hardly able to raise five pounds of steam, and the *Florida* wallowed along at a snail's three knots, making her northing slowly, crossing the Great Bahama Bank, running up The Tongue of Ocean toward Nassau, passing Green Key of grim memory, and then she sailed slowly into Nassau Harbor with the brilliant Stars and Bars snapping in the fresh breeze.

Things hadn't changed much in Nassau. The American Consul raised particular hell when the *Florida* was allowed as much good Welsh coal as she wanted, while the Union vessel *Dacotah* had recently been doled out a meager twenty tons.

Twenty-six of the *Florida's* crew jumped ship at Nassau, and a Negro crimp, for gold, brought out eighteen men in a tug, with fishing poles in their hands to fool the authorities, only to be promptly sworn into the Confederate Naval Service aboard the *Florida*.

The Federal ships off Abaco Light had been tipped off that the raider was at Nassau, but before they quite reached the harbor the *Florida* was making full speed out into the Queen's Channel. It was a close call, for a big Yankee side-wheeler sighted the raider and started in pursuit, under full sail and with her big paddle wheels beating up a yeasty storm.

The big Yankee hung on like the bulldog she was, and just before dusk she had forged to extreme gun range for the third time that long day.

The crew lined the rails watching the Yankee. "She'll make it," grumbled Able Seaman Simmons.

"When then?" asked Apprentice Seaman Brinker.

Simmons spat over the side, turned his hand upside down by the side of his neck, tilted his head, thrust out his tongue and rolled up his eyes. "Hung for pirates we'll be, lad."

"Enough of that talk!" snapped Mister Read.

Clint Wallace had been training with his gun crew. They had their drill down pat. He was more than proud of them, for his experiences on the *McRae* had taught him the value of good gunnery and a precision gun crew. He looked toward the Yankee.

Dallas Longbow, First Loader, glanced at Clint. "Mebbe we can try a shot at her, sir."

"Too far," said Clint.

"For us, but not for them," said Second Loader Tack Beaseley.

Even as he spoke a gun thudded off on the Yankee and the shot plunged into the ocean a scant hundred yards behind the speeding raider. It was top-hole shooting in the rising wind and pitching sea.

Clint looked at sky and sea. The Yankee had the odds with him, but the weather was getting bad. Clint knew they were heading north, to raid along the New England Coast, but unless the Yankee let up, they'd have to cut for cover somewhere.

In the hours that followed, the raider ran into a hard blow and she pitched and wallowed under reefed canvas, while somewhere far astern the Yankee still hung on.

Clint was on his forecastle watch at midnight staring into the wet blackness. There was nothing to see but spume and darkness. He huddled into his oilskins. They had ripped under one arm and water seeped in. He hadn't ripped them himself and the only other person who had worn them had been *Mister* Robert Lester, the elegant. No apology; no offer of payment or replacement; nothing.

Clint raised his head to peer into the howling murk and his wet hair almost stood on end. An apparition had appeared in the darkness, a huge man-of-war with great thrashing paddles, plowing through the storm. "Steamer! Dead ahead!" screamed Clint.

The *Florida* sheered to one side and the great vessel shot past. "That's the *Vanderbilt*," said Midshipman Floyd as the Federal ship wallowed astern. "Eleven-inch guns."

The raider's crew moved swiftly. All lights were doused and power was shut off from the propeller while the *Florida* slowly wore ship to face in the opposite direction; her forward funnel was quickly lowered to the deck and a tarp was thrown over it.

It wasn't a moment too soon, for the big Yankee came crashing back through the seas. "Have you seen a two-funneled ship pass this way?" hailed an officer from the deck of the *Vanderbilt*.

Maffitt picked up his trumpet. "Aye, we did! Moving

fast she was, passed us by a few fathoms, going the other way."

"Thank you, sir!"

"No bother at all!" yelled Maffitt. "Good luck to ye!"

Then they parted, Yankee and rebel, in the midst of the howling storm. John Maffitt shoved back his cap and wiped the sweat from his face. "This is too close," he said. "Ho for the Spanish Main!"

And so it was. She headed for the homebound track of China and East Indian clippers, with banked fires, her propeller raised into its well so as not to drag, and all canvas set. There would be good hunting on the Spanish Main.

They raised her on February 12, 1863, at longitude 65 degrees 58 minutes west; latitude 24 degrees 1 minute north, somewhere well east of the Bahamas and north of Puerto Rico at four bells in the afternoon watch. A great white-winged three-masted ship under all plain sail. She was a sure enough Yankee, for no one else could build a ship like *that*.

The Stars and Stripes crept up to the peak of the *Florida*. The clipper slowly changed course and crowded on more sail. She was fast, a real greyhound of the high seas. Two hours logged past and the *Florida*, crowding on all sail and full steam, was gaining half a mile an hour. It was the sixth hour of pursuit when the *Florida* had inched up to within three miles of the clipper.

"Mister Wallace, you may open fire when you are ready, sir," called out Captain Maffitt through his trumpet.

"Load!" snapped Clint almost like an echo.

The First Loader slid in the red flannel powderbag, and the Second Loader slammed it home with the copper-tipped rammer. A wad was inserted, slammed home, followed by the shell and another wad. Clint cocked the gun lock and capped it. He crouched behind the rounded breech to sight. "Train left!" he said. The gun moved when hauled by the tacklemen. Clint turned the elevating screw and then lowered it a little. He stood up. "Stand clear!" he said. He waited for the slow uproll of the raider and then smoothly pulled the lock string. The gun slammed out a crisp report and a thick mouthful of smoke, shell, and flame. The stinking smoke blew back against Clint, and then he saw the thin white spout of water rise where the 110-pound projectile had struck the water two ship's lengths behind the clipper.

"Load!" snapped Clint.

Again the smooth and swift routine. Clint fired again. The spout was in line with the speeding clipper but still well astern. Someone laughed on the quiet deck of the raider. Clint turned quickly to see Bob Lester leaning languidly against the gun he captained, one of the broadside 6-inchers. Clint flushed. "Load!" he commanded.

This time the 110-pounder was within half a ship's length of the beautiful stern of the clipper. Bob Lester snickered again.

"Look!" yelled a seaman from the maintop.

The clipper had clewed up and was backing her yards. It was eight bells in the afternoon watch. The sun picked out the house flag of the clipper snapping in the wind. Yellow, red, and yellow in three broad horizontal stripes, with a huge white "L" on the central red stripe.

"A. A. Low and Brothers," said Averett studying the house flag through his glasses. "They pioneered the long China runs. Fine ships. The *Great Republic* and the *Samuel Russell*. Goers."

"What ship is that, sir?" asked Midshipman Floyd.

"I can't say. I know one thing: I've never seen a more beautiful ship in my life."

He was right. It was a magnificent product of Yankee shipbuilding and rigging. With her varnished masts and spars, pure white sails, glistening black hull, and broad gilt band, she was like a picture ship upon a picture ocean. A helpless and beautiful thing waiting for the lean and hungry raider to close in on her.

The Stars and Stripes were hauled down on the raider, and the Stars and Bars replaced them. The *Florida* circled the clipper twice. "It's the *Jacob Bell* of New York," said Captain Maffitt. "I've seen her before. A record breaker on passages from New York to India, New York to San Francisco, and back again." There was an odd tone in his voice, almost as though he wished he had not caught this beautiful vessel. "Cutter away, Mister Read," he said at last. "Bring her captain, papers, chronometer, and above all, her flag."

"Reefer," said Read to Clint.

Clint stepped into the cutter. She struck the water with a splash and whining of boat fall tackles. "Take over, reefer," said Read.

"Fend off forward! Cast loose the after fall! Cast loose the forward fall. Shove off forward! Shove off aft! Out oars! Stand by to give way! Give way together!" Clint rapped out his commands and the well-drilled crew had the boat under way, surging against the low swells, forging toward the great clipper. Clint held the tiller and as the cutter pulled away he saw the face of Bob Lester and the sarcastic grin on it. Try as he would, Clint never seemed able to get anything but criticism and sarcasm from the midshipman.

"Strike your colors, sir!" Maffitt trumpeted to the *Jacob Bell*.

There was no response. The *Florida* was hardly seventy-five yards away. Her gun ports were open and her broadside guns had been run out.

"Strike your colors, *Jacob Bell!*" roared Maffitt sharply.

The Stars and Stripes came down at a run just as the cutter bobbed alongside the Jacob's ladder.

Clint had never seen a better built or more lovely ship. In the long time that it took to ferry crew and passengers over to the *Florida,* he had plenty of leisure to look about. Her captain claimed she was carrying English property. Sixteen thousand chests of the finest tea; one thousand, three hundred and eighty tons of it; cassia, camphor, matting, thousands of fans, sandalwood, lacquerware, shell and ivory, temple bells, and thousands of cases of firecrackers. Value, ship and cargo, slightly over two million dollars!

Clint wandered about her that night. Live oak, locust and pine, cedar and rosewood, bird's-eye maple and satinwood had gone into her building. The cabins were exquisitely paneled in rare woods and filled with carved furniture covered with Chinese satin, while beneath her bowsprit, staring moodily over the ocean, was the figurehead of Captain Jacob Bell, her builder.

There was no hope for her. In the main cabin they piled the exquisite furniture and poured buckets of melted lard and butter over it. In the forehold they piled combustibles with lard and butter. In the huge main hold, among the tiers and tiers of rare tea they dumped a barrel of whale oil.

Clint and Mister Read stood alone on the teak deck at eight bells of the afternoon watch the day after they had captured her. She rocked gently in the swells with a creaking of blocks. "Savez" Read looked about. "All right, reefer, let's touch her off."

Clint felt a lump in his throat. He walked aft to the main hatch and called down. "Touch her off, Simmons!" Then in the main cabin he ignited the mess on the floor. When he regained the deck, he saw smoke curling up from main and fore hatches. The three of them dropped into the cutter as the sky grew dark with approaching dusk, while smoke wreathed up from the great ship they had left.

The *Florida* headed south through the darkening seas while fire began to dance up the tarred rigging of the *Jacob Bell* and flared along the varnished yards and dry canvas of the bunted sails.

The *Florida* was miles away when the firecrackers blew up in the hold of the clipper. Her masts fell like great trees into the sea, and the gutted hulk lay afloat like a trough of coals on the dark sea beneath a funeral pyre of smoke.

The course of the *Florida* was shaped for Carlisle Bay in the Barbados, while the jack-tars aboard the raider sipped the finest of fragrant *kysong* tea from the lost *Jacob Bell*.

CHAPTER EIGHT

The Burning Wind

"Cutter away!" crackled the command from the quarterdeck of the *Florida*. "Mister Lester! Take command of the boarding party! Mister Wallace will do the incendiary honors!"

The cutter struck the water with a splash. The sea was running high and the cutter heaved up and down like a cork. Clint took the tiller and gave his orders to the well-trained crew, while Bob Lester stood in the stern sheets staring eagerly at the tall, bark-rigged vessel. "Good hunting," he said almost to himself. He turned quickly. "Watch your helm, Acting!"

Clint flushed. The boat was being well handled, but trust Mister Lester to find fault. She rose high and came down hard, splattering foam and water.

The hunting had been good in the days since the magnificent *Jacob Bell* had perished. The *Florida* had coaled at the Barbados after a stormy passage, stormy not only for the raider but for Acting Midshipman Clinton Wallace as well. Twice he had been sharply reprimanded for carelessness, although it had been the fault of *Mister* Lester, and once Clint had been "mastheaded" for arguing with *Mister* Lester in front of the grinning crew. But the hunting *had* been good.

They had left a story behind at the Barbados that they were bound for the Caribbean to cut out a California steamer on her way from Panama to New York with gold. They had, instead, sailed down to the Line. Early in March they had gaffed the *Star of Peace* with a single shot from Clint's beloved forward pivot gun. Bound home from Calcutta with one thousand tons of saltpeter for the DuPont firm. The gun crews of the *Florida* had had fine practice on her from half a mile and she had burned with a flame that could be seen for twenty miles. Later the *Aldeberan,* bound from New York to Brazil with flour, beef, pork, hams, live lobsters barreled in ice and seaweed, brandies, wines, rum and whisky, and to top it off, thousands of clocks, had flared like a torch.

Then it had been the Yankee bark *Lapwing* in the Sargasso Sea, from Boston to Batavia, laden with smokeless coal and just at the time *Florida's* stokers had been scraping the bottoms of their bunkers. The raiders had found a fine family carriage consigned to a gentleman in Java on the deck. The *Lapwing* had been made into an auxiliary and renamed the *Oreto Number Two* under the command of Lieutenant Averett, armed with two twelve-pound howitzers, crewed with twenty men, and set off on a raid of her own, with a rendezvous at the equator.

The *Florida* had then set afire the bark M. J. *Colcord,* laden with flour and bacon for Capetown. Later they had rendezvoused with the *Oreto Number Two* to find that Averett was full of excuses and hadn't found a single prize, so Maffitt had sent him off again, to meet later at Fernando de Noronha, Brazil's penal rock island.

The week of April 17, 1863, thirty miles below the equator the *Florida* struck again. The huge ship *Commonwealth* of New York, 1,300 tons, bound round the Horn for Frisco, with a cargo insured for $370,000.00, and one third of it consigned to the military at San Francisco. New York papers aboard her had news about Abe

Lincoln replacing fumbling General Burnside with "Fightin' Joe" Hooker. Federal gunboats were on the hunt for the pirate Maffitt in the Caribbean. The *Commonwealth* had burned beautifully that hot night.

"Easy there, Acting!" snapped Lester, as Clint brought the tumbling cutter close to the side of the tall bark. She was named the *Henrietta*. Lester stepped easily from the surging cutter onto the ladder as the boat rose high, then the cutter dropped swiftly. On the next upsurge Clint went aboard, and as he did so he remembered he had not brought his sword with him, having a holstered navy Colt at his belt.

He was on the deck of the Yankee when he noticed the fine sword Lester was wearing. It was familiar; it was *too* familiar.

The bark was the *Henrietta* of Baltimore laden deep with flour, kegs of lard, and thousands of candles. She would burn like an inferno, thought Clint, as he walked aft into the captain's cabin while listening to *Mister* Lester's rattling voice as he took full control. The sun glinted from Clint's sword at *Mister* Lester's side.

Young Brinker followed Clint into the cabin. "Here, sir?" he asked.

Clint took the captain's chronometer from the bulkhead. "Yes, Brinker," he said quietly.

The boy set to work. He was one of the best incendiarists aboard the *Florida* by now, with special techniques of his own. He took out his sheath knife, drew out the drawers from beneath the bulk, smashed them, and shaved them down to kindling. He scattered newspapers over the wood, then piled broken furniture atop that, adding the oil from two lamps. The reek of the oil rose in the cabin.

"Sea is rising," said Brinker.

The ship was lifting and falling heavily. Clint nodded. "Wait for the word, Brinker," he said.

"Aye, aye, sir."

Clint went about his business, overseeing the men in the holds. When he returned to the deck, the cutter was returning to the *Henrietta* after taking over the last boatload of ironed prisoners.

"Touch her off, Acting," said Mister Lester from the quarter-deck.

"She'll burn fast," warned Clint.

Lester's handsome face reddened. "Touch her off!"

Clint glanced at the cutter making heavy way against the tumbling seas. It might be a close thing. He gave his orders, and the three fires were started. Brinker came up to Clint and glanced at the boat. "A little too fast, Mister Wallace!"

"Yes."

The flames were leaping and crackling when at last the cutter came alongside and the seamen dropped down into her. Clint looked aft. Mister Lester was standing by the wheel examining a sextant. He made no move to join Clint. The fire was gaining swiftly. *"Mister* Lester!" called Clint.

"Nervous, Acting?"

"Oh, you bumptious, pigheaded ..." said Clint under his breath.

The cutter was thudding hard against the wallowing side of the burning bark. The coxswain looked up desperately. "Can't hold her here much longer, Mister Wallace!" he said.

Clint bit his lip as he watched Lester stroll casually aft. "Found a fine sextant here," he said. "Just what I've been looking for."

"No looting. Captain's orders," said Clint.

The gray eyes studied Clint. "He doesn't have to know I've taken this, Acting."

"No looting," said Clint stubbornly.

The wind shifted and sent a wave of smoke and heat over them.

"Mister Lester!" yelled the cox'n, "I can't hold her much longer!"

Lester slid the cased instrument inside his coat. "Just keep your mouth shut," he warned. "Get into the boat."

Clint swung down the ladder and dropped into the pitching boat. He took the tiller and then he knew what the coxswain had been up against. The scend of the sea was driving her hard against the wallowing hull and the wind pressure was keeping her there. It would take maneuvering to get her clear without being damaged or swamped.

There was no sign of Mister Lester for some time as the boat crew fought desperately to fend off. Then he looked casually over the rail, chewing on an apple. Suddenly there was a sharp explosion and the hull of the bark shook. Flame and burning brands shot out over the side of the craft and fell hissing into the sea. Mister Lester didn't hesitate. As he stepped into the boat, another explosion shook the bark.

"They's some barrels of gunpowder in the tween-decks!" yelled a seaman. "Spaced apart they was, but if they *all* go up!"

Lester paled. He gripped the tiller. "Shove off forward!" he yelled excitedly.

"No!" cried Clint above the battering of the wind.

But it was too late. The bow swung out and the wind and the scend of the sea caught the boat and slammed it back hard against the side of the ship. Young Brinker screamed and when the cutter swung away again, he pulled his right arm from the sea. It had been smashed flat. Clint felt sick. "Shove off aft!" he commanded. "Out oars! Stern all! Pull! Pull! Pull!" The cutter slowly backed away from the ship. "Oars!" cried Clint. "Stand by to give way! Pull hard starboard! Hold water port!" The cutter turned to parallel the heaving seas. Now was the delicate time. "Pull hard starboard! Back water port!" Slowly, ever so slowly, she turned and the grandfather of all waves crept up on them. "Give way together! Stroke! Stroke! Stroke!" The wave swept harmlessly up against the stern of the cutter, lifted her high, higher than the decks of the burning ship, then let her slide down into a long trough.

The cutter was brought alongside, the falls made fast, and she was raised dripping from the sea. Brinker was tenderly carried below.

The *Florida,* close-reefed in a tumbling sea, bore away from the furiously blazing *Henrietta.*

It was a quiet ship that night. The surgeons labored over young Brinker as the hours went past and at dawn, just as the first light paled the sky, young Bennett Brinker, enlisted as being eighteen years of age, but actually fifteen, the only Brinker boy left out of three sons, one dead at Shiloh and the other dead of camp fever at Manassas, quietly slipped his cable and sailed for mythical Hi-Brazil.

They buried him at noon. The slight body, sewed into a hammock, with a 110-pound shot at the foot, slipped from the board over the side while the Stars and Bars were held back, and a volley rang three times over the tumbling seas.

"Mister Wallace," said Captain Maffitt quietly, "please report to my cabin at once."

Mister Robert Lester, Passed Midshipman, was waiting in the cabin. John Maffitt took his seat and looked up at the two young faces. "What happened?" he asked.

Bob Lester spoke. "The boat was not properly handled, sir. She slammed back against the side of the ship while young Brinker was fending off."

"I know that, sir. Have you any excuse?"

Lester flushed. "I was not in charge of the boat, sir."

Maffitt looked up at Clint. "Well?" he asked dryly.

"I have nothing to say, sir."

The pleasant faced changed. "That is for *me* to say, Mister Wallace! I watched you through the glass. You were in charge of the incendiary party. You knew what her cargo was! I saw those explosions! It is by God's grace alone that you were not blown up with that ship! Why didn't you leave earlier?"

Clint could not speak. The midshipman standing beside him did not speak.

"Well, *Mister* Wallace?"

"Perhaps the coxswain might throw some light on it, sir," said Clint at last.

"Perhaps."

The coxswain was sent in. He saluted and removed his cap. Maffitt eyed him. "Coxswain," he said quietly, "what happened beside that ship?"

"The wind and waves were too strong, sir. The scend of the sea forced us against the ship. The young gentlemen took a long time to come into the cutter. The first command was to shove off forward, which, in my opinion, begging the young gentlemen's pardons, sir, was the wrong thing to do. The bow swung out and the sea slammed it back. Poor Brinker never had a chance. Poor lad. I ..." His voice trailed off.

Maffitt eyed Clint. "I have seen you handle small boats before, sir. Why did you make such a mistake?"

"I did not give the command to shove off forward, sir."

In the silence that followed, even above the rushing of the sea against the side of the ship and the howling of the wind through the taut rigging, Clint swore he could hear the separate ticking of each of the captured chronometers hanging in a neat row on the bulkhead.

"Who gave that command?" asked Captain Maffitt. "You, Coxswain?"

"No, sir!"

"You, Mister Lester?"

Again the multitude of ticking, ticking, ticking ...

"No, sir," said Mister Lester.

Maffitt's steady eyes flicked from Lester to Clint and

then back again. "Coxswain, who gave that command?" he asked.

"I don't know, sir. I heard it clearly but could not tell who it was. Mister Lester or Mister Wallace."

"Thank you, Coxswain. Dismissed."

The man saluted and left the cabin.

Maffitt stood up and paced back and forth. "One of you gentlemen is lying. I will not probe into it. Sufficient to say that the whole affair was badly handled. The fires were started too quickly. There was too much delay in leaving the ship. There was utter carelessness in getting the cutter away. A man was horribly injured and died in great pain because of the carelessness of the man who gave that order."

The *Florida* dipped up and down.

"A man can make mistakes," said the officer quietly. "We all do, but they are honorable mistakes for the most part. The Confederate States of America has been pleased to commission us as officers and gentlemen. When we touch at the first Confederate port, gentlemen, I shall ask that both of you be relieved from duty aboard this ship, unless, before that time, the one of you who is responsible for the death of a fine young seaman sees fit to confess.

"Until the time we do touch a Confederate port, I cannot afford to spare any of my officers. Therefore you will remain on duty. Dismissed, gentlemen."

They stepped outside into the companionway and Clint looked at Lester. "Well?"

"You were the boat commander, Acting."

"You gave the command."

"Can you prove it?"

The ship swayed up and down. "No," said Clint quietly. "But there's such a thing as conscience. Mine is clear, at least."

Lester smiled thinly and raised a fist. "Smell that, Acting," he said. "I can use it if I have to."

Clint grinned. "Now?" he said softly. "Now, *Mister* Lester?"

"All hands on deck!" rapped out a shrill command.

They sprinted for the ladder and went up it like monkeys.

"All hands shorten sail!"

They went up the shrouds and in the fierce wind Clint seemed to ease some of the bitterness he had against Bob Lester as he fought the elements to get in the thrashing sail.

The three-masted ship was making fast time, and when the warning forward pivot gun cracked she ignored the warning and kept on, raising more kites, crowding on all her canvas.

The *Florida* was under sail at the time but she didn't seem to be footing as fast as the fleeing Yankee. "Lower the propeller," ordered Captain Maffitt. "I want full steam."

The banked fires were raked and sliced, then a thick layer of black coal covered the glowing red bed, and as the *Florida* kept on under sail, losing a little every half-hour, the steam pressure crept up in the gauges. Then a thick wreath of smoke blew from the twin funnels, the engines were engaged, and the big propeller began to turn, driving the slim raider on at twelve knots.

At one-mile range the forward pivot gun cracked again and the stranger let fly her sheets and wallowed in the heaving seas.

"Mister Lester!" called out Captain Maffitt. "Take command of the boarding party! Mister Wallace, take charge of the incendiary party!"

Clint ran toward the cutter. Here it was again, the same deadly combination of Lester and Wallace, a tumbling sea, and a ship to be torched.

She was the *Oneida,* ninety-five days out of Shanghai, bound for New York, laden with tea and bolts of Chinese silk. The cutter plowed back and forth hauling prisoners, bolts of silk, the flag, charts, and chronometer, while Clint and his men readied the fine ship for burning.

Clint stood by the starboard rail watching the cutter at the side of the *Florida*. Simmons came up beside him. "All set for the match, sir!"

"Hold it for the word, Simmons."

"Touch it off," said Mister Lester from the quarter-deck.

"A mite early, if I may say so, sir," said Simmons.

"Touch it off!"

Simmons looked at Clint, from whom he usually took his orders. "Go ahead," said Clint quietly.

The fires were crackling below when Clint saw the cutter come alongside. The wind shifted and a runnel of fire raced up the port shrouds of the foremast and danced crazily out along the lower yards, licking hungrily at the canvas.

He looked about and saw Simmons running from forward. "She's going fast, sir!" he said.

"Where's Mister Lester?"

Simmons stared at him. "Ain't he in the cutter?"

"No!"

The flames now raced up the main shrouds and licked at the yards. Shreds of burning canvas began to drop on the decks. A hatch cover began to burn.

"Ahoy!" cried the coxswain. "Time to leave there! Ahoy!"

"Get aboard the cutter!" snapped Clint to Simmons.

"Where are you going, sir?"

"To find Mister Lester."

Simmons stared at him. "You won't have a chance, sir!"

"Get aboard!"

Simmons shrugged and scuttled down the ladder.

Clint brushed a burning shred of canvas from his coat. The last time he had seen Lester he had been on the quarter-deck. Clint ran aft. "Lester! Lester!" he yelled.

No answer. He glanced over the side. The cutter crew were fending off and batting at shreds of burning canvas and rope that had dropped on them. "Shove off!" yelled Clint. "Wait fifty yards from the ship! Stay to windward!"

Flames and smoke were gushing up from the open hatches. Clint hesitated, then plunged down a ladder to the tween-decks into a smoky haze thick with the smell of burning tea and silk. "Lester!" he yelled.

There was no answer. Clint ripped loose his neck scarf and wet it with water from a breaker racked to a bulkhead. He tied the wet scarf about his nose and mouth and began to probe his way into the thick, smoky darkness. His head reeled and his breath was coming in short gasps when he slammed a shoulder against a cabin door and burst into a stateroom. Bob Lester lay on the deck and he did not move.

Clint swiftly tied the midshipman's wrists together with his handkerchief, then raised the hanked arms over his own head and straddled the unconscious reefer. He began to crawl through the thickening smoke toward the nearest ladder, dragging the unconscious body beneath him. Slowly he went, foot by foot, his head reeling and his hands stinging from the heated deck, until he reached the ladder.

He dragged Lester up the ladder rung by rung and reached the deck in a thick haze of smoke and flame shot through with burning eyes of canvas and rope floating down from aloft. Somehow he got Lester to the windward rail, hoisted him up, and then looked for the cutter bobbing on the water a hundred yards away.

"Look out, sir!" shrieked Simmons. "The mainmast!"

Clint turned. The great spar was tilting slowly toward the side of the ship as the shrouds and stays were burned through. There was no time to waste. Clint pulled Lester up on the cap rail, got a good breath, then heaved him over the side. Clint pulled off his shoes, ripped off his swordbelt and sword, frock coat and cap, climbed up on the cap rail, and arced cleanly into the sea just as the mast fell slowly and heavily to smash through the rail within a few feet of where he had been standing.

He went down deep and then curved slowly up again, breaking surface close beside the bewildered face of Bob Lester. "Are you all right?" yelled Clint.

"Yes."

The cutter was coming close to them with great sweeps of the oars and now strong hands caught hold of both boys and heaved them into the stern sheets. The cutter wallowed deeply as she was turned, then shot away on a course for the raider as the foremast fell, followed swiftly by the mizzenmast. The *Oneida* was burning like a torch.

They clambered over the *Florida's* rail as the cutter was hoisted up. "Fine work, Mister Wallace," said Captain Maffitt.

"Thank you, sir."

Bob Lester brushed back his wet hair. "Thanks, Acting," he said quietly.

Clint did not answer. He turned on a heel and walked to his quarters in the steerage. His sword was gone because of the carelessness of Mister Lester.

Midshipman Floyd, now Acting Master of the *Florida,* came into the steerage and watched Clint. "That was smartly done, Wallace," he said at last.

"Thanks, Mister Floyd."

"It was a close shave for you. You could have saved yourself first, and no one would have thought unkindly of you."

"I would have done the same for a Yankee."

"Yes, I suppose so."

Clint turned. "What's wrong now?" he demanded.

"Nothing. Except that the man tried to make up to you."

"I want nothing from him!"

Floyd shrugged. "It takes a big man to save the life of

another man. It takes a bigger man to accept a man whom he has had reason to dislike."

"I want no preaching, Mister Floyd!"

"I suppose not." The Acting Master turned and was gone.

Clint dropped into his bunk and looked up at the deck above him. The cruise was going well. They had been seventy days on the raid, and according to Maffitt's calculations they had destroyed six millions dollars' worth of Yankee ships and cargoes.

He felt the *Florida* heel off on a new course, bound for Fernando de Noronha. Maybe he would have a chance to get on one of the auxiliaries of the *Florida*. It would be better for him and perhaps for the *Florida,* but he knew he would hate to leave her.

CHAPTER NINE

Fortune Favors the Brave

Fernando de Noronha loomed out of the ocean, a gigantic granite hump two hundred miles from Cape St. Roque. The *Florida* rolled gently in the sea, moving slowly away from the huge rock cairn. There had been disappointment at the rock. The *Alabama,* under command of Captain Raphael Semmes, had been there just the week before on *her* raiding cruise, and aboard her had been John Maffitt's son Eugene, serving as an officer.

The reception of the *Florida* had been cold. The raider was again low on coal, but a Brazilian man-of-war had appeared and her polite but insistent captain had ordered the *Florida* to leave and take her prisoners with her, despite Maffitt's appeals for pratique, the communication between a ship and the port in which it arrives, or a license or permission to hold intercourse and trade with the inhabitants of a place after sanitary inspection or quarantine.

The fact was that Brazil was getting worried about the power and wrath of the United States Navy, and besides, the coffee market of the north, for her great armies, was a lucrative one.

There were two other ships on the heaving waters, moving slowly away from the *Florida* on divergent courses.

One was the *Oreto Number Two,* now under command of Acting Master Floyd. The other ship was the *Kate Dyer,* captured by *Oreto Number Two* through a simple ruse. *Oreto Number Two* had been the Yankee bark *Lapwing,* laden with coal and with a fine carriage destined for a gentleman in Java, upon her deck. The crew of *Oreto Number Two* had sawed off a thick spar, painted it black, and placed it upon the carriage wheels for a "Quaker" gun. The bluff had frightened the skipper of the *Kate Dyer.*

The *Florida's* bunkers were filled with coal from *Oreto Number Two.* The auxiliary had orders to meet the *Florida* off Rocas Island, midway between Fernando de Noronha and the Brazilian mainland.

It had just chimed eight bells to mark the passing of the second dogwatch, and the *Florida* was slipping easily across a moonlit sea when Clint went below to his quarters, which he still shared with Mister Lester. A quiet enough place it was too, for two midshipmen, as Quartermaster Billups had remarked, for they did not speak to each other, nor had they since Lester had thanked Clint for saving his life.

Clint placed a hand on his bunk and bent to open a drawer beneath it. His hand felt something hard under the blankets and he stood up and threw the blankets back. A leather case lay there. He picked it up and opened it. It held a fine sextant, beautifully engraved, and Clint immediately recognized it as the one Bob Lester had taken from the *Henrietta* despite Captain Maffitt's orders against looting.

Clint's face tightened. Just that very day the Master-at-Arms had shaken down the crew's quarters to look for loot. They were commerce destroyers, not pirates, and it would not look well to the rest of the world if the crew were allowed looting in any form. A rumor had drifted about the ship that the captain wasn't above having the steerage and officers' quarters checked for loot as well.

It would be just like Bob Lester to plant his stolen sextant in Clint's bunk and let him take the blame for looting. Clint eyed the beautiful precision instrument. All such instruments had been collected to be turned over to the Navy Department for reissuance to Confederate ships. There was a dearth of such instruments throughout the South, as there was a dearth of many other things.

His temper was boiling swiftly and the safety valve was beginning to hiss. He threw the sextant on Lester's bunk, yanked the door open, and strode swiftly along to the nearest ladder leading up to the main deck. The *Florida* was ghosting along easily with a soft musical washing of water against her sides and the thrum of the tropical wind through the taut rigging.

Passed Midshipman Bob Lester was standing near the foremast watching some of the hands skylarking. Two of them were sparring in an exaggerated style, while two others were Indian wrestling. An English seaman was softly playing a flute.

Clint walked around to face Bob Lester. "You've done it now," he said quietly.

The handsome midshipman straightened. "What do you mean?" he asked coldly.

The sailors stopped skylarking and the music of the flute died away.

"You figured there might be a shakedown of the steerage by the Master-at-Arms," said Clint.

"That's so, but what has that to do with me?"

"You're sure you don't know?"

Lester reddened. "Look, Acting," he said insolently, "I don't know what's bothering you, but I'm not in the mood to listen to it."

"You'll listen to it, all right!" Clint stepped back a little. "You once held up a fist and said you could use it if you had to. Put it up again, *Mister* Lester!"

Lester smiled coldly. "With pleasure," he said. He raised his fist and Clint instantly slapped it aside.

The men were all on their feet now and Mister Hoole came forward. "What is this, gentlemen?" he asked.

Clint looked at him. "It's skylarking time, isn't it, Mister Hoole?"

"It is."

Clint reached out and slapped Lester hard across the face, knocking off his cap.

"Just a minute there!" said Mister Hoole.

"Let them go to it," a quiet voice said. "Savez" Read came forward. "This has been coming for some time. Fair and even. Skylarking time." He smiled. "Right, gentlemen?"

Rob Lester nodded. He peeled off the white shirt he was wearing and stepped back, raising his fists in approved fashion.

"Form a ring!" said Seaman Simmons.

Clint shucked his coat and shirt and stepped forward.

"Ready?" asked Mister Read.

Roth boys nodded.

"Time, gentlemen," said "Savez."

Rob Lester moved swiftly, and his attack was so sudden and so skilled that Clint was sitting on the deck with a stinging midriff and jaw before he quite knew what had happened.

Lester stepped back, threw a few hard shadow punches, bounced around lightly on his feet, and then coolly eyed Clint.

Clint got up slowly. He raised his fists and moved in. This time he managed to tap Lester two or three times at a distance without hurting him before he landed hard against the fife rail of the foremast and went down on one knee. He shook his head. The blow that had felled him had come out of thin air.

Lester smiled. "I may not have mentioned previously that I was champion of my class at The Citadel."

Clint got up. This time he let Bob come to him, and the taller boy moved in cautiously, feinting and ducking until he managed to clip Clint on the jaw and stagger him. He rushed in to finish the job only to walk into a hard left fist that glanced from his nose. He bent over from a right to the midriff, and the left seemingly came up from the deck to connect solidly under his chin. He sat down hard and stared up at Clint in surprise.

Clint threw a few exaggerated punches, bounced high on his feet, and then smiled down on the surprised midshipman. "I may not have mentioned," he said archly, "that I was champion of my class in the forecastle of the ol' *Creole Queen.*"

Simmons slapped his thighs. "That Mister Wallace," he said delightedly. "Always good for a laugh, he is."

"Yeh," said *Mister* Lester softly.

"Time, gentlemen," said Read.

This time they went round and round. Bob, the sparring master, and Clint, the hard in-fighting bulldog, who took three punches to get one in, and the odds were even up. Clint felt a tooth crack and his mouth tasted salty from blood, but he had the satisfaction of seeing a "mouse" under one of *Mister* Lester's beautiful gray eyes.

"Time," said "Savez" Read.

Clint dropped onto Seaman Simmons' knee, and one of the sailors swabbed his face and shoulders with a sponge. "He's shifty, he is," said Simmons, "but he'll not last."

Clint's breath was coming hot and heavy. "Sure, sure," he said, "and I wish you were out there to tire him out."

They met in the center of the ring. Clint had noticed that every time Bob threw a hard right hook he invariably dropped his left. Three times Clint was staggered by that vicious right before he went under it, then rose high to come across Bob's lowered left with a sweeping hook that drove *Mister* Lester to the deck. Flecks of blood spewed from his mouth and stained the planking.

Clint stepped back and waited. "Enough?" he said.

Lester smiled thinly. "Oh, no, *Mister* Wallace," he said as he got up and raised his fists.

Lieutenant Hoole looked quickly at Lieutenant Read. "If the Old Man hears about this ..." His voice trailed off.

"Let them go to it."

Both boys were tired now and each punch needed an effort, and the effect of them, unless one of them was lucky, didn't amount to much. The *Florida* lifted and swayed and the rising and falling deck wasn't of much help as far as footwork was concerned. Three times Mister Read stopped the fight and asked them if they wanted to go on, and neither one of them would quit.

Clint shook his head as Bob landed a hard one-two. He sank a weak left into his opponent's midriff, then danced back. Bob was throwing that right hook again, where he lowered his left. Three times again, and then Clint tried the same counterattack he had tried before and it worked. But the results were slightly different, for at the same time he rode over the lowered left arm with his sweeping right hook, Mister Lester fired a right cross to the chin that shook Clint to the heels. The *Florida* surged a little and Clint went down, and something fell heavily across his chest. Clint was licked. He had closed his eyes so as not to see Mister Lester's grinning face.

"What do ye call a thing like that?" asked a Limey seaman.

The quiet, amused voice of Lieutenant Read came to Clint. "Why, I'd call it a draw, and a mighty good one too."

"Depends on who gets up first," said Mister Hoole sagely.

Clint opened his eyes and looked full into Mister

Lester's face, not inches from his own, battered and bruised, as his face was battered and bruised. Mister Lester grinned weakly. "We can always get up together, Acting," he said.

And so it was. The two of them got up together and the crewmen cheered.

"What is this, gentlemen?" demanded a familiar voice.

They all turned to see Captain Maffitt standing beside the mainmast. "Skylarking, sir," said Lieutenant Read.

"I see." Maffitt studied the battered faces of his two lowest ranking officers. "Main trestletrees, gentlemen." he said politely to Clint and Bob.

"Doesn't the captain mean the main trestletrees for one, and the fore, or mizzen trestletrees for the other, sir?" asked Lieutenant Hoole.

Maffitt shook his head. "I think I made myself clear enough, gentlemen. Up with you!"

Wearily they climbed the ratlines, slid in through the lubber's hole, and rested against the topmast and lower mast doublings.

Minutes ticked past and then Clint said, "It was a good fight, *Mister* Lester."

"Yes."

"But the reason for it has not been forgotten by me."

"I wish I knew what it was, *Mister* Wallace."

Clint scowled. "There you go again! You planted that sextant from the *Henrietta* in my bunk so that the Captain would think I had looted it, instead of you."

The boy was puzzled. *"Me, Mister* Wallace? The sextant was for you. I knew you wouldn't speak to me, so I left it there for you. Captain Maffitt had told me to keep it when I turned it in to him. He said the Navy needed instruments, and as I was on the lowest rung of the ladder to being a future admiral in the service of our country, I'd need a good sextant as well as any other naval officer."

"Good heavens!" said Clint explosively. "Why didn't you tell me?"

"As I told you, you wouldn't talk to me."

Clint stared at the boy. "Thanks," he said.

Lester smiled. "I told the Captain about the mess I had made in the cutter that day when the *Oneida* was burned. All of it was my fault, and every day when I saw your accusing looks, I felt worse and worse. But it wasn't easy for me to come to you. Here they had made me a Passed Midshipman, more by a fluke than anything else, and you were only an Acting and a better seaman and gunner than I'd ever be. I was jealous and I made it hard for you because of that jealousy. It was the wrong thing to do, but my parents were so proud of me being a midshipman on the *Florida* that I just couldn't go to the Captain and ask to be reduced. It was wrong, *Mister* Wallace."

"My friends call me Clint, Bob."

The handsome boy thrust out a hand. "Shipmates?"

Clint gripped Bob's hand hard. "Shipmates!" he said.

"Sail ho!" cried a lookout.

"Where away?" called out Mister Read from the quarter-deck.

"Broad on the port beam, sir!"

"Can you make her out clearly?"

"Aye, aye, sir! A fine brig and a fast one! Yankee, from the cut of her sails!"

"General quarters!"

The alarm sounded throughout the ship. Two bruised-looking reefers slid down backstays to the deck and took their posts at their guns as the raider changed course and headed for the brig.

The brig was a beautiful ship and a fast sailer but the warning gun shot across her lovely bows stopped her. She was the *Clarence,* Rio de Janeiro to Baltimore, with ten thousand bags of coffee in her holds consigned to the U.S. Quartermaster.

While the crew was being removed from the brig, preparatory to burning her, Captain Maffitt and Lieutenant Read were in deep conference aboard the *Florida*. In a short time word was passed to the boarding crew on the *Clarence* not to set the torch to her. Messrs. Maffitt, Read, and Company had other ideas.

Captain Maffitt had the crew assembled at the break of the quarter-deck. "Men," he said, "the *Florida* will have to move north. It will soon be too dangerous for us here in the South Atlantic. Lieutenant Read has suggested that he take the *Clarence* and a score of men, proceed to Hampton Roads, Virginia, a stronghold of the Federal Navy, and Army as well, to cut out a steamer or gunboat of the enemy. Lieutenant Read thinks this is entirely feasible by using the brig's papers and carrying only a small crew, thus to pass Fortress Monroe. If this is not possible, he has volunteered to attempt an entrance into Baltimore Harbor to fire the Yankee shipping there."

Bob Lester whistled softly.

"The *Florida* will rendezvous off the New England Coast, somewhere off Nantucket, with the *Clarence*." He paused. "God willing, men."

The crewmen and officers eyed each other, wondering who would be chosen for the daring raid.

Maffitt paced back and forth. "Lieutenant Read has asked for twenty men, Assistant Engineer Brown, and Quartermaster Billups. I do not wish to lose them, but I must give Lieutenant Read every advantage, and so they will go. Mister Read has asked for two junior officers as well."

The *Florida* creaked in the gentle swells. Clint softly sucked in his breath. Oh, if he could only go!

"Passed Midshipman Robert Lester will go," said Captain Maffitt.

Please, sir, thought Clint.

"And Passed Midshipman Clinton Wallace."

Why not me instead, thought Clint? Acting Midshipman Clinton Wallace was as good as Passed Midshipman Clinton Wallace. *"Passed* Midshipman Wallace!" he yelled, and then his face grew crimson as he saw the grinning faces of officers and crew.

"I took it upon myself, *Mister* Wallace, with the approval of the other officers, and I'm sure the crew as well, to promote you, sir."

"Thank you, sir!"

Maffitt's face clouded. "I wonder if you men will thank me later on," he said quietly. "No matter! To business! There is much to be done."

By early morning of the next day the *Clarence* was armed and provisioned and ready to go. Read stood on his own deck at last, with his crew, listening to the last words of one of the greatest raiders of them all.

"If you find it impossible to enter Hampton Roads, you will continue up the coast toward Nantucket. The *Florida* should be there by about July 4, unless we are sunk.

"If we *do* meet we'll sweep the coast together! You might make a capture or two on the way up. You'll be on your own. No orders to hamper you. Your success will depend on yourselves and your sturdy hearts! Cast off there!"

The lines were loosened from the *Clarence* and then hauled inboard. The brig drifted away from the sleek raider. When a hundred yards parted them, the sails of the brig were loosed, sheeted home, and began to fill. "Dip our colors, Mister Wallace," said Captain Read.

The colors dipped and the *Florida* dipped hers in return.

Maffitt stood by the weather rail of the raider. He raised his trumpet. "Remember, *Mister* Read," he called, "fortune favors the brave!"

Clint watched the *Florida* set course for Pernambuco.

She was beautiful and she was his ship, but a sailor goes where he is ordered to go, no matter the heartache. "I wonder if we'll ever see her again," he said quietly.

"I wonder," echoed Bob Lester.

Fortune favors the brave.

CHAPTER TEN
A Toy Raider and Quaker Guns

The *Clarence* had been allowed only one six-pounder field howitzer by Captain Maffitt for heavy armament, with rifles and pistols for the crew's sidearms. But seamen are famed for their handiness, and in a very short time five more "guns" peered from improvised ports on the brig. "Quaker" guns, made of sawed-off spars, painted black and mounted on dummy carriages. Captain Read had also ordered a makeshift bridge rigged for him upon which to take his stance, telescope thrust under arm and long reddish mustache flaring in the sea breeze.

The *Whistling Wind* was the first prize, captured 250 miles west of the Bahamas, loaded with coal for Union Admiral Farragut's Gulf Blockading Squadron. She burned beautifully. Next was the schooner *Alfred H. Partridge*, bound for Matamoras, loaded with arms and clothing for Union sympathizers in Texas. She was bonded by Captain Read, and the skipper was asked to deliver the cargo to Confederate citizens in Texas. Captain Read and the gallant, though small, crew of the *Clarence*, didn't know anything at that time of the underhanded business of Yankee traders clearing Northern ports for ports in Mexico, where cargo was transshipped to "rebels" in Texas, for an almighty neat profit, while Yankee boys were dying on the bloody battlefields of Virginia.

Off Cape Hatteras they captured the brig *Mary Alvina* on a fine June day. She was bound for the port of New Orleans with commissary stores for the Union forces there. She burned well too.

Captain Read had been studying newspapers picked up aboard his prizes, and he had also questioned officers and crews of the vessels. Fortress Monroe was stopping all comers. Only ships carrying government supplies could enter Hampton Roads. The original papers of the *Clarence* could get them into Chesapeake Bay, but not a fathom further.

The *Clarence* was directly in the well-beaten track of the Union ships that constantly shuttled between the blockade bases on the Southern Coast and Hampton Roads. Read decided to cruise north, hoping to capture a prize that would have papers able to get him into Hampton Roads. They had been uncommonly lucky so far. Fortune favors ...

The big bark-rigged vessel appeared out of the dawn mist off the Virginia Capes which were just visible off to port of the *Clarence*. The breeze was fair and the ship was fast. Both ships were within plain sight of each other, but the brig had no chance of overtaking the fast Yankee.

"Savez" Read scratched at his growing red beard. "*Mister* Wallace," he snapped. "Close those gun ports! We can't outrun that bark but maybe we can outsmart her! *Mister* Lester, hoist the United States flag upside down!"

Bob Lester stared at his commanding officer.

"Jump and make it so!" said Read.

Lester hauled down the flag, turned it upside down, and hoisted it again. It was the traditional distress signal of the sea.

The bark began to change course and headed for the *Clarence*.

"*Mister* Wallace!" said Read. "I want you and ten men in the cutter. No uniforms! No rifles! Just pistols!"

The bark closed in until she was within hailing distance of the *Clarence*. "What's wrong?" came the hail.

"Lower away!" said Read.

The cutter went down at a run and was cast loose from the falls, to be rowed toward the bark. Meanwhile, on the deck of the *Clarence* not a soul showed.

The cutter was close to the Jacob's ladder of the bark. Read stepped onto the ladder. Clint made the cutter's painter fast to the bottom of the ladder and followed his skipper, and in turn he was followed by the boarding party.

A dignified man waited on the deck. "What is the trouble, sir?" he asked Read.

"Nothing, sir. For us, that is. Trouble for you though." He took a pistol from beneath his coat and cocked it. "Your ship is my prize, sir. I am Captain Read of the auxiliary ship, *Clarence,* Confederate States Navy. Be kind enough to show me your papers and log, sir."

It was that easy. She was the bark *Tacony,* in ballast from the Union base at Port Royal, bound for Philadelphia. Read studied her log and learned what he had already suspected; the *Tacony* was a far faster sailing ship than the *Clarence*. She was almost ideal for an auxiliary raider, but she could not enter Hampton Roads or Baltimore according to her orders. Captain Maffitt had ordered a rendezvous off the New England Coast, somewhere off Nantucket, and time was running short. They would have to sail north, but there would be good hunting there too.

Clint leaned against the rail, watching the men of the *Tacony* being ironed. He looked beyond the *Clarence* and saw another ship, a schooner. "Look, sir!" he called.

Read grinned piratically. "*Mister* Wallace. Take the

cutter back to the *Clarence,* get a few more men, then get me that fine schooner."

The schooner *M. A. Schindler* was caught and fired in half an hour, and while the cutter was pulling back to the *Clarence,* yet another ship came into view, heading for the burning schooner.

The cutter pulled hard for the *Clarence,* and Clint's heart sank as he saw the second cutter being rowed slowly between the *Clarence* and the *Tacony* with the six-pounder in it.

But Midshipman Robert Lester was up to the occasion. As the ship approached and came within hailing distance, he had the false ports of the *Clarence* dropped, and the wooden snouts of the "Quaker" guns peered menacingly at the new arrival.

"Don't shoot!" yelled the captain of the vessel.

She was the schooner *Kate Stewart,* and there was no chance of burning her for she carried twenty women on board, bound for Mexico.

Captain Read transferred all his prisoners to her and bonded her. When the *Kate Stewart* touched land, and it would be certain to be the nearest port, the Federal forces would know that an auxiliary raider was loose along the coast. There was no other choice. Captain Read bragged steadily about a rebel high-seas fleet that would soon scourge the coast, hoping it would have some effect.

Later, the brig *Arabella* came by, laden with neutral cargo, and was allowed to continue on her way.

At high noon they touched off the *Clarence* for a gigantic coffee roasting. Thousands of burning bags of Brazilian coffee beans filled the sea air with their odor.

The *Tacony* headed north under full sail.

It was a busy place off the Delaware Capes. The brig *Umpire,* Cuba to Boston with sugar and molasses, burned sweetly. That same night a Federal man-of-war questioned the *Tacony* about "rebel pirates," and was given accurate misdirections. Just before daylight another Yankee bulldog appeared and was also given directions. The first Yankee had been sent northwest and the second one to the southeast.

June was running out quickly while the *Tacony* forged northward, ever northward, with her now disreputable-looking crew. On the 20th the huge packet *Isaac Webb*, with seven hundred and fifty passengers aboard, mostly immigrants, was stopped, bonded for a fraction of her value, and allowed to proceed. Not so the fishing schooner *Micawber*, which got nosy and was burned for its pains, while the passengers on the *Isaac Webb* got down on their knees and prayed for deliverance.

On the 21st it was the magnificent new clipper *Byzantium*, full of coals from Newcastle, and she burned swiftly, as did the *Goodspeed* later that same day.

The *Tacony* closed in on the New England fishing fleet on the 22nd, for the waters were full of Gloucestermen and Cape Codders out for the summer catch of halibut, cod, and mackerel. Five of them flared up on the 22nd; eight within the next few days were captured and six of them torched, while one was filled with prisoners and sent to port. The eighth was saved for another purpose.

On the 24th it was the gigantic *Shatemuc* bound for Boston with hundreds of Irish immigrants aboard her, which was stopped by the *Tacony*, and a $150,000.00 bond signed.

The mackerel schooner *Archer* lay close alongside the *Tacony*, while the colors, armament, and some stores were transferred to her from the bark. It was to be Read's third flagship.

It was past midnight when the tired crew were finishing the hard work of transferring the last of the stores. "Savez" stood on the deck of his latest ship, and when the job was finished he spoke quietly to his crew. "We've learned there are over twenty Yankee gunboats searching for us. They have a complete description of the

Tacony and it wouldn't be long before they spotted her. The *Archer* looks like dozens of other fishing craft of her type. She is only ninety tons, sails well, and is easily handled. No Yankee vessel would dream of suspecting us now. This gives us a chance to dodge about a bit for more prospects."

The men nodded. The sails slatted in the slight breeze and the two hulls ground together.

Read paced back and forth for a moment. "It is my intention to follow the coast still further north, with the purpose of burning the shipping in some exposed harbor, and perhaps of cutting out a fast steamer for our next ship."

Rob Lester whistled softly as he looked at Clint.

"You wanted to be a hero," said Clint dryly.

Read looked at his watch. "Touch off the *Tacony*, Mister Wallace. She should burn well."

The *Archer* moved easily off into the darkness of the predawn while the tall *Tacony* flared up against the night.

Portland, Maine was somewhere in the offing as the *Archer* moved slowly through a clinging fog. It was close to noon, but one could hardly tell it was so.

Clint peered through the opaqueness. He was tired. They were all tired aboard the *Archer*, for these had been trying though successful days since they had left the *Florida*. Clint wondered where she was now. Still raiding, penned up in a neutral harbor, or at the bottom of the sea as so many of her victims were.

"See anything, Clint?" asked Bob Lester. Fog.

"Yes, and more fog."

Clint looked at the midshipman. They had grown to be shipmates since the fight they had had aboard the raider. "What do you think about 'Savez's' plan, Bob?"

Bob shrugged. "Daring. Not prudent. But daring."

"I agree." Clint strained his eyes at the drifting fog. An hour ago he could have sworn he had seen a Yankee man-of-war, gun ports open, and great Dahlgren guns peering myopically and hungrily at the little schooner. "Do you think we'll get away with it?"

"No."

Clint rubbed his tired eyes. "If we don't, we'll be killed or captured. I don't mind being killed, but I sure don't want to be captured."

Bob laughed quietly. "I love the way you put that."

"I mean it," said Clint stubbornly. "I won't be taken prisoner, Bob."

The midshipman looked at Clint and placed a hand on his shoulder. "Neither will I."

"We'll stick together then?"

Again the pressure on the shoulder. There was no need to speak.

"Look out!" yelled Clint.

"What is it?"

"Port your helm!" screamed Clint back to the man at the wheel.

It was too late. The bows of the *Archer* struck a low-lying dory, and as the planking of the small boat splintered beneath the forefoot of the schooner, two oilskin-clad men leaped for the bowsprit of the *Archer* and caught it. Clint and Bob hauled them back to the deck.

"Whew!" said the biggest of the two fishermen. "That was right close now."

"Sorry about your dory," said Clint. Neither he nor Bob was in uniform, nor were any of the crew.

The second fisherman shrugged. "Third time it has happened to me. What boat is this?"

"*Archer*, out of Southport."

The man nodded. "I'm Albert T. Bigger; my mate here is Elbridge Titcomb. We be Portland men."

Clint nodded toward Bob. "Bob Lester there. I'm Clint Wallace."

"Where ye bound?"

"Portland," said Clint on a hazard.

"Ye're off course then."

Bob leaned casually against the foremast. "You know the way?"

Bigger grinned and spat over the side. "Blind, in fog, or any other way. Born and bred in these waters I was."

"What's going on here?" asked Captain Read.

Clint turned. "We ran down their dory, Captain Read."

"Sorry to hear that." Read eyed them. "We're trying to make Portland, men. We heard that a rebel raider was burning ships all along the New England Coast."

"Sho!" said Titcomb.

"We figured we might be safe at Portland."

"Sure will! We got Fort Preble there."

"Yup," said Bigger, "and the *Caleb Cushing* too."

"The *Caleb Cushing*?"

The Maine man grinned. "Sure been out to sea a long time. She's that new revenue cutter. Neat hull. Very fast they say, and handy too. Mounts a 32-pounder and a 12-pounder."

"You don't say?"

"I *do* say! She's moored out in the roadstead. Just two weeks under commission. Fine ship, sir. Fine indeed."

"Any other new ships in the harbor?"

"The *Chesapeake*. Fast steamer. One of the best. A New York liner."

"Then there's the *Forest City* of the Boston line," said Titcomb.

"Very interesting. Just where are we, mates?"

"Casco Bay."

"The fog is lifting. You'll con us in?"

"Certainly."

The fog was fading away. A light breeze was dissipating it. Bigger took his place beside the helmsman to con the *Archer* in.

Titcomb kept eying the few men on deck. "Sure don't talk like State of Maine men to me," he said to Clint.

Clint had his left hand on the butt of the navy Colt he had in his pocket. "No?"

"Nope." Titcomb shifted his chew of tobacco. "Who be ye?"

Read was near the wheel. He grinned at Clint. "Tell him, reefer."

"This is the Confederate States Ship *Archer*, commanded by Lieutenant Read, C.S.N."

Titcomb laughed and slapped his thighs. "That's a good one."

Bigger took the wheel. It was sundown and the light breeze carried them right into the crowded harbor, a craft hardly different from dozens of others. The anchor plunged down and the *Archer* rounded into the wind.

Bigger smiled. "You'll ferry us ashore, Captain Read?"

"No," said "Savez."

Bigger stared at him. "But why?"

Read took out a Colt. "This is why. Iron these men, Mister Lester. Take them below!"

Clint grinned as he heard Titcomb telling Bigger, "But he did tell me who they was, Albert! Trouble is, I never believed him!"

"Savez" Read surveyed the harbor with his telescope in the fading light. He whistled softly as he studied frowning Fort Preble. He whistled a little louder when he saw the spick-and-span *Caleb disking* riding at anchor, but he whistled loudest of all when he saw the big and trim *Chesapeake* at her wharf. "Council of war, mates," he said.

They gathered in the cabin, crowding it to the bulkheads. Not a one of them looked like the smart sailors who had been on the *Florida*. Bearded, dirty, and thin, they looked more like pirates.

"I'd like to take the *Chesapeake*," ventured Read.

Engineer Brown shook his head. "It would take hours to get up steam, sir. We wouldn't have the men to get up that steam or to hold the vessel against the troops they would be sure to send against us."

Read nodded. He tugged at his reddish mustache. "There is still the *Caleb Cushing,*" he said. "It's our best bet. Agreed?" He nodded in satisfaction. "Let us pray, gentlemen."

The *Archer* rocked easily in the ground swell as a score of rebels, in the middle of a harbor in Maine, hundreds of miles from the nearest rebel ships and rebel forces, prayed for success in their daring plan.

Read raised his head. "Three men will take the *Archer* to sea. Myself and the remaining nineteen men in the two small boats, oars muffled, will row over to the *Caleb Cushing,* at moonset, which is timed for 1:30 A.M. The *Archer* will be leaving harbor about the time we attack the cutter. If by any chance we *don't* capture the cutter, we will have no means of escape other than the two small boats. You know how far we can get in them." He looked from one man to the other. "Any questions, gentlemen?"

No one spoke.

"Fortune favors the brave," said "Savez" Read quietly.

In the dimness of the deck the raiders got ready. Pistols were cleaned and reloaded. Cutlasses were wiped free of rust and sharpened. Oars and rowlocks were muffled with rags. Now and then one of the raiders would look across the harbor toward the schooner-rigged *Caleb Cushing,* but then his eyes would wander to Fort Preble and the muzzles of the huge guns leering out over the quiet harbor. One shot from one of those would be enough.

The moon rose and seemed to sail across the waters for an incredibly short period of time, and then it was on the wane.

Somewhere in the quiet harbor a ship's bell rang twice clearly and then once again. Three bells of the middle, or churchyard watch—1:30 A.M. by landsmen's time.

"Boarders away," said "Savez" Read.

One by one they dropped into the boats until only the three men who would sail the *Archer* to sea were left.

The boarders had helped raise the sails to catch the dawn breeze, and the anchor had been hove up short.

"Good luck," the three men said.

There was no answer from the two shadowy boats as they moved slowly out over the darkening waters toward the *Caleb Cushing*.

CHAPTER ELEVEN

The Last Prize

The dark waters lapped against the sides of the boats. Clint Wallace had the tiller of the first boat, with Lieutenant Read beside him in the stern sheets. The second boat, steered by Bob Lester, was a boat's length astern of Clint's.

The strokes were slow and steady, and when the lapping of the water became too loud against the bows of the boat, Clint motioned to the oarsmen to ease off.

Read's left hand closed on Clint's shoulder. Something loomed up through the darkness. It was the *Caleb Cushing*, riding easily at anchor. Clint signaled to his oarsmen to stop. They drifted slowly toward the cutter. "Now?" whispered Clint to Read. The officer nodded.

Clint stripped off shoes, trousers, and jacket. He had strapped a belt about his waist with a sheathed knife attached to it, and a hard lignum vitae belaying pin hung in a loop from the belt. Clint let himself down over the transom into the water. It was cold, but not uncomfortably so.

Mister Read took the tiller. Clint swam slowly, using a breaststroke until he saw a wet head bobbing up and down in the water. It was Bob Lester. This was a plan they had worked out with Read. Bob and Clint swam together, rounding the bows of the cutter, and then drifted along the starboard side until they saw a ladder. Clint gripped it and eased himself up with his head just above the cap rail. A dim glow showed from a lantern near the binnacle and the riding lights flickered in the stiff offshore wind. There was no one in sight on the deck.

Bob came up after Clint and the two of them stepped to the deck. The steady dripping of water from them sounded inordinately loud. Bob walked softly forward while Clint walked aft. There was no one in sight, but the cutter certainly would not be unmanned.

Clint turned to signal to Read, and then he saw the blue-clad figure staring toward the dim boats in the water. The man opened his mouth to call out, and Clint swung up the belaying pin and placed it neatly and with despatch just behind and over the man's right ear. He sank to the deck with a loud grunt.

Read's head was just showing above the rail when another man slid back the hatch of the after cabin and looked toward Clint. "That you, Jenkins?" he asked.

"Aye," said Clint. The man had sounded like an officer. "Aye, sir!"

"You sound odd. What's wrong? Are you wet? Come, man, speak up!"

Clint retreated a little. The officer came forward. "Why do you walk away?" he demanded.

A head came up over the rail and a pistol nuzzled into the ribs of the officer. "This is why, sir," said "Savez" Read. "Don't make a noise. Raise your hands."

Clint quickly searched the officer for weapons and found that he was unarmed.

"Who are you?" demanded the officer.

"Lieutenant Charles Read, of the Confederate States Ship *Archer*. You are my prisoner, sir!"

"I don't believe you!"

Clint smiled. "Look," he said.

One man after another came over the rail and moved immediately to the task he had been instructed to perform. Bob Lester led some of them down into the forecastle to capture the men still asleep in their hammocks, while others checked the after quarters.

"Now, sir," said Read, "do you believe me?"

"Yes. I am Lieutenant Dudley Davenport, acting in command on this vessel."

"Where is your commanding officer?"

"The captain died a few days ago. Lieutenant James Merryman, his successor, is not expected to reach Portland until tomorrow." He laughed dryly. "We were to go to sea when he arrived ... to look for rebel raiders off the coast!"

"You won't have to now. You have a small crew aboard, sir."

"Half of them are on liberty."

Read beckoned to Clint. "Iron this gentleman and his resting sentry to the foremast, reefer."

The raiders began to get the cutter ready for sea. The sails creaked slowly up, and the capstan clicked steadily as the anchor was hove up.

Clint got dressed and checked the guns. They were new guns, of a type with which he was not too familiar. "Parrotts," said Read of the guns. "Good weapons."

Bob Lester was drying his hair, and then he raised his head. "The wind, sir," he said quietly.

The wind had died away suddenly. Lieutenant Davenport laughed. "It usually does about this time, gentlemen." He laughed again. "The tide is setting in. *Bon voyage!*"

Read bit his lip. "Reefer," he said to Clint. "Get both boats forward, pass towing lines to the cutter! We'll tow her out to catch a wind."

"Do," said Lieutenant Davenport politely.

And so it was. The two pulling boats worked like a team until the heavy cutter began to move slightly and then had way on her, but it was slow, it was so slow!

The cutter would have pulled easily enough under better conditions, but the tide was against them and the men were tired, for none of them had slept since the night before. Clint pulled stroke in the first boat and his muscles, hardened by the months at sea, seemed to lack elasticity and life. Back and forth, with a long pull, back and shoulders, then feathering the blade to keep even the slightest wind from slowing it down. No one spoke in either boat as they pulled steadily.

Fort Preble was so close; it was *too* close. The dew glistened on the snouts of the great black guns. There wasn't any sign of life on the ramparts but there must be sentries on duty, and within a few minutes, if the alarm was raised, those big guns could be manned, loaded, and fired.

"How big are them guns?" asked Dallas Longbow suddenly, almost as though he had read Clint's thoughts.

"Twenty-four-pounders and thirty-two-pounders," said Clint at a guess.

"Columbiads?"

Clint shrugged. "Rodmans, Columbiads, Parrotts, Dahlgrens...what difference does it make?"

They stroked on.

"How far can they shoot?" asked Tack Beaseley.

"Depends on shell weight, powder charge, wind, and so on," said Clint.

The *Caleb Cushing* veered a little in the pull of the tide and the two boats seemed to be standing still. They pulled stronger.

"Two miles?" asked Beaseley.

"Yes."

"Two and a half," said Dallas Longbow.

Stroke, stroke, stroke, and the boat seemed to inch forward, and still there was no wind.

"Three," said Seaman Jim Yancey.

"Two," said Beaseley.

"Three!"

"Two, I said!"

"Shut up!" snapped Clint. "What difference does it make?"

Inch by inch and foot by foot until the sweat was running down Clint's body like a stream and the wind was gone completely. But the tide was there, against them, and the weight of the heavy cutter and the tired muscles and weary minds.

"They say the Yanks have a 20-inch gun somewheres," said Seaman Simmons. "Kin throw a 300-pounder shell."

"Hawww!" said Dallas Longbow.

"Kin!"

"Can't!"

Clint rested on his oar and felt a blister break. He turned and looked at the dim, straining faces behind him. "Listen," he said quietly. "Once more! Just once more, and so help me, I'll break the loom of this oar over somebody's thick skull!"

The boat was quiet for three minutes. "Spoilsport," said an indistinguishable voice from up forward.

Clint couldn't help but grin. They were tired but their spirit was good.

Hour after hour and no relief. There wasn't any. Now and then a man would rest on his oar, but not a man of them asked for relief. They were beyond gunshot range of Fort Preble now.

"Look," said Tack Beaseley. He pointed to the east.

There was a faint indefinite lightness in the sky. The false dawn. Almost immediately the cutter seemed heavier and more sluggish. Clint stared at it. "Oars," he said. The oars rose dripping from the water. Clint stood up and took off his cap. The wind caressed his hot brow. "The dawn wind," he said. He bowed his head to pray.

The boats bumped alongside the cutter and were hoisted aboard. The sails were run up and they caught the wind. The cutter heeled a little as she started her run to freedom up Casco Bay.

"Listen!" said Bob Lester.

The wind carried the sound of many churchbells to them from Portland. "It ain't even Sunday," said Tack Beaseley.

"No," said Lieutenant Read. The wind ruffled his flaring red mustache. "It's the alarm, boys. They know we're out here! Whistle for a wind!"

They whistled. Clint thrust his sheath knife into the mainmast to bring on a stronger wind. The sails flapped.

The wind did freshen. Read shook his head. "We're whistling too soft, for a soft wind. Whistle loud for a gale, boys!"

"The sails are asleep, sir," said Quartermaster Billups. And so they were, just full and not flapping. The *Caleb Cushing* heeled a little and the chuckling of the water under the forefoot was a merry sound to the tired men.

The increased wind brought the louder sound of the bells to them across Casco Bay. Lieutenant Read studied the shore with his telescope. "Mister Wallace," he said quietly, "be so good as to take command of the 32-pounder. Mister Lester, captain the 12-pounder."

Clint walked to the big gun and called out the names of men for a gun crew. "Cast loose and provide," he commanded. Then it was ready for loading, with charges, wads, and shells.

"Load!" said Clint.

Charge, wad, shell, and wad, were sent in and rammed home. Clint cocked and capped the gunlock and attached the lockstring or gun lanyard. "Run out!" he said. The tackles groaned as the heavy gun was run out ready for firing. Clint turned and saluted. "Gun ready for firing, sir," he said smartly.

Read nodded, then took the report of Bob Lester. There wasn't anything else to do but sail and wait. The Yankees would be out soon enough with blood in their eyes.

In an hour they could see twin columns of smoke rising from somewhere in the harbor. Later the columns of smoke began to move out of the harbor and onto Casco Bay. The columns got closer and thicker.

Then Lieutenant Read lowered his telescope. "Two steamers," he said to his crew. "Big steamers! Loaded to the guards with troops and guns and making fast time. One of them is the *Chesapeake,* the New York liner. The other is probably the *Forest City* of the Boston fine. There is a smaller vessel astern of them. A steam tug. Other small craft behind the tug, but I can't make out who is in them. Probably spectators coming out to see the end of us rebels."

The men grinned expectantly.

Read smiled. "Well, they say congressmen came out to Bull Run in July of '61 to see us rebels get a thrashing. They do say the congressmen beat the Yankee soldiers all the way back into Washington!"

The men began to laugh.

The *Caleb Cushing* was making good time now, but the steamers were coming up fast astern, thrashing the water with their paddles. The morning sun glinted on the brass barrels of artillery pieces on their decks and on the bright bayonets of the troops aboard.

"Mister Wallace, I make it about two miles. You may open fire when ready, sir," said Lieutenant Read.

"Stand clear," said Clint. He bent over the breech of the gun. "Train right...train right...train right...Hold it! Train left a little. Hold it!" He elevated to maximum, then stepped aside with lockstring in hand, waited for the slow uproll, then pulled the string. The big 32-

pounder spat flame and smoke. A moment later a spout of water splashed fifty yards off the port bow of the speeding *Chesapeake,* which was outdistancing the *Forest City.*

"Excellent practice, Mister Wallace!" said Read in delight. He clapped his hands together. "Let's have more of the same, sir!"

It was tophole shooting at that range.

"Run in!" ordered Clint. "Swab!" He thumbed the vent.

The gun was drawn back and the wet sponge slid in and out of the smoking muzzle and was held aside, blackened and steaming.

"Load!"

Powder charge, wad, shell, and wad were slammed home hard. Clint capped and cocked the gunlock. "Stand clear! Run out!" He bent over the breech. "Train left! Hold it! *Steaaady!*" He depressed the muzzle a little. "Stand clear!" He pulled the lock string.

The shot plowed up the water neatly on the starboard bow of the fast *Chesapeake.* The next shot was ten feet from the side of the hull, while the third shot landed on the port side not fifty feet from the paddle box.

"Racketed!" said Bob Lester. "Fine shooting, Mister Wallace!"

"Thank you, Mister Lester," said Clint dryly.

Then the fine big steamer turned and bore off.

"She's running away!" said a seaman. He wiped a dirty, powder-blackened face.

The *Chesapeake* came close alongside the *Forest City,* and the two steamers followed the *Caleb Cushing* at a safe distance.

The raiders wet dry lips while watching their two pursuers. Both guns were loaded. Rifles, pistols, and cutlasses had been issued. Water tubs had been placed on the decks and sand was spread to prevent slipping on blood.

Lieutenant Read watched the two Yankees through his glass. They were not dropping back, nor did they come up into range either. They had a lot of respect for that 32-pounder captained by a seventeen-year-old midshipman.

Then the steamers parted company, one to port, the other to starboard, opening out like the points on a great pair of pincers, and inside the pincers was the little *Caleb Cushing*, moving along under sail. Faster and faster the steamers came on.

"Hold your fire," said Mister Read. He tugged at his long mustachios. He eyed the steamers and the sails of his prize, then looked at his score of weary and dirty men. "I think they mean to ram us, men," he said. "We can perhaps place a shot in a boiler or a paddle wheel. The odds are against us. They can circle about us like hawks and rake us with gunfire and then ram. We won't have much of a chance."

The cutter dipped and rolled in the freshening wind. The steamers were laying down plumes of thick smoke as rosin and turpentine were heaved into the fires to get up full heads of steam pressure.

Clint Wallace glanced at Bob Lester, and the words they had spoken to each other before they entered Portland Harbor came back to him. "I won't be taken prisoner...Neither will I...We'll stick together then..."

Minutes ticked past as the steamers seemed to grow larger and larger and more ominous-looking at the same time.

"Savez" Read climbed up on the starboard main shrouds and looked at the *Chesapeake* and the *Forest City*, so much bigger than his little command. There were hundreds of soldiers on those two ships, many fieldpieces barricaded by bales of cotton, and trouble for a cargo.

The raiders eyed Lieutenant Read.

Read looked at his men. "Men, this is our last chance. You have written a glorious chapter in Confederate naval history. We have our choice: fight or surrender. Which shall it be?"

Twenty-two men spat out one word. "Fight!"

"Fight it will be! Battle stations!"

The Confederate flag was run up to the peak amidst cheers from the raiders.

CHAPTER TWELVE
Battle Stations!

Clint Wallace stood beside his gun on the forecastle deck watching the approaching steamers. Lieutenant Read had taken his station beside Clint. Clint saluted. "Lieutenant Read, sir, it would be my pleasure to have you command this gun."

Read shook his head. "You've done fine, reefer."

"I insist, sir."

Read smiled. "Well, all right then, but you must act as gun layer."

"Aye, aye, sir."

It was quiet on the heaving deck of the cutter as she sailed steadily on toward the open sea.

A gun coughed and smoked on the foredeck of the *Chesapeake* and the shot splashed two hundred yards behind the *Caleb Cushing*.

Read grinned. "Open fire, Mister Wallace."

"My pleasure, sir! Run out! Stand clear!" The gun roared back and the 32-pound shot struck full and fair just under the cutwater of the steamer.

"You may fire when ready, Mister Lester," said Read gravely.

The 12-pounder's first shot struck the lower rail of the *Forest City* and its second shot tore off a flagstaff. The two guns roared steadily, echoed by the barking cough of the fieldpieces on the two steamers. Gun smoke and funnel smoke lay thickly on Casco Bay, raveled by the offshore wind.

A shell tore through the mainsail of the *Caleb Cushing*, and another smashed through the taffrail within a few feet of placid Quartermaster Billups.

Then it was load, fire, run in, swab, load, run out, and fire again while the stinking gun smoke blew constantly across the decks of the cutter.

Shells struck the water on both sides of the cutter and just astern, sending up great spouts that showered sails, decks, and men, but the gun-firing never slackened.

Read smiled. "They aren't too anxious to get close," he said. He slapped the hot breech of the 32-pounder. "Good practice! As long as we can fend 'em off, we won't have to worry."

The steamers were wary and even though the fieldpieces cracked constantly they were hardly allowed within accurate range, and the veil of smoke between the steamers and the cutter wasn't conducive to good artillery practice. Besides, the cutter was small and handy, and the 32-pounder on her forecastle deck had two fine big targets neither of which carried an ounce of armor. If one of those shells hit a paddle wheel or a boiler, it would be all over.

Clint glanced at Lieutenant Read as the firing stopped on the *Caleb Cushing* to allow the blinding smoke to blow away. The officer's jaw was set and his eyes were half-closed. The fight was still going on, but how long could they last?

A shell smashed the fore topmast and the shattered wood came down in a tangle of rigging and canvas. Seaman Simmons went up the shrouds with a boarding ax in his hand and cut loose the snarl.

The steamers shifted back and forth. They had the

speed and the maneuverability, and those Yankees could handle ships.

The 12-pounder stopped firing.

"Open fire, Mister Lester!" spat out Read.

"We can't, sir. We've run out of ammunition."

Read tugged at his mustachios. "You're sure, sir?"

"Yes, sir."

Read shrugged. "Well, we still have a gun. Keep up the fire, Mister Wallace!"

"Aye, aye, sir!"

A shell smashed through the starboard rail of the cutter just forward of the quarter-deck and tore through the deadeyes of the port main shrouds, then plunged into the sea.

The men paled. If that had gone off!

Shot after shot until the 32-pounder was too hot to touch. Forty-five minutes of almost continuous firing. "Run in! Swab!" commanded Clint. He thumbed the vent and waited until the blackened dripping swab was withdrawn from the smoking gun muzzle. "Load!"

The men teetered on their feet waiting for the shotman to bring up the next projectile.

"Load!" roared Clint.

No shotman. Clint turned angrily to look at Tack Beaseley. "Where's that shotman?"

"Here, sir," said Shotman Stackpole.

"Where's the shot?"

Stackpole shrugged and held out his dirty hands expressively. "There ain't any left, sir."

Clint stared at the man. "You're sure?"

"Positive! They's five hundred pounds of powder left in the magazine but not one shot left in the locker!"

Read wiped the sweat from his powder-blackened face. "Did you check the reserve locker?"

"It's locked, sir!"

"Who has the key?" demanded Read of Lieutenant Davenport.

The Federal officer smiled. "It's lying at the bottom of Casco Bay, sir."

A man snatched up the rammer and waved it over his head as he walked toward the Federal officer. "You ..."

"As you were!" snapped Read. He paced back and forth. "We'll have to break the locker open then!"

Davenport shrugged. "It won't be easy. It's iron-bound."

Read plunged below and a few minutes later he was back on deck and his face was set. "No chance of getting into that locker," he said. "Cram anything you can find into that gun, Mister Wallace!"

They picked up iron belaying pins, blocks, tools, and other odds and ends, crammed them in on top of a wadded powder charge and fired at the steamer closest to them. But now it seemed that the Yankees suspected that the cutter was low on ammunition. They edged closer and closer while the raiders frantically searched their craft high and low for anything at all that they could fire at the enemy.

Clint and Bob plunged below. They hunted throughout the wardroom for anything to fire. "Nothing," said Bob despondently.

Clint looked into the pantry. A red, round Dutch cheese, just about the size of a 32-pound shell, lay on a platter. Clint snatched it up.

"We need crackers if we're going to mess," said Bob with a grin.

"Mess? If we can't sink the Yankees, we sure can stink 'em, mate!"

They hurried up on deck and Clint held up the cheese for the raiders to see. "The last shot in the locker, mates!"

He carried it to the gun and waited until powder charge and wad were inserted, then gently rolled the heavy cheese into the muzzle and heard it settle down against the wad.

"Wait!" said Lieutenant Read. He eyed the two steamers. "Get the prisoners up on deck!"

The white-faced crewmen were bundled into a boat, and the keys for their irons were tossed in at their feet. The boat drifted astern with the men frantically waving at the *Chesapeake*.

Read looked at his men. "I won't let them have this vessel," he said quietly. "Mister Lester! Lay powder trains to the magazine. I want fire materials ready fore and aft; I don't have to show the men of the old *Florida* how to do that! There's five hundred pounds of good Yankee powder in the magazine. It should make quite an explosion."

The raiders scattered to do their work. Read walked to the starboard rail. "Lower both boats," he said quietly. They were lowered and towed alongside. In a few minutes the men in charge of powder train and firing materials reported to him. There wasn't much left to do.

The *Chesapeake* and the *Forest City* moved in, closer and closer, and the *Chesapeake* picked up the original crew of the *Caleb Cushing* from the boat which Read had set adrift. They would know now that the *Caleb Cushing* was helpless.

The sun was at its zenith. The powder smoke had blown away. The wind freshened a little. The end was near for "Savez" Read and his men.

Read glanced at Clint. "You may fire when ready, Mister Wallace," he said seriously.

"Run out!" said Clint. "Stand clear!" He stepped to one side and pulled the lockstring and the gun smashed back against its hurters. Something splattered against the bows of the *Chesapeake* and it immediately slowed down and lost way.

The ripe odor of strong cheese mingled with the gunsmoke odor on the decks of the cutter.

"Well done, Mister Wallace," said Read gravely. He

looked about at his men. "Prepare to abandon ship! Haul down our colors, Mister Lester!"

They soberly watched as the blackened and tattered flag came down. "Abandon ship! Mister Wallace and Mister Lester!"

The two midshipmen saluted their commanding officer.

"Mister Wallace, set fire to the powder train. Mister Lester, start your fires fore and aft first, however."

Clint looked at Bob Lester, then at Lieutenant Read. "Sir," he said quietly, "we don't want to surrender!"

"Neither do I, reefer. Have you any other ideas?" Read gestured toward the approaching steamers. "They'll be on us in a few minutes."

Clint looked at a battered dory lying on the deck. It had been struck by shell fragments but it would still float if buoyed up by empty water kegs and breakers, and there was a lug sail, mast, and oars in it. "Sir, I'd like to go over the side with that dory and take my chances at sea."

"They'd see you! How far do you think you'd get?"

Clint smiled. "I'll turn it over in the water, sir, and get beneath it. They may not bother to examine it. It looks pretty bad, sir."

"Yes," said Read thoughtfully. "You have my permission."

"We can torch the cutter, sir, then slip over the side and drift away before the charges go off."

"We?"

Clint nodded. "Yourself, sir, Mister Lester, and myself."

"Aye, sir!" said Bob Lester.

Read eyed the boat, the two earnest midshipmen, then the oncoming steamers. "No," he said quietly. "They'd look for me, reefers. Besides, I won't leave my men. But you can go." He held out a hand. "Good luck! Fortune favors the brave!"

They ran to the dory, lashed kegs and breakers

beneath the thwarts to buoy it up, then lowered it quickly over the side. Bob Lester turned it over. It was on the far side of the cutter from the two steamers.

"Savez" Read buttoned up his coat, adjusted sword and pistol, slanted his cap at a rakish angle, tugged at his flaring red mustachios, then stepped into his waiting boat. Both boats shoved off, and the raiders began to row toward the nearest steamer.

Clint crawled to the forecastle, staying well below the railing. He started a fire there, then crawled aft to start a fire in the main cabin. He crept up on deck and peered through a hole in the bulwark. The two boats had stopped three hundred yards from the cutter and the men rested on their oars, watching the cutter, while one man in each boat waved a white flag toward the two steamers.

Clint crawled to the place where the powder train started. He took a match from a block and struck it against a coaming. He touched off the powder, heard it fizz and hiss, then scuttled swiftly to the side of the cutter, wormed his way through a shattered hole, and dropped into the water beside Bob Lester. Lester grimaced. "If that goes off before we drift far enough away ..."

They ducked under the dory into the dimness below. There were several holes in the sides and through these came shafts of sunlight. They held onto the thwarts and kept their mouths and noses above water.

Minute after minute ticked past. Far down the bay they could see the little *Archer* beating its way to sea with hardly a chance to escape now from the Yankee steamers. It would do the boys little good to try to reach her.

"I can't stand much more of this," whispered Bob.

"You'll have to!" said Clint fiercely. "Or I'll give you another beating like I did on the *Florida!*"

"Beating? *Who* gave *who* a beating?"

"Shut up!" said Clint.

Minute after minute. The water lapped at the sides of the slowly drifting dory.

How far were they from the doomed cutter? Maybe they were still right next to it!

Clint cautiously thrust out a leg. If he touched stout planking his heart would stop. He did touch something but it didn't quite feel like planking.

Bob Lester grinned with a pale face. "It isn't the cutter, mate, for I've been feeling for it for ten minutes! That's my leg!"

Clint was just working up to peer through a hole when a tremendous blasting noise came to them, and an instant later the dory heaved and rolled in a heavy sea, while the water pressure about the bodies of the two boys seemed to grip them like a firm but watery fist.

Something hit the top of the dory, and they heard water splashing all about them as debris struck the surface. The dory rolled and Clint got a quick glimpse through a hole. A great wreath of smoke hung over the sunlit waters where the *Caleb Cushing* had been. Beyond that he could see the two boats filled with the raiders, close by the side of the *Chesapeake,* and armed men in blue aiming bayoneted guns at the men in the boats.

"Well?" demanded Bob.

Clint sank down. "Now all we do is wait, mate," he said philosophically.

And they waited, and waited, and waited, until suddenly Bob hissed at Clint. *"Listen!"*

A familiar sound came to them: the creaking of oars in rowlocks and the lapping of water against something other than the sides of the overturned dory.

"You think there's any of them left out here, Sergeant?" a voice asked so startlingly close that Clint winced in surprise.

"Hardly likely, Sam. Bodies maybe, if there was any of them left aboard the cutter. But with that blast it ain't likely even a body would be left. Besides, they would have sunk anyway."

"Yeh."

Oars creaked again. "Look at that dory," another man said. "Stove in, she is."

"We could tow it back to the *Forest City,*" said the first speaker.

Clint stared at Bob Lester. Bob raised a hand up out of the water and crossed two fingers.

"Get closer to it," the sergeant said.

Both boys hardly dared to breathe. The dory bobbed slowly up and down, and Clint wondered whether or not the water was clear enough for the Yankees to see their legs through it.

Something bumped against the side of the dory with a clattering noise. The other boat. It ground hard against the dory.

Then suddenly something thin and bright probed through a hole in the boat, paused, then drove in hard, and the tip of it struck Clint in the chest, and the pain of it almost made him scream in agony. It was a bayonet. He felt the blood start from the wound. The bayonet was withdrawn and then plunged in again but this time a hand was between the tip and Clint's chest. The hand of Bob Lester.

Clint quickly raised a hand and held the blade as it was withdrawn, to wipe the telltale blood from the bright steel.

"Nothing," said Sam at last.

The boat slowly moved away and the two boys looked at each other in relief. The pain in Clint's chest and in Bob's hand was nothing compared to the intense relief they felt.

In a short time they heard a steamboat whistle, then the hurried thrashing of great paddles. The dory moved up and down in the waves created by the passage of the steamer, and then it was bobbing gently on the swells.

Clint peered through a hole. One of the steamers was standing up the bay, while the other was close by a schooner that was letting down its sails. It was the *Archer,* captured with her crew of three. There were many small boats floating near where the *Caleb Cushing* had gone down. A fair-sized catboat was tacking about and two old men in her were picking up salvage. Even as Clint watched, they headed for the dory. "Catboat coming, Bob," he said.

"For us?"

"Looks like it."

"You have your knife?"

"Yes."

They looked at each other. There was no need for further speech.

The catboat bumped against the dory. "Looks like she's in fair shape, Seth," said a nasal voice.

"Make a line fast to her, George. We can patch her up."

They heard fumbling, and then the catboat moved slowly toward the harbor. "Now," said Clint.

The two of them ducked under the side of the dory, gripped the keel, pulled themselves over the bottom and dropped into the cockpit of the catboat. Clint held his blade against the throat of the whiskered Yankee at the tiller, while Bob held his point against the back of tire other man.

"Tie them," said Clint.

They worked fast. Both men were tied and gagged, then placed in the low cabin of the catboat. Clint took the tiller and steered for the open sea to put distance between them and the other boats.

At dusk they placed both men into the dory and Bob rowed them to a small islet, cut one of them loose, then swiftly swam back to the catboat. It would be hours before the two angry men could patch up the leaking dory enough to make it safe to get to the nearest inhabited land, and by that time the catboat would be well on its way. But to where?

The sun dipped down and was gone, and darkness spread over the heaving waters while the catboat footed steadily out to sea. There was a full water breaker in its cabin and some food as well. Not very much, but enough for a day or two.

Bob Lester had the tiller and he sat hunched up against the evening chill with an old blanket about his shoulders. He looked at Clint. "We've come a long way from the *Florida,* mate. Lower and lower. First the *Clarence,* then the *Tacony,* then the *Archer,* the *Caleb Cushing,* a stove-in dory, and now a catboat. The whole coast might be alerted by now that two rebel reefers are beating to sea in a stolen catboat. By daylight we'll be too far out for anyone to think we're just sailing or fishing. What do you think we should do?"

Clint shook his head wearily. "Head in to the coast, abandon the cat, then try to work our way south."

"It's a long way home, mate. A long way home."

There was a faint light from the rising moon but between the moon and the sea there was a thickening wraith of fog. They had no idea where they were. They couldn't see land; some time before they had seen faint lights far astern of them, although whether on land or on a ship they couldn't say.

The fog was coming down fast and they knew they were drifting steadily out to sea.

It was almost midnight when Clint heard the first of many foghorns they would hear that lonesome night. But they saw nothing. Nothing but the heaving waters and the damp, drifting fog. There was no compass in the boat. No way to navigate and no way to see the stars for a fix even if they had had the instruments to do so.

Maybe a Yankee prison would have been better at that. Clint Wallace thrust the thought from his mind. Don't give up! Fortune favors the brave!

CHAPTER THIRTEEN

To Live to Fight Again!

The sea was calm and the fog hung low over it, distorting sounds that seemed to come and go. Clint Wallace stood in the cockpit of the catboat trying not to look at the ever-present fog. Bob Lester was asleep on one of the cockpit seats. His wounded hand had become infected and it was red and swollen. There were no medicines aboard. Indeed, the food was all gone and there was hardly a mouthful of water left in the breaker.

Three days of drifting, drifting, with a slight breeze now and then that hardly flapped the canvas. The first two days they had heard foghorns, and once they had heard distant voices, but they had seen nothing but the eternally heaving waters.

Clint was rigging a fishing line. They had to have food. But they needed water most of all. Somewhere Clint had heard of compressing the flesh of fish in a cloth to wring the juices from it. The thought was distasteful but his thirst was great.

Suddenly he lifted his tired head and looked at the wall of fog. He had heard a faint sound toward the bows of the boat, whichever direction that was. The water lapped against the sides of the hull and the canvas flapped fitfully. A block creaked.

The sound came again, a steady, beating, rhythmic sound, and one that was familiar. His tired brain refused to function. He stared in the direction of the sound and noted that it was steadily getting louder and much closer. Frash-frash-frash ... He had heard that sound before. But where? Louder and louder and then suddenly out of the swirling, drifting vagueness of the fog came a harsh blasting sound. A foghorn! Those were great paddle wheels! "Bob!" he yelled.

The midshipman sat up and stared at Clint.

"Listen, Bob!"

Frash-frash-frash...Then the harsh blatting of a great foghorn.

They stood staring into the milky fog.

"She's close!" said Bob.

"Too close! Look!"

A great bow had thrust itself through the fog and was driving directly down on them.

"Over the side!" yelled Bob.

They struck the cold water simultaneously, and just as they came to the surface they saw the bows within fifty yards of the bobbing catboat. They swam desperately and did not look back as the bows knifed cleanly through the catboat, spewing wreckage to either side.

The huge hull hurtled past and Clint had a quick look at the name in gilded letters on the fine trail boards of the great steamer...*City of Manchester*.

The paddles were beating up a yeasty storm. A man called hoarsely from the deck of the steamer. The waves swept the two boys up and down and then the teakettle stern shot past them and Clint saw the name again. *City of Manchester,* Liverpool.

The sound of the paddles slowed down and then stopped. "Ahoy out there!" a man yelled in an unmistakable English voice.

"Ahoy! Ahoy! Ahoy!" screamed the boys.

The paddles moved slowly, then came the whining of boat tackles and the sound of a boat striking the water, then quick commands and the sound of oars striking the water.

In a few minutes they had been picked up, brought to the steamer, bundled in blankets, and taken below. A chin-whiskered officer came in to see them. "Captain Milas McKay, *City of Manchester,* Boston to Liverpool, gentlemen!" he said. "I'm terribly sorry I ran you down."

"We're not, sir," said Clint. "We were out of water and food and didn't know where we were."

"You're a long way out at sea and right in the steamer track."

Bob shrugged. "We were lost, sir."

"Fishermen?"

Clint glanced at Bob. "Yes," he said quietly.

"So? From Portland, by any chance?"

"Not exactly," said Bob.

Captain McKay smiled a little. "You don't sound like Yankees to me."

"I ..." said Clint, and then his voice died away as he saw the look on the captain's face.

"It's been quite a start to this run," said Captain McKay. "Yankee warships all over the place, challenging every ship, looking for some rebel raiders. Pirates, they called them."

"So?" said Clint.

"Yes! They captured a crew of them near Portland some days ago. Brought them up to Fort Warren for imprisonment. Seems as though they captured a Yankee cutter right in Portland Harbor and got away with it and then their luck ran out. They were captured, but they blew the cutter up first."

"Very interesting," said Bob dryly.

"Seems as though two rebel midshipmen were missing

though, supposedly blown up on the cutter. Boys about your age, too."

"Sad," said Clint.

"Yes, indeed! Well, it's no concern of mine. I have a run to make to Liverpool. Sorry I can't take you back to your country, gentlemen, but in Liverpool you can contact the United States Consul and I'm sure he'll take care of you."

"Oh, certainly!" said Bob Lester. "He'll take care of us all right."

"They say the raiders originally were part of the crew of the C.S.S. *Florida*. Fine ship. I saw her built in Liverpool. Called the *Oreto* then. Some dodge, the rebels building both the *Florida* and the *Alabama* under the noses of the Yankee Consul."

"Ha! Ha!" said Clint.

McKay smiled. "They do say Mister Bulloch, who had the cruisers built, is arranging for more of them to be constructed in England or France. I suppose, if a person wanted more information on them he could see Mister Bulloch about the mysterious craft."

"If he wanted more information he could," said Bob Lester wisely, "couldn't he, Mister Wallace?"

"Oh, certainly, Mister Lester."

"Good Yankee names those, Wallace and Lester," said Captain McKay. "Odd thing though, the names of the two missing rebel midshipmen were Wallace and Lester. No relation, I'm sure."

"None," said Clint.

Bob shook his head.

The captain walked to the door, then turned. "Get some rest," he said. "You'll dine with me this evening in the privacy of my cabin. You might be interested to hear of those new vessels Mister Bulloch is building."

"We will indeed, sir," said Bob Lester.

The door closed behind the captain.

Clint grinned at Bob. "Our luck holds, mate," he said.

Bob nodded. "You know, mate, if we can't get a berth aboard one of the new vessels, mayhap Captain Maffitt *might* just possibly get to Europe. I heard him mention once that he hadn't been in France for many years and that France was quite sympathetic to the rebel cause."

Clint grinned. He lay back and closed his eyes, feeling the easy lifting and swaying of the fast packet as she breasted the Atlantic on her way to Liverpool. Fortune favors the brave! They had lived to fight again!

GLOSSARY OF SEA TERMS

BACKSTAYS—Lines abaft a mast, used to steady and support it.

BARK—A sailing vessel with three or more masts, square-rigged on all save the aftermost, which is fore-and-aft rigged.

BLAKELY—A heavy cannon of British manufacture.

BOATSWAIN—Pronounced bosun. An unlicensed officer in charge of the crew; a sort of straw boss, usually in charge of all deck work aboard a ship.

BONDING—A bond was given by the master of a captured ship in the name of the owners, stipulating that in consideration of not burning or otherwise destroying the vessel, the captors would be paid the sum of the bond within six months after the ratification of a treaty between the United States Government and the Confederate States Government.

BRIG—A vessel with two masts, square-rigged on both; also the ship's prison.

CATBOAT—A small sailing craft, pole-masted. The mast is stepped far forward and carries a single sail.

CAT'S-PAW, OR CATSPAW—A light current of air that disturbs the surface of the water during a calm.

CHRONOMETER—An accurate ship's clock, used in navigation.

THE CITADEL—The Military College of South Carolina in Charleston.

CLEWED UP AND BACKED HER YARDS—To truss up the sails of a ship and to turn the yards so that the ship loses way and drifts.

CLIPPER SHIP—A large sailing ship, usually full-rigged, with exceptionally fine lines and a huge spread of canvas, that could carry a large amount of cargo; noted for beauty and speed.

COXSWAIN—The man who usually steers a small rowing boat and has charge of it.

CUTTER—A nautical word with a number of meanings. It can refer to a large rowing boat; a single-masted sailing vessel with a deep and heavy hull; or a sailing or steam vessel used by the old Revenue Service, now the modern Coast Guard, for patrolling, law enforcement, saving of lives at sea, and many other duties.

CUTTING OUT—To send an armed party in small boats to destroy or capture an enemy vessel in a harbor or other place where the larger ship cannot go.

DAHLGREN—A heavy naval cannon of American manufacture.

DEADEYES—Three-holed wooden blocks through which the lanyards that connect the shrouds with the ship's side pass, originally named "deadman's eyes" because of the resemblance to a skull.

DEFILADE—An obstacle in the way of gunfire which prevents the projectiles from reaching their target.

DORY—A small, flat-bottomed rowing boat noted for its seaworthiness, usually used for open sea fishing.

DOUBLINGS—The place where the masts are joined together; the lower mast to the topmast and the topmast to the topgallant mast.

FIFE RAIL—A wooden railing about the sides of a mast, on the deck, wherein belaying pins are placed to hold lines and halyards.

GIMBALS—A device which allows a suspended body to incline freely in any direction, used aboard ships to keep compasses, chronometers, lamps, etc., level when the ship rolls.

HI-BRAZIL, ALSO HY-BRASIL—A mythical place where sailors are supposed to go after death to enjoy ease and pleasure throughout eternity.

HYDROGRAPHY—The science of measuring and describing seas, lakes, and rivers in so far as regards their usefulness for purposes of navigation and commerce.

KNOT—A division on the log line answering to a mile of distance. A nautical mile is 6,080 feet, while a land mile is 5,280 feet. The nautical knot is used as a measurement of ship's speed.

LA CONFEDERACION DEL SUD—Spanish for the Confederation of the South, or the Confederate States of America.

LUBBER HOLE—The hole between the head of a lower mast and the edge of the top, through which sailors may mount without climbing outside the rim by the futtock shrouds.

MANIFEST—Actually the ship's passport, containing all the documents necessary to enter or clear a port, the names of the owners, charterers, together with the nationalities of all members of the crew, the ship's contents or cargo, consignee and origin, destination, and all marks and symbols.

MASTHEAD FOR YOU—A custom in the old navy whereby a culprit would be sent aloft for a number of hours to sit on the crosstrees high above the deck no matter how foul the weather to repent of his sins. In the modern navy it means to stand before your commanding officer to answer for your misdeed.

MIDSHIPMAN—A naval cadet, one of the lowest grade officers in the line of promotion in the old navy; nowadays a student at the United States Naval Academy at Annapolis, Maryland.

PACKET RATS—The tough seamen who crewed the fast packet ships of the North Atlantic between Great Britain and the United States and Canada.

PACKET SHIPS—Fast sailing ships that carried passengers, mail, and cargo across the North Atlantic.

PARROTT—A heavy cannon of American manufacture.

PRIZE MONEY—Money awarded to the officers and crew of a naval ship for capturing enemy cargo vessels. The amount was regulated by the value of ship and cargo, and allotted in shares on a sliding scale from the commanding officer down to include the lowest member of the crew.

PROVOST GUARD—Military police used to keep order in camps and also in towns near camps, their authority usually extending only to members of the military forces.

RATLINES—Light horizontal rope fines running across the shrouds, thus forming a rope ladder used by seamen to ascend and descend the masts.

REEFER—An old time nickname for a midshipman.

RODMAN—A heavy cannon of American manufacture.

SCEND, OR SEND, OF THE SEA—Motion of the waves, or the angular displacement upward of a vessel's hull.

SCHOONER—A vessel with two or more masts, fore-and-aft rigged.

SEXTANT—A navigational instrument for measuring the altitude of celestial objects and their apparent angular distances, thereby determining the latitude and longitude of a ship at sea.

SHROUDS—The most important parts of the standing rigging of a ship; heavy ropes or lines running down from the mastheads on either side to steady the mast against side pressure and also from being bent forward.

SKYLARKING—To engage in hilarious or frolicsome sport, playing tricks or games aboard ship.

SLIPPED HIS CABLE—Seaman's term for one newly dead, comparing his lot to that of a ship which has left its anchor behind and gone to sea.

STEERAGE OFFICER—One who has quarters in the steerage of a warship, i.e., on warships the quarters assigned to the junior officers, forward of the wardroom.

SUPERCARGO—The business agent of the owner aboard a ship.

TEAKETTLE STERN—A rounded stern as opposed to a flat transomed stern, so called because of its resemblance to one half of a teakettle.

THWARTS—Seats in a rowing boat.

TRAILBOARDS—Ornamental scrollwork on both sides of the bow of a ship, usually carved and picked out with gilt, and sometimes, but not always, bearing the name of the ship.

TRESTLETREES—In a ship one of two strong bars of timber fixed horizontally on the opposite sides of the masthead to support the frame of the top.

UNCLE JONATHAN, COUSIN JONATHAN—A nickname for the United States that preceded that of Uncle Sam. It was also used as Brother Jonathan, originating during the Revolutionary War, when any patriotic American was so called. George Washington started it, by referring to Governor Jonathan Trumbull of Connecticut as such. Jonathan Trumbull gave freely of food, ammunition, and advice to the new army. When in doubt Washington would say, "Let us ask Brother Jonathan." Later the nickname was applied to the Continental Congress and still later to the United States.

WEARING SHIP—To turn a vessel around, so that, from having the wind on one side, you bring it upon the other, carrying her stern around by the wind.

WEATHER RAIL—The rail on the side of the ship against which the wind is blowing, as compared to the other rail which is then called the lee rail. By custom, when the commanding officer of a ship was on his quarterdeck he took his station at the weather rail, while the other officers took their station at the lee rail.

WHITWORTH—A long-range breech-loading rifled cannon of British manufacture, some of which found their way to the Confederacy.

TAKE A LOOK AT ARIZONA JUSTICE AND THE LONELY GUN:

Two Full Length Western Novels

Owen Wister Award winner Gordon D. Shirreffs spins tales of the old west that are exhilarating and bigger than life. You'll find two such full-length tales in this double volume sure to please even the most discerning consumer of Western fiction.

In *Arizona Justice*, when Rowan Locke rode into Llano with a marshal's badge in his pocket and the iron will to bring back a killer, all he heard talk of was the terrible Donnigans, those five wild-tempered brothers who thought they were above the law.

In *The Lonely Gun*, Case Hardesty had to cross what the Conquistadors called the Devil's Highway on foot—or die. It was the highest, driest, meanest desert in northern Mexico. Hot on the trail behind him were the outlaws he'd taken for $20,000—and behind them the lawmen who had sworn death to the lot of them.

In one hand he held a Winchester, and in the other a salt sack stuffed with enough bills to buy a ranch in Sonora—if he made it. If he didn't, well, there was plenty of space for a grave out on the Devil's Highway...

"The joy of reading Shirreffs' work is in his mastery of pacing and his tough, gritty prose." – **James Reasoner, author of Outlaw Ranger.**

AVAILABLE NOW

ABOUT THE AUTHOR

Gordon D. Shirreffs published more than 80 western novels, 20 of them juvenile books, and John Wayne bought his book title, Rio Bravo, during the 1950s for a motion picture, which Shirreffs said constituted *"the most money I ever earned for two words."* Four of his novels were adapted to motion pictures, and he wrote a Playhouse 90 and the Boots and Saddles TV series pilot in 1957.

A former pulp magazine writer, he survived the transition to western novels without undue trauma, earning the admiration of his peers along the way. The novelist saw life a bit cynically from the edge of his funny bone and described himself as looking like a slightly parboiled owl. Despite his multifarious quips, he was dead serious about the writing profession.

Gordon D. Shirreffs was the 1995 recipient of the Owen Wister Award, given by the Western Writers of America for "a living individual who has made an outstanding contribution to the American West."

He passed in 1996.

Printed in France by Amazon
Brétigny-sur-Orge, FR